"Well, Charita," he said, "I have decided, for several reasons, that you will marry me."

Her spoon slipped, and fe‌‍‍‌‍ the saucer with a clatter. Her pink mouth o‌‍‍‍‍‍‍‍‍‍und came out.

He went on. ‍‍‍‍‍‍‍‍‍‍‍ed taking care of. I need a wif‌‍‍‍‍‍‍‍‍‍‍‍‍‍‍. I like you very much, ‍‍‍‍‍‍‍‍‍‍‍‍. And you like me, do‌‍‍‍‍‍‍‍‍‍‍y for her reply.

Sh‌‍‍‍‍‍‍‍‍‍‍‍rt. "I—like you, yes, but ‍‍‍‍‍‍‍‍‍‍‍ . . . I might not be right for you. ‍‍‍‍‍‍‍‍‍e more sophisticated might be more to yo‍‍‍‍‍‍.

"But that doesn't mean I'd want to marry someone like that. I want a lady who is discreet, with a pleasant voice. Someone who would dress prettily and keep my home a home. You would do nicely."

"I would try very hard," she said soberly.

"Then go to bed, Charita, you are so weary. I promise you, it will be easier in Kyoto." He cupped her round face in his big hands and very gently touched his lips to hers.

He had just time to feel the softness of them and to smell the slight perfume she wore when she sprang back. She put her hands to her face and stood trembling before him. He realized suddenly that she was shocked. She must never have been kissed on the lips before. She was truly an innocent. He must go slowly in courting her. She was like the rare golden lotus, the nickname the Japanese had given her. With her pale golden skin glowing pink, her fragile beauty, swaying as in a wind . . .

Janet Louise Roberts

WARNER BOOKS

A Warner Communications Company

WARNER BOOKS EDITION

Copyright © 1979 by Janet Louise Roberts
All rights reserved

ISBN 0-446-81997-2

Cover art by Mort Rosenfeld

Warner Books, Inc., 75 Rockefeller Plaza, New York, N.Y. 10019

W A Warner Communications Company

Printed in the United States of America

First Printing: August, 1979

10 9 8 7 6 5 4 3 2 1

To Loretta—

With the memory of cherry blossoms
falling in still pools, and
Mount Fuji on a clear day.

Petals sketched in gold
Float on rippled silk to draw
Lord sun's loving gaze.

Golden Lotus

1

A white, driving rain lashed mercilessly at the fragile window panes, causing them to rattle and tremble in their wooden frames. Charita Atwood stood with her small, round nose pressed to the window, gazing wistfully outside at her once lovely garden now pounded beyond recognition into the muddy earth. The trees which had stood so gracefully were bent almost double, their few leaves stripped from the barren limbs.

How lonely it was here, despite the kindness of the neighbors. The road wound out from Sapporo on the island of Hokkaido, losing itself among the thick trees, then trickling into a dirt path which stopped abruptly about two hundred yards beyond their tiny Japanese house of natural wood. Few houses stood nearby; they were closer to the end of the road.

Her father loved the house and the distance from "civilization," which to him, meant Americanization. It had the atmosphere he wanted to complete his latest book on Japanese customs and mythology. Sliding wooden doors, a few modern windows, tatami mats on the wooden floors, the primitive means of plumbing and cooking—all were familiar to him—and spelled serenity.

Charita also was accustomed to such simple living. Her mother had died when she was three, and her father, a professor, had given her into the tender care of a Japanese couple. Oku and Helen Noguchi had been her dear foster parents, treating her like their own daughter, and their only son, Kanji, had been her true brother. Yet—this loneliness was hard to endure, especially since she was frightened.

The neighbors said the storms were bad here, that this one might be particularly severe. She had seen no one since early yesterday, when the winds began to whip up the low clouds into blackness, and the heavy atmosphere threatened rain.

In the next room, across from the living room, her father lay on his pallet. Robert Atwood lay on his back, and this morning his breathing seemed labored and hoarse. His hair was so white, his face pallid and lined. Charita had never seen him so ill. The doctor had come from Sapporo several times, and she had seen his gentle face harden and his lips firm as he treated the older man. She longed to ask questions, yet dared not hear the answers. Could her father, only fifty-four years old, be dying?

He had adamantly refused to go into a hospital. No, he must finish his book first. His work was his life. There was no arguing with him, he simply did not hear anyone. Then, two weeks ago, he had laid down his pen, smiled, and fallen over. She had gotten him to his mat and he had struggled weakly. "I am not yet finished," he had whispered, tossing his head restlessly.

Charita had soothed him with hot tea and gentle words, and he had slept. He had not really wakened often since then.

She had come to take care of him, and she *would!* But she was frightened, terribly frightened. The Noguchis had kept from her so much of the reality of life. Even when Helen's elderly mother had died, Charita had not been permitted in the sickroom or afterward, to help with the burial preparations. She must be shielded, protected, sheltered at all cost.

Her blue eyes gazed steadily out at the pouring rain, toward the muddy road. The great trees, stripped by the wintry winds, swayed in the passion of the surging wind. No one would be out today, it would be madness. Just now she wished there were a telephone; she would have phoned her parents, or Kanji, or . . .

Her eyes widened as a small tree near the road seemed to move. It came nearer, and she saw it was not a small tree, but a large man. He was wearing a tan raincoat, darkened and made useless by the rain, the tall boots to his knees must have been soaked through, and his head, Charita noted incredulously, was bared to the wind. It looked like he carried a box and a suitcase. He was coming here!

Who was mad enough to be out in this storm? She ran to the door, waited in an agony of impatience as the tall man struggled against the gusts of wind and rain to get up the stone-lined path. She slid open the door and the rain came in, lashing her dark blue kimono.

The man lifted his wet head and grinned at her, a slash of white teeth lighting his tanned face. "Hi, brought you some groceries," he said, as casually as though he had driven up in his elegant silver car.

"Brad! Mr. Livingston," Charita gasped, then tried to take the carton of dripping groceries from him.

"Don't touch it, honey, it's soaking wet. Where's the kitchen?"

She pattered before him in her house slippers, leading him to the small room that served as kitchen and storage room. Just in time, he set the carton down. The sides broke open, and fruit slid across the floor. She got down on her knees, gathered it up, and put it in a bowl. Apples, peaches —how had he found them? she wondered. And oranges! bright, pretty round balls—she hadn't tasted fresh fruit for weeks. She put the milk cartons into the tiny icebox and hoped they might stay cool for a time. The ice had melted two days ago.

Bradford Livingston divested himself of the streaming raincoat and hung it over a chair. Then he sat down to pull off the heavy boots, grunting as he tugged at the wet leather.

"How did you get here?" she asked finally. And why, she wanted to add. But one didn't ask the wealthy and superior Mr. Livingston *why* about anything. She had learned in the year of their acquaintance that he did what he wanted, when he pleased.

"Plane, hired car. The car broke down about a mile up the road," he said, rising to pad about the kitchen in his stockinged feet. He scrutinized Charita for a long time as she set away the boxes of rice, macaroni, tinned meat and chicken, fruit juice. "You look like something the cat dragged in. Get yourself a glass of milk and sit down," he ordered.

Charita gasped, then laughed, a delicate, melodic sound. Brad was as rude and abrupt as ever, but her eyes shone as she poured out a glass of milk. "May I pour some for you?" she asked politely.

"No, thanks, I'll get some coffee. Brought some instant; I'm not that fond of tea," he explained as he opened the jar and looked about for the tea kettle. She turned up the fire for it to heat and found a cup and saucer for him. He frowned his disapproval at her, so she sat down at the wooden table to obediently drink her milk, and savor his presence.

For such a big man, Brad was neat and quick in his movements. He prowled around the tiny kitchen like a great jungle cat, she mused, smiling at her fancies. He dwarfed the place, his head almost reaching the ceiling of the unpainted house. She watched him pour steaming hot water into the cup, stir it, and sit down opposite her.

"How is your father?"

Her face shadowed; she unconsciously nursed the halfempty glass of milk in her slim fingers. "Not . . . well. The doctor comes when he can. Father refuses to go into the hospital."

"That's like him. Set in his ways. I hope, young lady, you're not as stubborn of nature as he is."

She managed a smile at his teasing drawl. "You were most kind—to come," she said. "How did you hear?"

"Kanji. His folks wrote to him. I dumped everything in his lap and took off. They must have been out of their minds, letting you come here and nurse him. You're just out of school."

"He is my father," she said, her gentle dignity hurt. Sometimes Brad was just too candid and rude. She wasn't accustomed to it.

"I'll take a look at him. Can you manage to cook the meals? Or shall I get a woman to come in?"

She had managed for more than a month. "I can do it. It won't be steak—"

He grinned at her. "Poking fun at me for ordering steak wherever I go? I haven't forgotten our last dinner, Miss!"

Brad had invited Professor Atwood and Charita out to dinner, at an elegant restaurant near his home in Kyoto. Her father had ordered a typical multi-course Japanese meal, she, out of courtesy to him, had done the same. Brad had ordered a steak, "Well-done, with lots of potatoes."

Her father had kidded him. "We will never make a Japanese out of you, Brad! In the midst of the finest of Japanese luxuries, you choose a steak. Why did you come to Japan?"

"For good hand-labor on my jewelry," Brad said promptly. "And I found it. My staff works darn hard, and they turn out beauties. By this time next year, the company will be on its feet financially."

No one had expected otherwise. Brad Livingston was but thirty. Although young by the standards of American business, he had made one fortune already, and would probably make another in his Japanese venture. He was an inventor, chemist, a brilliant man, Kanji said, in awe and delight that this man had made him his assistant in the

Livingston firm. Professor Atwood had introduced Brad to various officials, translated patiently, obtained permission for him to build the factory and office. He cut through reams of red tape with patience and persistence, and within a year Brad had his jewelry business off to a successful start. It was a form of jewelry on which electroplating of gold was added. Charita did not pretend to understand all of the process. For Christmas, Brad had given her a delicately chased golden bracelet with matching button earrings. They were so exquisite she had not dared wear them. Certainly she had no dress that would do them justice! But now and then she enjoyed peeking at them in their lovely inlaid wooden box.

The wind howled and shook the panes of glass; even tucked against the shelter of the small hill at its back, the wooden house shuddered on its foundations. Brad was concerned.

"Is it always this bad in March?"

"It is usually raining and cold, but a bad storm is expected this week," she explained.

He nodded at her, "That's why I had trouble getting a plane over here! When?"

"Tonight, maybe, or later. It depends on how fast it moves."

"And you were going to stay here, alone with him?"

"What else could I do? The neighbors have been more than kind, but they have their own families to care for."

"You might have phoned," he said grimly and looked about for the telephone. Charita shook her glossy blue-black head.

"No telephone," she said, quivering a little in amusement at his expression of disbelief. He was not used to Japan yet? She was sure he had a telephone in every room of his smart home. She had not seen his house, but Kanji had been there, and had described it in awe and wonder. The best of both worlds, said Kanji: beautiful natural woods, massive

14

rooms, Persian carpets, paintings on the walls, a magnificent garden with a pool, sliding doors, servants— This house must seem like a doll's house to him, or—worse—like primitive living. Suddenly self-conscious, she bent her head, lifted the glass and finished the milk. It tasted good and fresh.

"I'll take a look at him," Brad said, finishing his coffee. He set the cup down with a decisive click, stood up and left the room. She followed him, moving softly in her slippers.

They looked into the room, then went in and stood silently beside her father's crude pallet. It was no better than a camp cot, she thought. He didn't believe in comforts for himself because he wanted to use his money for books, and for traveling throughout the country talking to people as part of his research.

Professor Atwood's breathing was more labored. Brad put his tanned cheek gently to the thin, narrow chest. He rose, looked at the gaunt face, the white skin stretched over the fragile bones, touched the forehead lightly. "No fever," he said.

She shook her head. "No, he is cold sometimes. Yet, he throws off the blankets when I put them on."

Brad gently replaced one blanket, tucking it around the shoulders, then moved away. He said nothing more. In the tiny living room-dining room, he moved to the windows and looked out. She wondered what he was thinking. Charita sat down in the wooden chair and tucked her feet neatly under it. She preferred sitting on cushions, but that was too informal before this big American. Finally he came to sit down near her.

"Nothing to do but wait out the storm," he said quietly. His gaze seemed to run lightly over her, as though in assessment. She wondered what he saw. At eighteen, she felt immensely younger than him—he was so arrogantly sure of himself, so experienced. He had traveled the world, whereas she knew only Japan.

"What do you do all day," he asked, when the silence had stretched between them.

Charita felt suddenly gay and giddy, so different from the way she had felt an hour ago.

"Paint and sew," she said, with a smile. "There is such peace and silence here, I have completed three paintings."

"I'd like to see them."

It was something to do, in that rain-lashed early afternoon, with the storm approaching. She got up and turned around the canvases stacked against a wall. They were small, all she had been able to buy in the town nearby. In Sapporo, she could have bought a large canvas, but she had no transportation. It had cost dearly to taxi out to her father; she could spend no more on frivolities.

Taking a canvas into his big capable hands, Brad studied each one in silence, before setting it down and looking at the next. Charita felt embarrassed by his intent scrutiny.

"These are very good, Charita," he said, then. "You have great talent."

She felt relieved and surprised. No one else had said that. Her foster mother praised every little thing she did, from cooking rice to serving tea to greeting guests. Her foster father knew little about art except that all in his family appreciated nature and gazed for hours at a flower, or Mount Fuji, on their few trips there.

"You are most kind," she said, formally. Maybe he meant to make her feel better.

It was as though he read her thoughts. "I don't flatter, honey," he said bluntly. "My business is art. You *are* good. You could make a career of this, if you wanted. It would take years, but you could."

She could not think that far ahead; in fact, at this moment, she could not even think past the night. She had begun to worry about where Brad would sleep. He must be accustomed to a big bed, and they had no beds, only tatami

16

mats and futons. Maybe he would go back to a hotel in Sapporo.

The wind howled unexpectedly, and she shuddered, gazing at the window. The tortured trees outside were bending double; even as they stared, one snapped in the wind and fell against the house. Brad was up in an instant.

"I'd better move that away from the house," he said, and went to pull on his boots and raincoat. She watched anxiously from a crack between the sliding doors as he tugged and strained at the large tree, to drag it away from the fragile walls of the house. He came back in, drenched, pushing back his thick chestnut-brown hair from his forehead.

"Some storm," he said. "Judging from the sky, I'd say we're in for a lot more of the same. Have any cards?"

"Cards?"

"Bridge, poker?"

"Oh—I am sorry, no. I do not play, nor my father."

"Don't worry, I'll live," he said dryly at the worry in her tone. He grinned at her, tipped up her chin with his finger. "How old are you, fifteen?"

"I am eighteen years of age," she said soberly, a little hurt.

"You look about five," and still grinning, he went out to the kitchen to shed his boots again. She heard him moving about, but stayed where she was. It hurt to be considered a child. Why, she didn't know.

He began whistling softly, and she felt comforted—she was not alone anymore. Even if he went to Sapporo tonight, he had come, and brought food and thoughtfulness. Charita was grateful. She went out to the kitchen to thank him, then paused, astonished.

In his stockinged feet, his jacket off, his silk shirt sleeves rolled up to reveal tanned, brawny arms, Brad was peeling onions. Rice was simmering on the stove.

"Oh, you are not cooking!" she breathed, shocked.

"I'm not? Then tell me what I'm doing, honey," he teased.

"But I will fix the meals. You have only to say you wish food, and I will prepare it."

"You sit down and watch. I've camped out many a time. You may fix the tea if you want," he added, as she hovered anxiously.

It was very strange, to let him do the cooking, which he did in the same efficient manner he tackled everything. The food, when he set it on the table, was delicious. He had opened a tin of tuna fish, the rice was fluffy and finely flavored with the onion, and he had sliced a plate of tomatoes and cucumbers. Charita had set the table and made the tea, nothing else. Now she ate with him, rather dazed and confused. Did American men do everything, even the work of women?

"I lived alone for years," he explained, as though he'd read her mind again. "Worked my way through college, worked at odd jobs in mining camps across the country. You learn to cook, or you starve."

"Oh, I see," she nodded. She didn't see, really. Were there no women about to provide food for him?

He ate briskly, as though his mind were on other matters and he were stoking up to rebuild his energy. Charita ate little, pushing the tuna around on her plate.

"Eat up," he commanded with mock fierceness.

She swallowed. "I am not very hungry."

"Comes of eating too little, at odd times. Go ahead, that's a good girl," he admonished, as he picked up her fork, lifted some food on it and put it to her lips. His dark brown eyes twinkled as she took the fork from him and frowned in confusion.

"You need someone to look after you," he said.

"I am old enough—" she began.

"But not grown up," he said, as though the subject were dismissed. "How about a peach, or an orange?"

She selected a peach. Brad washed it for her, then set it, cut, on a plate, and put it before her. He ate two peaches, relishing them as he let the juice run down his chin. He wiped it off and said, "I like peaches. Worked in Georgia once, helping at harvest. Never tasted anything like a fresh peach off the tree."

He began telling her about working on the Georgia peach farm, making it sound amusing and different. Charita listened, her blue eyes wide, fascinated. He had rarely bothered to talk to her, not like this, telling her about himself and his life. Usually the talk was business, between himself and her father. Or they discussed finding a house, hiring a staff of servants, and decorating his offices. Tonight was unusual.

She was considering a second cup of tea when her father called.

"Charita! Char—ita!"

She set down the cup, rose automatically, upset with herself. She had forgotten, for a short time, her father and his grave illness.

"Sit still, finish your tea. I'll go," said Brad, and pushed her gently back down again. He padded out into the other room, and she heard the voices—her father's so weak and thin and high, Brad's so deep and strong.

Brad came back. "He's thirsty. What do you give him?"

"Hot tea. Hot broth with a little rice. I can give him some beef broth from the tins you brought—"

"Good, you fix it, I'll feed him. We're going to talk a little. Why don't you rest, and I'll do the dishes later."

She set her lips. She would not have this rich, important man doing her dishes! The very idea was outrageous. She prepared the broth, rejoicing that she had something nourishing at last for her father. His stomach seemed to reject fish now, though he had always liked it.

Brad took the broth and disappeared with it. He was

gone a long time. She heard his voice from time to time. She heard little from her father. She poured hot water into the basin and started the dishes, keeping an ear cocked for sounds from the bedroom.

She had finished the dishes and the pans, and was hanging the dish towel over a rack, when Brad returned. His face was grave and distant.

"How is he?"

"The same," Brad said, unhelpfully. "I think he'll sleep awhile. Finished? Come on in the other room and put your feet up."

She was tired. The storm was hanging over them, making her feel curious and apprehensive, and weary of worry. Yet Brad was taking charge, and she was relieved of carrying all the burdens. She made one feeble effort to send him away.

"I thought you might want to go back to Sapporo to a hotel tonight," she began, as she sat down among the cushions in the living room. He had added fuel to the smoldering coals in the little hibachi, and the warmth was comforting. He didn't seem to mind, either, that she curled up in the cushions, instead of sitting formally on a chair.

"Out in this storm? Thank you, no. It's a good ten miles back to Sapporo, and the car battery is dead."

"I do not mean to sound ungracious," she said faintly, and a pink blush came up in her young face.

He looked at her, then at the fire, as he sat down in a chair. "Don't worry about me," he said.

"I'll prepare some tatami mats and a thick futon for you, and there are many blankets," she told him.

"I'll stay up with your father. I would appreciate a blanket—later on, honey!"

As he gestured to her, she sank down again on the cushions. He leaned back, easily, in the hard chair.

"So—you've finished school, Charita?"

She nodded. School seemed a thousand years ago, though she had finished just last summer, a little early for her age. Since then she had remained at home, helping her foster mother about the house, doing errands for her, mending, sewing, painting. They had not approved of her going out for a job. Besides, what would she do? They would not hear of her working in a factory, though there was a transistor radio factory in town.

"And did you enjoy school? What subjects did you like?"

"Oh—art, and history, and philosophy," she said absently.

"I was always onto chemistry, puttering around," he said easily. "Liked to fool with experiments. I blew up the lab once. Almost got myself expelled."

"You didn't!" She gazed up at him in amazement. He was grinning, she wasn't sure he was serious.

"Well, it wasn't entirely my fault. One of my buddies decided to play a joke on me. I was getting straight A's for identifying the unknown solutions they had us working on. But he substituted his own brew while I was out of the lab. When I came back, I added another chemical, and wham! Blew up sky high. Blew a hole in the ceiling. Was the professor furious! A fire started, they had to get out the fire trucks—"

He went on easily, telling her tales from school, from his many varied jobs, entertaining her, until she even chuckled from time to time. The wind rose outside, and beat at the windows, and shook the house, yet she felt cozy and comfortable crouched in the cushions, listening to his slow, easy drawl.

"Well, time for you to turn in, your eyelids are drooping," said Brad, at last. "Go on, now, get me a blanket, then get to bed. I'll be on sick call tonight."

21

She wanted to protest, but he was inflexible. Nobody said no to him, she thought, yet it was somehow nice to be taken care of, after the weeks of caring for a sick, tormented man. She went to bed, and to sleep, in spite of the howling storm.

She wakened with a jolt. The storm was shaking her. Then she realized it was Brad, moving her shoulder gently to rouse her.

"Come, Charita, wake up. Your father wants you." She sat up with a jerk, her heart pounding with alarm. His voice was so grave.

"What—what is it? He is worse?" She slid out of bed, conscious of the thinness of her cotton pajamas. He held the robe for her, as if it were a coat, and she slipped into it, as she put her feet into slippers.

"I think he is going down rapidly, my dear," said Brad, and put his arm about her shoulders as they went into her father's room.

The storm was howling more loudly. Trees lashed against the windows, as though all nature tried to enter and make them share in the madness. Brad had lit a candle near the bed. Her father's face seemed more white and strained. Yet there was a curious peace in it.

"Char—ita," he whispered, and she went to kneel down and take his thin hand in her warm ones. He felt so cold.

"Dear Father, rest, and get warm," she said gently.

"No. Must—talk. Brad."

"Right here."

He was at Charita's shoulder, his warmth like a furnace behind her, warming and strengthening her.

"I have—not provided for—my darling."

"Don't worry about it," said Brad. "She'll be taken care of."

"I have not—finished my—book. It might have—helped pay—" whispered her father.

22

She caressed his hand, pressed her lips to his fingers. "Don't fret, Father, I can earn my own living," she said, with more confidence than she felt.

A slight frown creased her father's forehead. "No—won't do—I wanted you—safe—"

"I'll take care of Charita," Brad said firmly. "Don't you fuss, now. I'll always take care of her."

"Promise—"

"I promise. You have my solemn word. You know I keep my word. You were of immense help to me, Professor Atwood," he added quietly. "I shan't forget that. Charita shall be like my own, I promise. She shall never want for anything."

Charita stirred, distressed by this exchange. Brad's big hand pressed on her shoulder to keep her still. Her father sighed, and lay back, she felt him slackening, and thought he had gone to sleep. "Thank . . . you . . ." he whispered, and his thin lips scarcely moved. "Char . . . ita . . . my dear . . ."

"Yes, Father."

She waited for what he would say. The silence went on, and on. The fingers in hers were lax.

The hoarse breathing seemed easier, in fact she could not hear the heavy, strained sound that had troubled her for days and nights. She waited, kneeling there, Brad's hand on her shoulder.

Then Brad leaned down and lifted her up, taking her hands from her father's. She protested, "Oh, wait, he was saying—"

"He is gone, my dear," said Brad, very gently.

No. She could not believe it. She bent down, to listen to the breathing, to touch her father's face.

"Father . . ." She sobbed once, a strained sound. Brad drew her up again, back into his arms, and held her solidly against his broad chest.

Her fist was clenched against his shoulder. Her shock was so great that she could not cry. That her father should die! That he had gone—he had left her—she could not believe it. It was too sudden—

And the storm raged outside, winds shrieking around the small house, where death had entered so quietly.

2

Brad tucked Charita back into her bed, ignoring her feeble protests. She was shaking, but she had not wept, and that worried him a little. Her control was unnatural for such a young girl. But she had been raised as a Japanese girl, and the Japanese valued self-control highly. Still—he wished she had broken down.

When she was down, he went back to Professor Atwood and did what he must. He was accustomed to death; he had met the grim reaper before, in mining camps, out in the wilderness; even on the Georgia peach farm.

Then he laid out several mats, set a futon on them, and unfolded several blankets. He lay down and stared at the streaming window panes. The storm was lashing on furiously and he hoped the small house would hold together. He had noticed that it was built against the side of the hill, no doubt to withstand just such onslaughts. The front to the sea wind, the back to the hill.

He lay awake for a time, thinking, a frown creasing his high, stately forehead. There were several possibilities of what to do with Charita. He could take her back to her foster parents, they were immensely fond of her. But they pampered her, and protected her, and in their small town she would never meet an American. He did not see her marrying a Japanese.

He might give her into the care of his business associates, Miles and Jacinda Snow. They were reliable, wealthy. Yet, Miles did have a bad drinking problem, which would trouble and upset Charita. Then there was Jacinda. Well, lately she had become so damned sarcastic and hard. He didn't want Charita to be exposed to Jacinda's cynicism. It would rub off, he felt. Charita was very young and vulnerable. This was a touchy age for her. She could go any way.

She was sweet, he thought, smiling at the thought of her innocent blue eyes, and her quick smile at some of his stories. She had dimples in her cheeks when she smiled and her laugh was low and pretty. She had attractive ways, and used her lovely hands in a graceful manner. Her shiny cap of sleek blue-black hair framed her face beautifully. He thought her too pale and thin, though. The past months had been hard on her. Damn it, they should never have let Charita come to take care of her father, especially in this isolated spot.

She was intelligent, had achieved excellent grades in school—her father had bragged about that, his eyes alight. She might be able, he had said, to help him gather his historical facts and put some material in order. Brad had thought at the time that it was a sad waste of a lovely girl.

Should she go on to college? She showed no signs of wishing that. But maybe she would want to. She was so polite, she might not have expressed her wishes. Also, she knew her father's financial situation. She might go to the States, to a relative, and attend college. Get her out of the suppressive Japanese atmosphere, show her some American good times. Might be a culture shock, but good for her. She was an American, after all, though she had lived all her days in Japan.

The rain had lessened to a steady drumming. He closed his eyes and willed himself to sleep. He could do nothing about Charita tonight, and her father was past helping.

When he woke, the windows were lighter, and the rain was softly throbbing. He smelled tea. Charita must be up. He got up, washed at the small hand basin, and went out back to the outhouse. Damn it, no girl should have to live like this! He had endured worse in the mining camps, but this was a civilized country—

He was frowning when he went into the kitchen. Charita gave him a quick look and smile. He saw her eyes were red-rimmed, covered hastily with powder, which had smudged in white streaks. Poor child.

He put his hand briefly on her shoulder. She felt so small. "I'll fix breakfast," he said.

She looked shocked, that amused him. "No, it is almost ready, please, Mr. Livingston. You will sit down, yes?"

He breathed an impatient sigh, and sat down to be waited on. Sometimes she did not even talk like an American. Professor Atwood should have taken her back to the States years ago, when her mother died. It wasn't right that she had been brought up like this.

Still, she was charming, and her ways were pretty. She served his coffee gravely, waiting to see if it was as he liked it. Then she took the hot plate in a napkin, and served the ham and eggs. For herself, she had juice and tea.

He reached over for the toast plate and put on it some pieces of ham and half an egg. He set it before her. "Eat that, my dear," he ordered. "You'll need energy."

Her pink mouth opened to protest, then closed again. She tackled it slowly. He ate quickly, thinking of what to do next. When she had sipped at her tea, and most of the food was gone, he said, "Who in the village takes care of the graves?"

Charita flinched, then quickly schooled her face to

calm. "The man lives but four houses from us. I will talk to him."

"You give me his name, and directions. I'll go. I have enough of the language to manage," he said. He patted her hand reassuringly. "It's necessary, honey. This rain doesn't look like it's giving up for a time."

"No, sometimes the rain lingers with a late storm such as this," she replied politely. Her fingers were cold.

Brad finished his coffee, then put on his now dry boots and coat and went out in the rain. It was a steady downpour, but the black clouds still loomed ominously in the west. He made the arrangements; the man was very polite, his wife peeking from the next room, obviously listening.

Professor Atwood's body was taken away, and later in the day, he was buried in the small graveyard of the village two miles away. Charita thought her father would like that because he was fond of the place and had made friends with the people. The graveyard had the simplicity and calm he had always sought.

In spite of the bad weather, a number of men attended Robert Atwood's funeral. Charita, sheltered by a huge black umbrella someone had produced, listened impassively to the service. It was partly Buddhist, partly Christian, Brad noted, shifting from one booted foot to the other, partly in English, partly in Japanese. Professor Atwood would have been pleased.

They returned to the small house. The car was still in the road, stuck in the mud, battery dead. Someone told Brad that the planes were grounded for the time being. No one was allowed up while the storm still threatened.

There was nothing to do but stay and keep cheerful, he thought.

Women scurried in and out during the late afternoon. They brought hot dishes of rice and steaming meat; they brought flowers, and talked in low tones to Charita while their men talked to Brad.

Charita served them tea, and answered all very calmly. Her control was amazing, Brad thought, watching her. Her hands shook, but she managed a bright smile from time to time.

As evening came, the house grew quiet. Brad served the supper on trays before the hibachi. Charita sat on cushions before her tray, curled up like a kitten. Brad's long legs bent awkwardly before him as he tried to get comfortable on the cushions. He was more at ease in a chair, and this food was strange to him. There were spices he didn't know, and exotic preparations. But it was hot and nourishing; delicious though unusual. Some thoughtful person had brought ice and he had been able to get the small icebox rechilled. Another man had told him, very politely, about the tiny grocery in the village. There he could get fruits and vegetables and fish.

"Tomorrow," said Brad, "I'll go find this grocery and get us some more food. Looks like we're stuck for a time. You don't mind much, do you?"

She smiled and shook her head. "I must sort through Father's papers, and see how far he went on the book," she said absently. She sipped her tea, gazing into the fire.

"That's good," he encouraged. Give her something to think about. "Do you think you can finish it for him?"

She brightened. "I might be able to. He had discussed the notes with me. Yes, I might—he had but three chapters more to write."

"That would be a fine thing to do." He had thought about getting her somehow into Sapporo to a hotel. Perhaps, though, it was better to stay here, let her face the fact of her father's death, occupy herself with his papers. They could pack up the books and papers and move out as soon as the storm quit.

That night, lying on the futon by the hot coals, Brad thought about Charita. He did not think she should come back here alone, nor did he want her to. It was better to finish up all business now and leave the house forever. He had another futon on top of him, and it felt good and warm and cozy. He had slept in tents, in the open near a fire, in primitive cabins, yet this was more comfortable than any of those places. It was a pity this simple house was so homey. This was all she had, he realized. What would happen to Charita?

The next day, several village women called again. They looked with bright dark eyes at Brad and at Charita, and whispered together. Damn it, thought Brad, as it dawned on him, the conventions were being violated! He was alone in the house with an attractive and vulnerable girl. He felt impatient, but it was the truth. Charita's reputation would be in shreds.

He was thinking, wondering what to do with his charge. The Snows were out: Jacinda was no caretaker of pretty young girls. She had no children of her own, and she wasn't exactly the motherly type. She would have screamed with laughter at the idea. And the Noguchis would be only a stopgap while he decided Charita's future. College, then?

He questioned Charita gently. "Have you thought of going on to school?"

"School? I have finished," she said blankly.

"I mean college—university. Is there anything you want to study? History? Or art—or teaching?"

She shook her shiny head. She almost looked Japanese, he thought absently, with her dark hair in a smooth pageboy style, and bangs over her wide forehead. Only her deep blue eyes betrayed her American ancestry. Her face was round and innocent and young. And her clothes!—Brad frowned at the dark kimonos and the schoolgirl uniform of blue jumper and white blouse. He longed, suddenly, to see her really well dressed, perhaps in a demure creamy white silk dress, or a festive deep blue taffeta the color of her eyes. He considered bright rose wool to bring out the roses in her cheeks—or something springlike, perhaps apple green.

"I had not thought of the university. I don't know if I could pass the examinations in the courses. I thought only of helping my father," her voice quivered a little. She put her hand to her mouth, and visibly schooled herself back to control.

"About painting, Charita, I think you would do well there," he said. Yet he knew that it took years of dedication and intensity and drive to make a career in art. There was so much competition in any of the arts. He would hate to see someone as gentle as she up against the ferocity of the drive for fellowships, the long years of struggling.

"I like to paint, but it is a hobby," she said quietly. "No, I must think of making a living. There is a factory in the village where my foster parents live. I think I could obtain a job there. The owner is a friend of my foster father."

Brad frowned, he didn't like the idea of that at all. Charita, soft and naive, in a factory, with tough, hardboiled men and women? No, never! Even if she lived at home, it would be too rough on her.

"Well, we don't have to decide yet, but I have an idea," he said slowly. The idea formed in his mind; he shoved it away, impatiently, yet it kept coming back. It *would* work, it *could* work! but he wanted to think about it more. He smiled into her questioning face. "Let me think it over a bit, Charita."

"Yes, Mr. Livingston," she said obediently. "May I serve you some coffee?"

"Why don't you serve me some tea?" he asked, on impulse. "I remember that tea ceremony in your home when I first met you. I think I would appreciate it more now. I didn't understand it all then."

Charita's face glowed with animation, and Brad silently congratulated himself on the idea. It would give her something to do, and it was a charming custom.

She went first to her bedroom, and returned, wearing a formal kimono of scarlet with yellow chrysanthemums embroidered all over it. It made a startling difference in her appearance. The colors gave a rosy glow to her pale golden skin and fragile beauty. Her blue eyes sparkled with pleasure as she brought the instruments of the tea ceremony, the bamboo ladle and dipper, the bowls, the bamboo whisk, the powdered green tea.

He watched her with some amusement, carefully hidden, and much pleasure, that he was not able to hide. He lowered himself to the floor, at her instruction, and sat among the cushions, as she knelt intently before the bowls and the small fire and kettle.

"Shouldn't I be reading some poetry, or something?" he asked.

She looked closely at him, to see if he was teasing. "You may, if you like," she said. She rose gracefully, and went to the book shelves, and returned with several volumes. "Here is your Wordsworth, and some haiku translated. You may read what you wish."

It was an odd but pleasurable pastime. He read Wordsworth for a time, glancing up to watch her serene movements as she went through the time-honored gestures of ladling the tea into the bowl, adding hot water with the dipper, then whipping up the water and powder with the bamboo whisk. Turning the bowl about, she served him the slightly bitter tea. He drank it solemnly, and returned to reading haiku.

"May I read aloud, or would it disturb your contemplation?" he asked.

"I would enjoy your reading," she said, formally, with a little smile dimpling her pinking cheeks. She didn't look so white and wan now, he noted with relief.

He read aloud to her as she drank the green tea, and served him the darker tea he preferred. They sat for a long time on the wood floors, with cushions to soften the hardness, and he read while she listened and commented with grave delight on the poems.

The wind rose, and the rains returned full force, but the pair engrossed in reading haiku scarcely noticed. It was a background for the quiet afternoon, and for a time, they could ignore the elements.

Finally Brad laid aside the books, and lay back lazily on the cushions. It had been an emotionally strenuous time for him, as well as for Charita. He had been fond of the professor, and he would miss him. The man had been good to him and Brad believed in paying his debts.

"Do you have any relatives in the United States, Charita?" he asked, as though idly.

A shadow crossed her expressive face. She raised her hands, palms outward. "My mother's aunt, a couple of cousins. They disapproved of her marrying my father. They said he was an idle dreamer, he told me. My father, a professor! How could they!"

"Do you still write to them?"

She shook her head, and he watched as the pretty dark hair flew about her shoulders, sparkling as it caught the glow from the fire. "No, I never did. They didn't write to us after mother died."

That was out, then. He would not push her onto unknown, unliked, and disapproving relatives.

"I'm almost alone in the world also," he said. "My father died when I was eighteen; my mother remarried, a man with a sixteen-year-old girl, Jacinda. We were both only children and got along well. When the parents divorced after much quarreling, we still saw each other. She is married and lives in Japan."

"That is nice for you," she said thoughtfully. "I am sorry your childhood was unhappy, though."

He shrugged. "I was pretty well grown, and off to college by that time. The early years were good, I have that to remember. It is nice to have happy times to remember."

"Yes," Charita said quietly. "One is soothed and made happy by the memories that are pleasant, storing them up like treasures of the mind."

She spoke so seriously that Brad was startled. Girls he knew didn't talk like that; they were flippant, or amorous, or aggressive. Charita was not any of those things.

The talk wandered to her father's book, his other works. Charita spoke of them well, her face glowing with pride. She had evidently read and enjoyed them all, and was well-versed in Japanese myths and legends, and the country's history.

Brad slept well that night; he had made up his mind. The days passed easily.

There were the books to pack carefully in the packing cases Brad was able to find. They stuffed rice paper around the rare, precious volumes that the professor had used in his research. The current manuscript went into a smaller box, which Charita would keep with her. A single suitcase was sufficient for her clothes. Brad made a mental note of that; she must be outfitted.

A few neighbors still called, but the darting looks at Brad and Charita told their story. Although Charita seemed unaffected by it all, he was determined to still the gossip before they departed.

The dreary rains had finally begun to let up. Brad stirred himself, contacted the garage in the village. A man picked up the car and worked on it, promising to have it ready in a couple of days.

He went in search of Charita after the long trek back from the village through the mud of the single-lane tracks. He left his boots on a newspaper in the kitchen.

Charita was kneeling before a bookcase, absorbed in one of the books she was supposed to be putting into the packing case. Her father had not been rich in furniture or money, but his library was that of a connoisseur.

"Charita, let's have some tea and coffee—and we'll discuss plans," he said briskly.

She looked up from the book, her blue eyes vague, then gradually focusing on him. "Oh, yes, Mr. Livingston," she said, and gracefully moved to get up.

"Thought I told you one hundred times to call me Brad," he said amiably. The thought of being called Mr. Livingston all the time made him flinch; he wondered if she felt he was too old, if she saw him as an elderly friend.

"It does not seem respectful," she answered, preceding him to the kitchen. Today she wore the neat schoolgirl uniform of navy blue and white, with the little insignia of her high school. She seemed younger than ever.

But he had made up his mind.

"Call me Brad," he said firmly, and sat down, letting her fool with the tea kettle and cups. She enjoyed it, and he wanted to concentrate on keeping the right tone with her.

"Yes—Brad. You are most kind to me."

The kettle boiled; as she poured the hot water into the cups, he stirred his absently. The fresh milk was gone long ago, the rice and tins of meat were almost finished. They should leave soon. He felt a little regret. The small house had been peaceful, away from the world.

"Charita, I have been making plans. Today I reserved two places on the plane for us for Wednesday, to return to Kyoto."

Her eyes widened, she gazed steadily at him. "Yes —we must return to our duties," she said, with a wistful sigh. "I shall return to my foster parents—yes?"

"No," said Brad. "I have been thinking seriously about that. I promised your father I would take care of you, and I will. If you are away off in that village, I can't keep an eye on you. You have no other relatives you care about— right?"

She nodded. "Except my brother, Kanji."

"Um—yes." Kanji was a handsome rascal, Brad thought. He was about as capable of taking fatherly care of a girl like Charita as a happy young stallion in a field of frisky mares.

"What—did you think about?" she asked timidly, as he stirred and stirred his instant coffee.

"Well, Charita. For several reasons, I have decided that you will marry me."

Her spoon slipped and fell into the saucer with a clatter. Her mouth opened; no sound came out.

He went on, very briskly. "You need taking care of. I need a wife; I am thirty and not married. I like you very much; I respected your father immensely. And you like me, don't you?" He waited anxiously for her reply.

She seemed to find her voice with an effort—"I—like—you, yes, but Brad—Mr. Livingston—Brad—"

He continued, in his take-charge manner, avoiding that troubled gaze of hers. "The sensible thing is to get married. I am sure you will take care of my home very capably. You are schooled in housekeeping, you speak Japanese, you are —very attractive. I need a hostess, as well as a wife. You will fill the role admirably."

"I—will?" She sounded dubious.

He nodded convincingly, pretending to himself that it was a business deal that must be put over. "Right. You are a lovely girl, you will become a beautiful woman. I'm a bit older than you are, but that is no matter, is it?"

She shook her head in silence.

"Well, then, we shall get married in Kyoto. I know a minister who will do the job—"

"I always thought . . . I would be married in a Shinto ceremony," she said softly, her gaze on her swirling tea.

"Well, we can do both," he said recklessly. He was willing to promise anything at that moment.

"We could? That would be pleasant. And I would

invite my foster parents and Kanji, and my school friends—"

"Splendid. And I should invite my business associates."
He was beginning to relax and enjoy himself. The worst was
over; she was starting to accept the idea.

"But I might not be right—for you," she said soberly.
"I mean—someone more—of your taste. Kanji said you
admire brilliant and sophisticated women."

He silently cursed the talkative Kanji. "But that
doesn't mean I would marry one," he said firmly. "I want
a lady who is discreet, with a pleasant voice that does not
rasp the nerves, who dresses prettily, and makes my house
a home. You would do that, wouldn't you?"

"I would try very hard," she said soberly. She sighed
a little. "I have nothing to bring to you, no dowry," she
said, her mouth drooping.

"It is a little unusual, but I am sure your father's
books are a fine dowry. And your own mind and heart," he
added.

She seemed a little comforted.

He went on, quickly, "Well, that is settled then. I will
tell your neighbors, so they will be reassured that you are
in good hands. I think they worry about you."

"Yes, they are most kind," said Charita. Her face did
not change from its innocent glow. She did not even realize
that they were gossiping about her, concerned about her
reputation and future.

She submitted docilely to Brad's plans. She packed
her suitcase, finished packing the books with his help. Brad
spoke to the next woman who came in, and the word flew
about the small village like wildfire. Many came the next
day to bring small gifts and wish them well.

"It is only a poor thing, but it wishes you well. May
you remember your insignificant neighbor when you look
at it," said one woman, coughing behind her hand, as she
presented a magnificent black lacquer jewel box to Charita.

"It is very beautiful and will remind me of your goodness and kindness to me," said Charita, always graceful with the right words. She beamed at the woman.

Every gift, no matter how small or large, received her grateful thanks and was placed carefully on a table. A silk scarf of a violet-purple hue was received and the right words said, along with a strand of pearls from the man who ran a factory in the village. Some brought paintings, one gave a small statue of the goddess Kuan-yin, the Goddess of Mercy. Charita exclaimed with pleasure over this and handled it tenderly. It was of painted wood, and the face was marvelously well done, with a tender expression.

Some brought painted fans, some small cups and tea-pots, or lengths of cloth in beautiful weaves. All were received with the same courtesy from Charita. Brad tried to echo her gratitude but feared he could not equal her exquisite manners. Still, the visitors seemed to approve of the "big American man" to whom she had been betrothed, and many of the ladies seemed much relieved that her future was assured.

Many of the men spoke of the kyoju, the professor, to Brad. He was a man of learning and gentleness, and they had respected him and spoken more freely to him than to many Americans. "He lived our ways," said one man, with wonder.

"He admired your ways immensely," Brad told them. "He thought you had found the secret of a full and rich life: contemplation, mercy, peace."

That pleased them, and Charita smiled at Brad glowingly.

Then came the task of wrapping up all the gifts again and finding more boxes to put them in. It would be a job to get them all to Kyoto, but Brad knew Charita well enough to know she would not leave behind a single cup or piece of cloth. It would be a gross insult, and she would never be guilty of that.

She was weary when she had finished. She stretched

her arms, and put her hands to her head. Brad went over to her. It was late, past midnight, and they must get the plane the next day, after the ride to Sapporo.

"Go to bed, Charita, you are so weary. I promise you, it will be easier in Kyoto." He cupped her round face in his big hands, and very gently touched his lips to hers. He had just time to feel the softness of them, and to smell the slight perfume she wore, when she sprang back. She put her hands to her face, and stood trembling before him. He realized suddenly that she was shocked. She must never have been kissed on the lips before. She was truly an innocent.

He must go slowly in courting her. She was like the rare golden lotus, the nickname the Japanese had given her. He had heard the name several times in the past couple of weeks that he had been here. She looked like a lotus, he thought now, with her pale golden skin glowing pink, the fragile beauty of her form, swaying as in a wind.

"Go to bed, Charita," he said again, and turned her by the shoulders gently toward her room. "I'll wake you in plenty of time in the morning. Sleep well."

"Sleep well," she said in a muffled tone, and disappeared into her bedroom, closing the door after her.

He went to bed on the mats, thoughtfully, his arms crossed behind his head. He smiled to himself in the darkness. He had a gem of a bride, he thought. A real innocent, a virgin of such purity and sweetness—how had he come to be so lucky? He must take care of her, must not shock or distress her. But one day he would waken her to passion—and then—then—she would be truly beautiful to him.

3

Brad made things move so smoothly, with seemingly such little effort. Charita watched him discreetly behind her lowered lashes as he drove into Sapporo, his hands easy on the wheel of the automobile.

He handled everything with an economy of movement that fascinated her. Even people. She watched him with the woman at the airline counter. She was bowing and smiling, eager to please. The car was left with her; she would arrange all, she assured Brad. Another man came up, anxiously, to make sure the big American man was well cared for. He also assured Brad the seats on the airplane would be of the best; he regretted so much the first-class seats were all gone, but they would have the first row of economy class. The hostess would be notified to look after them.

Brad turned back to Charita. The suitcase was sent on its way. She huddled into her shabby tweed coat, a little large for her. The coat was a gift of an English friend of her foster parents and was warm, but next to Brad's casual, well-dressed form, she felt uneasy. She thought he did not approve of her school uniform, but a kimono did not fit under the tweed coat, and she had nothing else.

He smiled down at her, and took the box she was

clutching. She carried the manuscript and her father's papers with her. She trusted no one with the box, except Brad.

"We'll go right to the gate, Charita. Only twenty minutes until the plane leaves," he said easily.

She nodded, and let him guide her down the long corridors, around corners, through doors, past officials. Brad took care of everything, the showing of papers and passports, of tickets, of speaking to everyone, of finding the way. She recalled as a nightmare the trip from her foster parents' home near the Inland Sea to Tokyo, the change of planes to Sapporo, having to find her way, bewildered by the vast airports, the crisp officials. This time all she had to do was trot along beside Brad and let him manage.

Very soon, they were in their seats on the airplane. She had the one next to the window, and the hostess wanted to serve them tea or coffee or juice immediately. She was hovering over them solicitously as two men brushed past her rudely, jarring her. She turned with a set smile, and greeted them.

They were short, stocky Japanese, with broad faces, from the north of Japan, thought Charita, listening to their accents as they demanded to know where their seats were. The hostess settled them in the row behind Charita and Brad, and politely served them.

Their black eyes had swept over Charita and Brad, frowning at the Americans. They looked tough, she thought. She did not know why she shrank from their gaze, but felt instinctively that they were of a much rougher lot than she was used to. She knew farmers and villagers, ones who might look as though they lived a poor, hard life. Yet their faces were gentle and kindly. These men had set scowls, and tough, low growls were their way of communicating.

She forgot them as she sipped some hot tea, and thanked the hostess in English. The girl obviously wanted to practice her knowledge of English. It was important for the growing tourist trade, and she might get a job on a more important airline if her English were better.

The lights flashed, a soft bell sounded, and Brad leaned over to make sure Charita's seat belt was fastened securely. She watched his big hands test the belt. He was so close to her that she could smell his faint after-shave lotion, and see the slight bristle on his face. He had had to shave with her father's razor, there was no electricity in the house.

"All set?" he smiled down at her. She nodded. She felt funny in the pit of her stomach, and it had nothing to do with the way the airplane lifted smoothly into the air from the Sapporo airport. The two weeks alone with Brad were gone; they were going back to his big, important world, and she had promised to marry him.

To cover her uncertainty she peered from the small window of the plane. The trees were beginning to show green; further south there would be more green, and perhaps the cherry trees would be coming into bloom. It was late March, and she had missed the beautiful changing of the seasons in her foster parents' home on the Inland Sea. There, she would have watched the first daffodils come out, the first buds of the fruit trees, the pinking of the cherry, the yellowing of the forsythia. But perhaps Brad had all these in his gardens in Kyoto—

His home. Her mind scurried away fearfully from that thought. Had he really meant to marry her? And when? After some years? She had no trousseau ready. A Japanese girl would have been preparing for more than a year to have lengths of brocade made up into kimonos; the beautiful obis would have been prepared; large chests of cedar wood, with gold and silver handles and inlaid work, would have been purchased, and filled with silks and undergarments and household goods.

How did Americans marry? She had no idea. She had not even thought about it.

"What is worrying you? Does the plane bother you?"

Brad's voice in her ear shocked her back to the present. She shook her head, smiled at him bravely. "I was thinking . . . about the future," she said softly. "I do not know—what to do next."

"You let me worry about that. You just sit back and do what I tell you," he said, with a twinkle in his eyes and a smile on his lips.

She laughed a little, he seemed to mean for her to do just that. He took her hand in his, and began to smoothe her slim fingers.

"Next—" he said. "Well, we'll get to Kyoto airport, hopefully in good time. I telephoned my secretary, she will meet me, and also my stepsister Jacinda and her husband. I thought you would stay with Jacinda and her husband, Miles Snow, for a few days. I want to get organized for the wedding."

When her eyebrows crinkled in doubt, he reached out with his free hand, and smoothed them back in place, teasingly. "It will be—soon?" she asked, slowly.

He nodded, easily, as though it was all in a day's work. "Right. Jacinda has good taste, and will want to get dresses and manage everything for you. But her taste is definitely too sophisticated. I thought you and I would go shopping for things. You'll want a white wedding dress and a veil. And some pretty dresses and hats and shoes, and all the accessories."

"It will be—so expensive. It is something I should bring as my dowry," she whispered, biting her lips. "Oh, Brad, we should wait. My foster parents will advise me."

"No need," he said. "We talked about all that, and I want to arrange things myself. I can see you in peach satin, and sapphire blue wool to match your eyes. Yes, I definitely want to do things my own way." He smiled, but she heard the firmness behind the tone.

"If I were Japanese, I would be purchasing boxes of kimonos," she said, not wishing to offend him, but worrying

43

about the details. She hated to come poor to him. It was a shame for her. "A Japanese bride goes with her parents to purchase and have made up many beautiful kimonos of silk and brocade, and they are part of her dowry."

He bent over and kissed her nose. She blinked at him.

"Darling, you are not Japanese, and I want to have a say in what you wear," he said firmly. "I have to entertain a great deal. It will be a relief to have a wife like you, to manage everything and still look pretty. You may buy as many kimonos as you like—after we are married—and wear what you will. But I want to be consulted. Okay?"

She swallowed. With an effort, she said, "Okay," brightly, and let him change the subject to his home in Kyoto. She listened, fascinated, as he told her about the house, the gardens, the servants. He entertained mostly in restaurants, but he wanted to change that, to be able to entertain British and American guests in his home, as they expected. The customs were different.

They changed planes in Tokyo, and she went along obediently wherever Brad directed. She did notice that the two tough-looking Japanese seemed to have the same destination that they did, following them to the next gate, to take the plane to Kyoto. Again they sat behind Brad and Charita on the plane, in first class this time. They also had an argument with this hostess; she could not hear what they were saying, for their backs were to her, and the girl had a low, polite voice.

A man from the airline came onto the plane, the hostess murmured to him. He talked to the two men, some money exchanged hands, he gave them a receipt, and left the plane. The men settled down to talk to each other in hushed, angry tones.

Brad was up front, talking to one of the pilots. He seemed to know so many people in Japan, Charita thought. Or perhaps with his easy charm he made friends everywhere.

She settled into her seat and gazed curiously out the

window. She had seen little of Tokyo; it was a huge, bustling city, and the airport seemed to teem with people. She saw Japanese women in dark kimonos that indicated their marital status, and girls in bright kimonos that showed they were not married, and more girls in English- and American-style clothes, with their little feet in high heels. She wondered if Brad would want her to wear very high heels. She could manage about one-inch heels, but the two- and three-inch ones hurt her feet.

The rumble of the two men behind her reached her ears. There was no one else in first class. "Gold formula . . ." one said. "Must get . . . important."

"The master will be . . . angry . . . must get gold formula. No word . . . three weeks . . . his anger is bad —he is too powerful. No good word, ahhh, how he will be angry."

Her curiosity was aroused. She listened more intently, bent over the newspaper Brad had put in her hands. It was an American paper he had picked up in the airport to read.

"Gold . . . important . . . where does he keep . . . Master will be furious—"

They said it again and again; she caught the words in Japanese as they mumbled and fussed at each other. She caught something about "laboratory . . . someone must go there and get inside . . . the man has ordered much supply . . . if we could find out what he has ordered—"

She gazed thoughtfully at the newspaper, not seeing the words. She knew little of business, but Kanji had told her once that his work was very important. Business people were always trying to steal the secrets of a business, he said, and if they could manufacture a similar product before the prototype was patented, it could bring much money. He was proud that Brad trusted him to help make up chemicals. But only Brad made the final mixture, and only Brad was in the laboratory when he finished the gold jewelry. Was it something like this?

She felt sorry for whoever these men were after. They would be cold and ruthless in their efforts to get his secrets. Why had they been in Sapporo? Was the laboratory there? She thought about speaking to Brad about it, but he lingered with the pilots until the lights flashed.

Then he returned to his seat. "I was able to call my office," he said, at once. "It's all set. We will be met. Are you all fastened in, honey?"

Her seat belt was not fastened. He frowned, and fastened it for her, carefully testing it. Then he fastened his own, and took her hand.

She forgot about the two men behind them. Brad's hand was big and firm, with calluses on the palm, revealing how industrious he was. He dressed so smoothly, with such elegance, that one forgot he worked very hard. Her father had said he was one of the most dynamic men he had ever met. "He makes me feel weary," he had added ruefully. "Such energy. Such attention to details."

Tears sprang to her eyes. Her father would never again speak to her of his work, of his thoughts and feelings. She had not been able to spend much time with him, but he had come regularly at least once a year to her home with the foster parents, and spent a week with them. He had been someone of her own, her very own. Now she was alone in the world.

"Honey?" Brad's voice breathed in her ear. He kissed her cheek. "Tears?" he whispered.

She dashed them from her eyes and smiled, ashamed of herself. To lose self-control, and in public! "Forgive me," she murmured.

His hand squeezed hers. "We'll be able to talk, once we are home in Kyoto," he comforted her.

She could not speak. She felt such a mixture of confused emotions. Panic at the thought of marriage to this big man, practically a stranger. Pride in him, for being so big and successful—but why did he want to marry *her*?

Obligation, she thought sadly. The Japanese were very careful always to repay debts, if possible a hundred times over. They hated to be in debt to someone, because it meant such an obligation. Was that what Brad felt?

Her father had helped him tremendously in the beginning, she knew that; Brad had said, over and over, that he was immensely indebted to her father. Did he feel, then, that he could discharge the debt only by marrying Charita and caring for her? Responsibility was so serious. Obligations and debts of gratitude that would burden him for a lifetime. She stifled a sigh.

They came down soon in Kyoto, it was only about an hour's journey. She felt more and more strange, detached from herself, as though someone above looked down pityingly on this little girl in the too-big homely tweed coat and the schoolgirl uniform, sorry for her, wondering what she would do.

The lights flashed on, they unbuckled their belts. Brad said, as everyone began to crowd the aisles, in a hurry with their briefcases and large traveling bags and important airs, "We'll wait till they get off. No hurry."

They sat there quietly. The stewardess came over to them after most had left. "Is all well?" she asked.

Charita smiled up at her. She looked a nice girl, so polite and kind and pretty in her uniform of kimono and sandals. "All is quite fine, thank you so much," Charita answered in Japanese.

The girl beamed, and bowed low. "Ah, you speak Japanese so very well," she said, in surprise.

Charita thanked her again, and Brad stumbled through some words in Japanese as well. The hostess bowed them to the steps; they got off, Charita still clutching her father's manuscript box. Behind them, the two tough Japanese men followed closely, silently.

She caught one glimpse of them as she turned at the bottom of the steps. They were staring at her, black eyes beady and cold, their broad faces expressionless.

They went on; she waited for Brad. Brad had turned slightly from her, greeting a big man who had strode across the airport from the terminal.

"Hello, Frundsberg," said Brad. "Nice to see you! Are you off to the States?"

"Hello, there, Livingston! No, no, just to Tokyo on some pressing business. Anxious to be on— Where have you been? I tried to call you last week."

"Up in Hokkaido," said Brad, and the two big men stood a little aside to talk. Charita eyed the stranger curiously.

He was as tall as Brad, husky, older, maybe forty-five years of age. His hair, which had looked blond, had gray in it also, she thought. His eyes were a piercing blue; he smiled often, creasing the lines of his big face. He spoke with a husky German accent. He looked nice, rather fatherly, she thought.

She was observing the two men when something bumped against her so hard she went sprawling, the manuscript box flying from her arms. She had been jolted so swiftly that her breath caught and she could not scream out.

She had thrust her arms out to protect herself and felt them scrape on the rough concrete. Her knees hurt, as she had tried to catch herself. She half turned, still lying on the ground, and saw what had hit her: A baggage truck, laden with luggage, had knocked her down.

Her eyes widened in horror. The truck was backing up, slowly, deliberately! The driver could not see her, he was backing toward the next plane!

"My God!" Brad cried suddenly. He dropped his briefcase and raced to her. He yelled at the driver, and at the same moment, threw his weight against the truck, holding it in place, and shielding Charita.

The driver stopped the truck, peered around. His face registered comic incredulity. As he hopped down, the great truck wavered.

"You idiot!" yelled Brad. "Get that away from here!"

The driver was bowing to the ground, he was apologizing feverishly in Japanese, he was an abject criminal, he had been terribly negligent. Brad cursed him fluently, and sent him on his way. Then he dropped down to where Charita lay on the ground.

"My darling, my darling, how are you?" he inquired apprehensively, cradling her in his arms. She could not catch her breath. Her hand went up to clutch him, then halted, as she stared at the bleeding palm.

The hostess came down the steps, clattering on her sandals. She rushed over to them, kneeling on the concrete beside Charita, her face reflecting her concern. "What is it? What happened?" she said, in great agitation. "I saw that truck—"

Frundsberg came over to them, gathering up Brad's briefcase and Charita's box on the way. "My God, what an idiot!" he rumbled, in fury. "He could have killed the girl! Do you know her, Livingston?"

"My fiancee," said Brad, his mouth tight. He bent over, picked up Charita, and began to carry her to the terminal. Frundsberg and the hostess trailed after them.

Inside the door, people gathered around, exclaiming about the terrible accident. Charita felt very shaken and sick. She was trembling and felt very embarrassed by all the attention.

"I am—all right," she faltered. "Please—put me down —I can walk—"

Brad set her down gently in a chair and knelt to see what damage had been done. His face flared in anger as he saw her badly scraped hands.

"And her poor legs," whispered the hostess, in sympathy. She sheltered Charita discreetly while Brad lifted her skirt.

"I saw the whole thing! Criminal carelessness," rumbled Mr. Frundsberg. He deposited Brad's briefcase and the box next to Charita, gazing down at her, troubled. "What shall I do, Livingston? I can get a doctor—"

"No, no, just let me—go home," muttered Charita, wanting badly to cry. But one did not cry in public.

Her knees were scraped badly, her legs had several gashes and they stung terribly. She dared not close her hands, they hurt so. She blinked back tears. Brad rose, touched her head carefully. Her little tweed hat had fallen off, her hair was mussed.

"Does your head ache?" he asked gently, pushing back her bangs to see if there were bruises.

"No . . . I fell . . . on my hands and knees—" she whispered.

"What is it? What's going on!" demanded an imperious high shrill voice. A tall attractive blond woman pushed her way through the crowd, followed by a tall red-faced man. "Brad, what in the world are you doing?"

"Hello, Jacinda. Got the car here?"

"Yes, outside," she said briskly. She stared down at Charita. "This can't be the fiancee! My God, Brad, she's a schoolgirl!"

The hostess had opened Charita's coat and was examining the hurt knees. She half looked up, to Charita's face, then down again, her lips compressed. "She should see a doctor," she said in a soft polite voice. The other woman's voice overrode hers.

"Brad, I insist on knowing what is going on! Where is your fiancee? And what happened to this girl? Miles, get a chair, we'll see her to some welfare place before we go on—"

Brad got up, his face flushed with anger. Charita felt so humiliated she could not look up at him.

"Jacinda, lower your voice now," ordered Brad, in such a cold snappy voice that Charita cringed. "Miles, do get a chair, we'll get Charita out to the car. Where is Pearl?"

"I am here, Brad," said a soft, pretty voice, and a Japanese girl managed to get through the curious crowd hovering about them. She stared down at Charita; Charita gazed back at her.

She thought she had never seen such a pretty girl. Pearl had short black hair and bangs like Charita's. But her dark, almost black, eyes were self-confident; she was doll pretty in a red kimono with a gold and silver obi. Her creamy face was perfectly made up with a little rouge, a bit of lipstick; the long lashes were untouched, sweeping the cheeks in a manner Charita intensely admired.

"Charita, I'll introduce you presently. Now we'll get you to Jacinda's apartment and get a doctor for you." Brad had recovered from his shock, and was in command again. He took the wheelchair Miles brought, thanked the hostess charmingly, pushed back the crowd. He took Charita through the hallway. She vaguely remembered that Mr. Frundsberg had patted her shoulder as he set her father's manuscript box on her lap. Pearl had taken Brad's briefcase as though it were her right.

Jacinda tried to talk to Brad as they went, but he silenced her impatiently. "Not now, Jacinda. Pearl, stop at the phone and get a doctor to come up to the Snows' apartment. I'll see you there."

"Yes, Brad."

Pearl went off efficiently, still clutching his briefcase. He wheeled Charita out into the parking lot, transferred her to a huge black limousine, to the front seat beside the driver. Jacinda and Miles Snow slid into the back as Brad got into the driver's seat.

"Oh—our luggage," Brad said.

"I'll get it," Miles offered and quickly took the tickets and got out. "You go on, I'll bring it to the apartment." He slammed the door and strode away, as though glad to be off.

Brad's mouth was set in a grim line as he drove them through the heavy traffic. Charita had closed her eyes and laid her head back. Maybe the nightmares would go away. Her father's death, the plane ride that always made her dizzy, then that accident. It was so humiliating, so clumsy of her, she thought. What Brad's friends must think of her! And his secretary, Pearl, so exquisitely dressed and coolly competent. She had looked disdainful and disapproving. If only Charita could be alone and cry. It would help so much to cry.

Once out of the traffic Brad drove like the wind, and the blond woman in the back seat said little. Charita felt her coolness like a north wind at her back, but she was too upset to do anything about it. Slowly, the drive soothed her.

"Brad, her room is ready, but I think she might be better off at a hospital," Jacinda began at once when they arrived.

"If you can't take care of her," Brad said with deadly politeness, "I'll take her to my house immediately."

"Don't be silly! Of course I can manage." Then the woman was silent again.

At the apartment building, Brad carried Charita tenderly inside and to the elevator. He did not put her down until he had reached the spacious apartment and carried her into the room Jacinda indicated.

The room was lovely, the walls painted a cool, silvery blue. The low bed was wide, and against one wall stood a pale wood dresser and a mirror framed in bamboo. There was a breathtaking view of Kyoto from the windows. Brad laid Charita gently down on the bed, then stood looking down at her anxiously.

"I'll find out if the doctor is coming," Jacinda said crisply.

"Ask the maid to bring some hot tea!" Brad called after her.

He sat down on the bed beside Charita. "My poor darling, I wouldn't have had this happen for the world," he said so gently that tears sprang unbidden to her eyes. She tried to blink them back, but they rolled slowly down her cheeks. He bent and kissed them tenderly away. "I meant for you to be so happy," he said, under his breath. "What happened anyway? Did you trip?"

She shook her head. "I did not see the truck . . . I must have been in its path. I felt a push and it sent me sprawling down. And when I turned, it was backing toward me again."

"My poor love," he said, and kissed her mouth softly. Charita felt strangely soothed by his kiss even though at first she had been frightened.

The maid clattered in with a tea tray, and gave a sympathetic look toward the girl on the bed. Charita sat up. Brad held the cup for her to drink, while the maid watched and smiled. Charita felt she was calming.

Then they heard a door bang abruptly open. Miles' voice called, "I found only one suitcase for the girl, they must have lost the rest of her luggage. Where's Brad?"

He came to the bedroom door, repeated the message. Brad said, "There was only one case. The rest is coming on later. Where is Pearl?"

"She's here. And the doctor is coming." He stared curiously at Charita. "How's the little girl?" He sounded more sympathetic than his wife, but there was still a cool drawl to his tone.

"Her hands and knees are still bleeding. I expect she'll need a tetanus shot as well." Brad stood up. "You lie down, honey. Get some rest. We'll bring in the doctor. Had enough tea?"

She nodded and whispered, "Thank you." Charita felt terribly tired and frightened. This was not at all what she had expected of her trip, not this strange arrival and the unfriendliness of Brad's friends. They treated her like a child. Did they think he had gone mad, to think of marrying her?

Brad and Miles left the room, and the maid lowered the blinds and closed the silver and blue paisley drapes. She whispered around in her sandals, and finally left with the tray. Charita tried to relax.

She could hear the voices in the living room, that smart gold and silver room she had just glimpsed as she was carried in. Jacinda's voice was unusually loud, carrying into Charita's room and invading her thoughts.

"Now, Brad, tell us the whole story," the woman said in a commanding tone. "What in the world happened? Just because her father died, why in hell do you feel you have to marry that child?"

Brad hushed her, but the voice had echoed so. Charita flinched, and felt herself tensing again. *That child. Have to marry that child.*

She shivered. In the aftermath of the journey and the accident, she felt so alone, so wretched. The pain in her hands and her legs was not so awful as the ache in her heart. Brad had soothed her, said he would marry her. But it was impossible, wasn't it? Why would he marry a child like her?

She grasped the thought of seeing her foster parents. If only her dear mother was clucking over her and taking care of her. She must go soon to them, and leave these strangers. She did not belong here.

4

Charita remained in bed for two days. In spite of the stinging pain of her hands and knees, she would have gotten up and moved about. But Mrs. Snow coolly refused to allow her up. Charita had the feeling the woman wanted to keep her out of sight and out of mind.

Brad came visiting twice a day. On his second trip, he brought her a dazzling diamond ring. The enormous stone was surrounded by small, vivid blue sapphires set in platinum. Charita could not believe something so lavishly beautiful was hers.

He slipped it on her small finger and cocked his head, appraisingly, then smiled. "Perfect fit," he said, satisfied. He had fastened a little bit of string around her finger before he left her the first day, tied it, then carefully slipped it off.

She studied the ring with sober blue eyes.

It fit her beautifully, but must have been horribly expensive. She sighed. Somehow she had to tell Brad she could take care of herself, that he must not take on this burden of responsibility for his lifetime. She would return to her foster parents and find work. It was the only solution.

"You don't like it?" Brad asked, teasing her. "I'll bring you an assortment, rubies, diamonds, emeralds—"

"Oh, Brad, no!" She shook her head vigorously. He brushed back her fringe with gentle fingers.

"Feeling better?" he said, seriously. "I have the addresses of several fine dress shops, and I am longing to get you fitted out. The wedding is set for a week from today, which will give you time to notify anybody you want to attend."

A week from today! Oh, no! Charita wet her lips, sitting up straight from the supporting pillows. Jacinda Snow had brought her a beautiful blue silk nightdress, and soft white mohair bed jacket with silver satin ties to wear over it. She had been kind, in her cold way. "Brad, I must talk to you. This—this has been too sudden. You must think over carefully—I mean, I would wish you to consider what you wish to do—"

He put his hand over her mouth. "No more," he said, with a laugh. There was a darkness in his eyes she did not understand, as though behind the laughter there was concern, or trouble. "We are going to be married, and you are going to be a beautiful wife, and make me very happy. Don't you want me to be happy?"

Put that way, what could she say? Jacinda Snow came in and lounged against the end of the bed in her ice-blue silk dress, her blond hair short and tightly curling about her ears. To Charita she seemed so efficient and smart. The maid had said Mrs. Snow and her husband were both lawyers; very smart and very rich, she had told her in awe.

"Her scratches are healing nicely," said Mrs. Snow, in her clear, high voice. "Just one on the right hand is bad, take a look at it when the bandages are off, Brad. I was concerned about that."

His face shadowed, he took her right hand gently in his and tried to peer under the bandage. They both did seem concerned. "We'll have the doctor again tomorrow morning," he said. "How is your shot reacting, Charita?"

"I'm all right," she said. She felt exhausted, and it was an effort to keep smiling.

She was better the next day; and the following day, she was allowed to get up and get dressed. Mrs. Snow had gone out and bought two dresses for her, and Charita put on the blue print smock with the wide white collar and white cuffs. She thought the soft blue pretty, the color of hydrangeas. She tried to thank Mrs. Snow.

"Don't thank me, thank Brad," said the woman, with a wave of her long slim hand. "You do look pretty," she added graciously. "The tweed coat will have to do for today, but I think Brad will dump it in the trash bin after he has bought you some others."

She mixed kindness with such subtle cruelty, that Charita never knew where she was with her. She could not fence with her, could not match the sting in her words. It would be very discourteous anyway; after all, the lady *was* her hostess.

Brad arrived about ten, and looked delighted to see her up and waiting for him. "You look lovely, and with much better color, darling," he said, and bent and kissed her lips. Jacinda was watching. Deeper pink came to Charita's cheeks. "Thank you for looking after her, Jacinda."

The woman shrugged, lifted her coffee cup again. "No trouble. The maid does it all," she said.

"Well, we'll be off," said Brad, and took her away with him. He said no cruel words about her tweed coat, but she noticed that it disappeared at one shop. She had a new tweed suit. The colors were a blend of soft heather and cream, and Charita wore a cream cowl-necked cashmere sweater under the jacket. A matching tweed coat fit precisely to her young form and completed the elegant outfit. Brad bought her another coat of pale blue, and a matching twill suit with contrasting wine piping, and a dress of soft blue silk. Then she began to lose track.

He seemed to delight in watching her parade before him in the dresses. She was a perfect size eight, easy to fit, and the saleswomen brought dress after coat after suit for her to try on. Charita had no idea what he had chosen until the boxes were opened in her bedroom back at the Snows' apartment.

There was a full-length dress of pale cream satin which was to be her wedding dress. Senior saleswomen had chosen for them a short lacy veil attached to a cream satin cap of pearls that just fit on Charita's silky black head. Matching pale satin high heels and pretty shimmering stockings were added to complete her bridal ensemble.

There were boxes of pantyhose in varying shades. There seemed to be hundreds of matching undergarments in white, cream, and blue, petticoats and brassieres and panties of the most sheer fabrics.

The maid hung up everything for her. Charita was lying down, at Brad's urging. She would join them for tea when she had rested, he had said firmly. The maid exclaimed over each garment, held it up for Charita to admire, then hung it away in the huge wardrobes.

There were five coats. She counted them, shaking her tired head. However would she wear them all? And Brad had mentioned something about getting furs for her for next winter, but that would wait.

"Lovely, exquisite," cooed the maid in Japanese. It was a bond between them that Charita spoke Japanese, and the maid had been very attentive to her. Now she held up a pale pink full-length gown of softest chiffon, with a butterfly short cape effect over it. With it were pink slippers to match the dress, and more shoes in boxes. Black shoes, brown, blue ones with high spike heels, pink and rose and violet.

The maid smoothed out a soft violet wool dress, sighed over it, hung that away. There were more boxes to open. She was enjoying it more than Charita, who was wrestling with her thoughts.

Brad was arguing with Jacinda, she could hear his voice rumbling, and the woman's clear voice rang out sometimes. "A fool! I never thought you would be such a fool, to fall for a little doll—why she is scarcely out of school! She has no brains to speak of—"

Brad's voice rumbled. Charita strained, ashamed of herself, but anxious to hear if he would defend her intelligence. She leaned back with an aching head as the maid chirped admiration over a pert cherry red wool dress with brown wood buttons, and a matching little red hat, and red shoes.

Brad returned to her room, entering after the briefest of knocks. Charita looked at his face; from the lines about his mouth and the flash of his eyes, she thought he had become angry. But he smiled at her, and helped her gently from the bed.

"Come and have a bit of food, darling, you must be worn out. I have to get back to the office for a time, but I'll be back for dinner. Meantime, I want your list of guests for the wedding. Your foster parents, of course, and Kanji—"

She went out to the other room with him. Jacinda had disappeared, and a maid brought a large tea tray, and poured for them. There were little cut sandwiches with tuna, mushrooms, and cucumbers, along with a plate of little pastries, covered with chocolate icing and butterscotch and meringues. How Kanji would have enjoyed these, thought Charita. He had such a sweet tooth.

Her throat was grateful for the tea; the warmth helped dispel the lump of fought-back tears. She told Brad who she would like invited, and he wrote them all down carefully. There were not many.

"Oh—and Brad—we must send gifts to Sapporo, to those who gave us gifts," she said timidly. He frowned, in surprise.

"Gifts—to them?"

She nodded. "The custom is to choose some item, such as a large silk handkerchief with embroidered initials in the

59

corner to commemorate the date of our wedding. That will be sent to everyone. The stores will do this. Only the scarves or handkerchiefs must be chosen, and the names given to the store."

He seemed surprised and interested, and she explained more about that custom. It helped dispel her fright and despondency. He appeared genuinely interested in this. He promised to take her to a store soon after their wedding, with a list of the names of those who had given gifts, and arrange it all.

"We might as well wait," he said, with a little grimace. "Presents are pouring in at my house. I haven't opened them; that will be your pleasure, my dear. Not in my line! And besides, they are more for you. I poked at some of them, and I think they are linens, and china, and household goods."

"How like you, Brad," said Jacinda, entering. "At Christmas, you used to poke all your presents and guess what was in them. And guessed right ninety percent of the time, I might say."

She seemed cool and uncaring and laughing, not like the furious-voiced woman Charita had heard from her bedroom.

Brad laughed, and stood up. "I must be on my way. Pearl will think I'm lost. She'll have letters for me to sign, and a few people to see. I'll try to get back here by seven. Charita, you'll stay up?"

She nodded, and he bent and kissed her forehead, and left. She studied the bottom of her teacup intently. She felt uneasy there, alone with Jacinda. They had scarcely talked.

The door slammed somewhere, the elevator rumbled. Jacinda got up and poured some tea for herself. She took no sandwiches; she was slim and quick on her feet. Charita noted her shoes, of cream silk, with three-inch spike heels.

"Pearl," said Jacinda, at the window, staring down. Charita wondered if she were watching Brad get into his large black limousine. "Pearl. Now, there's a problem—"

Charita drew in to herself, curling up her legs under her in a small defensive motion. She did not speak, holding her breath. Jacinda meant something.

"Pearl. Did you know—" Jacinda turned around and studied Charita's small round face curiously. "Did you know that she is Brad's mistress?"

Charita gasped. It was like cold water from the sea flung in her face from a careless hand.

"No?" asked Jacinda. "Well, he probably doesn't think it matters. He won't marry her, she is Japanese. It has gone on for a year now. Poor Pearl, how she must have felt when she saw you! Looking like a Japanese girl, yet an American, suitable for Brad to marry. Yet I don't suppose she ever expected him to propose. She is too good a secretary! Nothing like eating one's cake and having it also. Men in Japan seem to be good at that. And I understand the women don't even try to protest. Isn't that right, Charita? You understand the customs here better than I."

Her bright green eyes were watching Charita's like a cat at a mouse hole. Charita held her control. She looked down at her hands, at the diamond surrounded by sapphires that sat so firmly on her slim brown hand. Brad had put it there, and kissed her hand. He had bought her clothes, he had been kind to her when her father died.

She felt so numb. It was best to feel this way. If the numbness wore off, she would be hurt. She might cry, and she would not cry in public. Especially before this woman!

"Nothing to say?" Jacinda smiled, pacing the floor like a sleek cat. She wore a long emerald green housecoat that reached to her ankles, and the skirt floated about her trim ankles and high-heeled shoes. Her blond hair was set off by the emeralds at her ears, an emerald of immense size adorned her right hand. From Brad? Somehow the delicate design reminded Charita of the few examples she had seen of Brad's workmanship.

"No," said Charita, her throat tight. "Will you have more tea, please?"

" 'No, will you have more tea, please?' " mimicked Jacinda, her voice rising. "My God, you are cool. Maybe you're smarter than I had figured! Caught him, by God, when no one else could! You, just out of school, with your innocent baby blues! And coming back from your father's funeral with Brad's ring practically on your finger! By God, maybe I have underestimated you!"

With relief, Charita heard a key in the door. Miles slammed in, slammed the door shut, called out in a booming voice, "Anybody home? Jacinda, you here?" He came into the living room, grinned at them. His walk was slow, unsure. He reached out to a chair to hold himself up.

"Drunk already? A bit early in the day, isn't it, Miles, darling?" Jacinda turned on him like an elegant cat. Her smile at him was tinged with bitterness and malice. "It gets earlier and earlier. Did you go to the office at all?"

Miles grinned at her. "What the hell do you care?" he snapped. Charita realized, with horror, that they quarreled like that, with bitterness and stinging words, and grins, to show they were not hurt themselves.

She rose, and excused herself politely. She did not think they even heard her. She retreated to the blue and silver stillness of her room, and with relief, sank down into a chair.

A dress was laid out on the bed, a new dress. The bright cherry red with the wooden buttons, and the red high-heeled shoes. She stared blankly at it. Then she shivered.

Brad—and Pearl. Lovely Pearl, his secretary, his more-than-secretary. Brad would never marry Pearl, but he would keep on seeing her every day—and some evenings. It was the Japanese custom, said Jacinda, wasn't it, Charita? Wasn't it the custom here?

She put her hands to her face, but the bandages reminded her of her injuries. Only small bandages remained, but they bothered her. She sighed deeply, and slipped off her dress, to put on a robe and lie down for a time. Maybe Brad would not return, maybe he would stay with Pearl—

She bit her lips, lying on the bed, stretching out with a weariness which had nothing to do with overexertion. She was tired to the bone. Her father's illness, the long months of worry and work, the death, the airplane flight, the accident in the airport— All were as nothing compared to this new burden.

What could she do about it? Brad was evidently going through with this marriage. Why? It was obvious to her that he felt an obligation because of his promise to her father which had come about because he felt he owed her father a debt.

But he must not pay all his life! And she could not, would not pay also!

A mistress already . . . Charita shivered in the warmth of her blue robe, and turned over gingerly to lie on her side, and gaze out to the purpling dusk of Kyoto. Lights were blinking on all over the city. Somewhere out there Brad was working and signing letters and Pearl was hovering over him. Maybe they were talking, maybe Pearl was asking when she would see him again—alone.

To Charita, Brad had seemed so fine and wonderful. She felt hurt then, and disillusionment. She had put that lively god on a pedestal. He was a very important man, and to him she had attributed many virtues. He was thoughtful, he was kindly, he took his vast duties seriously. He had been good to her, so very good.

She thought of the afternoon when she had made tea for him in the ceremony, and he had read poetry to her. She had felt so close to him then, as though to a kindly brother, older and imperious and dictatorial, but still a kindly brother. Marriage had seemed like a solution to her problems. He wished it, she would do it.

But now? How could she now?

The maid tapped softly on the door and entered

quietly, her sandals slap-slapping on the polished wood floor. "Miss Charita? You will get dressed now for dinner?" she asked eagerly. It was exciting for her, someone young in the house to be cared for, someone gentle and pretty, with so many new bright clothes. It made her days interesting.

Charita sat up slowly. The maid was picking up the cherry red dress, setting out the shoes. "No, not those," said Charita. "I will wear a kimono tonight."

The maid looked puzzled. She had seen the kimonos, she had hung them in the closet, wondering at the ideas of the Americans who enjoyed wearing the Japanese costume, when the American and French styles were so glamorous and different. "Kimono? Tonight? When your betrothed comes?"

"Yes," Charita nodded her head vigorously. The maid shrugged, and took out the red kimono with the red and yellow chrysanthemums embroidered on it. She laid out the gold and silver obi. She helped Charita into the undergarments, the kimono, the sandals, over the white socks. She fastened the obi skillfully. "You are most kind," Charita murmured.

The maid beamed at her. "How lovely you look, you are not offended if I say you look like Japanese girl?"

Charita smiled. She was not offended. Tonight, she indeed felt like a Japanese girl being bartered off, and this she would not obey. She would not be impolite, no, she would be most courteous. But no compromise would she accept. Nor would she be a sacrifice for her father's debts to Bradford Livingston.

She heard the murmur of voices as she went out to the hallway. She hesitated in the doorway to the brilliantly modern living room. Mrs. Snow looked up impatiently, her emerald cigarette holder held in one long slim hand over the ashtray.

"We don't want supper yet," she said, curtly, and

turned back to Brad. Charita had seen the gleam in her green eyes, the cold look.

Brad glanced up, then stood quickly. "Charita!" he said, surprised. "You are wearing a kimono tonight."

"Yes," she said, coming into the room slowly. Mrs. Snow had pretended to think she was the maid, but no maid would wear such a highly decorative kimono while serving dinner. She knew, that woman knew—and had been deliberately insulting.

She seated herself carefully in the chair Brad indicated, one of the silver plush armchairs.

"You know, I thought it was the maid," Jacinda laughed. She fit another cigarette into the emerald holder. "Really, Charita, you are full of surprises. With all the pretty dresses Brad has so generously bought for you—"

"Charita may wear what she chooses, Jacinda," Brad said abruptly, displeased. Charita noted the lines about his eyes and mouth.

Miles arrived soon after, breaking the awkward silence. He was wearing a fresh gray silk suit, his face sullen and red, as though he had had another drink or two.

He stared at Charita. "Well, well, how pretty, my dear," he said, and wandered over to the liquor cabinet. How much they drank, Charita thought with dismay. Her father had some sake from time to time, but it was usually on some ceremonious occasion. Miles gulped off whiskey as though he craved it.

The maid announced dinner. Brad took Charita in, and she sat docilely across from him. Jacinda kept the conversation flowing, with her glib, bright remarks. Brad said little, Miles responded only when directly attacked by a sharp barb from his wife. Charita poked at her food, she was not hungry. She had been silently rehearsing what to say.

"Well, Brad, what shall we do this evening?" Jacinda asked, wiping her scarlet mouth on the fresh white napkin, leaving an angry red smear. She tossed the napkin down carelessly, it slipped to the floor. "We could go out to a nightclub, Charita is much better. Though I do think she should change her dress!" She laughed, as though amused, but the green eyes were cold.

Charita spoke up politely, her voice clear, her chin raised. "I wish to speak to Brad alone for about half an hour. That is all. If you will be kind enough to permit us to speak alone, I shall be grateful."

As though she had thrown a stone into the clear water, the silence rippled out and out, in ever-increasing waves. Brad cleared his throat.

"Use my study," said Miles, before Brad could speak. "Feel free. I'm going down to the bar."

Jacinda began to frown. "Now, Miles, I want to go out later, you know I planned—"

"Go without me," he said rudely. "You'd rather have Brad anyway." He left the dining room and they heard him stumbling in the hall. He cursed a table for being in his way.

Brad took Charita's arm and escorted her formally to the study. His mouth was grim. They went in, and she sat down weakly on a chair near the desk. Brad sat down on the edge of the desk and looked at her. She felt at a disadvantage, he was so much taller, and now he seemed to loom over her.

"Well, Charita? Are you unhappy about something?" he said quietly. "Don't worry about Miles, he isn't your problem."

She had been vaguely sorry about Miles, and puzzled, but she wasn't worried about him. Her own problems were more immediate and dangerous. She shook her head.

"No, Brad. I must tell you something." She paused. The speech she had rehearsed seemed cold and stilted. She searched for fresh words.

"Aren't you feeling well? Did we go too hard today?" He was very gentle and concerned about her, as over an invalid.

She took a deep breath, looked down at the ring, and began. "While I am most grateful for your kind attentions and many goodnesses to me, I cannot marry you," she said, not having planned it that way at all.

"What?" he snapped, and she felt him tense, too near her, as though a panther flexed his muscles to jump.

She tensed also. "I wish to express to you my grateful appreciation for all you did for my father," she grappled frantically for her set speech. She licked her soft lips. "You have been exceedingly kind to me. However, I feel . . . I cannot . . . I mean, I am not ready . . . I cannot marry you—oh, please, Mr. Livingston, I cannot marry you!"

She saw the brown hand nearest to her clench slowly, the fingers drawn into the wide palm. She dared not look at his face. He was silent for a minute.

"What made you panic, Charita?" he asked, very quietly.

"Panic?"

"Yes. You were quite willing to marry me. You seemed —happy, and even relieved. Don't you like me?"

This was worse than she had believed possible. She had thought he would be relieved, and grateful. She tried again.

"You are very kind—"

"The hell with kindness." He had not raised his voice, but she flinched from his words. "The hell with gratitude. I thought you liked me, that you felt at ease with me. I realize it is sudden, but damn it all, Charita, you need a home, and this is no place for you. Jacinda is acting like a bitch, and Miles has been staggering around drunk. No, we're going through with it, and I'm going to take care of you! I promised your father—"

"That is just it," she said hurriedly, as his voice rose a little, and the fingers clenched and unclenched. She watched that large brown hand, fascinated. Why was he upset? She had thought he would be glad. "You owe my father some debt for helping you with your business. However, it was his pleasure to do this for you, and you have hired Kanji, my foster brother, which pleased Father immensely. He owed much to my foster parents and he was glad some of the debt was repaid. However, you repaid the debt to my father when you were so kind to me and took care of Father—"

"Charita, will you please stop talking about debts and repayment and all that foolishness?" he snapped, harshly. "I don't give a damn about all that. You're going to marry me because you're young and alone in the world, and I need a wife and I want you for my wife— My God, do you hate me?"

"No, no," she whispered, shocked. "I have been trying to say, I admire you, and respect you, and you are most kind—"

He groaned aloud, and shoved back his thick chestnut-brown hair impatiently. He stood up and began to pace the large study. She watched him. Five steps to the bookcase, back to the window with eight paces, and another six back to the desk, then back to the bookcase—he came to pause before her, and stuck his hands in his pockets.

"Now, Charita," he said, as though he gripped firmly at his patience. "What do you feel about this? Why are you suddenly coming up with objections? Are you feeling panicky? Or do your injuries hurt?"

She wet her lips again. Her throat seemed dry, but she could not swallow. "I—I feel it is too sudden," she managed to say. "My foster parents are not here to advise me. And you—you are doing this because of some debt of gratitude to my father."

"No, I am not," he said at once. She managed to look at him fully. His dark brown eyes gazed down steadily at her. "No, no gratitude, no debt. Now, what are your objections?"

She could not say it, she could not say the words about

his mistress. She sighed. "I cannot go through with it," she said, with sad bluntness. "We do not know each other, it is not the American way," she added hopefully. "In Japan, one arranges the marriage with a go-between, and she tries to match—"

"I don't give a damn in hell about what is done in America or in Japan, or what the usual is! Charita, this is between you and me. I am going to marry you, and you will be ready in four days, or by God—" He stopped, as though with an intense effort, and turned back to stride to the window. From there, he tossed at her, "Do you dislike me, do I offend you?"

"No, no, of course not, you have been most generous, most kind and considerate—"

"God give me patience!" he roared suddenly at the window. He came back to her, scowled at her. "We are—going—through—with this wedding," he said, slowly and distinctly. "You give me no good reason for calling it off. Now, do you want to go out to a nightclub tonight, or not?"

She stared at him, then rose, with dignity, and gathered her red robes about her. "I cannot marry you," she said with finality, her head high. "It is impossible. That is all. Goodnight, Mr. Livingston."

He cursed under his breath, his long arms reached out, and he swept her to him. Paralyzed, she felt him press her head against his arm, she could not move from the tight grip of his arms. Wide-eyed, she stared up at him, then blinked, and closed her eyes as his brown face came down near hers. His mouth closed on hers, fiercely, bruising her lips and chin. He kissed her, ferociously, his arms gripping her.

She was too shocked to protest. She had never been held so before. No one had violated her gentle spirit or her young body. She trembled in his grip, unable to believe this was happening to her. He brushed aside the edge of the kimono, to reveal the white skin of her shoulder, and a bruising kiss pressed on her throat, slid over to her arm, down to her breast. He kissed the slight curves there, as though he would eat her, she thought later.

Then abruptly he let her go. He was breathing fast, his face was flushed, his dark eyes sparkled with a fire she did not understand.

"The wedding will take place as scheduled," he said, standing about two feet from her. She felt the heat from his body like a furnace before her. She felt scorched by the fury of his passion, not understanding it at all. "I'll pick you up at ten tomorrow morning, we'll go to the New Miyako Hotel to make final arrangements. You want a Shinto ceremony and a Christian one, don't you? Good, that will make it all nice and tight," he said, with an edged mockery.

She backed to the door, bewildered, her blue eyes large and afraid. She reached for the knob. "I cannot . . ." she whispered.

"You will. You promised." He opened the door for her. "Dream about me, Charita," he said, as she fled down the hall.

She flinched from his angry mockery. As she reached her room and opened the door, she heard Jacinda's voice. "What's going on? Brad, where are you going? You said we'd go to a nightclub—" Her voice was angry and plaintive.

"Not tonight. I'll see you tomorrow. See that Charita wears an American dress tomorrow, that red one with the red shoes!" Brad slammed out of the apartment.

Jacinda came in search of Charita, but Charita was safely locked in her room, trembling. When Jacinda called out to her, Charita said, "I am going to bed."

"At nine o'clock? Don't be silly! Let me in, I must ask you—"

"Please, leave me alone!" Charita cried, and put her face in her hands. Her skin felt burned where Brad had kissed her. Later when she removed the kimono, she found several small bruises purpling on her delicate skin. It was as though he had branded her with his fire.

During the next few days Charita tried again to protest about the marriage. But Brad would not listen. Heedless of her pleas, his mouth set in a grim line, his dark eyes flashing with determination, he swept her through the arrangements.

The wedding took place at the elegant New Miyako Hotel, in their wedding rooms. A Shinto ceremony had been arranged by the delighted management. Rarely did an American couple wish this ceremony. It was a good omen, thought the Japanese guests. To them it showed that this man who was setting up a business in their country was fond of their customs and respected their beliefs.

Charita looked pale and bridelike in her cream satin, with the short veil. She moved through the rituals numbly. Aware all of the time of Jacinda's disapproval and anger. Aware of Brad's repressed rage. Her foster parents came only in time for the first ceremony.

She wanted to hug them and beg them to carry her away. Dear Oku Noguchi stood beaming at her from behind his spectacles, his eyes sparkling with pleasure and pride. "We are so very happy for you, dear little daughter," he said. "If only we had had time to purchase bride clothes for you, and garments of kimonos and obi. Still, we shall arrange for kimonos to be sent to your new home. We wish you not to forget your old parents."

Helen Noguchi was less restrained. She held Charita tenderly to her, her crinkled face lacy with wrinkles. They had been older when Kanji had been born, and had had no other children. Charita had been her dear unexpected daughter, so good, so obedient, so talented with her art.

"How beautiful is my daughter! How angelic in her robes! The ceremony is precious to me, you are following the dearest wishes of my heart. I will speak to Mr. Livingston

71

and remind him that you are most precious of jewels given into his care."

She did that, and Brad listened respectfully, smiling down from his height, bending to put a kiss on her wrinkled cheek. "I will take great care of this jewel," he said, without an edge to his voice. He seemed gay and younger today, his eyes sparkling, his manner gracious to all the guests.

The first ceremony took place in the room set aside for the Shinto rites, before the priest, who blessed them, and bound them together in the old manner. Candles were lit for them.

The second ceremony soon followed, in another room, in the Christian manner, before a Protestant minister attached to the consulate. He was solemn, a little nervous, not quite sure he was doing the right thing when he did not know the bride and groom, and the Shinto ceremony had come first. But he was reassured by the smart presence of the many American and British guests he knew, Mrs. Snow in her emerald green silk, and the son of the assistant consul Donald Raglan, seated next to Mrs. Snow.

"The parents couldn't come, official business. Mother was upset, she wanted to walk out and come on over," Donald said breezily to Charita, after the ceremony. He kissed her, smiling. "There, I've wanted to do that since I first saw you in pigtails. You're a lucky fellow, Mr. Livingston!"

"Very lucky," said Brad. He kept his hand on Charita's arm, or his arm about her waist, possessively, as though worried she might slip away. She smiled and smiled, even when Pearl Takahashi came up to them.

The young secretary was elegant in a pale gray silk, her short black hair smartly groomed, pearls in her little ears. She bowed before Charita, and repeated the conventionally graceful words of congratulations. But Charita looked into the dark eyes and saw anger and fierceness there.

"You are most kind," said Charita. She wondered how

she would feel if her lover were marrying another woman. She would not have been able to attend the ceremony, she knew that. Pearl had been at both ceremonies. She had helped arrange the flowers also, Brad said casually.

"My secretary is a Pearl," he said, making a joke and a pun. Pearl smiled gaily at him. Only Charita seemed to feel her hurt and pain. The girl had admirable self-control.

Kanji Noguchi was there also, looking elegant in a new blue suit, attentive to his parents. He was a good son, though he had had to leave them in their village and come to Kyoto to find work. He seemed to admire Brad. He squeezed Charita's hand, and whispered, "You have the best man in the world. I will burn incense for you and whisper prayers many days and nights, for the joy of your marriage. Dear sister, my heart wept for you there in Hokkaido, but I knew you would be safe and cared for with Brad there."

He spoke in Japanese. Charita felt tears coming, and tried to blink them back. But they clung to her long lashes, and blurred her blue eyes. Brad turned, and spoke sharply, "What did you say, Kanji?"

Kanji looked embarrassed. "One speaks to one's sister," he mumbled. He did not want to repeat his praise of the man to his face, it was not seemly. One made less personal remarks, of his intelligence and his goodness.

"Please speak in English. I want Charita to become more American," Brad said curtly.

Charita was glad her foster parents were not near to hear this. Kanji gave him a thoughtful look, his face smoothed to blandness, which meant he was putting on a cloak of caution. He bowed. "As you wish, always," he murmured in English.

Brad looked annoyed. Charita gave a little sigh, and shifted from one aching foot to the other. If only she could have worn sandals today—but no, two-inch heels on the cream satin slippers were the thing, the bridal shop clerk had convinced her.

She met more of Brad's friends and business acquaintances. She looked about for the big kindly bear of a man, Karl Frundsberg, who had been at the airport, but he was not present. Some of the people were business associates, workers in Brad's jewelry firm, lawyers that Miles and Jacinda Snow knew. Both Americans and English seemed to think Charita had made quite a catch; she overheard some catty remarks about his wealth and her poverty, which she thought in bad taste as well as wounding. His Japanese friends and hers were much more polite.

She longed for the wedding reception to be over, yet dreaded it. Would they go away on the train to a resort, the way newly married Japanese couples did, to return with glowing faces and demure manners, to settle down to their new lives together? Brad had said nothing of it, he had not suggested that she pack her suitcases. The maid would manage all, he had said.

The multi-tiered white wedding cake was cut, and eaten, and exclaimed over. They drank wedding punch and wines with some two hundred guests, and finally the event was over. Brad took her out a side door, helped by Kanji, and they sped away in his huge shiny black limousine, with a chauffeur today.

They arrived in about twenty minutes at an enormous gray stone house, set on a hillside, some distance away from other houses. They entered by the red-painted gate, and went up the walk, and Charita wondered if this was a new kind of hotel, it was so large.

"Here we are, home, Charita," said Brad. Someone opened the door, she saw a kimono-clad back bowed low. Brad bent over, swept her up into his arms, the long white skirts hanging over his hands, and carried her inside. He smiled at the beaming servants lined up to greet their new mistress. He introduced her to each one, they bowed low, smiled, seemed genuinely glad to meet her.

She answered each in Japanese, and the smiles grew wider, even incredulous. The new mistress-san knew their language! What a wonder!

"I'll show you to your room. This young girl is your maid, darling," Brad said, indicating a petite girl with huge dark eyes. "She'll help you change to something comfortable. I thought trays in the living room, all right? And some tea for you."

He was thoughtful and kind, Charita reminded herself to stem her increasing unease. No one could have been nicer on Hokkaido. She followed Brad to the room, then gasped as she saw how spacious it was.

The room was decorated with blue silk walls, deeper blue draperies over the wide windows, with Venetian blinds which could be adjusted to admit light but keep out the brighter sun. A king-sized bed took up one side of the room, covered with a blue satin bedspread embroidered with peacocks and flowers.

A mirrored sandalwood dresser was set against the opposite wall, with a matching wardrobe nearby. Charita saw the clothes set inside; someone had been busy today, for all her dresses hung there, with the shoes neatly on shelves below. And her five coats—

"I hope you like it, darling," said Brad, and went away. The maid helped her change to a blue kimono, seeming a little surprised at her choice. Charita had been longing to get into sandals all day, and she rubbed her feet thankfully before slipping into the white socks. The maid seemed shy, and said little, but peeped with interest into the wardrobe and the dresser drawers.

The maid showed her to the living room, not a grand one, but a smaller one at the back of the house, "for the family," murmured the maid timidly.

Brad was waiting for her, lounging in a deep, comfortable chair. He got up; he had changed to a pair of gray trousers and a short gray jacket of velvet. He smiled at Charita, and nodded. "More comfortable, eh? We'll have tea in here, and an early bed for you. It's been a long day."

"Yes, a long day," she echoed soberly. She seated herself, as he seemed to wish her, in a chair, though she longed to sit on the floor among cushions. There were deep cushions on the wine-colored sofa and chairs, with rose cushions set about on the floor. "This is a most beautiful house, Brad," she commented shyly.

"I hope you will enjoy it. I'll show you about tomorrow night," he said.

"Thank you."

"I had wanted to take you on a honeymoon, but I can't just now," he said, and ran an impatient hand through his hair. "Work has piled up, there's something only I can do —I'm sorry about this. We'll get away in a month or so."

Alone with him. She stared somberly at the floor. The housemaid brought a tray of food, a butler followed with a tray of tea and coffee and set them within easy reach of Charita. She busied herself with pouring, and handing cup and saucer and sandwich plates to Brad.

Brad did not seem to feel any constraint. He chatted easily about the wedding, asked several questions about her friends there, especially Donald Raglan. She explained they had gone to high school together; he had been in her home several times.

"Seems a nice chap."

"Yes, he is most pleasant."

She began to yawn, from nerves, politely shielding her mouth with her hand.

"To bed with you," said Brad, more cheerfully. "You go ahead, darling, I'll come in presently."

She froze. Come in—to her room? The night she had dreaded had come, and she was not prepared. She had thought only to get out of the wedding, then to get through those ceremonies and reception without screaming to be let free. And now?

She managed to say good night, and left him. The maid helped her undress; she had set out a peach-colored nightdress that was a little nothing of silk and lace. Charita washed off her makeup, which Jacinda had applied rather heavily that morning, and slid into bed, to wait, her heart beating so hard it hurt her.

Brad came in soon. She felt like she was choking as he entered the room. He wore only a silky robe and matching pajamas. He turned out the lights as he came, and the room was a blue dusky hue.

He slid into bed with her, and at once pulled her to him and put his arm about her. Charita tensed and felt as though she had stopped breathing. Brad paid no attention. He bent over her, and his lips went to her face. Gently, he explored her face, kissing her soft cheeks, her lips that tasted like fragile honey blossoms. His kisses trailed down her throat, all the while holding her possessively.

Charita could not endure the closeness or the heat of his body. The way he held her waist and shoulder hurt her tender flesh. "Please—do not—oh—please—do not—" she managed to choke out.

"Don't be silly, darling. We're married," Brad said, against her breast. He nuzzled her gently as he kissed the velvet skin. He would leave more bruises, she thought vaguely, but tried to brace herself to endure his kisses. This was too quick! Too brutal! She felt panicky and wished she could get up and run . . . and run . . .

Oh, why had she agreed to marry him? She did not want to marry anyone! It was horrible—to feel someone so big and hard and so close. She had never shared a bed, even with a girl friend from school. She squirmed and tossed her head frantically from side to side as he moved his exploring hands over her.

"Hold still, love," he whispered. He rose above her

77

then, and pulled up her night dress. For a terrible moment, she felt pain as his hand moved between her thighs.

"Don't—don't!" she cried.

He bent and kissed her mouth, to stifle her cries. He tried to soothe her. "It'll be all right, darling. Don't worry, I'll go slowly. Charita! Stop that—" She was slapping at his hands, trying to get away from him.

"No, no, it is hateful, don't! Oh, please, leave me—"

"Leave you!" Brad was suddenly angry. "Damned if I will! This is our wedding night. Damn it, Charita, didn't Jacinda talk to you?"

For an awful moment she thought he meant about Pearl being his mistress. She lay immobile, and he took advantage of her stillness to come completely over her, and try to do something—painful—to her. Unable to restrain herself, she cried out and pummeled his chest with her small fists. Tears began to flow down her cheeks.

"You are hurting me! Please, it hurts—"

Brad rolled over beside her, where he lay taking deep breaths. "Charita," he said, a biting tone in his voice. "Did Jacinda talk to you about tonight? About sex?"

"No," she said quietly, and he groaned.

"Damn that woman! I told her to. Oh, well, perhaps it's for the best. She's a damned cynic," he said, and got up. She put her hand to her mouth to stifle a sob. She had angered him again, but she could not help it, she hurt so.

He sat down on the side of the bed, and pulled on his robe carelessly. He reached out, touched her face—felt the wetness. "Poor child," he said, more gently. "It's all been too sudden, hasn't it? Look, darling, don't cry. I'm going to sleep in another room after I have a cold shower." His voice sounded grim under the gentleness. "Tomorrow night, we'll have a talk. You sleep in, and get some rest. Okay?"

"O—kay," she managed to say.

"And don't worry! It'll be all right." With those words, Brad got up and left the room.

Charita turned over and tried to stifle her sobs in the pillow, but they overcame her. She felt so horrible! Another night and she would have to endure this. And again, and again—after all, this *was* marriage, and she had given herself to him. Brad Livingston was a very possessive man and somehow she knew he would not give up what he had. He was a hard man under the kindness. He never gave up what he took, and he had taken her, for life.

Silent sobs shook her slender body as she realized it was her wedding night, a night supposed to be joyful and warm and loving. . . .

It was a long while before Charita Atwood Livingston fell asleep.

5

Kanji Noguchi raised his head from the papers coverng his desk and thoughtfully watched his boss as he prowled the room restlessly. It was extremely odd. Brad Livingston had been married only yesterday.

Yet when Kanji had come in this morning at nine o'clock as usual, Brad had been there before him! Kanji had been stunned to see him.

Brad had mentioned casually that he could not take a honeymoon journey just yet, that there was too much work now. But last night had been his wedding night! Surely no one could leave such an enchantingly pretty bride as Charita early the next morning! Had something gone wrong?

He looked down again at his books. He was violating the man's privacy by his rude thoughts, Kanji decided, and concentrated on studying the entries intently. Brad trusted and relied on him more and more, and Kanji was immensely proud of this trust.

Only a year ago, Kanji had been working in the factory of the transistor radio company in his home village. He hated the work, yet thought he was tied to it for life. Slowly he would move up in the ranks. In ten years he might expect to be a supervisor in one section, in twenty years a supervisor in a larger area, forty years to retirement. The thought was deadly, yet it was all he could hope for. His parents were not wealthy, and there were so many intelligent men of his age wanting work.

Then Professor Atwood had brought Bradford Livingston to the home of the Noguchis. They had greeted Brad warmly, tried to help him solve his problems. Mr. Livingston had come to Japan to look for men who could hand-craft precious gold into the designs he created.

Mr. Livingston had said little, he had let Professor Atwood speak for him. He seemed to observe, to sit with his hands quiet, his eyes intent, while he listened all the time.

Kanji had been pleasantly surprised at the end of the evening, for this big, important man with much money had turned to him and said, "Will you come and work for me? I want to train an assistant in Japan, and you speak English very well. I think we could work well together."

He had said it so casually, Kanji had thought at first it was merely a compliment to his parents for bringing him up so well. When the man continued, he had finally understood that he meant it!

To live in Kyoto! To work with fine jewelry and be the assistant of a brilliant inventor, a chemist. It was not to be believed!

But Bradford Livingston knew his own mind, and knew men. Before Kanji knew it, he had been moved to Kyoto, set up in a splendid apartment near the factory he helped Brad to rent. He was given such a large salary, that he could send money home to his parents regularly! He even hoped to save up enough one day to marry, to buy a home, to buy a car. He was deeply involved in hiring the skilled men who would do the jewelry in the workshop. So much trust for Kanji. So much important work!

Then Brad had said, "Oh, you should have a car. Let's go out and get one for you."

Kanji well remembered the joy of that day. Brad had gone with him to an automobile dealership. Kanji had pointed to one small secondhand car, but Brad had shaken his head decisively.

"I don't go for secondhand cars, you buy someone else's mistakes. No, let's see that one," and he pointed to a splendid large red Lincoln Continental.

Kanji had not believed it, not even when Brad pulled out his checkbook and paid for it, and put it in Kanji's name. The car was part of his work, his boss said casually, and shook off Kanji's stumbling gratitude.

"Nonsense, you need this, part of the job. Now, let's get back to work. Oh, do you have a driver's license?"

That was all, such a big gesture, such a fine gesture. One dared not say to him anything was needed, for Brad would buy it at once. They all understood that and were careful not to speak before him. He would have paid for a flat for Pearl, but she shook her head. "No, no, it would be bad for my reputation!"

Mr. Livingston had grinned. "Oh, that! All right, I'll just raise your salary. I couldn't have gotten along without your good work. How much do you need?"

No one could be as generous as this man, so casually generous. He paid the craftsmen so well that Kanji had had to protest politely. "It will set all the craft guilds against us, Mr. Livingston! You must pay the right rate."

"It's too small, how can the men live on it?"

"They will manage."

They settled for a figure halfway between what Kanji suggested and what Brad wanted to give. The men came eagerly to work, and now they had twenty men working in the beautiful well-lit rooms below the offices.

He had rented an entire building. He had wanted to buy it, but that could not be permitted without much "red tape," as Brad called it. So he was arranging slowly to buy it, and meantime it was rented. He had ordered the walls painted a soft blue and cream, easier on the eyes, he explained. He had installed new light fixtures, to enable the men to work better at their detailed and intricate work.

Each man had a worktable of his own and was shown general designs, bracelets, necklaces, earrings, or rings, and told to invent his own versions of them. The freedom to create was so alien to them, that at first Brad had had to be in there continually, encouraging them to continue with the work, to finish a piece without waiting for his approval.

"That's great, that's lovely, go ahead." He delegated Kanji to look at the work, and approve it, he had other work to do. Kanji, with great trepidation, went ahead, and was amazed when Brad would nod his head and assure him that was fine.

The pieces were molded in silver, then a gold process was applied which turned the finishes a pearly pale gold, in such exquisite, shining colors that they were snapped up in Japan and America. No one knew what comprised the process, except Brad. When a number of pieces were ready, he would close the factory and work by himself in the chemistry laboratory next to his office, mixing the chemicals, working through the night, until every piece was finished.

When the workers came in the following day, the chemistry lab was cleared of all chemicals, and the pieces stood shining and beautiful, propped in trays, ready to be polished and rubbed with soft cloths, and set into velvet trays for display.

Brad told no one about the formula, it was in his head, he said. He had warned Kanji and Pearl that the formula was a secret, an invention of his own he meant to keep to himself.

Such an invention! Kanji would look at the jewelry and sigh to himself, that Brad had worked something out like this! So beautiful, so unusual. It was simply advertised as "gold-plated silver" with 14-carat gold, and that was all. But it was more than that, he felt sure. He admired Brad deeply. The jewelry sold very well, Brad was pleased with it. He had more commissions than he could fill. The rings were made of gold, and the workmen would take them and set in the diamonds, the rubies and sapphires, the pearls, that Brad supplied, all of the finest quality, and they sold for large sums. Everyone admired the pearly gold jewelry.

Brad had been striding about, studying the papers in his hands. He thought on his feet, he said. He came to a stop before Kanji's desk. Kanji sprang to his feet, he could not stop this respectful habit, though Brad often frowned and said, as he did now, "Sit down, Kanji. You know, we're going to have to expand. There are more orders than we can fill, and I'm not even trying."

Kanji's face glowed. "Yes, Mr. Livingston, you are most successful. All admire your beautiful jewelry."

"I have other ideas," said Brad, thoughtfully. "There is a red-gold and an amber-gold I have created. I haven't even started to make those yet."

Kanji stared at him, scarcely breathing. The man spilled over with ideas! He was a miracle-worker! Such a businessman, such an inventor, such a brilliant chemist!

"How can I help you?" he breathed anxiously.

"Keep your eyes open for more workers," Brad said, and laid the sheaf of papers before Kanji. "And take a look at these orders. Enough for the next year, I'd say. We can't do them in time for Christmas unless we get more help. That means setting up another floor for worktables. Let's see about fixing up the ground floor—part for workrooms, and part for a display store. I wish we could get permission to buy this building! I hate to do all this, only to find we cannot keep the building."

Kanji wanted burningly to help him. He hovered over the account clerks, he kept things going when Brad was away, he oversaw the workrooms, encouraged the men. But this was not enough! Brad was ambitious, and Kanji wanted him to have everything he wanted.

"I will see the men again today," he said. "If it will

please you, I will suggest with much care that a bribe might be offered—"

Brad's hand went over his face. "Is that necessary?" he asked wearily.

Kanji bent his head. "I fear it is," he said, subdued. "The man who owns the building is arranging for the marriage of his third daughter and needs much money for her. If it might be suggested that a sum of money could be added to the price of the building, yet given to him in an envelope without being spoken of—" He broke off, his head still bent. "I am ashamed, Mr. Livingston, that I speak of this. You are a man of much honor—"

"I understand how it is," said Brad. "It's done in the States also, though not quite the same way. All right, Kanji, go ahead. Talk to him and figure out the sum needed, delicately. I'm sure you can handle the situation. I would blow it—"

"Blow—it?" asked Kanji, puzzled.

"Mess it up," Brad explained. "I don't have your tact." He grinned, and to Kanji it was like the sun coming out from behind a cloud. "You handle it, Kanji, I trust you."

"I shall do my very best," said Kanji, still awed and frightened by the responsibility given to him. He was but twenty-six! He now earned more money than his father had earned in his lifetime, more than any of his acquaintances, even those ten years his senior. He could marry soon—if all went well—

He could marry—

He put the thought out of his mind, firmly. He must not "blow it" with the important meeting of the man who owned the building. He telephoned and politely made an appointment in a tea shop near where the man worked, and went out to see him.

All went well. The man was burdened with debts, for he had four daughters and no sons. The dowries, he told Kanji, were eating up all his savings. Kanji listened with great sympathy, told him with quiet confidence that his boss was of a great understanding and wealth. They talked back and forth, and Kanji came away with the agreeable feeling that another meeting or two would see them settled on a sum.

He returned late to the factory, disappointed to find that Brad had left. Still, it might be better to wait and see the man again, and try to get things settled. Brad got impatient with the intricacies of such details, and wanted only to hear of results. He left a note on Brad's desk: "All is going well. I shall see the man again on Wednesday. I hope to have good results of this before long. Kanji Noguchi."

He had trained himself painfully to leave out all he would have written in Japanese to a superior who was of his own country. He had never forgotten how Brad had exploded on receiving his first painfully composed note: "This pitiful piece of humanity begs humbly to inform you who is a master of great and intelligent wisdom that four poor and ignorant workmen have been employed to dare to work on your designs of such elegance—"

"My God, what in the name of Heaven have you said here!" Brad had put the note under Kanji's nose and raved about it for ten minutes. "For the love of God, write clearly. Leave out all those poor miserable worms, or by God I'll go right out of my ever-loving mind!"

Kanji tried to explain that he was being respectful, but Brad would have none of this. The second note received the same reception, with even more force in it. The third note had been torn in two and thrown with great accuracy into the wastebasket some ten feet away.

"Kanji, you don't talk like this. Don't inflict those notes on me! Write in clear English. Just say what you have to say, and quit! God's sake, I'm begging you!"

Kanji had worried about it and talked to Pearl, who had worked for Americans for three years. "He means it," she said. "Leave out all that guff."

He had been shocked to the core. "Guff? What is this? You do not respect him? You do not wish to say the proper words to him?"

Pearl had turned up her elegant nose. "I wish to please him," she said in her clear, bright voice. "He wishes to be treated like an American. So I write clearly and say just what is to be said, no more. No guff!"

He admired Pearl at times, she was a most efficient secretary. They had been quietly engaged for ten years, since their parents had arranged it. They had been young, he was but sixteen, and she was twelve. But both were only children, and their mothers had been close friends.

Now Pearl would not even talk about marriage. That was in the past. She had left home, saying her father beat her mother, and she could not endure it. Not endure it! He was sorry that her father was brutal to her mother, but for Pearl to leave home, take jobs with American firms, learn to live in an apartment of her own by herself—and cut her hair short, and dress smartly in American styles— All this had shocked him deeply.

Pearl was an admirable and intelligent girl. She had had two years of college before she left home. She had refused to return to college, for she had said she must earn her own living.

Kanji went out to her office, and sat down, waiting. She was typing a long list of names. He waited patiently while her fingers flew over the electric keys. By the tilt of her head, he knew he had but to say a word, and she would tell him to leave her.

She was becoming as independent as an American girl, and it troubled him.

He waited until the list was finished, and she had rolled the paper out of the typewriter, proofread the list, and set it aside.

"I wish to take you out to dinner, Pearl," he said. When he saw her stiffen, as though to object, he added quickly, "I am most tired, and I think you are also. I should like to dine quietly with you, and speak of the day."

He made her curious, her dark eyes sparkled a little. "Well—maybe. But no personal talk, Kanji."

"When is there not personal talk between us?" he asked reasonably. "We have known each other many years, and we work in the same firm."

"You know what I mean!" She got up briskly, put the cover on her typewriter, locked away papers, then glanced around as though to make sure all was in order. Finally she was ready.

He let her go out, then locked up after her. The burly night guard was on duty and Kanji spoke to him before they left. Because of the precious jewelry inside, the building was guarded night and day. The watchdog was a huge one, with sharp eyes and a growl that made one's spine curl in fear.

They went out to Kanji's car. He unlocked it, and helped her in. He closed the door and went around. He felt jubilant inside himself. Today he had done some good work for the boss he worshipped, and tonight he would have dinner with the girl he adored. It was a good day. Perhaps his luck had changed completely the day Brad Livingston had hired him. He hoped so.

He took her to dinner in an American-style restaurant he knew she liked. He preferred Japanese himself, but they were most expensive now, and anyway he wanted to do what Pearl wished.

He ordered for her, shrimp and vegetables, and a crisp salad, and the same for himself. A bottle of white wine came, and the waitress opened it for them, and poured it out, bowing to them. Kanji tasted it, and nodded, the way he had seen Brad do. He watched his idol so closely, he could imitate to the least nod the way Brad looked and moved and acted.

"Ah, that's better," Pearl sighed, moving her shoulders in the deep blue dress. She wore dresses like the American women, and he thought she looked beautiful. But never so beautiful as in the rare times now that she wore the kimono and obi. "I was tired, Kanji."

She spoke naturally to him tonight, as though weariness had worn down her resistance. No one sat near them, and he bent toward her urgently.

"Pearl, you know what is in my heart. I wish to take care of you always. Will you permit me to speak to your parents about marriage, perhaps in a year?"

She straightened, and her head bent. She moved the wine glass carefully with her tapering fingers, so graceful and beautiful.

"Kanji, I do not wish to insult you, nor make you angry. Our friendship goes back a good many years."

His heart began to sink. Was she going to refuse again to set a wedding date?

"It troubles me to see you work long hours, to live alone," he said quietly. He longed to put his hand on the graceful one near his on the table, but it would insult her. One did not show affection in public. The GI's kissing and hugging girls on the street made many Japanese sick at their stomachs, it was so vulgar.

"Do not worry about me, I can take care of myself," she said brightly.

"I wish to speak to your parents," he persisted.

She shot a dark look at him. He admired the long lashes, the beautiful shape of her eyes. How he longed to put his hand on the creamy pearl of her cheeks, to touch the blue-black of her straight short hair. "There is nothing to talk about," she said curtly. "I write only to my mother. I never go home, nor do I speak to my brutal father! He knows what I think of him!"

"Pearl!" he gasped. "He is your father!"

Her lovely mouth set in stubborn lines. "I told him when I found him beating her yet again, with a walking stick, that I would never return home, nor speak to him again. Nor will I! He is a rough beast, and I detest him with all my heart!"

He was silent, aghast. No matter what happened, one's parents remained one's parents, and entitled to one's courtesy and respect. He himself had been revolted when he had learned of the man's behavior. But one did not discuss it, it was between husband and wife.

"Kanji," said Pearl, her eyes downcast, her mouth demure once more, "if I did marry you, would you beat me at times?"

He hesitated, cautiously. This could be a trap. Yet honesty compelled him. "It is—the custom, Pearl. If it became necessary, I would have to do so. A man is nothing if he is not the master of his wife and his family."

"There," said Pearl, nodding her head vigorously. "You admit it! No, I shall remain single all my days if I cannot marry a man who would treat me with respect and reverence! No, I shall not marry soon, perhaps never."

He was silent, troubled. He could have lied to her, yet he had always dealt honestly with her. There was a blunt honesty about Pearl that had always attracted him. He wanted to promise that he would never beat her. But he was a man. It was the custom. And she could be infuriating. If she were to defy him in public, if she were rude to his parents or to hers, or were to neglect the children, it might become necessary to beat her. It caused him a curious pain to think of hitting her, of reddening that lovely golden-pearl skin of hers. He had to bite his lips to control himself, he felt sick over it.

"You see, Kanji," she continued, over another glass of wine. Her eyes glittered at him in the semidarkness. "I want to be a modern girl. I am a woman of today. You are a traditionalist. Your family were samurai. You are not the kind of man I could ever marry."

He put his hand to his face as though she had struck

him. He felt insulted, ashamed, angry. He swallowed hot words. They could not quarrel in public.

She waited, then added, quietly, "I reject the arranged marriage, made between our parents. I will tell my parents so."

"No!" he forced himself to say. "Pearl, you will not! It would hurt my parents so much."

She hesitated. He knew she liked and admired his gentle parents.

"Well—we could wait a time, then tell them slowly."

He wet his lips. This was going all wrong. "We have been engaged for many years. If you wish to wait another year—I will wait. But could you not begin to purchase your dowry? You will wish kimonos and obi, and many boxes of sandlewood. I know your parents wish to begin this. Your mother asked me when they might buy some boxes and begin."

"Tell them no," said Pearl, defiantly. She got up and reached for her small handbag. "Let us go, please. The answer is no."

They went out to the car after he had settled the bill, and bowed to the waitress and the owner of the restaurant several times, and complimented them on the meal. No matter how miserable one felt, one must pay one's respects. Pearl bowed only slightly, and they looked at her curiously.

He took her to her flat, and stopped the car. "You will think this over," he suggested, hopefully. "The marriage has been planned these many years. I have looked to the time when it would be my great privilege to take care of you—"

She tossed her head. "I can take care of myself! I prefer to remain single, like the American and English girls! They have true freedom. If they marry and do not like it, they get divorced!"

He sucked in his breath in shock. That she could think it, even say it!

In silence, he saw her to the door, bowed deeply to

her, and murmured his gratitude at the pleasure of her company that evening. When she had gone up the stairs, and out of his sight, he turned and went back to the car.

He felt numb and sick. He started the car, but dared not drive on until he was in control again. Pearl had rejected him so firmly. Never before had she spoken with such finality. She had forbidden him to tell Brad she was engaged to him. But he thought it was because she wished to work and save money for the marriage later.

Now—now—a snake of doubt was crawling through his mind. Could the gossip be true? He had denied it, laughed at it, but now it returned to haunt him.

Some said, some asked, some whispered, that Brad's secretary was more than respectful of him. She spoke pertly to him, and he laughed. Could it be true? Were they—lovers?

Surely not. Surely Pearl would not forget her honor, her modesty, her upbringing. But when she and Brad were together, Kanji had always found himself watching them closely. They were good workers together, as though they knew each other's minds.

Could it be true? Could it be that Pearl loved her boss, Brad Livingston? She had been angry and upset over his marriage to Charita, Kanji knew that. She had said the girl was not right for him, then had closed her lips tightly over any further remarks.

Did she love him? Did Brad love her? Had they become lovers? Was Pearl Brad's mistress?

All Kanji's pleasure in the day was gone. He went home to his handsome flat, the one in which he had taken such pride. He left his car in the garage without the last happy pat to the wheel he usually gave his pride and joy. Nothing seemed to matter beside the enormous worry—

Did his betrothed love another man, and had she surrendered her body and her honor to him? A man now married to his beloved sister, Charita? If she had, could

92

Kanji marry her? She had refused to marry him, yet—yet her parents had promised her. It had been decided years ago. Was she so modern she would reject the promises of her honored parents?

Worst was the picture of Brad's hand on Pearl's shoulder as he stood casually behind her, looking at the pages in the typewriter, laughing with her over something. They appeared so intimate, so close. Had his revered idol dared to take his girl and treat her like a mistress?

That night Kanji could not sleep. He walked slowly about his apartment, thinking about Charita, thinking about Pearl, his Pearl. Late that night, still pacing, he was the picture of a man in pain.

6

Charita wandered slowly through her new home. She had been married for a week now. Still, when someone said, "Mrs. Livingston," she looked about to see who was addressed, then felt foolish.

She did not feel married. After that first disastrous night, Brad had slept in his own room, and they never spoke of their wedding night. He often worked late, coming home tired and silent, eating in silence, as though he did not notice what he ate. Would it always be like this, Charita wondered dismally.

Her small, slim hands twisted together. She could not settle down to anything. She had tried to paint in the pretty cool room which Brad had told her was set aside for her work. He gave her everything, she did nothing for him.

Charita had always worked. Even when she was a small child, she had had her duties. At first, it was helping with guests, serving tea, then dusting and sweeping or helping to prepare meals. She learned how to do many things useful in a household. She would make up the beds, setting out mats, placing the futons and pillows just so. She was especially adept at making pretty flower arrangements.

Here, there was so little to do. The maids and the houseboys did everything. Indulgently, they did let her arrange the flowers, and extravagantly admired her artistry. But that could not occupy one all the long day.

What did other married women do? Charita recalled her foster mother, always bustling about to make her small family comfortable, her rosy face beaming at them. Mr. Noguchi was very good to his wife. They were old-fashioned, and they kept the traditional ways. But never had he insisted on her eating after the others were finished, nor did she dine on cold rice in the kitchen, the way some women had to. No, she ate the good fresh food with the family, not the leftovers. Mrs. Noguchi obeyed her husband in all ways. She bowed to him. In the bath, she scrubbed his back. He had the first bath, and she had the last one, especially in the early years when hot water was scarce.

Charita sighed as she wandered from room to room. In this grand house, there was plenty of hot water, and Brad took showers! He had never asked her to scrub his back; she blushed now with embarrassment at the thought. He fixed his own drinks when he got home from work. He expected the servants to do the work of the house; consequently, Charita had little to do.

She thought of Jacinda Snow, the only other married woman she knew at all well. Jacinda was in her office all day. At home, she did nothing but drink, or change her clothes and be hostess at the dining table. There was no role model there.

Charita returned to the living room and surveyed it appreciatively. The wall-to-wall carpet was of thick gray plush, with a curving deep blue line in it. The draperies were of sapphire blue, drawn now to cover the French windows. Behind them were thin white lace curtains, so fine she scarcely dared touch them for fear they might tear.

The room was more crowded than the usual Japanese room. She supposed that many of these objects were collected during Brad's extensive travels, which he had mentioned only casually.

A black lacquer Japanese screen stood in one corner. Covering the screen were delicately drawn gold lacquer figures. There was a curved bridge, with a lady in kimono and geta daintily stepping across. Trees and flowers in gold surrounded the delicate bridge. Around the black borders were stamped shells, flowers, birds, and a family insignia of an old Japanese samurai house.

In another corner stood a plain black table, and on it an exquisitely made Chinese Kuan-yin in blanc-de-Chine porcelain about twenty inches high. Charita went over now, and gently touched it, curving her finger over the lovely lines, admiring the detail of the beautiful face. Charita thought of the painted wood Kuan-yin she had received as a wedding gift, still in its decorated wood box. Everything here was Brad, nothing was Charita. She felt a stranger in the house. Yet he had waved his hand, and said, "All this is yours, Charita." He seemed to mean it.

There was a carved mahogany cabinet against the far wall. One day she had opened it and looked at all the objects there. A celadon jade hand of Buddha had captured her attention for a time. There were some unusual orange red and black pottery jars Brad had told her were from Greece. She wondered who had created the handsome angular figures of dancers and bulls on the ancient pieces.

Brad had also collected wood figures from various African nations. She had gazed curiously at the ivory elephants, and other animals with long curved horns she could not name.

Nearby was the impressive stereo. In the evenings sometimes Brad would put on records and play enchanting music for her.

There was a color television set and sometimes Brad would turn it on, chuckling at the samurai plays. He said they were like Western cowboy films. He seemed fascinated by them, but she thought they were most exaggerated and undignified, real samurai were not really like that. They did not bother much about women. When the castle was attacked, they left the women there for the next warriors. But she did not tell Brad that.

Charita sank down on the deep gray plush velvet sofa and brushed down the skirt of her dress. Brad liked her to wear American dresses, but when she was unhappy and depressed, she put on a kimono. It made her feel like herself, her old self, once more. This evening she wore a blue silk dress with a full pleated skirt and graceful butterfly sleeves. She hoped it would please him.

She glanced at the clock once more. It was only five o'clock and she assumed he would be home in another hour or two.

Then she heard the car, and tensed. It roared past the windows, back to the garage. The chauffeur had driven him to work this morning, and Brad had climbed into the back seat with his portfolio already out, his papers in his hand. He scarcely noticed her wave good-bye from the door.

When she heard his step in the hallway, she looked up nervously. Would he be tired and grim, or smiling, with his shoulders back?

He was smiling when he entered the room.

"Good evening," she said . . . rose in greeting.

"Hi, honey," he said. He came to her and brushed a quick kiss against her lips. That was about the only way he touched her now. "You look like a pretty doll. I'll wash and change, it'll take me about fifteen minutes," he crossed the room quickly and was gone, again.

A pretty doll. Was that how he thought of her? Charita's mouth curved down ruefully. She sat down but jumped up again and went to tell the maid to bring ice. The maid was already appearing with the bucket, and gave Charita a wide smile and a bow. She set the ice bucket near the bottles and crystal decanters on the liquor cabinet, and departed with another bow. She would bring the tea tray when Brad came in.

Brad came back dressed in a pair of tan casual slacks

and a dark brown turtleneck. Charita thought how nicely the sweater complemented his dark hair. The maid came in with tea. "How's the day, honey?" Brad asked, filling a glass with ice, then pouring whiskey into it. He gulped down the first swallows, then came with his glass to the sofa.

"It went well, thank you," said Charita politely. It had dragged, actually, but she certainly could not tell him that. She held the pretty cup and saucer. White, rimmed in gold, with a tiny golden flower design in the center. Brad stared at the delicate hands perfectly framing the cup.

He sat down beside her. He watched her pour out the tea for herself. As he nursed his whiskey, he seemed thoughtful.

"You're bored, aren't you, darling?" he asked finally.

"I do not wish to complain ever!" she said passionately. "You have been very good to me, you have been so kind—"

His hand, chilled by the glass, touched her lips to silence her. He was grinning, lines carved beside his firm mouth. "I warned you about that gratitude bit, love," he said. "No more of that. Our marriage is starting off slowly, but things will pick up. When I get the work sorted out, we'll go off for a honeymoon."

"Oh," she said. She had wondered because Brad had said nothing about it. Yet—yet a honeymoon would mean sharing a bed with him, and the thought made her hot all over again. That terrible first night!

"What is the Japanese word for love?" he asked, casually, leaning back against the sofa and putting his free arm about her shoulders. It made her quiver a bit.

"It is *kōi*," she answered faintly.

"Does that mean to love, or is it a lover?"

She thought about that. His hand was closed firmly about the curve of her shoulder; it was difficult to concentrate. "*Kōi* is love. *Koi-suru* is to love. *Koibito* means a lover, or a sweetheart."

"Koi," he repeated. Charita wasn't sure if he was

trying out the word, or addressing her. She sipped her tea, with a shy glance toward him over the golden rim.

"Does the work go well?" she asked politely.

"Well, Kanji is a treasure. He takes a load off my shoulders. I have to push him to take responsibility, though. He seems to be afraid I will be offended if he makes decisions."

"It is not the usual way in an office," she offered cautiously. "One usually meets in a committee, my father says, and a decision is reached by all."

He shrugged and grinned down at her so charmingly, her heart seemed to turn over in her chest. "Committees aren't my thing, honey. They bore me to tears." The maid was hesitating in the doorway. "Oh, is dinner ready?"

She bowed low, murmured, "The poor miserable food awaits the hopeful pleasure of the master." Brad groaned.

Both Charita and the maid looked at him anxiously, but he was laughing. "I'll get used to it."

At the table, Charita noticed that he ate hungrily, and that there were tired lines around his eyes. He worked so hard, and for such long hours, that her heart felt very soft toward him. If only she could help him! He had rested in her house on Hokkaido, and the weary lines had been wiped out, but now they were back. If only he could rest more.

Perhaps he missed the gay parties he went to with Jacinda and Miles. After dinner, as they settled themselves back in the living room, she said timidly, "If you wished, you might go out to parties. I do not mind, really," and then shrank as he glared at her.

"Go out? To what parties?" he asked.

"I only meant—perhaps you wished to visit your friends. To be amused. It must be dull for you with only myself—"

He was shaking his head, his face relaxing. "I'm glad to be alone with you, Charita. I get very tired, must be getting old. It is pleasant to be with you, and not have to run around. They are leaving us alone because I told them to. Since we are just married, we have an excuse!"

It was puzzling to her, but she accepted it. Brad turned on the record player, and put on a Chopin étude, which he knew she enjoyed immensely. He came back to the sofa, sat down beside her, and slipped his arm about her. One hand pushed her head gently down on his shoulder, and she let it remain there. His free hand gently caressed her arm, in time to the music. It was soothing, yet exciting, to be close to his warm body, and feel him relaxing beside her.

They sat quietly like that for some time, enjoying the music and their quiet. At the end of the evening, Brad said, "To bed. I have to get up early. Good night, darling." He kissed her lips gently, turned her shoulders toward her room, and he went to his.

Charita lay awake for a time, thinking about him. He was so tired, did he have to work so hard? Was there no way she could help him? He had helped her so much on Hokkaido, she did not know what she would have done without his strength and decisiveness. Somehow, she had to help him.

The next evening, Brad came home early once more. "All goes well," he announced cheerfully at dinner. "I think I'll get my building. Today, Kanji, who has been arranging the transaction, gave me the report that the money has been settled on, and we have only to draw up the papers."

"Oh, that is good, I am glad for you," she said, happy to understand him for once. "And it gives me much pleasure that my foster brother is much use to you. He is always good and works hard, and respects his parents. He is a fine man."

"Yes, he is," said Brad thoughtfully. "What was your relationship with him, Charita?"

Her forehead wrinkled. "He was my brother," she said, worrying her lips with her small teeth. "Is that what you mean?"

"Yes—of course," said Brad shortly, and poured another drink. He came to sit beside her once more, and put his arm about her closely. He seemed more possessive tonight, insisting on her sitting right next to him as he talked.

She listened quietly to him as he talked of the volume of jewelry orders. He was swamped and had asked Kanji to find more workmen, and they were ordering more worktables.

"May I one day see these workrooms?" she asked timidly. "It would be a great pleasure to see the place where you work."

"Of course, honey. I'll take you with me tomorrow, and send you home with the chauffeur." He caressed her right hand as he continued to talk enthusiastically of the work. "I have always enjoyed jewelry designing, but never had enough time to do it all myself. Now I am getting someplace. The Japanese are excellent workers with all the patience in the world, and they carry out ideas magnificently. I like to stroll through the stores and see the lacquer and the tapestries and carvings. Infinite patience! By the way, if you ever want to go shopping, wait and go with me. I don't want you out alone," he added, so casually, she did not realize at first what he had said.

"What do you mean?"

"Charita, it is dangerous. You are now married to a wealthy man," he said, very gently. He gazed down intently into her upturned face. His fingers smoothed her cheek. "I do not wish to upset you. But you could be in danger, and I won't have anything happening to you. I will not have you go alone anywhere. You may go with Jacinda and Miles Snow—"

She could not imagine wishing to go anywhere with them! It must have shown in her expressive face.

He added quickly, "Or with Kanji and his parents, though I would prefer to be with you at those times. But never, *never* go out alone."

He saw her troubled expression, bent and kissed her nose. "Now, I've made you unhappy. Believe me, I don't wish you to be unhappy," he said lightly. "There are penalties attached to wealth, and this is one. So, you will obey me in this, won't you?"

She agreed; after all, in the marriage ceremony she had promised to obey him in all things. She was accustomed to going out alone. She enjoyed walking alone. Looking quietly in shops, selecting fruit and meat in the markets, or painting supplies in art stores. She enjoyed browsing through bookshops. It seemed that all this was the beginning of the end of her freedom.

The next morning, she put on a pink linen dress with a cutaway stand-up collar and was ready at nine when Brad was. She was happy to be going out with him, and color bloomed in her cheeks as she gazed about eagerly. The chauffeur drove them today. Brad sat in the back with her. He had a portfolio beside him, but he kept it closed. He held her hand, and together they looked out at the bustling city of Kyoto.

"Would you like to visit some places, Charita?" he asked, noticing the way she strained to catch a glimpse of the outline of a temple.

"Oh, please, when you have the time—" she agreed enthusiastically. "I should like to see the Sanju-sangendo again, and the Kinkaku-ji, and the Kokedera—"

"Wow! What are those things?" he joked.

She laughed with him, and he squeezed her hand, and then played with her fingers. "Sanju-sangendo is a most beautiful temple, a national treasure," she explained. "The lovely thousand-armed Kannon is there along with other figures of much interest. Father took me there one time, and explained them all to me."

"We shall go, and you shall explain them all to me," he said, with a smile. "And what are the others?"

"The Kinkaku-ji is the beautiful Temple of the Golden

Pavilion. It has a most serene garden. The Kokedera is the Moss Temple. It is a garden and pools all set out with moss, and so quiet and green, like an outdoor temple. My parents took me there, and we strolled for an hour or two, and never said a word. It is most calming to the spirit, like a place in Paradise."

"Then we'll have to go there," said Brad, seeming more interested in the shine of her blue eyes than the thought of visiting temples. "Here we are, now. Wait till I come around."

Charita noticed he gave a quick look around before he got out, and that a guard stood near the entryway to the factory. The chauffeur opened the door, and Brad came around to help Charita out.

Brad was wondering if this was such a good idea. He had received a couple of anonymous warnings through Kanji that the factory was under watch by some thieves. It might be that the jewels and gold were too tempting to be left alone. But they would not come in the daytime, he thought.

He helped Charita out of the car, and was delighted by the peach-bloom of her cheeks, the sparkle in her eyes. She had been very quiet and withdrawn since their marriage, as though all the liveliness he had admired in her had been quenched.

He showed her the first floor, explaining how it would be made partly into more workrooms, partly into a great showroom, where they would sell the jewelry that was of lesser quality. Most of the more valuable items were made to order.

Then they went up the stairs to the next floor. Charita gazed with wide-eyed wonder at the twenty worktables, with the men in their blue kimonos intently bending over their work or soldering or gently melting the silver pieces into jewelry. Brad took her over to one of the tables. The man jumped up at once, and bowed low. Charita bowed to him, and said a few graceful shy words, in Japanese.

"This is Mrs. Livingston," said Brad proudly, when he could get a word in. The man bowed even lower, several times, jerkily. He was overcome with the pleasure of being introduced to the wife of the big boss.

Brad urged him to show Charita what he was doing. The man showed his tray, with the different gauges of silver wire, and explained that he softened them with his torch until the silver was pliable. They were bent into bracelets. Decoration was added with his chasing tools and sharp-pointed fine files. The needle files were for the most delicate designs, the riffler files for reaching inaccessible places. He was working on a brooch, and explained how he would solder the fastener onto the back after the design was completed.

Brad introduced Charita to several others, being careful to take her to the men of most seniority. They would be insulted if he passed them over for younger and less experienced men. One craftsman showed her the ring he was working, which would hold a two-carat square-cut diamond eventually. Another showed her an elaborate necklace which would take many days of painstaking work to complete. Link after tiny link of silver was added, then glowing topaz would be set.

Brad thanked his workmen, and took Charita up to the next floor, to his laboratory and offices. She knew Pearl, they bowed several times to each other as he watched curiously. It seemed to be a game to see who could bow the most times and be the last to bow. Pearl won, for she kept on until Charita gave up. Kanji was smiling from his desk, standing there deferentially until Charita came over to him and bowed. They did not shake hands. The Japanese valued their own "personal area," and one did not come close and touch, Brad had discovered. Perhaps because space was so precious to them, they did not invade another's.

Brad took her into his office. "Papers all over, darling."

"You are very busy. Thank you so much for showing me the place where you work. Now I can imagine you working here," she said, with a shy smile that showed her dimples.

He was enormously pleased that she would admit this. "Oh, come and see my laboratory, also," he said, taking her arm. He unlocked the door, and led her in.

She looked about curiously. The walls of the large room were whitewashed and bare. There were large vents in the ceiling, opened to the sky when unlocked. The acids Brad worked with were too dangerous to be handled without proper ventilation. He also had a ventilating system to be used in rainy weather or on cold days.

The vats he worked with were of enameled iron. He used gold anodes in them, and made up a fresh batch of chemicals for the purest, most beautiful results. The supplies of potassium cyanide, potassium gold cyanide, caustic potash and potassium sulphite were kept in tightly covered bins or bottles, in a locked storage cupboard. He reordered and picked these up himself, and paid in cash, so no record would be kept of what he bought. He added a few other ingredients in his secret formula, so that the finish would be the unusual pearly gold which made the jewelry so popular.

"How do you use these?" asked Charita, indicating the vats.

He took her over to one. "This is called electroplating. It requires some chemicals to be mixed in the vat. Then the jewelry is hung on wires, and dipped into the chemicals. When the pieces come out, they are covered with gold."

"Oh, I see," she nodded her head, but looked blankly at him. He smiled gently at her. He didn't really want her to understand too much, it would be dangerous.

"And do you wear a white coat, the way they do in American films?" she asked.

He chuckled a little, and unlocked a cupboard. There

105

hung his white laboratory coats. He put one on, and paraded for her, grinning.

"You look so smart," she said admiringly.

"Thank you, darling! Now, I must take you down to the car. You'll go right home, won't you, and not go to any temples, no matter how you are tempted?"

She nodded. "Yes, I will," she said simply. "Thank you so much for allowing me to see where you work. You will—be home in good time tonight, for the dinner?" she added shyly.

"In good time." He drew her to him before they went out to the other office, and kissed her gently on the lips. "All right, now I'll let you go."

She was blushing and sparkling when they went out. Pearl and Kanji jumped to their feet, but he drew her past them. Downstairs, he saw her into the car, gave the chauffeur directions, and sent her home. The day guard was watching closely, his guard dog at his side.

Brad felt happier that day than he had since their marriage. Charita wanted to share his life, to know what he did, to think of him. That was a step in the right direction. He knew he had terrified her the first night, and had vowed to woo her gently and slowly. But patience did not come easily to him.

Once he had thought he would never marry. The experience of his parents had put him off marriage completely. He thought of those early years with remembered pain.

His father, Hal Livingston, had been a brilliant but cold businessman. Brad could still hear his mother screaming at him, "You don't give a damn about me! All you care about is piling stocks on bonds, making another million! You don't even care about your son!"

Brad had been crouched outside the window of his father's study, the baseball forgotten, his young limbs shaking.

His father had said coldly, "No one means anything to me, Annette. My son will inherit all this—what else does he need? And you—all you care about is your painting! Don't pretend to me! The boy is only someone to be shown off to company, or stuck in one of your sentimental gooey creations!"

She had screamed again, and flung a vase at him. At the crash and cursing, Brad had stolen away, shaken to the depths. He kept hearing his father's harsh words, "No one means anything to me."

His parents had divorced. He never saw his father again, because the man went off on a venture to Columbia, lost everything he had, and died in the jungle crash of his private plane. His mother had worked hard to support herself and Brad, her paintings sold well, and she had married Jacinda's father briefly.

However, the quarrels and screaming went on. His mother was artistic, temperamental. Brad, looking back, understood her a little better now. She had craved admiration and support, the warmth of loving solace. She had never gotten it. She had set up a studio in New York and painted cover illustrations and ads until her death several years ago.

Brad had inherited his father's sharp business sense, his mother's creativity. But he cringed from scenes; he had avoided close emotional ties with anyone. He felt fond of Jacinda, but knew she could take care of herself.

Only Charita had wakened something different in him, a need to cherish, to possess, to claim, to adore. She was, he mused, like the flowers and butterflies he had drawn in secret, under cover of economics texts and notebooks on business administration.

He had gone to Europe alone, tramping with backpack in the early years, staying at luxury hotels a few years later. He had wandered in art museums, strolled along canals to study the fragile structures of Venice, sat for hours sketching in outdoor cafes and beside rivers in the countryside. It had all added up somehow. He had started one jewelry firm, used his knowledge of science and business to make a success of it. His first million was the most difficult, the second easier.

Then he had begun to feel a lack in his life—a need to love and be loved. He had a wish to share what he had struggled so hard to achieve. Yet how he shuddered from thoughts of marriage—screaming accusations, tears, cursing, blows, then cold, furious silences.

Charita had begun to change him, he realized. He loved being with her, in silence and peace. She seemed like her nickname, Golden Lotus, blooming in fragrant silence.

He worked hard that day, throwing off the decisions and plans like fury, wanting to be done early. To go home to his wife! He had never felt like this before. He had always gone out with girls. Some, he had admired. In between jobs he would have an occasional affair. Work had always come first; he had always been intensely wound up in his work. He had made his first million before he was twenty-five, and now was well on his way to his third.

But all that was of lesser importance than the task he had set himself, which was to woo and win the wife he had chosen. She was gently bred, so differently from himself, of another culture and background. He wanted her love and devotion directed all to him. He had always been a possessive man about his work, his business, the works of art that he had collected. Now he felt even more possessive about his wife.

He left at five and was home in good time, though the traffic was as maddening as always, horns honking, taxis shooting out from all directions. It amazed him that the courteous Japanese were such madmen behind the wheel. Kamikaze drivers, Kanji called them.

Charita was waiting, in a long gown of summery yellow, with a beautiful pearl brooch at her throat, one he had given her. He was intensely pleased to see this. She rarely wore jewelry; he had wondered if she even liked it. She seemed brighter tonight, was more talkative, eager to hear what he would say.

The telephone rang at four in the morning. Brad rolled over, groggily, lifted the receiver, and blinked at the crisp voice in his ear.

"Mr. Livingston? I regret so very much to inform you that your factory has been broken into. This is the Kyoto police. Would you be so very kind as to bring your honorable self to the factory at once?"

"My God! Yes, I'll be right down."

He pulled on his clothes, and went off in the car. He had told a sleepy maid where he was going; he wondered if she had understood his message in halting Japanese. Traffic at night was nothing, he was at the factory in less than half an hour.

The police waited for him, and Kanji, in a dark blue slack suit, his hair mussed. Kanji was grave.

"Mr. Livingston," he said, at once. "The guard has been shot, and will not be moved until he has spoken with you."

Brad went over to where the man lay on a stretcher. He knelt down. "What is it?" he asked in slow, distinct Japanese.

"I will die," murmured the guard. "I have failed my trust. I do not deserve to live."

Brad stared up at Kanji. "Does he mean this?" he whispered. Kanji nodded soberly.

"He has disgraced himself," whispered Kanji. "And his guard dog, which he has owned eight years now, is also dead."

Brad thought quickly. The man's dark, pain-filled eyes were fixed agonizingly on his face. He was a burly, silent man, devoted to his job and his dog. He lived alone in a slum section of Kyoto; Kanji had found him.

"You must not die," Brad said. Disregarding the Japanese habit of not touching, he put his firm hand on the man's broad hand which lay so limply on his stomach. His head was crudely bound, blood seeped through the bandage, and there was another temporary bandage on his side. "You will be needed here. You are a very strong man. They must have sent three or four men to overpower you."

"Four," whispered the man, his eyes lighting a little in pride.

"You see? If word goes out that you are not here any longer, there will be more trouble. No, you must go to the hospital, and do all that the doctors and nurses tell you. Then you must return quickly to your job here. You are necessary to us."

"Truly?"

"It is true," said Brad solemnly. "In the meantime, we must hire several men to take your place until you return. And I myself will find another good guard dog for you to train. I am most sorry your dog is dead, in the performance of his duty. He died nobly." He could see the body of the animal, shot through several times. He also had put up a good fight.

"You are the most gracious nobleman, the most good and wonderful—" began the man weakly. Brad stood up, and motioned to the stretcher carriers, and they took him to the ambulance.

"Kanji, go with them to the hospital, follow in your car," ordered Brad. "See to it that he has the best care, and bill it to me. And if the occasion comes up, tell that man he is needed. If he kills himself, I'll be furious!"

"Yes, boss!" Kanji said, and turned to his car.

"And come right back! I'll need you!"

"Yes, sir!"

Brad followed the patient policemen into the building. He stared grimly at the blood on the steps. The guard had been surprised on the first landing. The worktables had not been overturned, nothing much had been touched there, to his surprise.

"Upstairs, if you please, Mr. Livingston," said the English-speaking chief of the police unit. He beckoned respectfully with his fingers and palm.

Brad followed him up to the third floor and found chaos. Pearl's desk had been ransacked, papers thrown about. So had Kanji's. Inside Brad's office, the work had been thorough. Every drawer was out, papers spilled all over. Some jewels in a locked box had been taken, but not the best ones, he was relieved to see. They had tried to open the safe, where the finest jewels were kept, but had not been able to. He had foiled them with the intricate locks, the several doors. Perhaps the guard had discovered them before they could do more.

Kanji returned as they were trying to discover how much had been taken. Brad set him to work figuring out the value of the gems. By that time, Pearl had come. It was six o'clock; he wondered tiredly how she had heard about this.

She set about straightening the papers. Papers? Then it hit him. The gold formula. The thieves had not just been after gems and gold and silver. They were after the formula!

He had it in his head, and he decided it would stay there. He had been urged by Miles Snow and Jacinda to register it, to patent it in the States and in Japan. But under the Freedom of Information Act, as soon as the patent was granted, it would be published, and anyone could see it and use it.

Even while it was being registered, during next year while it was being researched by patent lawyers to make sure it was original, someone could obtain access to it.

The policeman had been poking around, now he opened the lab door. "Mr. Livingston, oh, my!" he gasped. Brad went over and looked in.

Someone had tried to get into the cupboards which held the chemical supplies. It was a mess. The doors were half off their hinges. The empty vats had not been touched. So they were after the formula, Brad knew it now.

The police were curious, he could see by their eyes. The sergeant asked politely, "You will file charges, Mr. Livingston?"

"Yes, I'll do that. I'll come with you as soon as we complete the list of gems missing. I guess they were after the gold also," said Brad, though he knew that was not true.

"And the papers, you have some secret papers?"

"Not really," said Brad. "Those are orders from companies and individuals who wish jewelry made for them. Nothing anyone would want, or could use."

"I see," nodded the policeman.

All the time, Brad was thinking to himself, savagely, that the peace and quiet had been too good to be true. Someone was after that gold formula. Someone knew it was an original formula, never before used, and wanted it. Someone who must be in the jewelry trade himself. Someone—but who?

The gems stolen could be replaced, though he was relieved that the ones in the safe had not been taken. Some belonged to clients, some wanted their gems remounted in modern settings of a simpler design than past decades. He would have hated to have lost them. But others were insured and replaceable.

Only the gold formula was unique, and must remain so. He would tell no one. He would not even patent it. And he would continue to mix the chemicals himself. He would have to. No one else could be trusted to keep that secret.

7

Charita understood that Brad was very upset about the break-in at his factory. She was more disturbed that the guard had been shot. What if the men had attacked Brad? She shivered with fear at the very idea.

More guards were hired, four during the day and four at night, with their guard dogs. Brad was very quiet in the evenings for a time.

Jacinda phoned several times. He refused her invitations impatiently. "I'm very busy just now, I have little enough time alone with Charita," was what Charita heard him say on the telephone.

He listened as the other woman spoke. Charita could only hear the high clear tones, not the words. Brad scowled, his mouth clamped shut in the way he looked when he was furious.

When he spoke, his tone was very smooth, very cold. "I am sorry you feel like that. You do not know her. Later on, when you are better acquainted, you will understand. No—no, don't keep on about it—no, don't plan anything—"

When he hung up, he looked very displeased. Charita tried to pretend she was reading a glossy magazine he had brought to her, showing American fashions. He came and sat beside her, and put his hand over the magazine.

"Has Jacinda phoned you while I was not here?" he asked.

Her eyes widened. "No, nobody has telephoned to me," she said. "Why, what is wrong?"

"Nothing. Never mind." His face relaxed. "Jacinda has a way of twisting things about. She makes me furious sometimes. Fortunately, I know her well!" he added, and took out his pipe.

"But what has she asked?" persisted Charita.

"Nothing much. Only that you didn't want to go out shopping with her." He watched her face keenly.

Charita bit her lips. "I don't, but I have never said so," she said honestly. "I need nothing, you have supplied all my wants. Why should I go shopping with her, or with anybody?"

He laughed a little, and kissed her cheek. "That rarely stops a woman, that she has everything," but he seemed quite satisfied with her reply.

"I did receive a letter yesterday," she said nervously. Her fingers twisted together.

"Yes? From whom?"

"From my parents. That is, my foster parents. Mr. and Mrs. Noguchi. They beg to come to visit, and bring my dowry."

His eyebrows drew into a frown. "Bring what?"

"My dowry," she said. "It is the custom. You see, they consider themselves my parents. Wait, I will get the letter."

She went quickly to her room, and returned with the letter. He did not read it.

"Tell me what they said," he told her.

"Well—they have bought two sandalwood chests with the clasps in bronze, gilded," she said, scanning the letter. "And they wish to present to you the kimonos and obis, the lengths of brocade—"

"But I told you, Charita," he said, coldly, his eyes

flashing, "I will provide all you need! They need not bring anything. I am sorry they could not come early to the wedding, but it was short notice—"

"Yes, and father could not leave the factory for several days without permission. He begs your forgiveness for that—"

Brad made an impatient sound. She looked at him pleadingly. He rubbed his hand over his face.

"Please, Brad," she begged in a low tone. "They are anxious to do this for—for me. They used to say when I married a fine man it would be the second happiest day of their lives."

"Second to what?" he asked, in a barely tolerant voice.

"Second to the wedding of their son, Kanji, of course. And they said they would provide my dowry of kimonos and linens and china."

He was visibly restraining himself. "There is no need for that," he said. "I will provide everything. If you want kimonos and obis, I'll take you shopping—"

"I need nothing! Only it is for their honor and their pride, you see, Brad," she explained patiently. She put her small hands on his, and he turned his over to grasp her fingers. His face softened. "Please, Brad, allow them to come, and to give their gifts. It means so much to them."

"Well—all right, honey, if you want. Only you must tell them tactfully not to bring much, and we don't need any more china! And as for the dowry—"

"Just the chests and the silk brocade," she said hastily.

His face smoothed. He leaned forward and deliberately kissed her lingeringly on the lips. Her eyes closed involuntarily, she savored the feel of his strong hard lips against her soft pink mouth. He smelled of shaving lotion and tobacco; there was a slight bristle to his cheek. Her lips quivered, and moved, gently, against his.

He put his arms about her and drew her close. His lips pressed harder on hers, he felt so hard against her body, his chest against her soft round breasts. She gasped a little, her hand went to his shoulder, meaning to push him away. Instead, her fingers closed over the rough silk of his jacket.

When he raised his head and smiled down at her, she could not meet his gaze. She felt on fire with embarrassment and a new, unfamiliar emotion rising in her. He drew her back gently against his shoulder, and she rested there, her cheek on his silk shirt. She heard the pounding of his heart, like the waves of the sea against the shore.

She was relieved, yet puzzled, when again she went alone to bed. Was he not going to repeat that experience of the first night? He seemed to like kissing her. She didn't know whether to feel insulted that he did not wish to embrace her body or to feel relieved that the ordeal would not be repeated.

The Noguchis came the following week, the second week of May. The azalea was in bloom, in pink splendor on the bushes in the beautiful garden around the tiny pool. Peonies had begun to bloom in pink and white nearby. And the reddish purple wisteria vines trailed over the stone house, making it glorious. She was happy that the house and gardens looked their best. She had told the servants to prepare a Japanese bedroom for her parents, and a Japanese tearoom.

They had been happy to obey, curious and friendly and welcoming to the Japanese parents of Mrs. Livingston. Papa-san and Mama-san would be most welcome there, they assured her. They brushed and aired the rooms and the futons and the tatami mats, and found an elegant black lacquer tray with tea service especially for the parents' bedroom.

Charita arranged the flowers carefully. She set her

own Kuan-yin of painted wood in an alcove, and before it placed a low celestial blue bowl of azaleas floating in water, and in another corner a large blue and white vase with cut pussy willows and peonies.

Kanji and Pearl went to the railroad station to meet his parents and bring them to Charita. Brad came home early to be there, and waited with Charita. She wore a blue and gold kimono today; with a gold and silver obi, and blue-painted geta outdoors as she gathered the fresh flowers. Entering the living room through the French doors, she shed her geta and moved on stocking feet to the vases there.

Brad looked up from studying a magazine. He stared at her.

"Wearing Japanese today?" he asked.

"Yes, in honor of my parents. You do not approve?"

"You look very charming," he said. His face seemed closed, his eyes speculative. He watched her arrange the peonies in the green vase to set on the floor near the white Kuan-yin. "You do that beautifully," he said. "I suppose you had lessons in it."

"Mama-san taught me," she said.

His mouth tightened, he seemed about to speak, then buried himself in the magazine again. They both heard the car at the same time. Charita's face lit up, she felt breathless with joy. Her dear parents were coming, the first she had seen them since her wedding day, when she had not had much opportunity to speak to them. Now they would have a good long visit, a whole week!

Brad went to the door, shaking his head at the houseboy, who fell back to wait discreetly where he could see the honorable parents enter. A maid peeped from the back hallway. Charita stood behind Brad, eager to greet her parents.

Kanji escorted them up the stairs, and Pearl came behind them. Pearl looked almost American, thought

Charita, in her elegant dress gray silk, and the pearls at her throat and ears. She found time to wonder why Pearl came. Was this part of her duties as secretary? She knew the families had been close at one time, but now Kanji never spoke of Pearl's family.

Brad bowed to them, charmingly. Charita bowed again and again, then her mother enveloped her in a brief embrace, overcome with emotion.

"Dear Mama-san," whispered Charita, pressing her cheek against the wrinkled cheek of the gray-haired woman who had been her mother for most of her life.

"You look so beautiful," whispered her mother proudly. She would never dare say it aloud, it was not done. She caressed Charita's face with her little hand. She was so small, inches shorter than Charita, and Brad towered over them all.

They all went into the living room. Mr. Noguchi sucked in his breath in polite wonder. He spoke in Japanese, he did not know English nearly so well as Kanji, and when in an emotional situation he could not speak in a language other than his own.

"How magnificent is your house, Mr. Livingston! How honored are we that you permit us to visit our unworthy daughter—"

As he went on, Brad looked flushed, and Pearl turned up her nose slightly. Charita felt hurt. Her father was doing them an honor, he was being excessively polite and his words were of the best.

Brad thanked him, rather curtly, and Charita hastened to make them welcome. Her mother looked tired, and she showed her to their room. The servants were carrying in the boxes of sandalwood; they were large and heavy. She dared not look at Brad.

Her mother praised the room, in relief. "Soooo—you have a Japanese room for us! And a tearoom for us! How good you are, how you think of us! Such beauty in the room. You arranged the flowers! You are happy, my child?"

"Very happy," Charita assured her. She was happy today, to have her parents and foster brother here in her new home, to show them how well her new husband cared for her well-being. "He overwhelms me with new clothing and jewelry. He has every care for my safety. He does not permit parties until we are more acquainted, so I will meet his many friends gradually. We sit and listen to music of an evening, in peace, together."

"Ahhhh. That sounds good, my child. It was so sudden, the marriage, with no go-between," added her mother dubiously.

Charita took the opportunity to put in a tactful word. "He is an American, and only just becoming used to our ways, Mama-san. You must understand when he does not bow more than once, that it is not his custom, and he truly respects you and Father. He is most honorable and respectful of others, and has all care for his workmen in the factory. I visited the factory with him, and all look at him with eyes of wonder and admiration. It is truly a good place."

"Ahhhh," said her mother, and Charita knew the words would be repeated faithfully to her father that night, when the parents were alone.

They went back happily to the living room. Tea was brought in at once. Charita knelt to offer tea to her father first, and he took it, and sucked it in with appreciation. It was the best green tea. Brad made a slight face over it, but he drank a little. Kanji drank his, Pearl set hers aside after a few sips.

Charita wondered at Pearl, her face seemed so cool and aloof. Why indeed had she come, and why did Mr. Noguchi survey her with almost paternal pleasure?

"You look very well, Pearl," he said to her. "Your

work agrees with you? You are doing well, and reporting often to your parents?"

"I write to my mother often," said Pearl, after a quick glance at Kanji. "The distance is far, I do not go there."

"Ahhhh," said Mr. Noguchi, his face a little troubled, but still bland. "Your respected parents are well, I trust?"

"Well; I thank you for your kind words."

Charita wondered at her cool politeness. It was good of Mr. Noguchi to take so much trouble to inquire after her and her parents. The conversation changed, and she forgot the matter.

They went in to dinner. Charita herself served them, jumping up to put morsels first on her father's plate, then on her mother's. Kanji smiled at her with affection, but Brad frowned. Charita was so eager that they would feel at home and comfortable, she had ordered an all-Japanese meal, with raw fish, boiled rice, shrimp, hot vegetables, and tea.

After dinner, they had tea and coffee in the living room. Mr. Noguchi inquired politely about the business, Brad answered him warily. Kanji looked from one to the other, and finally intervened.

"Not much can be said of the work, my honorable father-san," he said, bowing low several times to his father. "It is in the nature of some secret work. Forgive our reticence."

"Ah, I understand," said Mr. Noguchi, who clearly did not understand. But he tactfully changed the subject to the beautiful garden.

Charita said she would show them the gardens the next day, when it was light.

Pearl and Kanji left about ten o'clock. Her parents were tired, they finally excused themselves, and went to bed. Charita went with them to their rooms, to make sure all was comfortable, and finally returned half an hour later to find Brad fuming.

"Is it necessary to do all this?" he demanded, as soon as she entered the room. "To bow to them again and again, to serve them yourself? I will not have you look like a servant!"

Charita gasped, her hand to her mouth, her eyes huge. "But—Brad, I show that I respect them, that I honor and welcome them!" she finally was able to stammer out.

"You are an American," he bit out. "Not a Japanese girl! I wish you would remember that! Perhaps I did wrong to keep you here, we should have gone at once to the States!"

She paled, frightened. "Leave—Japan? My people?" she whispered, and sank onto a cushion at his feet. "Oh, Brad, I beg you, do not be angry with me! I am a poor stupid woman—"

"Now, don't start that!" he groaned, and pulled her up into his arms, and set her on his knees. She felt the anger in his stiffened arms, but he was gentle with her, his hands holding her before him. "Now, Charita, eventually we'll go back to the States and live there. Not now. But I want you to forget all this bowing bit, and wearing kimonos all the time—"

She bent her head abjectly. He was angry with her, she knew it. "I wanted merely to please the good people who raised me after my mother died," she whispered. "I wanted—only—to thank them for their care of me all these years." Tears filled her eyes.

He was remorseful. "Now, don't cry, honey! Don't cry," and he bent to kiss the tears from her eyes, very carefully. She was still as he did this, holding her breath. She was coming to like his touch, he made her feel warm and happy sometimes. "Tomorrow would you like to take the parents to one of those places you described?"

He seemed determined to please her. "Perhaps to the Moss Temple?" she asked hopefully. "It is such a beautiful place, you will like it, I assure you."

"Very well. I'll tell Kanji to hold down the fort—"

"What fort?" she asked.

He chuckled, and she was so glad to hear it that she leaned back against him and put one slim hand on his big one. "The factory, I mean. It is a slang term. It means to take care of everything while I am away. Kanji can do that. We'll go to that Moss Temple. Okay?"

"Okay," she agreed and rubbed her cheek against his silk shirt. "Thank you, Brad. You are most good to me always."

He slid one hand under her hair, and caressed the back of her neck gently. "Only no more of that stupid humble woman, and that bowing, okay?"

"Only a little bowing, only a little stupid," she murmured, with a giggle.

She went off to bed much more happily then. She rose early and made sure hot tea was taken to her parents. Then she dressed herself in a shirtwaist dress of rose silk with swinging pleats. She added the pearls. She wanted to please Brad today.

They went to the Moss Temple then, and walked silently along the paths, gazing about in wonder. It was like finding peace in the heart of a storm. It had rained two days before, and the luminousness of the moss glowed all around them. The trees were gracefully bent, revealing many different hues of green and gold. And the pools in their various shapes were rippling. Charita had enjoyed her visits here in the spring, when the cherry blossoms added their soft pastel color, and in the autumn when the leaves turned vibrant crimson and orange. But, now, in the summer, was truly the best she decided. The various colors of palest green to deepest blue greens created an ethereal, almost underwater effect. She could tell that Brad was impressed by the beauty around him.

The party returned home in a tranquil mood that afternoon. They were settled comfortably in the living room, and the sandalwood chests were brought out. Brad watched as Charita opened the chests and took out the lengths of silk brocade, the many kimonos of crimson and blue and green, of gold and silver. Her parents had spent much money on them, and Charita was overwhelmed.

"You have done too much for me, my parents," she said, and knelt before them, and kissed their hands. "It is too much. I am not worthy of your many attentions."

The family spoke in Japanese, exchanging compliments, Charita protesting she was not worthy of their extravagant gifts. Brad watched them with growing impatience. It galled that he could not understand what they said. It made him crazy to see Charita on her knees. Finally he jumped up.

"Enough! It is too much, and unnecessary. I am her husband!" he thundered. "If she wants all these Japanese clothes, I will supply them! You need not have brought them! And I want her to dress like an American!"

"Oh Brad!" Charita breathed, horrified. Her father had turned pale with shock and suppressed anger, her mother held her hand to her heart. The serenity of the day was shattered. "I beg you—do not—"

"Get up!" he shouted. "I will not have you kneeling!"

He pulled her up roughly. He was furious! "Brad, please—not before my parents—" she whispered, pleading.

He glared at them all, then stormed out of the room.

Charita brushed her hand over her face. "I am so sorry," she finally whispered.

Her father sat there, his face stony, trying to conceal his hurt. Her mother shook her head slowly. "We should have thought," she murmured. "He is American, he is different. Does he not wish the dowry?"

Charita tried to think, fighting down tears. "He said —he said my father left his books and a good mind to me, and the manuscripts—he said they were my dowry. I needed no other," she tried to explain mournfully.

"I begin to understand," said Mr. Noguchi, relaxing a little. "Professor Atwood was a most honorable professor, a bright man of many gifts. Your honorable husband feels this was too much dowry for you. He is good man. He is ashamed that we do so much for you, yes?"

Charita, relieved, agreed with them. She praised their gifts again and again, thanked them for their great goodness, and then when they were appeased, and tea had been served, she went to find Brad.

She found him in his study. Papers were spread before him, but he sat with his head in his hands. The sight touched her. He looked so weary and so unhappy.

She came up quietly behind him, and gently touched his head. "Brad, pray forgive my stupidity. I did not consider how you would feel. I foolishly thought only to please my mama-san and papa-san. But my loyalty is first to you, my husband."

He leaned his head back against her breast. It was a strange sensation, but not unpleasant. She gently stroked his forehead, to smooth out the lines.

"Is it the custom? Those trunks, that silk?" he asked, in a strained voice.

"Yes, it is. A father will spend much money on a beloved daughter. You see, they think of me as their daughter. You know they took me in when I had no mother, and it would have hindered my father's work to take care of me. If they had not—I would have had to be taken to the States, to interrupt Father's work—or be left with unfeeling relatives who cared nothing for me. You see, they gave me love and care when I most needed it."

Her tone was unconsciously reproachful, and Brad sighed. "Yes, I understand. Forgive me, Charita. I forget life has not been easy for you."

"Yes, yes, it has been easy for me! Don't you see! *They made* it easy, they protected me, cherished me—" Her voice broke on the words. "They gave me a father and mother, and a beloved brother. I wanted for nothing. Father worked very hard for us all. I remember when our house was hard to heat, but we always had charcoal and good, warm blankets. Every summer, we went to the sea with Father, or to the mountains for two weeks vacation. How good they always were to me! And now this dowry, which cost them much— They need not have done it. Was I not their foster daughter, not their real one? Yet they wished me to have all they would have given to a real daughter. I will honor them all my life, as their real daughter."

He listened in silence as she tried to explain her feelings of gratitude to them. Her hand kept stroking, stroking over his head, as she tried to communicate with him.

Finally Brad reached up, took one hand, and put it to his lips. He pressed a kiss in the palm, then folded her fingers carefully around it.

"Okay, honey, I'll come and make my apologies," he said ruefully. "I guess I'm so jealous that I can't endure anyone else giving you presents. But I am grateful to them, for caring for you, and turning you into such a charming woman."

She didn't understand all he said, but was pleased and happy when she returned to the living room with him. Brad made his apologies with humility and charm. He had not understood their customs but Charita had explained them to him. He was most grateful for their kindness.

"And most of all, for your kindness to Charita when she was a young child, and needed you so much. You were so very good to her. She has become a charming and thoughtful and kind woman, and much is due to you."

The Noguchis listened with much pleasure which they tried to conceal. Mr. Noguchi cleared his throat, and made a long speech which Brad listened to with a smile. He was holding Charita's hand tightly all the time.

The evening ended pleasantly, with music on the

record player. Mr. Noguchi, after much urging, expressed a request for Beethoven, to Brad's surprise. It was his favorite composer, said Mr. Noguchi, but anything which Mr. Livingston cared to play would be most kind. They listened to the Sixth Symphony, and the peace of it remained with them as they retired.

Charita had donned her pink nightdress with the lace about the neck and short sleeves, and had slipped into bed. She lay with her hands above her head, drowsily, happy at the outcome of the day. A tap came at the door, the door opened softly, and Brad came in.

She stiffened in shock. He came into the darkened room. "Charita, I would like to sleep with you tonight," he said, and took off his robe.

She did not know what to say. She was paralyzed with fright, it was so unexpected. Brad slid into bed with her, and took her gently in his arms.

As though he felt her alarm, he told her, "I won't be brutal, the way I was, my darling. Don't worry, that was a terrible mistake. It won't happen like that tonight."

Charita managed to say, "It is for you to treat me as you wish, I am your wife." But, oh, how she dreaded it!

"Nonsense," Brad said vigorously. "I was rough with you. And you didn't have a clue as to what I was doing. We'll take it slow and easy. I want you to enjoy this."

He began to kiss her, his lips roaming over her face and down to her throat. His hands were gentle, moving the lace on her bodice to press kisses on her shoulders and down to her rounded breasts. Eyes tightly closed, she lay stiffly, fearing pain. But slowly, the warmth and ease of his manner relaxed her a little. Now she was more accustomed to his kisses, and the way he pressed her against his hard body.

He put one of her arms about his strong neck. Her fingers timidly moved over his head, enjoying the thick silky feeling of his chestnut hair. She thought of how it looked in the sunlight, with that reddish hue in the brown, and the way his dark brown eyes sparkled when he was happy. She wanted to make him happy, he had been so kind to her.

His hands moved slowly over her body. The silk nightdress slid as he stroked over it to feel the soft curves beneath. She caught her breath again and again, as his lips moved on her tender breasts, and his fingers slid up and down her silky thighs. He took a long time about it, whispering to her as he kissed her.

"You are so lovely, my darling. You are such a pretty girl. I adore the way you smile, with those dimples here," and he had to kiss them. "And your hair is so thick and soft and perfumed. I like it all down about your shoulders like this."

He went on praising her, sometimes in words that made the heat come to her cheeks, and, embarrassed, she was silent. But her hands tried to return his caresses, she stroked his neck and the hard muscular shoulders that loomed above her.

When he removed the nightdress carefully and gazed at her with an expression she could not define, she was frightened again, but she tried to conceal it. After all, it was his right, and she had her duty to perform. Only she hoped it would not hurt so much, and she would not be badly bruised.

Brad's fingers stroked delicately over her bare thighs, and between them. Charita gasped as he touched her intimately. He paused, then went on slowly, kissing her arms and shoulders, murmuring to her soothingly. Gradually, almost against her will, she felt heat rising in her body, coursing through her, until, startled, she felt burningly alive. Her whole being concentrated on him, on this new feeling flowing through her.

His hands moved over her again and again until Charita moaned and began caressing his back with a new

127

urgency. Finally he murmured in satisfaction, and slid up to lie over her, supporting himself on his knees and elbows, so he would not crush her slim body. She felt him try again, slowly, what he had tried to do before. This time he entered her and it did not hurt so badly. The pain came swiftly and suddenly, and then was gone.

"There, darling, are you all right?" he whispered, anxiously.

She managed to nod, and murmured, "It is all right." She hurt, but he seemed happy. She could endure the pain, for it was edged with sweetness. As he moved slowly on her, and then off, it felt better. He increased his pace and called her name. Then he slumped down on her, kissing her eyes, lips, ears, and murmuring soft words.

He held her in his arms and then went off to sleep. She lay awake, amazed and shaken. This was the next step in being a wife, she realized. What would come next, she wondered and drifted off to sleep in her husband's arms.

In the night, she wakened to hear the patter of rain against the French windows. Brad had gotten up to close them, and then returned to bed.

"Raining a little, looks like a storm ahead. Don't go out tomorrow, darling," he said, in a matter-of-fact way. "I'll go to the office. You'll stay in with the Noguchis tomorrow, won't you? Maybe show them your paintings, especially the one of the garden. That is exquisite, I want it framed."

"I will do as you say," she said shyly, as he gathered her into his arms possessively, and lay back to sleep. He pressed her head against his chest, she heard again the even strong beat of his heart.

"Good, you see that you do," and he chuckled; she could feel the rumble of it beneath his cheek. "Do you feel pain, at all, love?"

She blushed in the darkness, heat came all over her. "Just— a little—" she mumbled sleepily.

His hand caressed her hair lovingly. "I'm sorry, but it will pass. Take a warm bath tomorrow and soak in the tub. One of these days—or nights—you'll begin to enjoy this," he said, confidently.

Enjoy it? Would she? That first night, she had thought not. But tonight, he had been so gentle and careful, and she had liked his caresses and the new sensations he had aroused in her. Maybe one day she might enjoy it, but she was dubious.

She did not try to answer, and instead pressed her cheek against his hard chest, feeling the little tickle of the thick hairs that grew on his chest tapering in a line down to his thighs. She longed to touch him out of curiosity, but she did not dare. She lay quietly, and heard his deep, even breathing, and knew that she was fortunate. Her husband was gentle and good to her. She must remember how fortunate she was.

8

Charita enjoyed immensely the remainder of the week her foster parents spent with them. Brad took off from work when he could and accompanied them to temples, shrines, and gardens, so that the week stood out radiantly in her memory.

They all went to the Sanju-sangendo, the Hall of Thirty-three Bays, and Mr. Noguchi kindly explained to Brad and again to Charita the meaning of the statues that fascinated them. The Thousand-Armed Kannon was a marvelous image, and they gazed and studied it for a time.

They went another day to the Kinkaku-ji, the Temple of the Golden Pavilion, and after gazing respectfully at the wonder of the golden temple, they wandered about the gardens there. Brad had brought his camera, and they took turns snapping pictures of one another. Brad took several of Charita with her parents, she hoped they would turn out well. She enjoyed pictures so much, and would spend hours working on her lovely photograph albums with the covers of silk tapestry which her parents had given to her.

They went also to the Ryōan-ji, the Temple of the Peaceful Dragon, which had the famous "dry landscape" garden of raked sand and stones. It puzzled Brad, evidently, that it was really so small. They sat beside it on the raised steps for a time, silently contemplating the abstract arrangement of the various stones and boulders offering many possible levels of personal interpretation by the beholder until finally the serenity of the place began to reach him. Charita, with Brad's hand holding hers, felt it as he began to relax. He was usually so dynamic, so pulsing with life, so impatient to be on with the next job, that it was a relief to her when she knew he was relaxing and just contemplating the beautiful garden.

"That was unusual," said Brad, as they left, walking slowly around the pond where the trees bent lovingly toward the waters, and a few gracious white swans sailed majestically toward the bridge or the banks. "How much thought went into that, to make all appear just so."

Mr. Noguchi looked at him with calm approval. He thought more of Brad now, and had seen and admired the magnificent designs of his jewelry. Truly this was a man of imagination and goodness along with his wealth. Charita had indeed fallen into good hands.

He discussed the aims of Shinto on the way home, and Brad listened with interest, Charita observed. It was such a complex matter she did not understand it at all, she had merely grown up with the concepts and taken them naturally. She felt incapable of explaining to anybody, why the Japanese bowed to Mount Fuji, or became excited at the idea of an arrangement of rocks, or revered two huge boulders set in water and fastened with a rice rope.

Finally the day came when the Noguchis had to go home again. He had taken one week of his annual holiday to spend with Charita, and she told them again and again how honored she was that they had done this. It was a great thing for them to give up their journey to the mountains or the seashore, in order to spend the time with her.

"But it was a great pleasure to us," her father answered ceremoniously, with much bowing to Brad. "How kind you have been to receive us as guests, in your most beautiful home. One day, you must come to our miserable dwelling, though you will be uncomfortable there after such a life of ease as you have in this grandeur—"

Brad was getting flushed again, and Charita squeezed his hand hard to still him. He did hate all those self-effacing words, but her father could not be stopped, he would be hurt if anyone tried. Brad managed to contain himself, and even bowed several times to her father as they departed, which pleased Charita immensely.

"Whew," sighed Brad, as the door was closed, and Kanji took them off to the railroad station. "This miserable self is about bent double, and my stupid head may not be able to cope with my abject work today."

"Brad!" breathed Charita, rather shocked, and he laughed aloud, and teased her and made the dimples come in her cheeks.

"Now, I really must be off," he said, gathering up his portfolio. "I have spent a lot of time off the job this week—"

"Oh, you have, and I am most grateful, Brad," she said, earnestly. "I only hope you have enjoyed it a little bit, for I did enjoy it so very much. Your presence added to my pleasure in the temples and gardens—"

He bent and kissed her mouth, stopping the flow of words, a hard, almost brutal, kiss which quite stopped her breath as well.

"You may thank me tonight, when I have more time!" he laughed, lifting his head, his arm still about her slim waist. He looked down into her vivid blue eyes. "Appropriately," he added. "With kisses, and hugs, I believe. Good-bye, doll, take care of yourself!"

She managed to laugh uncertainly as he departed, for the chauffeur had brought around the black limousine. She waved to Brad as he left, and he waved back, smiling. Her heart felt warm as she closed the door, and went back to the now empty living room.

She hugged to herself the joy of the week. How

pleasant it had been to drive about with Brad and her parents, to see the beautiful places of Kyoto in their company. She would never forget the golden moments.

She hummed to herself as she straightened up her parents' former room, took the tray out to the kitchen. The maid was scandalized that she had done so much, and shooed her off very politely with many bows. Charita wandered back to the room she used for her painting, but she was still too excited to settle down.

A maid came for her. "The telephone for you, if you will please to answer it," she told her, with several bows. She plugged the telephone into the jack nearest to Charita, and handed the receiver to her with a big smile. It had been a most exciting week for them also.

"Hello?" said Charita, hoping it might be Brad.

The crisp cool tones rocked her back on her heels. She had almost managed to forget Jacinda Snow.

"Hello, Charita. So you're free at last. I want to take you shopping tomorrow," said the hard voice.

Charita bit her lips. She did not want to go. "Thank you so very much. You are very kind—"

"Good, meet me in town at the Kyoto Handicraft Center, I want to look around there first. Brad said he will send his chauffeur with you. But I'll have the car from then on. I'll see you at ten o'clock," and the phone clicked.

Charita stared blankly at the telephone. That woman was really very rude! She took for granted that Charita would go with her. And so did Brad. And she did not want to go—she did not!

She finally brought it up to Brad that evening, timidly. "Jacinda Snow telephoned, and wished me to shop with her tomorrow. But I really need nothing, Brad."

She watched his face carefully. It was bland, unreadable.

"I imagine she wants you to interpret for her, she

133

isn't very good at languages," said Brad. "It will do you good to get out, and I want you to become friends with my sister."

His sister. It was hard to think of that woman as Brad's sister. She stifled a sigh, and nodded, "As you wish."

Brad came to her bed that night, and once again he made love to her, so gently and sweetly that it did not hurt much at all. She lay in his arms afterward, timidly enjoying the touch of his lips against her cheeks, the lazy movement of his fingers through her thick hair.

"You are very adorable," he murmured huskily. "I'm not sorry at all that you are all mine to teach."

"Teach? About what?" she asked, against his bare shoulder. She touched her lips shyly against the bronzed hard arm.

"About love," said Brad. "I don't want anyone in the world even to kiss you. I am jealous of anyone you touch, even your mother!"

"Oh, Brad!" She smiled in the darkness. She knew he was very possessive, but that was ridiculous. Still—if he willed it this way, it was her duty as his wife to obey. It gave her pleasure that he delighted in her.

"Golden Lotus," he murmured against her cheek. "That is what they call you, isn't it?"

"Yes, it is what you call a nickname, a pet name. They began to call me that when I first came to them at the age of three."

"That is what you are like, a golden and cream flower, slowly opening your petals to reveal the heart of you." His voice in the darkness seemed to reach out and tug at her heart, and his hands on her became more urgent. But he seemed to restrain himself with an effort, and lay quietly against her, his long body hard against her softness.

He was gone when she woke in the morning, and

134

she was sorry. She enjoyed having breakfast with him, making sure his coffee was hot and black, the juice fresh and cold. She sighed as she showered quickly, and dressed in a slim sheath of cream lace and its little matching jacket. She studied herself worriedly in the mirror. Would she look fine enough to go out with Mrs. Snow? She added gold button earrings, and a gold and diamond brooch on her shoulder, and decided that she would do.

The chauffeur drove her in Brad's second car to the Kyoto Handicraft Center. She had to wait about twenty minutes for Mrs. Snow, and so she waited just inside the door, studying the exhibits with interest.

Mrs. Snow soon arrived, in a bright green car which she parked at the doorway. She came in, wearing a silk gown slit to above her knees, and the mandarin collar high about her thin neck. She took in Charita's simple lace dress with a long look, and her green eyes were more cold than ever.

"Well, let's look about," she said, and strode ahead on her needle-sharp high heeled shoes of green silk. Charita trotted after her, wondering.

The woman cast one look about the first floors, and said, "These are just junk," and went on. Charita blushed for her bad manners, and thought she did not know much either. The pearls were of good quality, the silks good. They were a fine representation of the country's products, and many tourists went there to buy because the employees spoke English and other languages.

They went upstairs to see the lacquer boxes. Charita stood silently as Mrs. Snow pawed over one and another, her long scarlet fingernails scratching more than one box. Finally she said, "No, these won't do. I want something of good quality."

The salesclerk exchanged a look with Charita, and Charita bowed low when she left.

"Well, let's find a better store," said Mrs. Snow, and

set off down the street so fast that Charita could scarcely keep up with her. She slowed down before a window. "There, that's an elegant dress. I can see you in it, Charita."

The dress in question was a low-cut blousy style of crimson, which did not appeal to Charita at all. She was about to say so, when Jacinda swept her inside. "We'll look at that one, in size fourteen," said Jacinda, loudly, pointing.

The clerk, bowing, looked distressed. She understood no English. Jacinda looked tense and exasperated. Charita translated for her, and added innocently in English, "But do you wear a fourteen, Mrs. Snow? That does not seem your size."

"No, it is for you!" she snapped.

"I wear a size eight," said Charita gently. "And my husband chooses all my clothing. I prefer to wait and choose dresses with him. His taste is very good for me."

This seemed to enrage Jacinda for some reason, her face turned pale with anger. She turned and marched out of the shop. Charita bowed to the clerk, said a few hasty words of gratitude in Japanese, and followed her.

Her feet were beginning to tire. Jacinda paused in the mad race down the street, took out a cigarette and lit it. "So Brad buys all your clothes," she said tightly.

"Yes, he is very good to me," said Charita, looking away from the cigarette. Several Japanese were gazing with disapproval at the woman smoking on the street. Some wore masks over their mouths and noses as protection against the air pollution.

"And I suppose he loads you with jewelry," said Jacinda, pausing in front of a jewelry store, to stare blindly at the array of pearl necklaces on trays, some pink pearls on black, some white on dark tan velvet, baroque pearls in exquisite brooches.

"Oh, yes, far too much, your brother is immensely

generous," smiled Charita, thinking that would please her.

The woman looked taut and strung-up. "Brother!" she spat. "He is not my brother! We are not related at all!"

Charita was silent, amazed. She always referred to Kanji as her brother, though he was no relation. Why was Mrs. Snow so angry?

They walked into the pearl shop. "I'll see the tray of brooches in the window," snapped Jacinda, and sat down at the table.

The man looked blank. Charita hastily translated. At her polite phrases in exquisite Japanese, the man beamed, bowed low again and again, and complimented her on the facility with which she spoke Japanese before taking the tray from the window and setting it before Jacinda.

She turned over the brooches with her long fingers, restlessly. The shopkeeper told Charita politely that the prices were set, and the jewelry of the best quality, from Mikimoto Company.

Jacinda picked up one piece. "How much is this one?" she asked. Charita translated the price for her. "Well, get him to cut down. Tell him I'll give him half," said Jacinda sharply.

"I beg your pardon, Mrs. Snow, but he has already said that the prices are set here. Also there is a sign in the window about that. You see—"

"Don't try to tell me how to shop!" cried Mrs. Snow, enraged. She threw down the brooch, and almost ran from the store.

Charita paused to thank the man, bowed to him several times, then slowly followed Mrs. Snow. She was amazed to see her in the next block, already. She went after her, but she was wearing shoes with heels, and they slowed her down. She saw Jacinda Snow get into the bright green car, about a block away from her. Charita paused at the corner, thinking Mrs. Snow would stop to pick her up. Instead the car picked up speed and roared past her. Charita stared after her blankly.

She could not take it in for a moment. She had a little money with her, Brad had told her to charge something to him if she found something she liked. Did she have enough money for a cab? Or should she phone home and get the chauffeur to come for her? Charita bit her lips in indecision.

"Charita! It's Charita! How are you?" The man stopped at her elbow, beaming at her.

She was ready to collapse with relief. "Oh, Donald! How good to see you!" They bowed to each other, Charita solemnly, and Donald with his big boyish grin.

"Well, this is a piece of luck! I've been thinking about you. I'm all alone, the folks are off on a tour to Hong Kong. How about lunch with me?"

"I should like that so very much! My feet hurt," confessed Charita, limping a little.

"What were you doing, shopping all by yourself?" asked Donald, casually. They turned to walk along the street. Across the way, Charita noticed a smart-looking girl in a gray suit. As she glanced again, she saw it was Pearl Takahashi. She waved and smiled, but the girl frowned at her, and after a moment, she turned and disappeared into the crowd. How odd. Charita thought perhaps Pearl was more conventional a Japanese girl than she seemed. She must think waving undignified.

"Well, I was with another lady, but she left," said Charita, more cheerfully. "Oh, do you have a car? How very nice. Would you take me home afterward? I hate to bother the chauffeur."

"Chauffeur, indeed. How grand you are," teased Donald, in his old manner. He took her arm, and helped her into his car. "What would you like, Japanese or Continental?"

"Oh, Japanese, if you do not mind," she said happily, settling into the small Datsun. "This is very nice! You have a job now, perhaps?"

He grimaced as he started the engine. "Not yet, I've applied all over the place. I tried at Karl Frundsberg's jewelry shop this morning. I don't think I made an impression. But I would love to get into that. I'd ask your husband, but he might feel he had to take me on because of our friendship, Charita," he added, artlessly. "I'd rather make it on my own, you know!"

"You have much honor, my father says," said Charita. Donald blushed under his tan, and smiled down at her.

"Well, enough of that," he said, with embarrassment. "How are you enjoying married life?" He had turned his attention to a great truck he wanted to pass, and did not see her face.

"It goes very well, thank you," said Charita politely.

"Well, Mother sent her regards, and said again she wished she could have attended your wedding. She plans to get something grand for you in Hong Kong. So don't be surprised! I'm putting off university for a couple of years, want to work in Japan for a time," he chatted on easily. He had always been easy to talk to, perhaps it was his parents' background in the diplomatic corps.

They went to a Japanese restaurant set in the midst of a lovely garden. Donald was able to get a table near the windows, and Charita gazed with rapture at the pond, the goldfish darting about in it were immense in size. Bushes of rose-colored azaleas set off the pool, while the other gardens were blooming with pansies of purple, cream, yellow, blue. She drew a deep happy breath.

She told Donald about her parents' visit, and the way they had gone about Kyoto with Brad. The conversation drifted to their school days, and when the waitress served them with their sukiyaki dinner they switched to Japanese to include the smiling girl in kimono in the conversation. They ate the delicious sliced beef and the vegetables, all stir-fried quickly on the grill before them by the waitress, who knelt as she cooked and served.

A big man had been observing them as they were lost in their conversation, chatting through the meal in Japanese. Now he came over to them. Donald jumped up, and bowed to him, Charita gazed up at him and smiled shyly; she recognized him.

It was the big graying fatherly-looking man she had seen in the airport.

"Mr. Frundsberg," said Donald. "How pleasant to see you. Isn't this restaurant fine, and the food delicious?" He was stammering around, unlike him.

"It is indeed good. And I am so happy to meet the new bride, Mrs. Livingston," and he bowed nicely to Charita.

"You are most kind," she murmured.

"I did not realize your knowledge of the language was so very good, Mr. Raglan," said Mr. Frundsberg, turning to Donald.

"Thank you very much. I went to high school here. In fact, Charita and I were in some of the same classes," said Donald.

"Indeed? You are friends of many years, then," he smiled. "I must congratulate Mr. Livingston once more on his good fortune in winning such a beautiful and accomplished girl for his bride. To combine grace, beauty, charm, and intelligence in one girl is indeed rare. How jealous I am of his great success!" he beamed at her, not seeming jealous at all, but rather pleased for her.

"I will repeat your kindnesses to my husband," blushed Charita.

He turned again to Donald. He said, in a lower, more businesslike tone. "We have been talking since you left the office. I am planning to enlarge the firm. I will need a young man fluent in both English and Japanese to help

140

with many activities. He would have to be adaptive and quick, and I think you may be the young man I am looking for. Are you interested, not in the job for which you applied in the factory, but in being an assistant?"

Donald gasped, then gathered his wits about him. "I should be most interested, and most honored, sir—"

"Good, good! Then come to the office tomorrow, shall we say at eleven? Good. We shall speak of this then, but I think you are the young man I am looking for!"

He patted Donald kindly on the shoulder, beamed at Charita, and ceremoniously took his farewells of them both. Donald sagged to his chair again, after the man had left the room.

"Well—am I in luck! You brought me luck, Charita," he whispered. He shook his reddish brown head in a daze, his boyish face shone. "A job with him! He has one of the top factories in Japan, for exporting to Europe. What an opportunity!"

"I am so very glad for you, Donald!" She was almost as breathless with excitement as he was. He was a dear, good friend of many years, and she was passionately interested in his welfare.

They finished their meal in great excitement, scarcely knowing what they ate. Donald took her home in his cozy little Datsun, and saw her inside. He drove off with a couple of triumphant toots of his horn, and she waved to him, smiling in delight.

"Charita, where the devil have you been?" Brad's harsh voice broke into her musings. She whirled around, eyes wide.

"Brad, you are home so early!"

"I thought you went shopping with Jacinda," he said grimly. He drew her into the living room, and shut the door with a bang. His fingers gripped her arm so tightly that they hurt. "What are you doing with that young man?"

She gulped, taken by surprise. How could she begin? "Oh, I met him on the street after Mrs. Snow—"

He shook her a little. "I have been phoning around, driving around, trying to find you. I thought you had been kidnapped! Pearl said she saw you with a strange man—"

"Oh, nonsense, Donald is not strange—"

His mouth grew thin and tight. "I think you had better explain to me what happened," he said curtly. "Now, Jacinda picked you up—go on from there."

It was like being in court, with a lawyer shooting questions at her and judging her at the same time.

She felt resentful. Jacinda had deserted her without explanation. She told the whole story, as simply as possible.

"And she just walked out, and drove away? That is impossible," said Brad angrily. "She knows how I feel about your being alone. I would never have allowed a stranger to take you out."

Charita tilted her chin. "What did Mrs. Snow say? How did she explain her actions in driving away and leaving me?" she asked simply, her eyes flashing with anger.

"She didn't say that. She just said you were very rude and unhelpful."

She swallowed. "I am sorry she felt that way. I explained as well as I could that the prices in the jewelry store were set, and I could not bargain for half price for her—"

Brad sighed deeply, let go her arm, and pushed his fingers through his hair. He looked tired and worried. Her heart melted.

"I am very sorry you had to search for me, Brad. Next time, I will telephone home and explain where I am going."

"There will not be a next time," he said shortly. "You'll go out with me or not at all!"

"That is foolish," she said gently. "I cannot stay home by myself all the time—"

"No? Do you expect to make more dates with Donald Raglan?" he flashed. "Well, don't count on it! I won't have it! You are not to see him again, not alone, do you understand?"

"But Brad—"

"I am late, I have much work to do," he snapped, and walked out. She heard the car on the drive, revving up with great noise. The excitement of Donald's new job had faded, so had the pleasure of seeing him again. Then the silence drifted back, leaving her alone and adrift in the midst of the silent house.

9

Brad set down his drawing pencil and sighed deeply. He had never found it so difficult to concentrate. In the outer office, Pearl's typewriter clattered on smoothly. Business was good, he had the figures before him. He had more orders than they could fill.

Yet he was unhappy and restless. He thought of Charita's reproachful blue eyes as he had stormed away from her this morning. She had simply asked if she might go out with Donald Raglan again to visit the Moss Temple, and Brad had shouted at her and refused.

He did not want to frighten her, but he had received several anonymous letters. Some threatened him, one warned that he had a beautiful young wife, and if he valued her life he would send money to such and such a place. He had ignored them, as always. A wealthy man was always the prey of cranks, and yet if anything happened to Charita . . .

I must tell Charita why I want her to be so careful, Brad thought. But he could see her golden skin paling, the fear in her beautiful eyes, the terror that would stalk her day and night. All he wanted was a peaceful, beautiful life for her, with him.

He savored the memory of her drowsy in his arms, eyes closed and slim hands clutching his arms as he finished their lovemaking. How sweet she was, so untaught and innocent. He enjoyed teaching her slowly what love could be. He wanted to treat her tenderly and gently, but sometimes his emotions threatened to overwhelm him. Then he had to lie back and take deep breaths, so he would not frighten her with wild passion. But, oh, she did drive him wild with desire!

Never had a woman made him feel the way Charita did. He loved her deeply, he realized, though she did not even begin to understand what love between them could be. He wanted to protect and cherish her all their lives. He needed to satisfy his primitive longings to keep her completely to himself. He did not want to share her with anyone yet, not even a child. But when she was more mature, he wanted children with her, a small doll-girl like herself, a sturdy boy. . . .

He smiled, picked up the pencil again, and began to sketch a design, dreamily. Something small and lovely, like Charita. A butterfly with blue wings, he thought, with delicate coloring and the most exquisite small antennae. A skimming of silver along the wings, blue enamel here, gold there. His pencil moved more quickly as he became absorbed.

Kanji came in the opened door slowly, hesitating. Brad looked up, absently. "Yes?"

"I beg your pardon for interrupting your thoughts," said Kanji, bowing several times.

"That's all right. What is it?"

"Mr. Miles Snow is here, he has an appointment with you regarding the corporation," Kanji said looking dubious.

"Oh, Lord, I forgot." Brad threw down the pencil. At least he had completed the design. "Show him in."

Kanji hesitated again, unlike him. "I wish to say— I fear he has been drinking. Forgive me for saying this—"

Brad stood up, his mouth grim. "All right, Kanji,

145

thank you. Show him in. Oh, and arrange to interrupt us with a long-distance call in about one hour, will you? And bring in a tray of hot coffee in half an hour."

Kanji looked relieved, and bowed his way out. "Yes, I will do this, thank you."

Miles came in grinning, his face red. "Got all your staff well-trained in bowing, have you?" he said jovially. "Never thought you would put up with all that, not you."

Brad did not smile. He indicated a chair, took out the papers briskly. Miles was drinking heavily these days, but he used to confine it to evenings. If he began drinking during business hours, heaven help him, and Jacinda. Perhaps this was why Jacinda was so edgy and upset all the time.

They began to discuss the matter of the corporation, about some legal tangle that had come up. Miles was usually sharp about this, he had practiced corporate law in Japan for several years, and in the States before that. But today he did not seem to have anything in order, and tried to hedge so obviously that Brad felt like choking him.

Kanji knocked and came in with a tray of coffee, pot and cups. He bowed, and set it on Brad's desk. "Your coffee, sir," he said. "And shall I pour it out for you?"

"Yes, thanks very much." Brad leaned back and waited. Even coffee would not help Miles much. He was only thirty-four years old, but already his stomach was distended and falling over his belt, his brown hair was lanky and graying, his hazel eyes were red-rimmed and bloodshot. A brilliant mind going to waste, thought Brad. He should never touch alcohol, it was sheer poison to him.

Kanji poured coffee, set the cups politely before them, and bowed his way out.

"I don't want this, I'll wait and have a drink later," said Miles, pushing the cup from him distastefully.

"I think it would do you good," said Brad curtly,

lifting his own white and gold porcelain cup to his lips.

Miles snarled, and the temper that boiled in him when drunk came to the surface. "Damn you, don't tell me what will do me good! You have a nerve! You have everything in the world! Millionaire businessman, a genius," he sneered. "God, how I hate it when Jacinda drags up your name at dinners! I can just hear her now—how brilliant you are, how marvelous, how kind, how everything that is masculine and virile—God, I could puke!"

"My sister has always been fond of me, but it sounds like she is going a bit strong," said Brad, attempting humor.

Miles slammed down the cup in his lax hand, and pushed back his chair, to stand unsteadily. He bent over the desk, pushing his flushed face at Brad's. "Sister, is it? Then what is your relationship, incest? I've had you crammed down my throat since before we were married! Well, by God, if you wanted her so much, you should have married her! Her great lawyer's mind would have found a way to do it!"

"Stop that," Brad said sharply. "We are fond of each other, but it isn't—"

"Don't feed me that! And so far as this corporation is concerned, you can go to hell! If you won't patent the formula, I can't do a thing for you, and that's final! So shove that up your—"

Kanji stepped in then, his handsome face registering amazement. "There is a long-distance call for you, Mr. Livingston," he faltered, in the silence around his entrance.

"I'll bet," snarled Miles. "Arranged, eh? I'll wait! Go ahead and take your fake long-distance call, and screw you both!" He staggered over to the window, and leaned at it, gazing out blindly at the glorious view of golden Kyoto.

Brad nodded Kanji away quietly, and he nodded and

shut the door behind him gently. He was a very understanding young man, thought Brad, gratefully.

"All right, Miles. So you're angry with me. You are also under the influence, as we say in the States. So why don't you go home, and get some rest—"

Miles swung around on him so quickly that he lost his balance. Brad hastened to catch his arm, the other arm came up to try to hit him.

"Come on, Miles! There is no point making scenes," said Brad tightly. Miles had been damned good to him in the past, or he would have thrown him right out the door by the seat of his pants. "You go on home, and we'll talk over the business another time. I have a damned good reason for not patenting this formula, but you won't understand it today—"

"Oh, sure, boy wonder has it all figured out. A lawyer by virtue of living near my wife!" sneered Miles. "Must have inhaled it when you were in bed with her—"

"Damn you, I never—" Brad stopped himself. No point in quarreling with a drunken man. He called for Kanji, got him to help him take Miles downstairs, and ordered a guard to drive him home in his car and take the bus back.

Brad walked slowly back up the stairs. He felt sick at heart. He needed a good lawyer, but Miles was getting beyond the point of helping him. And if he met with Jacinda and turned over all matters to her, Miles would get all the more upset. He had always resented his brilliant wife. Miles had his own talents, and they were good, but if Jacinda threatened to outshine him, it was only because she stayed sober during business hours.

Brad sank into his chair and stared blankly at the papers. He needed advice badly. He wanted to keep his gold formula a secret, and he thought it was the right thing to do. But if someone figured it out, or stole it, he was sunk. He would not even have filed for the patent.

Yet if he filed, anyone could get access to it. It would be open to anyone using the Freedom of Information Act, and his precious unique gold would be known to any rival.

Karl Frundsberg, the German who was one of his most staunch competitors, who already had some continental markets cornered would love to have it. He had tried to buy it from Brad, in fact, had offered him a million dollars for it, plus more to take over the factory and keep all his workmen. It might be the easy way out— But no, he loved that pearly gold hue he had invented, it was like his own child. He wanted to use it, and create beauty.

Brad was tired when he went home early. He wanted nothing so much as a cold drink, and Charita to sit beside him and curl up to him like a young kitten. He wanted to hold her hand, and listen to music, and think about how lovely she was.

He was shocked when he walked in the door and heard the deeper rumble of a man's voice from the living room. He shooed away the maid, and opened the door sharply.

Miles was stretched out in Brad's big chair, talking to Charita! His face was deep red, he was laughing at something she had said. Charita was seated demurely before a tea tray, but only she was drinking tea. When Brad came in, he saw the deep relief on her face. Her expression made him want to throw something. He put his hand gently on her shoulder, she attempted a bright smile.

"How early you are, Brad, that is good. Will you have tea with us?"

"I'm not having tea, honey!" Miles snarled. "I'm having another glass of whiskey, and if you're smart you'll have one also. Because when I get done telling you what your husband does with my wife—"

Brad's hand tightened on Charita's shoulder. "Darling, go to your room, I'll take care of this," he said

149

tightly. He could have struck Miles in his grinning face for daring to bring his sordid talk into Brad's peaceful home, and the shock in Charita's face was terrible to see.

Brad took Charita to the door, half-closed it after them. "He is very drunk. Ask the chauffeur to bring the car around, then go in the back where you can't hear him. When he is drunk, he doesn't know what he is saying."

Charita nodded, numbly, and Brad went back inside to Miles.

Charita went to notify the chauffeur. He came at once, and went to get the car out from the garage. He drew it up in the front, and prepared to wait.

Charita went back slowly into the hallway. She wanted to get away, yet perhaps if she served Miles more tea, he might calm down. He had been quite nice, refusing tea, but nice anyway, before Brad arrived. He had rambled on about when he was first married to Jacinda, and how happy they had been. The first days of their married life were wonderful, he had said.

They had gone on their honeymoon to the Caribbean, and had swum in deep blue waters, "as blue as your eyes, honey," said Miles. Days of swimming, nights of dancing. "Happiest days of my life. Then back to work. Damn it, how nice life would be without work."

She had smiled politely, yet thought he was wrong. She, herself, needed more work to do. How the time dragged until Brad came home from work. She felt so useless. Before, with her parents, or when her father was ill, she had worked so hard that she had slept hard and dreamlessly at night. Now she scarcely tired herself at all, and her nights were wakeful and she often lay awake and listened to Brad's steady breathing beside her, and wondered how she would get through another day.

A maid stood in the hallway, and Charita dismissed her with a soft word. She did not want the servants to hear the quarreling. Most understood English and would be sure to talk, they could not help gossiping to neighbors about their employers.

She arranged the vase before her with nervous fingers, adjusted the pussy willows, moved the azalea branch a fragment.

Miles' voice raised to a roar. "You made her your mistress!" he accused, over Brad's level tones. "My God, how can you excuse that? Do you want it all ways? You seduced her, I could see the change in her when you came! A year now! By God—I ought to have known something was up when she sent for you—"

Brad's soothing murmur grew harder. Charita could just hear his voice. "You do her a great injustice to say so. She wanted me to come and take advantage of a good business opportunity—"

"Take advantage! That's good! Hah, she was waiting to pop into your bed! You're the great idol of her life! Nobody compares with you, she said to me. Brad is so strong, so steady, so important, he's so clever, he makes money—"

"Cut it out, Miles, you'll be sorry you said all this tomorrow!"

"Sorry! No, damn you, I'll be glad! It's been buttoned up inside me for a year! And longer! We hadn't come home from the honeymoon before I got the word! Brad is so strong, he wouldn't do that! Brad could take care of this without effort. Brad wouldn't let a man insult her in public! Brad would do this—Brad is the great I-am; by God, I wonder she doesn't bow to you!"

Miles was snarling with laughter, choking with rage, spitting out the words so fast that Charita could scarcely understand them. She stood frozen near the closed door, unable to leave. Her face had paled, she felt dizzy.

Brad, deny it, deny it, she thought to herself. Tell him she is your sister, tell him! But Jacinda herself had said, angrily, that Brad was not her brother! Charita's hands clenched at her sides, sweat came out on her forehead. The rumble of the voices continued, finally they quieted.

She heard someone coming near the door. Brad. She turned and ran soundlessly back to her bedroom, and closed the door softly. She leaned against it, her breath coming in silent sobs. She put her fist to her mouth, to keep the sound from coming out; she heard the doors open, the men's voices in the hallway.

Presently the car started up, it drove away over the gravel, crunching along. Brad closed the door, and spoke to the maid. He came back along the hallway. Charita left the door, went to sit down in a chair near the window, and drew a book to her.

Brad opened her door for the first time without knocking. Somehow she resented that, as though he had intruded. She lifted a cool uncaring face to his keen gaze.

"Sorry about that, darling. Miles is a good fellow, when he is sober," said Brad, as though all the words had meant nothing at all. "When he's drunk, that's another matter. Raves on crazily. He didn't bother you, did he?"

Charita said, blankly, "I just offered him some tea."

"Well—" Brad hesitated, flexed his arms and rubbed his shoulders, wearily. "I'll get a long shower and cool down. Wear something pretty for dinner, will you?" He smiled, and closed the door after himself.

So it was to be dismissed in that manner. She longed to fling questions at him. But Brad would not discuss the matter, she realized.

She sat there for a little time, the book forgotten in her hands. Her thoughts were bitter. Pearl—and also Jacinda? Her husband's mistresses! Japanese men were like that, and a wife was supposed to ignore the matter and make him welcome whenever he came home. But somehow she had not thought Brad was that kind.

What did she know of men, though? Nothing at all. Her mind was whirling in circles, going back always to

152

that blunt harsh indictment. Brad had Pearl as his mistress, and also his stepsister, Jacinda. She had known they were close, Jacinda hung on him, his mouth softened when he spoke to her. Yet—yet—to be his mistress! She put her fist to her mouth again.

No wonder Jacinda had been angry with her. She probably thought Brad would remain faithful to Jacinda! And he had gone off and married a child, a young girl, innocent of the world. Jacinda must have thought he was out of his mind. After her sophistication and elegance, to marry a child! But of course Brad must be going regularly to her—

Or were those the ravings of a drunken jealous man? Was there no truth in the words? What could she believe? She tried to calm herself, she did not know whether she was upside down or not.

Finally she stood up and went to the wardrobe which held her immense assortment of new dresses. She fingered the kimonos wistfully—no, Brad would be angry if she wore one. She took down an ice-blue gown of shimmering beauty, with whirling pleats. Then with her mouth set, she put it back, and took down the blue and silver kimono, and got out her straw sandals and the gold and silver obi.

She dressed slowly, drawing it out. She longed for the old days in the home of her foster parents. If she were home with them, she would dress in a kimono, and go out to their warmth and loving concern. She would sit on the floor on cushions, and curl up, drinking tea, talking and chatting happily.

No more. Brad did not like her to chatter, he wanted her to talk intelligently and learn much. He had given her books to read—of United States history, American ways, English literature, and even a Bible and Commentary for her to study Christianity. As though she were a pagan!

Brad was in the living room when she entered. He had a glass of ice and whiskey at his lips as she padded in.

153

He set down the glass slowly on the table beside him, and his face got that closed-in expression she dreaded. But tonight she lifted her chin and returned his stare.

"You look very pretty," he complimented her coolly. "Blue is very becoming to you."

"I thank you," she said formally, bowing her head. She had dressed it with a fake chignon, drawing back her own hair and fastening it tightly beneath. She felt older, more mature, more dignified. Underneath, her heart felt as though it beat too rapidly, choking her. She shook her head at the offer of a drink. She had had enough of that drinking, the room reeked of liquor.

"Are you still sulking?" he asked pleasantly, picking up his pipe.

"Sulking?" How did he know how she felt, to think Jacinda was his mistress! That she should take it with a smile, and a bow, and all obedience to his wishes!

"About my refusing to let you go out with Donald Raglan," he said, stuffing tobacco into the large bowl of the brown pipe. He had changed to a light tan suit, and there were amber studs at his wrists and on his tie of cream and brown stripes. He looked handsome and un-caring, with his thick chestnut hair gleaming in the light of the lamp near him. "If you want to go back to the Moss Temple, I'll take you sometime. But you are not going to run around with any other man."

She started. She had completely forgotten Donald and his eager invitation. "He merely wished to celebrate."

Brad's dark brows drew together. "Celebrate what?" he asked.

"He has obtained employment, a position of great honor and respect. He was very happy. Since his parents are away in Hong Kong, he wished to take me out to share his happiness."

"Oh—I see. Where is he working?"

"With Mr. Karl Frundsberg, in his jewelry concern,"

154

said Charita proudly, her face glowing. "Is that not wonderful? Donald wished to—"

"With Frundsberg!" Brad had not raised his voice, but there was a menace in it which startled her. "What do you mean? Donald, your friend, has taken a job with one of my chief rivals, and you want me to congratulate him?"

Charita's eyes grew larger at this. "Chief rival? I thought you were friends!"

The big shoulders shrugged. "Oh, we get along all right. But he wants to buy me out. He's one tough man with his concern, a big German jewelry firm just opening a new branch in Japan. He has millions of dollars worth of business in Germany and France. So Donald is going to work for him! Doing what?"

"He is the assistant of Mr. Frundsberg, he said. I don't know what that means."

Brad's mouth was set. "Then I am sure I don't want you to see him again," he said definitely.

"But he is my friend of many years!" cried Charita. "You are being unreasonable, you are cruel—"

She wanted to fling all kinds of words at him, to accuse him of his affairs, to ask him why he would carry on in this way when he seemed fond of her. But she had no right to say anything. She was married, he had put his ring on her finger, he took care of her every need without question. She wore the clothes he had bought, the jewelry he chose. The very food she put in her mouth was what he bought for her.

"You can think whatever you choose," he said angrily. He set down the unlit pipe. "But you do—not—go out with Donald Raglan or any other man! Is that clear?"

"Yes," she murmured obediently, but she felt cold and weary. Her hands were trembling, and she folded them tightly together. He stared at her, waiting for more. She could say no more.

The maid came, bowed, and announced dinner. Brad nodded curtly. "We'll go in," he said. "Charita?"

He half-pushed her ahead of him, his hand on the obi at her back. She sat down at the table, her head bent unhappily. Brad gave her a warning look.

"I hope you are as hungry as I am," he said, before the maid. "The food looks delicious."

"Very good," she echoed. She felt as though she would choke over any food. She reached for the glass of juice before her, and sipped at it very slowly.

She felt weary and terribly unhappy, but appearances must be kept up. No one must be allowed to see how she felt. The servants were kind, but they were inclined to gossip, and Miles' visit had been food enough for their eager talk. She managed to smile, to take a bit of food on her plate, to eat a little.

Brad talked some, he told about an amusing incident with a traffic policeman. Someone had given him a new commission to do a complete set of jewelry, tiara, necklace and pendant, bracelets and rings, for an Arabian wedding. It would be an interesting task to design, using the symbols they wished. She brightened up a little, and listened with more interest when he spoke of this.

But presently he ran out of things to say. The rest of the evening was passed in silence. Brad put on record after record, glancing at her face to see if the choice pleased her. What did it matter, she thought forlornly, as she sat politely on a chair away from him.

She felt numb with hurt. When the numbness wore off, it would be terrible. When he came to take a cup of coffee from her, she flinched from his touch, and almost dropped the saucer. He gave her a hard look.

If she had known about him, about his many affairs, she would have refused to marry him, she decided. No, all she had seen was the kindness of a man who had respected her father. Her father was a professor, and Brad had honored him. Her father would have liked the marriage, she had thought that.

But rather would she have gone home to the Noguchis and taken a job in the monotonous work at the assembly line of the radio factory—much rather would she have lived in schoolgirl uniform and kimono—than live in the luxury he bestowed on her. For she would not have had to endure the humiliation and pain of knowing that her husband, scarcely married two months, had returned to his mistresses.

No wonder he did not want a honeymoon with her! It would have removed him briefly from the presence of Pearl and Jacinda, and who knows how many other women!

Brad took out another record. She had had enough. She rose to her feet.

"I am most weary. Pray forgive me if I wish to retire," she said, at her most formal.

His mouth was hard and straight. "Very well, go to bed. You do look tired, and I shall not bother you tonight," he said, sounding angry.

She bowed at the door, and left him, her back very straight. In the room, she was tempted to lock the door, but he would be most angry at that, so she did not.

She lay awake much of the night, listening to the sounds outside. A storm had come up, and the wind and rain beat at the bushes. Tomorrow, azalea petals would be strewn in the pool and on the ground in pink confusion. It was almost June, soon the other flowers would come, the roses and iris. She had studied lovingly the position of the various plants, and the gardener had counted to her what would be brought forth.

But who knew what would come forth? Tomorrow was uncertain, the future was dim. How could she endure a marriage like this? Anger between them, his hardness and indifference to her feelings. How would she manage to conceal her feelings? How could she receive him in her bed?

Charita cringed at the thought of it, of him coming to her, and pretending loving concern. She enjoyed his caresses, he was most gentle now. But knowing he might have come from Pearl—or Jacinda—or another woman—how could she accept his kisses and his embraces?

10

Jacinda sat in the deep silvery chair and crushed out another cigarette in the porcelain bowl beside her. Her mouth was thin and hard. She ruffled her long fingers through her brief silky blond hair, then carefully smoothed the strands once more.

She couldn't take much more. She was so confused and upset, she wanted to cry. And she never cried, never. She was a tough girl, she had always told herself. She knew what she wanted and where she was going and nobody would stop her.

But it hadn't worked out like that. Her world had started to fall apart when she was a child and had heard her parents screaming at each other. Her mother had departed, she never saw her again. Brad's mother had been her stepmother, she had known a brief relief in the sure presence of Brad, his crooked grin and wink at her when things went badly.

The scandal and divorce had scarred her. She had gone back to college, then to law school. By the time her father was on his third honeymoon, Jacinda had met Miles Snow.

Miles had seemed to the girl to be so much older, wiser, a lawyer of repute already. He was brilliant, and fun also. He could recite reams of poetry, he knew

Oriental wisdom and culture. He taught her about Zen and yoga, and laughed her out of the blues. She married him while still in law school.

Gradually she had learned that he was weak. Under the polished exterior he was like jelly, she thought bitterly. She had tried tactfully to prop him up, he resented it, and his tongue lashed at her. She had flinched from it, the screaming and accusations that were like her father's marriages all over again. She had tried to smooth things over. She had left him twice, then gone back at his pleading.

He needed her, he said. They would start again, he promised. And they did start again. They went to Japan, started over where no one knew them. A brilliant dual career, their own law firm specializing in helping Americans and Japanese business firms who worked together. A new social crowd, nights at country clubs, social afternoons with diplomatic crowds, welcomed everywhere.

But Miles was blowing it. Sky-high.

People were whispering, snickering. She hated it, hated it! Her hand trembled as she put the gold lighter to another cigarette. She was ready to leave him, but people did talk so. God, how they talked! And in Japan, where women did not usually work as lawyers, where foreign women were stared at and gossiped about—

How could Brad have married that stupid little schoolgirl? Her mouth closed hard over the cigarette, she drew a deep gust of smoke into her lungs. Every time she thought about it, her brain seemed to get red-hot with fury, until she was dizzy.

Brad. She idolized him, Miles had said. Not true. She was not so idiotic as to idolize any man. But Brad—She remembered the cool, incisive way he spoke, his sureness, his command . . . his compassion. Brad had always understood. She could ask him anything, he would do it, he would help her with money, advice, silent sympathy and the right words.

And he had married a girl of eighteen, a girl brought up like a Japanese girl! With nothing to her—nothing!

She closed her bright green eyes tight. Against the lids she saw Charita, with her wide eager blue eyes. Saw her as she had arrived at the airport in the too-large tweed coat, looking like an orphan or a refugee. She had not believed him when he had said he was going to marry the child! Marry her, for God's sake! She belonged in an orphanage!

Right out of high school! Knowing nothing about American ways and customs. No assurance, no poise, no sense of clothes, only a childlike body and mind, thought Jacinda savagely. Was that what Brad wanted? A child, to mold and shape, as he did one of his jewelry designs? He could not be so foolish! You didn't polish a bride the way you did a bit of gold.

Yet he had insisted she was the one he wanted. Said he owed her father much. Well, he could have paid off any debts by shipping the girl to the United States, sending her to a good college. That would have been plenty to do for her. But no, he had to marry her!

Jacinda's thoughts were too painful to be continued. She leaped up, began to pace about the room, her high-heeled sandals slipping on the polished floor, then across the silvery carpet to the golden draperies. She pushed one back and stared unseeingly at the golden haze over Kyoto. Damned place! Damned people! She was sick of it all.

Brad. She had been thinking this past year that her marriage to Miles was a mistake and that she and Brad were not related at all, though he treated her like a sister. He was so considerate, he did love her, she knew. If she got a divorce, he might marry her—

No, not now. He had married that fool girl! Again she strode about, kicking at a small precious Persian rug that lay before a couch. Her fingers clenched so that her long fingernails dug into her palms. All her foolish hopes and dreams punctured like a balloon. . . . Brad was stronger than she, she could have leaned on him. A man to lean on—

But no, he had married Charita!

And she was left with Miles, brilliant but weak, unable to resist just one more drink—wrecking their lives with his alcoholic binges—

It could have been so different. She had loved him deeply once, as much as she had allowed herself to love after the traumatic happenings of her girlhood. The pawing of her mother's lovers! How she had hated them, despised her mother. She had kicked one of the men in the groin—

At those times she had felt that all the hot baths in the world would not scrub her clean. She had affected tailored clothes, turned to the world of law, she would prove herself as good as a man, better! She cut her long blond hair short, she was brisk in manner, she knew where she was going. Men made no attempts to paw her now!

But if only Brad were free—

That girl was no good for him. She could not match his mind, his spirit, his strength. A child! She was not right for Brad. Jacinda had tried to convince Brad of that, he had only become angry. And Jacinda had had to let it go through, that farce of a wedding—a Shinto ceremony! Her nails dug sharply into her palms, until the pain recalled her to herself.

That was over, that ceremony. But one day Brad would realize Charita was no good for him. She wasn't right for Brad. And Brad would know it. He would quietly divorce her, provide her with plenty of money, send her away. Then, then he would turn to Jacinda—

Only she wasn't free—yet—

Jacinda turned sharply as the key fumbled in the lock, a man's soft curses sounded. The maid padded to the door, opened it. She heard the woman welcoming Miles as ceremoniously as though he were entering the apartment like a man, instead of a drunken sot! Men! Of all the men she knew only Brad was strong. Only Brad.

Miles stumbled into the room, the maid bowed and shut the door quietly after him. Jacinda watched him with angry green eyes, narrowed like a cat's.

"Late, am I?" he laughed, his red face grimacing. "Late, oh, yes. Stopped for some sake. That packs quite a punch! But I don't like the taste, I'll have a whiskey and soda, my dear!"

Mouth compressed, she moved to the bar, and filled the glass. He tasted it, then flung the glass at her, accurately, spilling it down her silky green dress.

"You bastard!" she hissed, furiously, as ice slithered down into her bodice. She fished it out, flung it at him. The glass had shattered against the wall.

He began to laugh. "Too much soda. Try again!"

"Fix your own drink, you sot!"

She turned to the door. He caught her arm, twisted it, and pulled her to him.

His face had turned ugly and menacing. "You've been meeting him secretly."

"Who?" she asked, coldly, as though unaware of the pain in her slim arm.

"Who? Who?" he mocked. "Your dear *brother*, Brad. I told him if he was your brother, it was incest!"

"What the hell are you talking about?" she asked, chilled with fear.

"Your hot pants, my dear! And the way Brad cools them! I told him to lay off you— Hey, that's good! Lay off—got that?" He began to laugh mirthlessly.

She caught her breath. Miles had surely not gone to Brad with his filthy stories—his accusations—

"You were supposed to discuss the patent today. What was decided?" she asked, very slowly.

"Not a damned thing, love! Not a thing! I told him

163

to keep away from my wife, and not meet her in secret! I know about your meetings in restaurants, and in bars, and in this apartment. Where do you sleep? Got a special apartment for him? Special to meet your lover?"

She tried to strike his flushed face. He caught her arm easily, and held her before him, studying her face with bloodshot eyes. She had only to keep cool, and retain her dignity and she could handle this.

"Where are you meeting him?" he snarled again.

She did not answer. She wished she were meeting Brad in an apartment, in secret. She wished she knew his skilled lovemaking, his tenderness, his caresses. God, how he would make love—

Miles struck her across the face. She staggered back, he caught her, and pushed her down on the rug. He straddled her, mocked her harshly as she tried to pull away from him.

"This is one afternoon when you'll forget him!" he whispered, his threat more deadly than his insults.

He yanked up the hem of the green silk dress, wet with the whiskey and ice. She fought him, her mouth tight. The dress ripped in his strong fingers. He clamped down her arms, and with one brutal lunge, forced himself painfully into her. Her thighs felt as though wrenched from their sockets.

"Don't! Don't, Miles! Stop that—you're hurting—" she finally had to cry out as she writhed under him.

"Why? Don't you remember what I feel like? Don't you remember how you used to beg for it?" he said, his mouth against her throat. His teeth bit at her soft skin, his hand pinched the soft flesh of her thighs.

She managed to lie still then, tears of pain and humiliation pouring down her cheeks, though she did not let a sob escape. She hated him in those moments, making her feel his male strength in her unready flesh. She thought briefly of the servants, but they would have scampered to the kitchen out of reach of his savage tongue. They would not dare come in.

He finished in her, and pulled out as abruptly as he had entered her. Then he rolled over heavily on the rug, his eyes closed. Jacinda waited. When he began to snore, she got up cautiously.

She was bleeding, her dress was a wreck and there were bruises all over her neck and legs. He would pay for this, she thought savagely.

She locked herself in the bedroom. The apartment was silent. Perhaps the maids had gone off, frightened by the sounds of her screaming. She took a quick cool shower, dried and powdered herself. Then she dressed as casually as though preparing for an afternoon out.

She hauled out two Vuiton suitcases and began to pack. Miles would sleep for a couple of hours, it gave her enough time. She put in her business outfits, her case of jewelry, a couple of evening dresses, sandals, shoes. All she would need for a time. If she had to come back for more, she would be sure Miles was out, or Brad with her.

Brad. She clung to the thought of him. He would help her. If only he had not married that girl. She hated that girl—so helpless, so clinging, so wrong for him—

She left the apartment, closing the door softly behind her. She carried her own cases down to the garage, not a servant was around, and she didn't want them to see her anyway. She managed to sling her bags into the green car and got in.

She drove direct to the small apartment she had rented with just such an eventuality in mind. She had known somehow that she could not endure much more of Miles. His drunks, his abuse, his attacks on her had grown much worse.

Jacinda did not allow herself the luxury of thinking for a time. Automatically she unpacked, telephoned for the telephone installer from the lobby downstairs, informed the apartment manager that she would not receive anyone.

Tomorrow she would call Brad, and give him her new address.

She ate sketchily at a tearoom nearby, and went back to the bleak apartment. She did not have her favorite paintings about her, the rooms were not decorated in her gold and silver colors. But she was alone, blessedly alone.

She went to bed and lay against the pillows, unable to sleep. She smoked one cigarette after another, and her mind began to function again.

She had always been proud of her mind. "A very bright girl," had read the early school reports. "Brilliant," said the college record. "Keen, unusual mind," said the law school.

But she had fallen in love with Miles, and married him. She had loved him once, as much as she had allowed herself to, cautiously, a little hopefully, wanting to lean on him.

It had gone wrong, all wrong. He was killing her love. She hated it that she worried about him still. Had the maids returned? Would they be able to put him to bed? He got chilled easily, she should have put a blanket on him before she left. What would he say when he woke up and found her missing?

She tossed and turned, pushed her head into the pillows. She turned on the little radio she had brought with her, but the chatter in Japanese irritated her. She snapped it off.

Was Miles awake, did he know she had left?

She had covered her tracks well, no one knew of this apartment, not even Brad. The manager had been well-bribed to feign ignorance of her presence.

When she got herself together, she would tell Brad. Go back to work in the separate office on which she had insisted. Refuse coldly to inform Miles of her whereabouts. Later, after her divorce, she might return to the States.

But first, she would wait to see what happened to Brad's marriage, how soon he wearied of the schoolgirl chatter of his little bride. Her lip curled in disgust.

What made people so crazy as to marry for love? Better by far to figure it out like a legal tangle, and have an arranged marriage, a marriage by the cool meeting of minds rather than the hot passion of bodies.

Jacinda—a brilliant businesswoman, she thought bitterly. She could sit in her office and advise a corporation how to manage its affairs, she could sort out a tax mess, she could cut through red tape with charm and finesse.

"But in love," she said aloud to the cheerless, impersonal bedroom, so unlike her glittering bedroom at home, "in love, Jacinda Snow, you are one damned fool!"

If only she could recover, and put it all behind her. Never would she make the mistakes she had made in the past. She would forget Miles, stop worrying about him, push him from her—

Damn it, she could call and ask the maids to make sure he was covered up, at least!

Her hand reached for the phone, then she remembered it was not yet connected. Oh, what was the use—why worry about Miles—he could damn well take care of himself! He would have to, from now on. She was through, finished!

11

Brad Livingston stepped out of the car, collected his briefcase, and nodded to the chauffeur. The car moved on toward the garage. He ruffled his hair wearily, as he walked toward the handsome house. He looked at it critically. It seemed so quiet, so peaceful.

Jacinda had finally left Miles, and Miles had come storming to Brad to demand to know where she was. It had been a very unpleasant afternoon. Brad was worried about Jacinda. She could take care of herself, she was a very capable person, yet he worried. He knew how deeply hurt she would be under her smooth, sophisticated surface.

What a mess people could make of their lives. He remembered when Jacinda and Miles had first married, how radiant she had been, how proud of her Miles had been, looking at her fondly, his lean face taut with emotion. They had seemed so suited, both so brilliant, both were lawyers, enjoying social lives and bright lights, laughing at the same jokes, keen to learn about Oriental matters.

He was grateful to them. If they had not come to Japan, he would not have thought of setting up business here, he would never have met Charita. His face softened as he went into the hallway, flung down the briefcase, and went into the drawing room. The maid picked up his case and padded softly after him.

Usually Charita was there, a sketchpad or book in her hands, dressed in something soft and lovely. Her blue eyes would glance up, she would smile—

Lately she had not smiled much. Her manner was more cool and distant, and she had him worried. She refused to say anything was wrong, but at night she lay still in his arms, and her coldness put him off.

The drawing room was empty. With Jacinda's disappearance on his mind, he turned sharply on the maid. "Where is she?"

"Livingston-san, she is in garden," smiled the maid, indicating the French doors with a graceful nod.

He drew in a deep breath. He had almost panicked. "Has she been out there long? It is hot today."

"Not long. Livingston-san is home early today," said the maid, bowing.

He went out the French doors into the gardens. Charita was sitting on the wooden bench near the pond, just gazing ahead of her. She was utterly still, her small hands folded in her lap, the deep blue kimono in graceful folds about her slim body. She did not hear him approach, when he spoke she started violently.

"Charita? I'm home, darling," he said, as casually as possible. He came up behind her, bent and kissed her dark head. Did he imagine she shrank from him?

"Oh, is it late?" She spoke as mechanically as a doll, her tones dull and lifeless. He eyed her keenly as he slipped down beside her, and put his arm about her. Her body stiffened, he did not imagine that.

"No, not late. I came home early. I've had an idea." He continued eagerly, in spite of her averted face. "What do you think of taking a long weekend, going off somewhere together? We haven't had our honeymoon yet. I thought perhaps to Mount Fuji—I hear the Hakone region is very beautiful."

169

She took a deep breath. "The work can spare you?" she asked.

She sounded reluctant, as though groping for an excuse. He frowned.

"The work can always spare me," he said. "It goes well, and Kanji is taking hold magnificently. I can't get away for a week, but I thought on Friday morning we'd take off—go for a long weekend, come back on Monday afternoon. Have you been to Hakone? Would you rather go somewhere else?"

She raised her hand to her face, seemed to brush at it, as though brushing off cobwebs. He studied the portion of her face that he could see, the long dark lashes shielding her eyes, the pink mouth so straight and tense, the pale cheeks, less golden now. "Where you wish," she said dully.

It was less than the enthusiastic response he wanted. His mouth set. He had to get away with her, alone for a time, and find out what was wrong. They were growing no closer, instead the distance between them was increasing.

"We'll go on Friday, then," he said gently. "Pack Western clothes, and a couple of kimonos. Kanji has recommended a Japanese-style hotel, where we can have a suite to ourselves. I thought it would be good to get away from everybody." He kept eyeing her keenly.

"Yes, as you wish," she said, submissively, and he longed to shake her and get the truth out of her. She was always so polite, sometimes he had no idea of what she was thinking. The fact that she wore a kimono today was a clue, it usually meant that she felt detached.

He stifled a sigh, and drew her up with him briskly. "Well, come along and get changed for dinner. We'll talk about our plans. I thought we could both take sketch pads and pencils with us, wander around and look at Mount Fuji and the flowers—the azaleas should be splendid at this time of year."

"Yes, ours are blooming very beautifully," she said,

with more life in her tones, indicating the pools of pink drifts on the bushes, and drifting in the pond, as petals fell from their branches.

"Very lovely," he said, standing with his arm about her and contemplating the sight. It did seem more peaceful here, after the turmoil of the day. "Oh, there are the early iris, what a lovely purple color."

"I was going to cut some for the drawing room, but I could not bear to put the scissors to them," said Charita, in a more natural way. "Are they not lovely against the green bushes?"

They walked slowly back to the house, speaking of the flowers, his arm about her waist, his head bent to her. He sensed she was deeply troubled; if only she would confide in him! Had she heard from her parents, bad news? Or was it something about their own marriage that worried her?

He meant to probe on the trip. She must be honest and forthright with him, or their marriage could not work. During dinner, they spoke of the journey, and she brightened somewhat. Perhaps she was just feeling dull and bored. She was used to being busy.

On Friday morning, they set out early. He was pleased to see brighter pink in her cheeks, and her blue eyes were sparkling. She had packed two suitcases, and he teased her gently about that. She blushed.

"The kimono and obi take up much room. Do you mind?" she asked anxiously.

"Not a bit of it. Some women can't set out for two days without four suitcases. You are most modest," and he laughed.

He felt free and joyous as they swung out into the traffic. They had started early to get ahead of the weekend travelers, and had to cope with the business traffic of Kyoto before they could get to the highways. He grumbled under his breath at the cars, and when they were finally free of the snarl he let out the big car happily. They had opened the windows, and the cool breeze stung their cheeks.

Brad had left Charita to her own bed these past several nights, hoping she would sleep well and get a good rest. He did not mean to let her alone during their brief holiday! He longed for her, his passion rose when he even looked at her. But he didn't want to scare her to death. She was learning to respond to him, but she was delicately and deliciously shy still. He was content with the situation, wanting to show her slowly all about the delights of being a wife. He meant to keep his desires under control, and be her gentle teacher.

When they had left the city behind them, the countryside intrigued him. Charita pointed out the unpainted wooden houses, where the rain and sun had turned them to marvelous shades of softest brown and gray, blending naturally into the fields and woods behind them. They looked at roadside shrines, at unpainted wooden torii—the gateways leading to more shrines. The impressive structures, with their slightly curved lintels, were like smiles, he said to Charita.

"Oh, yes, they are smiling at us," she agreed happily. "And how lovely is the wood, look at that one of pine. So lovely a color, so much prettier than the gaudily painted ones."

"I like the red lacquer ones, but they are still not so lovely as these," he agreed. "Your parents' home, is it of unpainted wood like that one?"

She nodded, "Very much like that one. It is of eight rooms, all on one floor, and the doors are of thick glazed paper, sliding back to admit the air. Only tatami mats are on the floor, and the floors are unpainted. It is most peaceful and soothing to the eyes, their home." She sighed wistfully.

"Do you feel homesick at times?" Brad asked, cas-

172

ually, his eyes on the scene ahead of them, the blue mountains in the distance.

"Oh, a little bit, at times. But our home is most beautiful," she said, with immediate reserve.

He would probe a bit more later, but for now he let it go. "They were very good to you, they are very kind people," he added.

"Yes, always. Father came about once a year to have a good long visit. He was welcomed so graciously, and we had much to talk about. How he would have rejoiced in your kindness to me! I think he—worried—about my future," said Charita.

"Yes, I expect he did. It would be hard for a scholarly man, such as your father, to manage a child and his difficult work."

"Yes, that is true. He thanked Mama-san many times for her gracious care of me."

"She raised you well."

"It is kind of you to say so."

From the corners of his eyes, he saw the small hands clench and unclench, more revealing than the polite calm tones of her voice. He did not know if speaking of her father did that to her, or what they spoke about concerning bringing up a child—but they would be closer by the time they went home, he vowed that.

Now the road was winding upward, bringing into view glimpses of Mount Fuji. Charita exclaimed, sitting forward like a child on her seat. He indulged her, but watched sharply to make sure her seat belt was fastened. She was not accustomed to the power of this car and the severe jolts when he was required to make sudden stops.

They wound in and out of small villages, alongside farms of tiny neat plots of fruits and vegetables. Ever upward, the car climbed, until they were in the coolness of the mountains, and now there were blue lakes to see, appearing suddenly beside the road. Once Mount Fuji was reflected briefly in one, and Brad let the car idle beside the road for a minute while they gazed at the exquisite view of the misty mountain reflected in the blue gray of the waters.

They rode on, now deep into the mountains. Wild flowers flung their brilliant scarlets and oranges and blues among the deep green of the mountain trees of pines and cedars. Clusters of white and rose azaleas appeared suddenly and were gone again. Mountain meadows rioted with purple and blue and pink among the deep green of the weeds and grasses.

Charita's cheeks were pink with excitement, and her eyes shone whenever she turned to Brad. "Oh, everywhere there is a painting," she breathed.

He smiled. "Wait until we get to the hotel. We'll sketch all day if you like."

They stopped for lunch about two hours from the hotel. They had their meal in a glass-enclosed restaurant with a glorious view of a lake, and Mount Fuji in the distance, with misty white clouds circling the head of the majestic perfect cone. Charita could scarcely take her eyes from the view long enough to eat. He had to tease her, and put more food on her plate, and coax her to try something.

"Here, some fish, darling, it's very good. They must have caught it early this morning."

She tasted, nodded dreamily. "So good. Oh, yes, a bit of the seaweed also," and she ate that eagerly, as though she had longed for Japanese food.

Did he try to make her too American all at once? He could not wipe out her past years as though they meant nothing, he thought tenderly. After all, they had made her the girl he adored. He listened to the chatter of the Japanese guests about them as they stole curious looks at his wife. How beautiful she looked today in the pale blue linen dress with the white collar and cuffs, her dark hair wind-blown about her golden lotus face. The dainty gestures of her hands, the soft chime of her voice, entranced him. The guests looked at him, so tall and bronzed and obviously American, to the girl—not a Japanese, yet—

The smart darkly-clad waiter hovered over them. He sensed their sincere interest in the scene.

"Tomorrow, maybe, Mount Fuji will be seen clearly," he smiled. "That will be lucky for you, yes?"

"Oh, I hope so," said Charita, and added in Japanese, "Is the air always so bright and cold and good?"

He beamed down at her, surprised by her speech. "It is often good like this. No pollution like the cities! I visited once in Tokyo, and the air—" He made a face, and she giggled.

They left reluctantly, but Brad was eager to get to the hotel early and get settled. Charita was more lively and spontaneous with her conversation now. Maybe that was all they had needed, to get away and be together.

They drove into the driveway of the spacious hotel in midafternoon. The drive was lined with azalea bushes and little beds of pansies, purple and gold and blue. Against the unpainted wood of the walls of the inn were the early iris, more purples and golds of softest hues against the brownish gray. Charita drew a deep breath of pleasure.

"It is so lovely, I shall enjoy it so very much," she whispered.

"Good. So shall I," he said firmly. They drew up, and a porter and boy came out to take their luggage and show them to their suite of rooms.

Charita gasped in joy when she saw the rooms. Brad felt more rueful, but not for worlds would he have dimmed her pleasure. But when he looked at the low seats —the tatami mats on the floor, and realized he would be sleeping down there—

He grinned at her. "Like it?"

She was radiant, her face showed her happiness. "It is so lovely, so calm! And look at the little garden outside!"

175

She stepped carefully around the small lacquer tables to peer outside through the slightly opened windows, into the little private garden, which opened on to the larger lawns of the hotel, sweeping down to a green valley. Beyond was the view of Mount Fuji, now purple in the distance. Charita clasped her hands to her breasts, surveyed it in rapture.

The boy left the bags, with several low bows, and murmurs of good wishes for them. The door closed, and they were alone.

Brad glanced into the suite. A large living room, with low tables of black lacquer, an arrangement of flowers in a shallow alcove, a beautiful still-life painting in gold and green above the flowers. In the bedroom were only the mats and a couple of tables. In a closet were the futons and pillows, which a maid would take out when evening came.

Charita turned from the windows. "May we walk soon?" she asked breathlessly.

"Yes, with sketch pads in hand, if you like," he grinned.

They had left their shoes in the space for them near the door. On stocking feet Charita went to the bathroom to peer inside. There was a huge, deep sunken tub, modern washbowl.

"I am spoiled," she laughed. "I am happy that we do not have to go outside for the facilities!"

Brad's mouth tightened as he remembered that primitive house on Hokkaido. He said, as lightly as he could, "I'm happy also. I like my luxuries. Hope there's plenty of hot water."

"There is also the pool," she said dubiously. "You might wish to bathe in the public baths."

"No, thanks! I haven't gotten around to that yet." He opened his suitcase, found hangers for his suits.

"Oh, let me do that," said Charita, and took the shirts from him quickly. She hung them up deftly, shaking out

176

the clothes with little pats of her hands, then turned to her own cases. He was relieved to see that she had put in some elegant evening dresses as well as two kimonos and obis.

Then they went for a walk, strolling around the grounds, smiling politely and bowing when they met the other Japanese guests, but not bothering with much except the view and each other. The gardens were laid out, some in flower beds, some in a simple arrangement of raked sand and rocks, soothing to the eyes. And always beyond was Mount Fuji, majestically looming in the distance, its cone crowned with the ever-present white snow and ice.

The evening was cool. Charita changed to an elegant rose brocade gown, full length, in which she looked like a princess, Brad thought proudly. She wore a diamond clip in her dark hair, more diamonds in her small ears, and a single gold bangle on her wrist. He wore a white tuxedo, with a black tie.

"You look most distinguished," said Charita, seriously. He bowed deeply to her, she bowed back, then spoiled it with a giggle. "You will soon bow as much as we do!" she sparkled.

"It's catching," he said, and offered her his arm. They went to the dining room for dinner, pleased when the waiter seated them near one of the huge windows overlooking the glorious views.

They could watch the sun setting behind Mount Fuji, the splash of scarlet and gold and orange on the snows, the melting purple shadows creeping through the gardens, the stars sprinkling the purple sky. Charita ate well, much better than she had been, and Brad found the leisurely meal a delight.

Charita glanced beyond him as they began dessert. She nodded, a questioning look on her face, then looked away. Brad turned about to see who she had acknowledged. He saw two short heavy-set Japanese men staring at him blandly, they had ugly short haircuts, stocky bodies, stuffed into nondescript blue business suits. They looked out of place in the elegance of the dining room, among guests in their silks and satins.

"Do you know them?" asked Brad, in a low tone.

"Don't you remember them? They were on the plane from Hokkaido to Tokyo, then on to Kyoto. They sat behind us." Charita looked down at her plate, frowning as though at an unpleasant memory.

Brad glanced back at them again. The men had risen and were moving away through the dining room. He saw a suspicious bulge under the jacket of the coat of the man who went second. He tensed. A gun?

"I vaguely remember now," he said. "Tell me what you know of them."

The waiter brought coffee. She waited until he had left, then murmured, "I heard them on the plane. They talked of—of a gold formula which they must procure for their master. It was very odd. Then I spoke to the hostess in Japanese, and when they realized I spoke Japanese, they glared at me very angrily. I don't know—" Her shoulders lifted in the rose brocade, and the soft lights gleamed on her bare shoulders. "They made me feel—odd. As though we were in a bad movie," she tried to laugh.

His mouth compressed. He tried to think clearly. Charita knew this much, would it be better to warn her? Many might be after that gold formula, it was becoming known. How was he to protect Charita? He didn't like it at all that the men were here. Had the men followed him and Charita to this resort?

"Tell me all you remember," he said, at last.

She closed her eyes, the better to recall, then recited all they had said. "It was not much," she apologized. "Maybe I am making something of nothing—"

"We will speak of it later," he said, in a low tone as the waiter hovered to pour more coffee.

The orchestra was playing dance tunes. Brad and

Charita moved to the dance floor, and for the next hour he was happily dancing, with Charita moving like a dream in his arms. He held her closely against him in the waltz, swirling her around and around until she giggled in protest. She even did the cha-cha, her eyes sparkling with glee at the steps she could do.

"You dance very well," he complimented, when they paused to have a drink at their table. She sipped cautiously at the champagne, wrinkling her nose at the bubbles.

"Kanji and I used to dance much. He was very good, he still is," she said innocently. "He would practice with me, as the parents watched."

Brad stifled the jealous rage that welled up. She did think of Kanji as her brother, not as a handsome, intelligent young man to be interested in. "He taught you well," he said. "And you had lessons in school?"

She nodded. "The waltz, the rumba, and other dances. It was a very modern school," she said proudly.

"I'm glad of it," he smiled, and filled her glass again. He had glanced about casually, not seeing the two stocky men. He hoped he was wrong about them, that they had taken themselves off somewhere.

About eleven, they retired to their rooms. He let Charita go first to the bedroom to undress; she was very modest and shy about undressing before him. When he went in, he found she was lying on one of the futons, her dark head on a pillow. She wore a pink gown with lace low about her shoulders. She turned her head away and shut her eyes as he shed his white jacket. It was then as he turned toward the windows, near the wardrobe, that he saw the bulky shadow at the window.

He caught his breath, the shadow had melted back, but he felt sure the person was still there. He felt for his own revolver, it was in the shoulder holster where he usually wore it.

He left it there, turning so Charita would not see the

dark leather straps. Easily he slipped on a velvet smoking jacket, leaving it open.

"Charita, about those men tonight. You said they spoke of a gold formula."

She turned back to him, sat up eagerly, forgetting the quilt that lay over her. He saw the warm tints of her skin under the rose silk, the dark mussed beauty of her blue-black hair.

"Yes, you think it might be your formula of which they spoke?" she asked, in a whisper.

He raised his voice. He wanted to be heard. "Yes, I think it may be. However, they are wasting their time. The formula is not written down, nor will it ever be."

Her blue eyes expressed her surprise, the fringes dark about them. "Why, Brad? Do you trust nobody?"

"Not exactly that. There is a proverb that says that when two people know a secret, it is no longer a secret. Much as I trust Kanji and others, I will not tell them. It is a dangerous secret."

The bulky shadow pressed closer to the window, risking being seen in the eagerness to hear. Brad kept a keen watch on it, from the corner of his eye.

Charita put her finger to her lip thoughtfully. "But, must the formula not be patented? Then many will know of it. It is the only safe way to keep it, is it not?"

"Oh, I may patent it eventually," he said lightly. "However, for now, I have not applied. I wish to keep the knowledge to myself, and only I will mix the chemicals used. That way I can be sure nobody will ever reveal it, no matter how innocently."

He saw the shadow coming closer to the window, and with a leap that drew a frightened shriek from Charita, he sprang to the window, pushed it back to the side, and grabbed at the chunky shadow. The man there gasped in alarm, and ran!

Brad was out the French window and after him, into

180

the dark garden. Two men were there, he saw, and his pace slowed. They looked the kind who would be expert in karate, and he wanted no part of the two of them. Angrily, he watched them melt into the shadows of the garden beyond.

He went back slowly. He had seen them, the moonlight had revealed one face, and it was that of one of the men in the dining room. So they were after him, and the gold formula. Well, he hoped they were convinced that Brad was the only one who had it. That way Charita would be safe.

Charita was standing on the futon, trembling with fear, when he came back in and closed the French windows. It was chilly outside, they did not need the windows open. He locked it firmly, relieved that it was glass and not glazed paper.

"Honey, I'm sorry," he began.

She ran to him on bare feet. "Oh, Brad, Brad, you—you went after them—I was so—scared—oh, Brad—" Her hands were shaking as she clutched at his jacket.

"It's okay, honey. I wanted to scare them off, and I did," he said gently, holding her in his arms, the slim silken form against him. "Don't shake like that, it's all over."

"The men—we must get the police—"

"They'll be far away. And what evidence do I have that they meant harm? They would only say they had strayed into the wrong garden," he said grimly. "No, forget it, honey. They'll stay away from you—from us, now," he said quickly.

She shuddered violently, and he moved her from him, and shook her a little.

"Get back under the covers, you'll be chilled. Go on, honey. I'll get undressed. We need some sleep."

"How can we sleep when those men—those men are out there?" she quivered.

"I shall sleep very well," he said with a smile. "Better the enemy you know than the one you don't know."

He grinned down at her as he tucked her into the quilt. She could not answer his smile. Her eyes had widened in horror as his jacket had fallen open. "Brad, you have a gun—"

"Precaution," he said. "I have a license for it, don't worry." He took off the holster, cursing himself for being careless, and set it near the pillow on the floor. "Just don't ever touch it," he added, carefully. "It is loaded, honey. A man like me has to have some protection."

She did not answer. He undressed, turned out the lamps, and crawled onto the futon, moving awkwardly on the floor. When he finally got onto the futon, and moved the quilt over himself, he found it was surprisingly comfortable. It was firm, yet yielding, like a hard mattress. Her mat was right next to his, he reached out and touched her arm. It was cold, she was shivering.

He moved over, and took her into his arms. "Sorry, honey, I've scared you half to pieces."

She pressed her face against his bare chest. Her face was chilled, her eyelashes fluttered against him. Her hands clutched at him as he held her quietly, gently. This wasn't the way he had planned their little honeymoon to go.

Presently the shudders ceased, and she moved her head so her cheek was on his shoulder. Her body became softer, curved to his, and yielding.

He pressed his lips to the bared shoulder under the lace, and felt desire rise fiercely in him. He adored her so much, he wanted her so; she was a fire in his blood. He kissed the shoulder, the delicate arm down to her wrist, kissed each finger, then back up to the shoulder again. He leaned over her, and began pressing kisses on the soft throat, up to the delicate ears, and then began a slow, tantalizing move over to her lips. When his hard eager

182

mouth finally closed on her mouth, he felt the movement of the pink lips, and knew she was answering him.

Slowly he courted her, slowly, there in the darkness, with only the moon peering kindly through the glass to watch them. He found the futons ideal for lovemaking, they were wide enough when they shared the two of them, and the floor was hard beneath.

He stroked his hands over her shoulders, and down to the soft, rounded breasts. She had the prettiest, most delicately shaped breasts, soft perfect cones, inviting his mouth and tongue. He tasted them and she trembled under his caresses. Her arms went up and around his bare shoulders, he felt her fingers digging into the muscles of his back.

"Let me . . . take this off . . ." he whispered, when the pink silk nightdress hindered him. She lifted herself, he pulled off the gown, and shifted himself to lie over her. Her arms came up again, closing about him, and burning desire took over. He heard her soft, hurried breathing, felt the tremble of awakening in her body, knew the silk of her under his own hard limbs.

He wondered vaguely if she were mature enough now to respond completely to lovemaking. She seemed eager tonight, after long weeks of being cold to him.

He decided to try it. He drew out the courting. He entered her slowly, then drew out completely, and felt her hips pushing up restlessly to his. He kissed her mouth with slow hot kisses, pressing his tongue into her mouth, touching her tongue, all the while his fingers moving over her breasts and shoulders. Then he moved further down, and concentrated on her breasts, taking the nipples in his teeth.

Then he would stop, and press himself ardently to her. He would enter again, slowly, feeling with delight the soft liquid response of her body. She was coming closer. Her reserve seemed to have been discarded with the nightdress. This time when he drew out, she murmured, "Oh, Brad . . . Brad . . ."

He caressed her again, again moving his lips down her smooth round thighs, to her knees, and to her small feet, then up again, to the thighs. Deliberately he pressed intimate kisses on her, she caught her breath, but she accepted them. The quilts had been tossed aside. On the futons they fought for sweet satisfaction.

He came to her again, and this time finding it impossible to draw out, he moved again, again, more deeply, more sharply, as she held him tightly to her with her fingers pressing into his back.

He played on her as he might have on a violin, coaxing sweet music from her delicate limbs. He heard her gasp, tense, and then came the response he wanted. She writhed in his arms, crying out softly against his shoulder. "Brad . . . oh, Brad I feel so . . . oh, Brad—" she moaned.

He held her tightly, rejoicing wildly in her feverish response, the first she had given to him, so completely and so fervently. At its height, he let himself go, and felt her delicate compressions holding his masculinity, as Charita lost all control over her body for mad moments.

When it was over, he drew out slowly, and lay back, breathing hard. It had been worth it, all his patience and coaxing and teaching. She was a woman now. He lay on his side, and put his arm across her, drawing her to him. He pulled up the quilts about her body, she would be chilled soon, and she lay like one dazed and faint from the furious emotions which had wrenched her.

When she had caught her breath, and the hard ragged breaths subsided, she moved weakly to face him. "Oh—Brad—what was it?" she whispered.

He smiled in the darkness, a little triumphant grin. He brushed his lips against her hot cheeks, against the silky disordered hair.

"Love, my darling. Complete love."

12

They slept late the next morning. Charita finally woke, and found herself curled up against Brad's naked body. She felt dazed, deliciously relaxed and warm, with his hard arm close about her.

A hot blush crept into her cheeks when she remembered the night before. How ardent he had been, she had forgotten everything in the need to fulfill the desire of her own body. She had been quite abandoned . . .

She scarcely knew how to look at him when he finally awoke, and smiled at her. He too seemed relaxed, that tired, drawn look gone. She put her finger gently in the deep crease of his tanned cheek, and he moved and kissed the finger.

"Hello, darling," he said.

She murmured "Good morning," shyly, and pressed her cheek against his chest, and felt the tickle of dark hair against her face.

"What would you like to do today?" he asked lazily, holding her softly.

"Oh—what would you like?"

He chuckled. "That would be more of the same as last night, honey! But I did have other things in mind."

She could not look at him. "What—other things?" she asked, in muffled tones.

"Drawing, sketching. I thought we might wander around and see if I can get some fresh ideas. I have felt a bit stale lately. Also, there is a fine ceramic museum near here. They are supposed to have some very old fine pottery and porcelain."

"The Hakone Museum," she agreed eagerly, sitting up, forgetting she had discarded her nightdress. His hand moved down over her back, and she tingled at the touch of his fingers on her spine. "It—it is supposed to be excellent—oh, Brad, you tickle!"

He laughed, and sat up. "Guess we'd better move." He glanced at his watch and whistled. "Ten o'clock! That's the latest I've slept in years."

She slid into her robe, and fastened it. "Do you mind if I use the bathroom first?"

"Go ahead. Better wear some slacks today, we may be walking in meadows and along country roads."

He watched her in lazy satisfaction as she moved gracefully to the bathroom on bare feet. She was so pretty, so sweet, and that cool, withdrawn look was gone. Last night had been terrific—it foretold well for their future. He was whistling softly as he got up.

When he was finished shaving, she had dressed herself already, in pretty pale yellow pants with pleats at the hips and matching pullover of paler yellow. She tied a silk scarf around the fuzzy collar about her slim throat.

"Golden Lotus," he smiled.

"More like a dandelion," she giggled, brushing vigorously at the dark hair, until it lay in a soft pageboy about her throat and cheeks.

The shadows were chased away from the blue eyes, the creamy face was pink-cheeked. When she was happy, she showed it. It was there in her radiant sparkle, the dimples he loved to kiss.

He dressed in a warm brown slack suit, for the wind was chilly on the mountains. He added the revolver in its

186

holster. Charita watched him silently, and some of the sparkle dimmed. When he had finished, he put his fingers under her round chin. "Don't worry, honey. I'm used to this. It's part of the business game."

She shook her head, troubled, but said nothing. They went out, got into the car, and went off for a late breakfast in town. The plump Japanese woman waited on them with many bows. A small child played in the sunlight coming through the opened door of the tiny restaurant, and Charita smiled at the round, eager face, the bright black eyes and tiny unsteady legs.

"You like children?" asked Brad casually.

"Oh, yes, so much. I used to take care of our neighbor's children. She had four children, and it was a burden when she did the garden and the laundry. So sweet they were."

"Good experience for you," he said, with a twinkle at her. She put her hand to her face, he reached over and took her fingers in his and gave them a squeeze.

They went on to the Hakone Museum. It was a beautiful building in an exquisite setting of a bamboo garden and moss garden, all overlooking a magnificent valley and the mountains beyond. They paused, silently gazing at the view, then went inside.

The first room was a large one, showing how the ceramics were made, how mended, the various procedures in creating the delicate beauty of porcelain. Charita lingered over them curiously, and Brad studied the photographs and the tools keenly. He wondered if they might one day go into that, as well as jewelry.

He murmured it to Charita, her eyes lit up. "How beautiful that would be! Is it possible?"

"If we can diversify that much. Don't know."

They went on to the other section of the museum; then presently one of the museum guides, seeing their interest, came to them, and began speaking of the treasures there. They had not enough room to show everything at once, so they displayed the marvelous Chinese and Japanese ceramics at different times of the year.

The man warmed to their interest, and began to tell them stories of the discoveries of the bowls. He pointed out the rare celadon of a vase, of a bowl. Charita sucked in her breath at the softest creamy green of the bowl, with its stylized lotus pattern. One vase of celadon was from the thirteenth century, and she marveled at that.

A bowl with three legs caught their attention. It had a soft purple glaze, from the Sung dynasty of China. The overall effect was of rose blue, with little bits of gold glaze in the trim still showing after many centuries.

Brad bent over the cases of gemlike porcelain, keenly studying the designs. His tanned face shone, he was happy looking at them, thought Charita, with relief. She had thought he might have planned this just for her amusement. It was good to know that he also enjoyed beauty. But of course he did, it showed in his work on the jewelry he created.

They stayed for three hours, going back again and again after the guide had politely bowed and left them to their silent pleasure. A blue and white glazed water pot and cover from the Ming period held them entranced with its intricate swirling designs in shades of blue. There were brilliant reds, one was particularly adorable with little children bounding on the sides playing with their toys.

When they left, they were still silent. Brad drove them away in the huge limousine, down the steep road, and turned off into a country road. He found a Japanese restaurant and they ate a late lunch there, of lake fish and rice, and more tea. Then they rode on, not talking much, but silently happy in their thoughts.

Brad finally pulled up off a dirt road, and parked the car. "That meadow overlooks Mount Fuji. Let's just sit for a time," he suggested.

Charita agreed, in a happy daze. This was such a perfect way to spend the day! Could he be truly happy, lazing away a weekend with her in this manner? From his face, he was, and she was delighted.

He carried their sketch pads, and a bundle of charcoal pencils with him. They walked into the meadow, after he had locked the car, and strolled about, gazing at times at the late afternoon views of the mountains, at the white apex of Mount Fuji, the distant hills. The meadows were sweet with late spring flowers, a few iris dotted them, a clump of azaleas bloomed richly with pink. Brad went over to it, carefully cut a spray with his penknife, and brought it back to where Charita had seated herself on a grassy knoll.

He set it down before him on his pad, and studied it intently. Then he took another pad, and began sketching it, stylizing it as he went, the blooms, the leaves and tendrils, the stems. Then he ripped that off the pad and began again, concentrating on the bloom itself. Charita watched him for a time, quietly, marveling as he began to create a jewelry design from the azalea.

Then the view drew her, and she too picked up a sketch pad, and began to draw Mount Fuji. It was so perfect, it had been done a thousand-million times, she thought. But it still inspired, and one's fingers itched to create another scene of it.

She did as Brad had done, stylized the view so that it could be a design on a flat background. It was fun to try it, and she worked a couple of hours on two sketches.

Brad had turned to work on a tiny wild iris, styling that also in a formal manner. The sun was slipping down on the horizon as they finally realized how late it was becoming.

"Ah, the sunset," murmured Charita, and reached out to take his hand. She felt the need to share the beauty before her. They watched together as the sun slipped down behind the mountain, blazing a fiery orange pattern across the sky and on the cold snowy slopes, before turning to the deep blue and purple of twilight.

They went back to the hotel, contentedly weary and a little amazed to find the day gone so quickly. They dressed for dinner. Charita put on the long silver blue dress Brad had chosen for her, with the diamonds again. This time her bracelet was of gold and blue enamel in a delicate flower design, one he had made especially for her.

They danced, ate, danced again, listened to the gay music, and relaxed. Brad was looking the guests over very keenly, Charita noted, and she too looked for those two rough Japanese men. But they seemed to have disappeared. Perhaps they had not been important, perhaps they were only two men on vacation, and had been curious about the two Americans, wondering why they would wish to come to a Japanese-style hotel.

Brad made love to her again that night, very gently and sweetly. Charita did not have the wild reaction she had felt the night before, but she was a little relieved not to. It had been so tempestuous, it had swept her so thoroughly that her mind had been swimming, as though she had a fever. She was not sure she wanted to try that often. It was delicious—but so like being on fire.

On Sunday they went out again, walking in the meadows, sketching, talking a little, hand in hand as they walked, looking into each other's eyes over a tea table, laughing at little things that caught their attention. They paused in the small town to enter an antique shop, but Charita would not choose anything to buy. Brad bought so recklessly for her, he gave her so much.

They sketched for a long time in the afternoon, having discovered a place along the lake where they could draw the blue waters and the reflection of a clear Mount Fuji radiant against the vivid sapphire of the sky. It was a perfect day of brilliant sunshine, a cool wind across the water, a few white clouds scudding before the wind. They

190

rode on a slow-moving ferry across from one side of the lake to the other, and back again, enjoying the wind in their faces. Charita put on a scarf to protect her head, and shivered in the cold, so Brad had an excuse to put his arm about her. Every direction of the ferry opened up new views of the pine-covered hills, the mountains, the arms of the lake, a small resort, a vivid red torii standing in the water.

On Monday morning, they started back to Kyoto. Charita felt a dim sort of sadness at leaving the mountains behind. She had been so happy there. She felt that Brad had also left his troubles behind in Kyoto, and had shed his problems for a time, for his shoulders were straight now, his laugh rang out. And the deep creases beside his mouth were laughter lines now.

"Did you enjoy that?" asked Brad. "I don't think I need to ask, you look happy." He sounded as though that made him happy also.

"It gave me so much pleasure," she murmured wistfully.

He put his hand over hers on her lap and squeezed it briefly before he had to put it back on the wheel. "We'll do it again soon, I promise, Charita. Our marriage is too important to let all that work get in the way of it."

"Your work is most important," she said politely.

"Life is more important," he said, as though surprised at himself. "I'm learning a lot from you, my darling."

"How do you mean?" she asked, startled, turning to look at him, loving the long straight nose, the arrogant turn of his head, the tanned face and strong hands, the thick hair that felt so unexpectedly soft in her fingers. "How can I teach you anything?"

He frowned slightly, not in anger, but deep in thought, as he negotiated a sharp bend and a steep drop of the road. "Well—a sense of values, I think. I was a pretty single-minded man in business for years, rather sour on life.

Nothing mattered but the jewelry business, making money and more money. Oh, sometimes I enjoyed good music, or going to an art gallery, things like that. But with you, I feel deeply content; life means more, is richer for me."

"Oh, I am glad," she whispered, more touched than she could have said.

"You know that book you were reading aloud on Zen? It begins to make sense to me. We'll have to find more like that," he said, with a smile at her, then a look back at the road. "Life whips past, a year is gone, ten years, and where am I? A person needs more to life than just doing a job."

"Yes, one needs to love and care for others," she agreed soberly. "One needs to be peaceful with himself, to have time to meditate and discover himself and others. Time to talk, to be silent. This time with you—has been most good for me, Brad," she added softly.

"For me also, the best ever."

She was quietly happy as they drew up in the late afternoon beside the house that was now home. The weekend she had dreaded had been a marvelous surprise, a series of surprises—all good except for that dreaded shadow outside the window. She still shivered inwardly when she thought of that man waiting outside, listening to them.

The houseboy ran out to open the doors, to assist with the luggage. The maid waited, bowing, at the opened door of their home. Twilight dwelt in blue and green over the bushes, the flowers, the pool.

Charita entered the house. The maid bowed low, but waited for Brad, following her.

"Livingston-san, you have much phone messages. Mrs. Snow-san, she call many many many times, she cry, she say where are you?" In her excitement the maid's voice rose. "I tell her, not know, go 'way on long journey. She cry more, she come yesterday, she angry. She say must know, must call."

Brad was frowning heavily. "I'll have to wait for her to call again, I don't know her number. Did she leave a number?"

"No, Livingston-san. No number."

The telephone was ringing then, imperiously. The maid dashed for it, Brad beat her to it. "Jacinda? Where the devil are you? Yes, I'll have to talk to you," he said, heavily.

Charita went on back through the hallway to the bedroom, so lovely and beautiful and peaceful. But her heart had dropped to her slim black shoes. Mrs. Snow was angry with him for going away.

And why did he not know her number? What was wrong?

Brad came back shortly, his face drawn. "Charita, I'll have to go out, I'm sorry. Jacinda is in trouble, and crying. Don't wait dinner, I'll grab a bite somewhere."

"Yes, Brad," she said dully, and turned her back to him to take up the sketch pad she had worked on that weekend.

He left at once. She felt as though she too could cry. Her bubble had burst, all the more upsetting because it had been blown up so high. Why had he bothered to take Charita away for a holiday? Jacinda was furious with him, and he adored her; he went running when she called.

The maid fussed over Charita when she could not eat dinner. "You eat too much on holiday? That matter? Why you not eat?"

"Just some tea, please."

Charita had changed to the yellow outfit he liked, with the fuzzy collar. But Brad did not come home in time to see her wear it. She finally went to bed at eleven, lying awake until she heard the whisper of the high-powered car turning into the graveled drive.

It was over, the dream. For some reason, he had wished to please Charita, and had taken her away with

193

him. Now he was finished with her for a time, the work—and Jacinda, and probably Pearl as well—would claim him, she thought bitterly.

Brad had left for the office before she got up the next morning. At least, he had left for the office—or Jacinda Snow.

Charita drooped about the house. She had thought about transferring her sketches into a painting of Mount Fuji, but all ambition and creativity had left her.

She put on her dark blue kimono with the silver streak through it for the afternoon. The silver obi had once pleased her with its silk brocade beauty, now she scarcely noticed it. She sat on the couch, staring blankly out the windows for much of the afternoon. She could not eat, she was desolate.

She had wanted too much, that was it. The gods had turned angry with her. She laid her cheek against a cushion, and closed her eyes. The maid moved in on soft feet. "Mrs. Livingston-san, you have visitor. May he be allowed to enter your room?"

Her voice was anxious. A married woman did not allow a man to call upon her. Charita sat up slowly, brushed back her heavy hair, and wondered how she looked. "Who is it?"

"Raglan-san, he say. He speaks in good Japanese!" The wonder of it threaded through the maid's voice.

"Donald Raglan? Oh, let him come in!" Charita grew more animated. A friend from home, a friend from her old carefree days. "And serve tea at once, on the gold and rose china."

"Yes, yes, Mrs. Livingston-san, it shall be done." The maid bowed herself out, and in a moment Donald came in. He burst in like a fresh wind, laughing, pleased with himself, his boyish face open and eager.

They bowed to each other as they used to as children when Donald came over to play with her. Then he beamed

194

at her again, saying, "How good to see you! I came over on Saturday, thought I'd call on you and Mr. Livingston. But you weren't home, and I am bursting with news!"

"News? You still have your position?" she asked anxiously. Whatever the news was, it was good, she could tell. But surely he had not thrown over that good job!

"Wait till I tell you!" He could not sit down, he wandered about the room, paused to admire the pearly white Kuan-yin, went on to the windows, then back. "Charita, I have a promotion already!"

Her mouth opened in shock. "You have not! It is too great an honor!"

He was laughing, his tanned face reddish with emotion. "Yes, I have. Let me tell you. Mr. Frundsberg was terribly kind but didn't give me much to do. He had me look around the factory, learn the workings, then I got stuck in an office with no letters to write or anything! So I started drawing some designs. Well! He came in one day and saw me doing it, and looked at them. I thought he might be mad! Was I scared! Losing that job right off, just after I had written the parents how well I was doing! But he wasn't mad, no sir!"

"Oh, tell me what he said!" Charita clasped her hands together in impatience.

The maid pattered in, giving Donald a disapproving look, and set the tea tray before Charita. On it was the best china, but the platter of little crackers and foreign pretzels clearly showed her opinion of the matter. This man was outraging her, she would not serve him good food!

Charita said, "Please bring some of the large almond cookies, also a plate of shrimp—Mr. Raglan is most fond of them." She nodded decisively, and returned the maid's look with a little glare of warning. "Mr. Raglan is a good friend of my parents, he often came to our home!"

195

"Yes, Mrs. Livingston-san." The maid bowed low several times, and went from the room.

"She doesn't approve, eh?" asked Donald frankly. "Well, I guess she's right. I would have waited till your husband was home, but Mr. Frundsberg gave me the day off to come see you, and I couldn't turn it down!"

"He gave you the day off?" asked Charita, puzzled.

Donald nodded, and accepted the teacup from her hand. "Yep. I think he wants to be in good with your husband! If you ask me, he admires Brad Livingston's work, and I bet I have the job partly because of our friendship! You notice I didn't get it until Frundsberg saw us together!"

The maid returned with a plate heaped high with the huge almond cookies that Charita adored, and a couple of plates of pink shrimp. She set them down carefully, then remained to serve them. Charita did not dismiss her, the maid was outraged enough. Even Donald, who understood Japanese conventions, knew he had not acted properly.

Donald went on chatting eagerly. Mr. Frundsberg had set him to work on some jewelry designs; he had shown him what he wanted in the way of some brooches. Donald was working on silver just now, later he might work in white gold. He had a commission from Germany for a fine set of gems to be set in silver. The work was marvelous, they had good workmen. He had his own drawing board, and Mr. Frundsberg encouraged him to go to museums and look at exhibitions.

Charita was on the verge of telling Donald about the Hakone Museum, then she remembered that Brad and Mr. Frundsberg were, after all, rivals, and she kept silent. She smiled, nodded, encouraged Donald, told him he was doing marvelously well.

"How happy your parents will be when they learn of this," she said.

His face shadowed. "Well—yes, I guess so. Of course

Dad wants me to go into the diplomatic corps. But I don't want to go to college yet. I might have to go back to the States for that. And Mother agrees with whatever Dad says."

Charita was silent in sympathy. Donald was an only child, and her fierce, unexpressed opinion was that they had neglected him shamefully. No wonder Donald turned to her and to the Noguchis for friendship.

The afternoon grew late. They talked some more, the maid had just brought fresh tea, and was standing with hands folded waiting, when the doorbell chimed. The houseboy answered, and came in bowing to the drawing room.

"Miss Pearl Takahashi wish to come in," he beamed.

Charita and Donald rose at once, and he showed the girl in. Pearl started into the room, then saw Donald, and a strong look of surprise and disapproval came over her attractive face. In fact, she looked rather ferocious, thought Charita. She carried a portfolio that looked like Brad's.

She bowed low, they bowed, again and again, until Charita gave up. "Please come in. We have just been given fresh tea, you will join us?"

"No, no, I cannot. I have some papers for Brad—for Mr. Livingston. I promised to bring them as soon as I had finished typing them out."

"He is not in the office?" asked Charita, then flushed. "But no—of course not. You will, however, join us for tea. It grows late, you work very hard for Brad," she had not missed that change from Brad's name to his more formal title.

Pearl reluctantly sat down, smoothed out her smart blue pleated skirt, straightened the corner of the white collar of her neat blouse. Her blue jacket was open, she looked the picture of a successful secretary and assistant.

The maid brought another cup, tea was poured, polite words exchanged. Donald knew Pearl, they had met several times. He did not speak of his work to her, so Charita did not either.

Finally Donald rose. "I must leave. Forgive me for coming when your husband was not home," he said deliberately to Charita. "I was most excited about the news."

She smiled at him, and bowed to him. "Please feel free to come anytime," she said defiantly. "You are most welcome in my—in our home."

She went to the door with him, to Pearl's evident disapproval, and saw him off. She returned to the living room. Pearl was standing, her face set.

"I must go also. The chauffeur is waiting for me. Forgive my abrupt departure," and she bowed again and again.

"You are most kind to bring the papers. I know you are a most valuable aid to—my husband," said Charita, smiling and bowing, over a burning, angry heart. This woman, her husband's mistress who dared to look outraged when she found Charita with an old school friend.

Pearl suddenly discarded her good manners. The maid had left the room. "Brad is too good for you!" she said passionately. "That you entertain men in his absence, when he works so hard for you! You do not appreciate him, his goodness, his devotion! A wife who welcomes the attentions of other men!"

Charita was appalled by the outburst. She raised her chin. "Mr. Raglan is a long-time friend of our family, he is welcome at any time," she said softly. Her blue eyes shone with rage. That this woman—*this woman*—dared rebuke her!

"Where there is no fire, there is no smoke," said Pearl, and turned to go.

"That is very true. You might also remember another proverb," cried Charita, forgetting her self-control completely in justifiable rage: "Obey the customs of the place where you are!"

Pearl looked intensely puzzled. "I do not know of what you speak," she said finally.

"Then consider another proverb: An evil act runs a thousand miles."

Pearl stared at her, then bowed and departed. Charita was shaking. To the empty room, she muttered, "And man cannot be told by looks!"

Brad seemed so devoted, so close to her, so loving. Yet he had not even stayed at the office today, he had probably run off to Jacinda! And his other mistress brought papers to him. Papers? Probably she was just checking to see where he was!

Did Brad think she would remain ignorant of all he did? Truly, rumors ran as fast in Japan as in other countries. He could not expect her to be fooled forever. Or didn't he care? Damn him, didn't he care?

13

Pearl was well aware when Kanji entered the office, paused and looked at her. She kept typing, the keys clicking efficiently, hoping he would go away.

He did not go. He sat down and waited. Her mouth tightened. He was so persistent! Why could he not take a hint? She had told him often enough that she could take the bus home, she did not wish a ride.

Finally the work was finished, she read it over carefully. She wanted no mistakes to mar her work for Brad. She was very proud of her job, the knowledge she had of English and of his work. Not many Japanese girls of twenty-two had such a responsible position, with such a salary! Pearl meant to earn every penny of it.

Kanji rose as she stood, and she went to put the pages on Brad's desk for his signature. He would be back later, he had said, to sign them and send them out.

When she returned Kanji was still waiting. She slipped on her gray jacket over the red and gray striped blouse, picked up her pocketbook, cast one last look over the office.

"I will take you home," he said.

"No, I thank you, I shall take the bus," she said. She moved to pass him. He put his hand on her arm.

"We must talk seriously, Pearl," he said, his dark face

intent. When he stood so close and touched her, she was very much aware of him. Kanji was a handsome young man, slim, with shining black hair he wore straight, and overgrown, friendly dark eyes and a full mouth that broke into an easy smile, yet he seemed unaware of his good looks. He dressed conservatively; he was responsible beyond his years. If only—But no wishing, she thought firmly.

"There is nothing more to say."

"My parents are distressed."

She was silent. So were her parents. She twisted the strap of her gray handbag.

"May I come to your apartment to talk with you?"

"No," she said flatly.

"Then come to my apartment," he persisted. "I wish to speak of matters which should not be overheard."

Her head raised. "I will not go to your apartment!" she flashed. "What would people—"

Mockery sparkled in his dark eyes. "You are a modern girl, Miss Takahashi," he said, with a show of respect. "You do not mind going to a man's apartment, do you? I am surprised at you. You boast of how modern you are. You work, you go about alone. You do not live with your parents."

She was silent, biting her red lips. She lived in a bed-sitting room, it was too intimate for any meeting. She had never invited a man there. The apartment manageress would be outraged, she might be asked to leave. Yet she did not want to go to Kanji's apartment. She suspected he might want to make love to her, to try to force the issue of marriage between them.

"Afraid?" asked Kanji, gently. "You need not be afraid of me. Am I not a dull, stupid fellow who has no aggression in him? Am I too little a man to attract you?"

Color came into her smooth creamy golden cheeks. She turned her head away, but the short, efficient hairdo did not conceal her expression. She brushed back the fringe of her hair nervously; she groped for words.

"Come," he said. "We will talk, and then have dinner together. It should not take long to straighten out matters between us."

He put his hand under her arm, and led her out. She went reluctantly. She half wanted him to be aggressive and push the issue. But when she was sane and cool, she wanted nothing to do with marriage. Not with Kanji, not with any man. Well, they might as well have their talk and get it over with.

They went down to his car, he unlocked it, and showed her into the seat, ceremoniously. She liked the luxurious feel of the car. It had been kind of Brad to insist on giving Kanji the car for his own use. It meant much to Kanji.

He said nothing as he drove, concentrating on the crush of Friday afternoon traffic along the wide streets of downtown Kyoto. He turned off then into the narrower streets nearing his apartment. She felt more and more apprehensive. There was something about the set of his jaw.

She remembered when they were young, and had first been betrothed, she had rather liked him. Their parents had met, and she and Kanji had met briefly. He was an attractive young man, he was polite to his parents and hers, and his voice had been gentle to her.

Yet her father had told her something of Kanji, how he excelled in judo and karate, how strong he was, how well he played soccer and baseball. "He will have strong sons," said her father, giving her mother one of those looks. He had had no sons by her at all, as he often reminded her bitterly.

The car stopped at the front of an imposing apartment building. Kanji got out, helped her out, locked the car, and they went inside. He bowed to the porter, who bowed deeply to him.

"I will need the car again. It is all right that I leave it in front for a time?" Kanji asked politely.

"Oh, assuredly, Noguchi-san." The man gave Pearl a curious look, took in her smart American-style suit, and bowed to her briefly. He was not sure of her status.

In the elevator, Pearl said dryly, "This will do your reputation no good, nor mine."

Kanji shrugged, apparently saving his ammunition. He opened the elevator doors, went ahead of her to his apartment door, unlocked it, and let her in.

She gave a little exclamation when she saw it. He smiled in pleasure at her looking about the living room and hallway. He had had his mother's help in furnishing the rooms.

It was of a quiet blue and silver design, with a smart carpet and matching draperies. In one corner was a small black lacquer table holding a precious Ming porcelain bowl in blues; in another, was the tokonoma—in it a fine calligraphic scroll containing a brief poem about a butterfly losing itself in a blue sky.

There was a deep couch of dark blue velvet, with silver cushions. Two matching chairs of blue velvet were contrasted with scarlet lacquer tables set comfortably near them. She could see briefly beyond the living room, to a kitchen and small dining room combined, set in fine pine furniture. Another door probably led to a bedroom and bath.

"You have a fine apartment, Kanji."

"Mr. Livingston was most generous to me," he said briefly. "Please be seated."

He did not offer to make tea. She was glad of that. She sank down in one of the velvet chairs, her hand instinctively caressing the material. How fine it was! Had he been preparing it long? It looked almost too large an apartment for one man.

He was studying her gravely, then he sat down opposite her. "Pearl, my father has had a letter from your father. Your honorable father is rather angry that no date has been set for an engagement, nor has he been informed concerning a dowry. He complains that he can make no plans until he knows the amount of the dowry, and your honorable mother wishes to begin purchase of the kimonos and obis, the chests and all the goods they want to give."

Pearl shot up straight. "They cannot go ahead with this!" she said rapidly, her slim hand waving in frustration. "I have told them I can take care of myself!"

"The marriage was arranged many years ago, the contracts were signed."

"They can be destroyed!"

"Have you told them this?"

Her head drooped. "No—my mother would receive— many blows—" she said in a low tone.

"I am sorry." He too was silent for a time, studying her bent head. "Pearl, cannot we go ahead with the plans? I am most fond of you. You will make a fine wife and mother of my children. You can see the apartment is ready for you. One day we will purchase a house."

"No!" she said violently, raising her head, and staring defiantly at him. "I worry about my mother, but not even for her will I give up my freedom!"

"You sound like an American girl, not Japanese," he said coldly. She saw the fist clench on his knee. "You are Japanese, even though you sometimes pretend you are not. The contracts were made."

"I do not wish marriage," she said bitterly. "I have seen no good marriages! Marriages are bad, they make bad relations. I prefer to remain single!"

He studied her worriedly. "You have never spoken so. Think of the good marriage of my sister, Charita. You admire Mr. Livingston as I do," he said, and she felt he was gazing intently at her, as though he would read her heart. "That is a good marriage, she respects him—"

She bit her lips against angry accusations. Twice she had seen Charita with that young American man! Her husband worked so hard for her, and saw nothing beyond his nose!

"My mother lives in fear. I don't want to live my life like that."

"I would not treat you like that—"

"You said you would beat me!"

"I did not say so. I said I would not promise that I would never beat you! It would take away my honor, my self-respect," he explained patiently. "That does not mean I would beat you!"

"But you give me no assurances," she said bitterly. "No, I thank you. I like my apartment, my solitude, my decision-making."

"But you are getting older. When will you wish to marry?"

"Probably never!" she burst out.

"Never to have marriage, never to have the pride of bearing sons and daughters? Pearl, Pearl, I cannot believe this—"

"How many times must I repeat to you that I mean this? The contracts must be broken, Kanji. I will not marry you."

"I should write to your father in this manner?" he asked, his voice rising. "You wish this?"

She pressed her hand to her forehead. "Please—not yet. Need anything be said?" she asked pleadingly. "I do not wish him to become furious with my mother. She writes that she has not been well."

She shook her head, tears sparkled in her eyes. Her mother was her one weakness. She hated her father for what he did to her poor gentle mother.

Kanji sighed. "We go around and around in circles which always come around again," he brooded. "I thought we could come to some agreement. We could announce the engagement, that will satisfy our honorable parents. They can proceed to buy the kimonos—"

"But they will want to set the auspicious wedding date! No, I do not want that! The arrangements will be like the tides of the ocean, dragging me with them!"

"In anger, you speak in poetry," he murmured, admiration in his dark eyes.

She shook her head impatiently. "Do not distract me with flattery! I do not care for compliments, they conceal the true meanings of the relations between people!"

"And what is the true relation between us, Pearl?" he asked. He stood up and walked over to the window. Her gaze followed him. Though not tall like an American, he was tall and well-built. Reluctantly she admitted he was handsome and charming. He was intelligent, he learned quickly, Brad said. But did she know him, his heart? No, she knew only that he came of kind parents, that he spoke well. What was that?

"I have always thought to marry you, Pearl," he said, without turning from the window. "I have fondness in my heart for you." His voice was a little rough and low. He was not accustomed to such a speech. "I have thought of no other woman like this. I wish to marry you, to protect and cherish you, to give you children, a home, for always."

She was silent, touched in spite of her turmoil of feelings. He was breaking through the barriers of their formality to tell her things he might not even in marriage.

"And you, Pearl? How do you feel toward me?" He turned to walk slowly to her. "Will you say you feel nothing for me? Will you deny that you like me?"

She did not look right into his face, she stared at her slim hands tugging at the gray gloves.

"I like you, Kanji," she said, in a detached manner.

"You are handsome, intelligent, you will do well. You will have no problem in finding another girl more willing to marry. As for me, I do not wish—"

"You offend me when you speak of this so lightly! Another woman! As though I would go out on the street and find another girl, when I am pledged for you, and our marriage!" Anger rumbled through his voice, shocking her. She stood up quickly.

"There is nothing more to be said," she told him formally. "If you will be so kind as to say nothing to my father for a time, you will be released eventually—"

He made an inarticulate sound in his throat. He grabbed her arms. Her shocked face turned to him. He had rarely touched her, never like this.

"Kanji!"

He grabbed her close, pulled her to his whipcord-hard body. She felt a thrill run through her, and a shiver of terror. What would he do? Never had she felt the warmth of a man's body against hers so closely, even in dancing it had not been so close.

"You like American ways. Maybe you like this—the way the movies do—" he said. He put his hand behind her head, held her steady. His mouth descended to hers, and she felt the strange hot touch of his mouth, so intimately against hers.

She was so stunned she could not move. He kissed her again, again, as though delighting in punishing her, as though learning to enjoy this brutal assault on her. His mouth moved to her cheeks, to her throat, forcing back her head so it hurt.

"You hurt—me—Kanji!" she tried to stop him. He kept on kissing her, bending her back so she could scarcely stand. Once unloosed, his kisses rained on her, his embrace was the act of an angry man who had been held back too long.

He held her tightly, he made her feel the masculinity

of his body against hers. She was intensely aware of him, tight against her. She felt as though he imprinted himself on her, and she would never be free of that print. Like a block print, her mind told her, in a daze. She would retain the image on herself forever.

He finally became aware of her helplessness in his embrace. She could not fight the hard muscular strength of his arms and legs. He loosed his arms a little, and looked down at her dazed face.

"Pearl," he said urgently.

She shook her head blindly. "Let me go. You shame me—" she managed to whisper.

He finally let her go. She gathered up her handbag, and walked to the door.

He followed. "You must not go like this. Wait, there is much to say. I will not do it again—please, wait, Pearl—"

"You have gone too far," she said, the blood draining from her head, leaving her dizzy. "You have gone—too far. I shall not meet you again—"

"Yes, you will." He followed her from the apartment. She felt in a panic, fearing the hardness of his arms, the brutality of his kisses. Were there bruises on her face? "We will talk again. I *will* see you. May I come for you tomorrow?"

"No. No."

She was ahead of him by just a few steps. The elevator door was open, about to close. Risking it, she dashed inside and the door closed behind her. She pressed the ground floor button with shaking hand, and kept the button pressed until the door opened again downstairs. Past the curiously staring porter, she fled outside.

She ran past Kanji's car, and down the street. Finally, as she realized people were staring at her, she slowed to a walk. She was out of breath, her hair mussed, her mind in a turmoil. What a fool she had been to take his dare, and go to his apartment! She would never go again! Never—never be alone with him again.

She found a bus presently, and took it to the center of town. She stopped at a small coffee shop, and mechanically ate a sandwich. She did not know if Kanji would try to go to her apartment that evening. She waited for a couple of hours, and furtively returned, looking about in agitation before she dared go down the street to her place. No one she knew was there.

She went inside her small apartment and shut and bolted the door. She felt shattered. Her little world had been blown to pieces. That Kanji had dared do this to her! He had always been a gentleman. Now she could never trust him again.

She felt half-sick, yet excited and keyed up also. She could not sleep well that night. She kept waking, as fragments of memory returned. That feel of his body against hers. That hard, masculine, tough body pressing to her small limbs. The way he held her so she could not get herself free. He was a tough man, all right. So hard and sure of himself—

But he could not have her! No, she was resolved on that. The engagement and contracts must be broken. She would not endure such an—an assault again!

She buried her face in the pillow and wooed sleep desperately, but could not forget the touch of his mouth against her lips and cheeks and neck. She had scrubbed the areas, but she could not scrub away the touch of his hard mouth, the lips that had sought for her softness. Oh Kanji, she thought, what have you done?

14

Brad Livingston parked the black limousine down the block, in front of a furniture store. As he locked the door and walked away, he looked about the neighborhood. It was a curious place for Jacinda Snow to choose to live. Yet this was the address she had given him.

Dark alleys ran crosswise to the main street. A grocery with an open market stood on the corner. As dusk came, children were running home, their shrill voices echoing. He smiled as one small girl stumbled against him and cried out an apology.

Her dark eyes gazed up at him. Her short dark hair was in bangs, like Charita's. He patted her head briefly. "Run home to mama," he said slowly in Japanese.

She bobbed a little curtsey to him, then ran on. He was still smiling as he approached the apartment house at the other end of the block. How Charita would have enjoyed the child. One day they would have a small girl, perhaps looking like that one, a round sweet face, large dark eyes fringed with long lashes, that dark straight hair framing her face demurely.

A car was moving slowly down the street, he did not notice it particularly. His thoughts were on Charita. After that heavenly weekend at Hakone, she was distant again, cool. He made love to her, but she lay passively in his arms. What was wrong? If only she would be frank with him! But her politeness was a barrier between them.

"Nothing is wrong," she insisted. "I merely have little to do. I must be more busy. I believe I shall paint another scene beginning tomorrow."

He had gone quietly into the workroom, her paints were hard and unused. Sketches were pinned to a canvas, but she had done no work. He worried about her. Her blue eyes were unhappy, her smile was formal with no sparkle on her face. And he had no idea what distressed her.

He sighed, shrugged off that worry for a time. He thought of Jacinda and her frantic calls to him. She had not gone to the office. Miles was off somewhere, probably drinking himself into a stupor. What a mess that marriage was, and it was ruining their business also.

He went into the hallway, searched the mailboxes for Jacinda's number, then walked up the stairs. At the crudely painted door, he knocked. This didn't look like a place for the smart, elegant Jacinda Snow.

Jacinda opened the door, said, "Brad!" He went in, and she flung herself at him.

He held her close to him, feeling compassion and impatience mingled. "What is all this, Jacinda?" he asked gently. "What kind of mess are you and Miles making?"

She drew back a little. She was fashionably dressed, yet the effect was not the same. Her face was white and drawn, even the makeup could not conceal that. The white silk suit with the green blouse the color of emeralds was her usual summer garb. But her eyes looked as though they had known many tears, and the red around them was not completely concealed by powder.

"Oh—Miles, I am finished with him," she said, her voice husky. She shook her blond head impatiently. "He drinks all the time now. Brad, I can't live with an alcoholic."

"I've tried to talk to him, you can't reason with him. I wonder if he should return to the States and dry out somewhere?"

Brad was thinking he would offer to pay for the treatment. Perhaps they needed money. Miles hadn't done much work the past year, he knew that. What a pity, because he and his wife had built up a good legal business.

"Perhaps. I don't care. I've left him, and I'm not going back." Jacinda reached nervously for cigarettes, extracted one from the crumpled pack, and lit it. The room gave the effect of shabbiness, though it was neat enough. Brad looked around slowly. How different from the shining gold and silver apartment, glittering in its elegance.

He sat down in the single large chair, and watched her gravely. She was puffing away, inhaling as though she lived on smoke. She was terribly thin and wan. This break-up was doing her no good.

"Jacinda, it won't help to hide out and hope events will settle themselves," he said, rather sternly. "It isn't like you to evade facts. Miles must be helped. I'll get him someplace in the States, if you'll take him over there—"

"I told you! I don't care what he does! He can drink himself into the grave if he wants!" she said passionately, waving one slim hand in agitation. "It means nothing to me. For once in my life, I'm going to think of just me! What I want, what becomes of me!"

She had always been self-centered, he thought. Perhaps in self-preservation, through the ugly marriages of her parents Jacinda had learned to fight for what she wanted. But it had made her hard and selfish at times. Only Miles had brought out the gentleness of love. What had gone wrong between them? Why did Miles drink so much?

"Well, all right. What do you want?" Brad asked reasonably. "Where do you want to go, what do you want to become?"

"You're laughing at me," she said sullenly. Her back was to him, she stared out the window blindly as the slowly blooming lights of the city block revealed the ugliness of the small neighborhood.

"When have I laughed at you, except in trying to jolly you out of the blues?" Brad asked gently. "Sit down and calm yourself, and let's talk reasonably. We used to be able to talk, you and I, Jacinda. Remember the days when our parents were first married? We would sit by the swimming pool, and laugh at the craziness of life?"

To his surprise and relief, she came back and sat on the edge of the couch. Her red mouth trembled into a smile, rather crooked, but a smile. "I remember. You were the one sane person in my life, always, Brad. I loved you from the first."

He felt a slight unease, but pursued that thought. "And I was very fond of my little sister, though you weren't so little. And how you turned into a beauty. Remember the time I escorted you to my college dance, and everyone fell all over you?"

"And I saw only you, Brad," she said, and put her hand on his as it rested on the arm of the chair. "It was always—you—always."

Her hand was hot and feverish. He did not withdraw his, but took her fingers reassuringly in his. He searched her face, she looked feverish. Maybe she was really ill, or on the verge of nervous collapse. Would she agree to going to a hospital?

"We can straighten it all out, Jacinda," he told her. "It will work out. We'll get you well and strong again—"

"I'm not sick!" she snapped, and her fingers closed tightly on his. "I'm not sick! I'm just fed up with my life!"

He was still, thinking about it. He would take her home with him, but that wasn't fair to Charita, he knew they did not get along well. And Miles would find her there and make them all miserable.

"What do you want to do, Jacinda? Have you thought about it? Do you want to remain in Japan and continue the business? You'll be welcomed, I know, even the men welcome you, however macho they are," he tried a light note. "You are known as a brilliant woman——"

Her shrill laugh startled him. "Brilliant! But a fool in love, I know!" she mocked herself. Her fingers hurt his hand. The nails were digging into his palm. "How, God, am I to work out anything? You got married!"

"And very happily," he said steadily. "Charita is a fine and lovely girl. I think I have waited all my life for such a woman, gentle and sensitive, artistic and thoughtful——"

Jacinda released him to put her hands to her ears. "Oh, God, stop it! She isn't worth your little finger! A stupid little schoolgirl! Oh, God, why didn't I stop that fool marriage! Now I'll be free and you won't!"

He tried to disbelieve his ears, and could not. His attention sharpened on her. Surely she did not believe—— She must be sick, and her fancies had turned to him, the one man she had always trusted.

"Forget that for the moment," he said quietly. "Jacinda, what have you thought about your future? I want you to be happy——"

To his surprise, she flung herself at him, landing on his lap. He stood up, revolted and shocked. She clung to his knees, kneeling before him, tears streaming down her cheeks.

"Brad, Brad, don't push me away! I couldn't endure it if you push me away! Everyone I ever loved—failed me —everyone but you—Miles, a drunk—Mother a—horror —oh, God, what shall I do——"

He bent to pull her up, she went into his arms, sobbing violently into his shoulder. He held her quietly, cursing his blindness. She was at the end of her tether. She had always loved him, but as a sister, he had thought. But they were not related. Miles' words to him began to make sense. What in the name of God had Jacinda said to her husband?

Her arms closed about his neck, she lifted her wet face. "Kiss me, Brad, tell me you do care what happens to me?" she pleaded. "Tell me—God, I'm so miserable."

He kissed her cheek gently, she tried to turn her head and kiss him fully on the mouth. He evaded her, and put her down strongly into the chair. "Now, Jacinda, be calm. We must discuss this quietly—"

"I don't want to discuss anyhing," she whispered, blindly reaching out for him. Her hand went to his knee. "Brad—make love to me—please—I want you, Brad."

He backed away, unable to conceal his revulsion. "Jacinda, you don't know what you're saying." He tried to smell the room, to discover if she had been drinking heavily. But her heavy perfume would have concealed all other odors, it was so strong.

"Brad—make love to me—come in the bedroom—it will settle everything— We should have married long ago. I never loved anybody but you. Brad—make love to me—"

His heavy hand kept her in the chair. "Stop it," he said, sternly. "You'll be sorry tomorrow that you said such wild things. You love Miles, you always have. We'll get you two straightened out, and it will be good again—"

"No, no, I hate him, he's cruel—look at my bruises— look at them—" Wildly, she stripped back the sleeves of her blouse. He stared at the bruises purpling on her arms. She opened the neck of the blouse, almost tearing it from herself. Bruises showed on her throat, on her breasts. "Look—what he did to me! Did you know Miles would do that? A good marriage—" She laughed shrilly, her green eyes staring wildly up at him. "Good marriage, hell! He hates me as I hate him!"

He could not endure cruelty in any form. He put his hand caressingly on her white neck, he thought of her as he had first known her, a pretty sixteen-year-old girl, in a bikini, her still coltish body stretched out beside the pool, as they laughed and joked to hide their tension and bitterness.

"I'm sorry, love, I'm sorry." He would send Miles to that sanitarium and dry him out, or get a divorce for Jacinda, Brad thought grimly. This would not do. He could not treat Jacinda like that.

"Love me—" she whispered. "I need love so much. I love only you—Brad!"

He had turned to the door. "I'm sorry, Jacinda, I must go," he said flatly. "Mixing us up won't do a bit of good. I'll try to get Miles straightened out, or send him to the States for treatment. Then we'll get you back to work, you always liked your work—"

"Brad!" she cried after him as he opened the door. "Don't leave me—don't leave me—"

"I'll talk to you again soon, Jacinda. Take care of yourself, get some food to eat," he said, in the opened doorway. He looked back at her briefly, his mouth gentled. She looked so pathetic, so lost, for such a crisp, sure woman. "Take care, love." He closed the door after himself and ran down the stairs into the night.

In the street, he paused to wipe his wet face with a handkerchief. Of course she didn't know what she was saying. She wanted to be comforted. But God—to invite him —He shook his head in disbelief and started toward his car.

The men crept up on him out of the dark alley as he was passing it. He saw them from the corner of his eye, and started to dodge. But it only deflected the blow. He felt it on his head, another on his cheek, and went down in the storm of blows that went efficiently over his hard body.

His arm protected his face, he kicked out at them, felt it connect. He yelled at them. "Damned dogs, get off

216

—damn you—" He yelled louder, hoping some store-keeper would hear and come outside, or someone turn on a light. Thieves thrived in darkness.

He heard an answering yell in Japanese. The men growled at each other, paused in their blows at his body. One tried to lift Brad, he was unable to do so, as Brad made his body as heavy and limp as possible.

He thought they said, "Another time—must carry off—" But the Japanese was strangled in their throats, the words were garbled in his dizzy mind.

The next thing he knew they had run off down the alley. The little Japanese policeman had panted up to him, his nightstick swinging from his wrist. "What happens here?" the man demanded, in Japanese, then realized the man on the ground was a foreigner.

He hesitated, torn between his desire to follow the attackers, and his wish to help the man lying stunned on the sidewalk. Compassion won, and he bent over Brad anxiously.

"I will take you to hospital," he said, very slowly, in English, touching Brad's head gently. "This hurt?"

Brad grimaced. "Very much," he said, slowly, in Japanese. "No. No hospital. Must go home. The address is—" And he repeated it slowly.

The policeman was intensely relieved that he could be understood. "But you must go to hospital. Wound cared for, yes?"

"I wish to go home. My car is—up the street—there —black—can you drive?" Brad felt as though his tongue was thick in his mouth. His brain was muzzy from the blows. He put his fingers to his cheek, looked at them. Even in the darkness he could tell they were sticky with blood.

But he was obstinate. He wanted to go home.

The policeman reluctantly agreed. He took the keys, went to the car, and very slowly, drove it back to Brad.

217

He managed to help him into the car, and drove him through the dark streets to the district where Brad lived. His breath sucked in with respect as he saw the grand house and the lighted windows.

The chauffeur came running when he saw the car approach. He helped Brad from the car, and supported on his broad shoulder, Brad managed to stagger to the house. A maid opened the door to them, bowing low, smiling until she saw Brad's face. Then she shrieked.

Charita ran from the living room. She saw Brad and gasped, her mouth opened in shock.

The policeman followed them in. Brad collapsed into a chair.

The policeman began to explain, painfully, in English.

"Please, in Japanese," begged Charita, bending over Brad. Her breath was caught in her throat as she saw the blood, the bruises, his weakened condition. "You must go to the hospital, Brad!" she exclaimed.

"No," he said obstinately.

He closed his eyes against the persuasions. Charita turned to the maid. "Send for the doctor, beg him to come at once," she said, in resignation.

Then to the policeman, she bowed, and begged him to tell her what had happened. Charita wore her blue and silver kimono with the silver obi. The policeman had been eyeing her out of the corner of his eye, unable to tell at first if she was Japanese or foreign. He finally decided she was foreign but knowing their ways and language, and began to tell his tale.

"And these men," interrupted Brad. "Did you see them?"

The policeman frowned in thought. "In the darkness, not able to see clearly. They seemed of stocky build, their accent was not of Kyoto. Their clothing was of dark cloth. I am sorry I know so little, Livingston-san."

Charita's wide distressed gaze met that of Brad, he

218

shook his dizzy head slightly. "It is good of you to bring home my husband," said Charita, with dignity. "May I please write down your name and station, that we may send thanks to you?"

He wrote them down plainly for her, in careful script, bowed deeply and left. The chauffeur had orders to drive him back to his station.

"A good man," said Brad in a weak voice. "Hadn't been for him, they would have beat me up good."

Charita said, "I think they did anyway. Why will you not go to the hospital?"

"Don't like hospitals." His grin flashed briefly. "Oh, get me to bed, will you?"

He tried to get up, managed it, stood swaying. Charita and the maid rushed to lend their shoulders on either side of him, and got him to his bedroom. She slid his jacket slowly from his shoulders, but he was biting back groans as she did so. The shirt was bloody, she removed it carefully. He was half-sitting, half-lying on the bed, his eyes shut.

Charita gritted her teeth. She found his pajamas, and dismissed the maid. Then she managed to take off Brad's trousers, and his underpants, his shoes and socks. She slid the pajama trousers on his long legs, and he lay back in relief. His forehead was beaded with sweat. Blood was streaming freely from his forehead cut, and dark bruises covered his arms, shoulders, back and chest. She could smell on him a dark, musky perfume also, and that sickened her.

Charita recognized that scent. She had smelled it often enough in the few days she had spent in Jacinda's apartment before her wedding. Brad had been with Jacinda. Probably in her arms.

It was midnight by the time the doctor reached the house. He examined Brad curiously, smeared him with ointment, studied the cut.

"It will need some stitches, perhaps the hospital—"

Brad gritted out, "No!"

The doctor, a small Japanese man of brisk, efficient manner, shrugged, his palms up. He brought out his equipment, and with resignation said to Charita, "Can you hold his head steady?"

"Get one of the maids," snapped Brad.

Charita shook her head silently, and positioned herself behind him, sitting on the bed beside him. Her arms ached before the doctor had finished, and she wanted to cry because Brad was hurting, and so was she.

But she held him very steady for the doctor's quick neat stitching. Six stitches were taken, then his face was washed with antiseptic and the blood cleaned away. A maid carried away the bloody clothes, and cleaned the room.

The doctor left some tablets. "You will take them, two tonight, and two more in the night if sleep fails you," he said. "Tomorrow morning, I will come again. If infection sets in, you will go to the hospital, if I must send two strong men to carry you."

Charita bowed the doctor out, and thanked him many times for coming in the night. He bowed back to her, and complimented her on her ability as a nurse.

After he had left, she went softly back to Brad. He was lying back on the pillows, his forehead furrowed.

He was not asleep yet. His pain-filled eyes gazed up at her. She smoothed back his hair softly. "You feel very bad?" she murmured.

"Like I've been in a football scrimmage," he murmured.

"Those two men—do you think—"

"Don't worry about it, honey. That's my job," he said, and took her hand in his. "Stay beside me, I'll go off to sleep soon."

But she couldn't help worrying. She sat beside him

quietly, without moving, until his relaxed hold on her hand told her he slept.

So much to worry about. She could not return to her room. She changed her kimono for a nightdress and robe, and returned to his room. The bed was wide, king-size the way he liked. Cautiously, she lay down beside him and covered herself with the sheet. The June night was not chill. She had turned the lights off, but she could see his form in the dusky room, lying beside her.

The attack. Where had it been? A bad area, the policeman had told her, a tough area. Why had he been there? He had obviously been with Jacinda.

That strong perfume, it was unmistakable. Expensive, musky, different. No other woman she knew had it. She sniffed. It lingered on in Brad's bedroom, even though the maid had taken away his bloody, torn garments. It was on his skin, she could smell it near her.

She lay on her back, staring into the darkness. She was upset about Brad, she had almost fainted when she had seen him coming in like that. All bloody and bruised, half-fainting himself.

Yet—that perfume on him—it made her feel tense and cold inside. Why had he been with Jacinda, so close that he still had her perfume on his skin? Had those long white arms been about his neck, had he clasped her close to him? Had he been—in bed—with her—those hours? Had he been so dazzled by her lovemaking that he had not taken care when he left her apartment?

Charita had heard that Jacinda had left Miles, Kyoto buzzed with the news. Miles was drinking heavily. He was calling everyone he knew to try to find out where his wife was. All were disgusted, and intrigued, and full of gossip. Two women of the American colony in Kyoto had dared to call Charita to ask if she knew where Jacinda was. She had said coldly that she was not aware that Jacinda had left Kyoto, and finally hung up on them.

Tense and unhappy, Charita lay awake, worried about the danger to Brad. Surely he must have been careless in leaving Jacinda tonight, or he would not have allowed himself to be surprised by those two men.

But his weakness and his injuries hurt her as though they were her own. She had felt the pain, and communicated it to her heart. Why, why, why?

Brad must be sorry he had married her, for if he had waited, he might have had Jacinda as his wife. Or was Brad the kind who preferred a variety of mistresses? He was a tough, passionate man, very masculine, very virile, thought poor Charita, with a sigh. He had proved that to her, beyond any doubt. Perhaps a wife was not enough for him. He had Jacinda—and Pearl—and who knew how many others?

No wonder Jacinda had warned Charita not to marry him! She must have hoped that the warning about Pearl would have been enough to make Charita refuse to marry him. She could not confess her own affair with him! He was practically her brother! And Miles knew about it which was why he drank, Charita decided. He knew his own wife was having an affair with Brad. That was the meaning of the drunken argument Miles had had with Brad.

"Oh, is there no way out of this confusion?" Charita thought, trying not to move restlessly for fear she would disturb Brad. "Shall I give him a divorce? Or does he wish to continue with the marriage, and have all the mistresses he pleases?"

The thought was sickening to her. She had enjoyed his attentions and caresses so much at Hakone; they had seemed to be alone in their own beautiful world.

Brad stirred, and awakened. He gazed up at her. "What happened?" He was frowning. "Oh, I remember . . ."

"Do you wish some water, or some hot tea?" she asked softly, sitting up.

"Water, maybe—"

"It is no trouble to fix tea, and it is soothing. I will make it with herbs," she murmured.

"Would you, darling?"

She slipped out of bed, padded to the elaborate kitchen with all its appliances, and made black tea with herbs. She came back, to find him propped up, his hand to his head.

"It is very much pain," she said sympathetically.

"Hurts like hell," he said briefly. "Sorry to wake you up, my darling."

She had brought a cup for herself. She poured out the two cups, and held his for him to drink. The lines in his face smoothed out as he drank.

"This is good," he commented. She smiled at him, and drank without speaking. She wanted to soothe him, to comfort him. It was odd, because she should hate him for what he was doing to her, yet she could not. She owed him so much, that she could never repay him. Her thoughts were chaotic as she slowly drank the hot tea.

"Shall you take the tablets of the doctor now?" she asked, when he was about finished.

He shook his head, then winced. "No, I'll sleep now. I don't like too much medication."

"He suggested them, if you were wakeful."

"Come lie with me, and I'll sleep," he said, and held out his arm.

She lay down beside him in the circle of his arm, careful not to put her head on his bruised shoulder. Soon she felt the slow deep breathing that meant he was asleep. Finally, she also slept, from sheer weariness and inability to find a solution to their seemingly endless problems.

15

Brad had said he wanted to get up the next morning. Charita persuaded him to wait for the doctor, who came at noon. By that time his pain was intense.

The doctor took off the bandages and examined the cuts critically. "They look all right today. I will come again tomorrow. Now for the ribs—"

"Ribs?" asked Charita fearfully.

"Yes, I wish to see if any are broken," said the doctor, and gave Brad a painful examination. The bruises hurt, but no ribs were broken, the doctor concluded.

"You are very lucky man, Livingston-san," said the doctor, sternly. "You are made of leather, yes? In any event, the leather is worn today, and you must remain in bed until it begins to shine again." He grinned at his own joke, and his merry black eyes sparkled.

"I have a great deal of work to do—" Brad stirred restlessly in the large bed, but his face was drawn and his eyes had lost their liveliness.

"So, so, nobody can do your work for you? You work alone in your big factory?" the doctor chided.

"Please, Brad, do listen to the doctor," urged Charita softly, her hand stroking his forehead very gently, avoiding the deep cut.

Brad shifted in the bed restlessly. "Well, I'll send for Kanji, and give him instructions—"

"Maybe tomorrow," soothed the doctor, and gave him some tablets which he had to take before the doctor left his side. They made Brad slide into a deep sleep, from which he did not awaken until about ten o'clock that night.

He woke refreshed, and cross, because he had lost a whole day. Charita chided him.

"He does what is best for you, Brad. You are ungrateful. He is very good to come to you, many doctors do not come to patients. Be grateful he did not force you to go to the hospital."

His brow smoothed. "No, I'll bet the hospital doesn't have as pretty a nurse as I have."

She flushed. "Now I know you are better!"

He chuckled, and stretched out, then stifled a groan. "God, if I had my hands on those creeps—"

"You will stay away from those men!" she said sharply, thinking of how dangerous it had been for him to meet Jacinda in such a bad neighborhood.

"I'll try, honey. I wonder if they—" He bit off the words, frowning at himself, and lay quietly thinking for a time. She moved about the room, straightening out the bedcovers, then went to get some hot tea and a couple of poached eggs for him.

She returned, and he sat up painfully to eat.

She was pleased that his healthy appetite seemed to have returned. He polished off the eggs and toast, drank the whole pot of tea, and said, "Tomorrow I'll have some steak!"

"If the doctor approves," she teased, with a smile.

"If the doctor does not let me eat something, I'll sneak out to the kitchen and prepare it myself!" Brad threatened, with his old grin flashing. He stretched cautiously when she had removed the tray from the bed, and nodded with relief. "Much better. The old ribs took a beating, but they aren't bent permanently."

He lay back. She was ready to sleep, having rested but little during the day. Brad was alert and bright-eyed. "I think I'll call Kanji tomorrow morning, have him come over," he mused. "I have some things to discuss with him. Those orders from France ought to be well underway—"

She let him plan on, took the tray out to the kitchen, returned to find him with a pad of paper and pencil, scribbling out notes to himself.

"Really, Brad, can't you forget work for a minute?" she asked crossly.

He glanced up, his gaze distant, then gradually focusing on her. "You could make me forget. Come on to bed, honey," he invited, then chuckled when she blushed and shook her head.

"Not to that bed, while you are wide awake," she dared to refuse him. "I'm going off to my bed, and you can stay awake and tire yourself as much as you wish!"

She started for the door, then repented a little.

"If you need me, knock on the wall, Brad, I will hear you."

He promptly reached out behind himself to knock on the wall, and she laughed, but fled anyway.

She was smiling as she shed her robe and crawled into bed. He could be such a darling and a tease, when he was not too tired and absorbed in his work.

Brad must have worked late that night, for when she crept into his bedroom at eight the next morning she found him sound asleep. And all about the bed were scattered notes in scrawled pencil, snatches of designs, scribbled memos to himself, part of a letter to a client. But he slept serenely among the pages. She shook her head at the sight.

She left him to sleep, which he did until noon. When the doctor came, he pronounced himself better satisfied. "But you will remain in bed a few more days, until the injuries heal and the ribs no longer hurt," said the doctor sternly.

Brad said, "Maybe another day, but no longer."

"You must listen to my good advice, Livingston-san," said the doctor shaking his head at him. "You can push your body to the limit for years, but eventually it will rebel! Be good to your body, and it will be good to you! Moderation in all matters! Common sense is the best medicine."

There was no telephone in the bedroom. When the doctor departed, Brad tried to crawl out of bed, but his legs disappointed him. He sat on the side of the bed and cursed them fluently.

Charita put her hands over her ears until he stopped.

"Please, Brad," she told him, distressed. "Please get back in bed. I beg of you!"

His mouth was set with impatience until he saw her eyes sparkling with tears. "All right, all right," he groaned, and lay down, and let her cover him. "But you call Kanji at the office, and ask him to come over after work. I want to talk to him."

"He has called this morning, he is anxious to know that you are well," she told him. "May he come now?"

"Yes, fine, tell him to come. Why didn't you say he had called?"

"Many have called," she said, with reserve. "Miles Snow, and Mrs. Snow have both phoned, and asked how you are, and Mr. Frundsberg who wishes to discuss a subcontract—did I say that right? Subcontract?"

"Put him off—put them all off," growled Brad. "Only tell Kanji to come, if he will be so good," he added, and teased her with his finger under her chin. "And smile for me, or I'll cry!"

Charita managed a shaky smile, and went to phone Kanji. Brad was so difficult to manage, she was amazed at herself for even trying. But it hurt her to see him trying to stagger around, pain on his face and stiff with caution.

Kanji agreed eagerly to come at once. He appeared in half an hour, and went in to see Brad. They talked for a time. Charita peered in at the door from time to time, worriedly, and finally called a halt when she saw Brad rubbing his forehead wearily.

"You must stop for today," she said firmly, entering the room. "Brad, you have given him enough to do, I am sure, to occupy him for a week!"

Kanji looked startled by her interference. Brad only grinned tiredly, and said, "Take away those cushions, darling, I'll lie down again. You have it all straight, Kanji, I depend on you."

Kanji stood up, and bowed deeply, respectfully, several times. "I am very honored by your words, and will do my poor best to manage——" He caught Brad's eyes, and flushed. "I mean—I will do as you direct, sir."

"I know you'll do a good job. And be sure to get Oboru-san to work on the French job. He has the most creative imagination and sense of fitness. I want this delicate and precise."

"It shall be done as you direct," and Kanji bowed again and again, backing respectfully to the door with a final bow.

"I will see you to the door, Kanji," said Charita swiftly, as he started down the hall. She disregarded Brad's call.

"Charita! I want you!"

Kanji looked back nervously. Charita grimaced. "I will send the maid with tea and sandwiches," she said, and gave the maid swift directions.

Then she turned again to Kanji. "I must talk to you. Perhaps in the gardens."

"As you wish, Charita." Kanji was puzzled, but followed her through the French windows of the living room to the gardens. They were glorious that sunny June day. The azaleas were still in pink and white bloom. The iris were radiant in purple and gold and creamy white. And the few rose bushes she had been able to coax to life were beginning to bloom, one yellow tea rose of exquisite shape. She paused to linger over that, with appreciation.

Kanji commented politely on the garden. "How beautiful is your magnificent garden, Charita. It gives peace of mind and food to the soul."

"I thank you. Please sit down here." They sat down on the rustic bench overlooking the pond. Her hands clasped before her. Kanji studied her face for a moment, then looked politely toward the pond and the large golden fish that swam quickly through the clear waters, and in and out of the golden lotus flowers on their large green platelike leaves.

"You have some trouble on your mind, my sister?" he asked, when she seemed to have a problem in starting to speak.

"And you also," she tried to smile, thinking of all the work Brad had given to him.

His face shadowed. She was accustomed to his face, she knew the shadows of his moods. He was a good-hearted, kind man, he had treated her with the gentleness of a kind elder brother since she had gone to them at the age of three, a bewildered small girl whose life had been shattered for her. She remembered how he had patted her on the head—the elder boy of eleven in his schoolboy uniform, seeming so much bigger—and said to her, "My parents shall be your parents. And no harm shall come to you! I am your brother now. And what a pretty little sister I have!"

"I am in deep puzzlement," he admitted slowly, gazing at the pond. "I am torn with my desires. I am bitter to confess I feel I know nothing about the woman I wish to marry."

229

She caught her breath. The woman he wished to marry? Who was that?

"Your parents—they have contracted—" she began delicately.

To her amazement, he nodded. "Yes, many years ago. I think you do not know that the honorable parents of Pearl Takahashi, not having a son, were eager to contract the marriage between us when we were yet small. It was done. Now, Pearl does not wish to regard the contract."

Charita put her hand to her heart. She had not felt so shocked for months, not since her father's death. Pearl—and Kanji—engaged? Betrothed for many years?

"I did—not—know this," she managed in a carefully neutral tone. Pearl and Kanji?

"Yes, it is true. In the early years, I did not see her but on the occasion of the signing of the contracts. Now, I have come to know her, we work together, we see each other. I thought with delight that this lovely girl would be my wife when I could afford to marry. Livingston-san has been extremely generous to this unworthy assistant. Now I can afford to marry—Pearl will not even allow the parents to purchase kimonos and obis and marriage chests of sandalwood." His head drooped in his shame.

Charita could feel her heart pounding in her chest. Her mind was in a dizzy whirl. Pearl, Brad's mistress, refusing to set a marriage date—

"What reasons does she give?" she managed to ask.

"I am frank with you on secret matters, because you are my little sister, and now you too are married," he said quietly. His face was flushed with embarrassment. He looked away from her toward the trees that sheltered the side of the garden. "Her father is most cruel to her mother. He beats her. He was accustomed to beating Pearl while she lived at home. This is why she left home, why she refuses to marry me. She asked me for a solemn promise that I would never beat her. I would never wish to do so, but how can I make solemn promise? It is to take my manhood from me! She is a liberated woman, she says. She will not marry without such assurance. She is bitter toward men, and she despises marriage."

Charita could scarcely get her breath at the confidences that tumbled from Kanji. She could understand why he did not confide in his parents, why he was deeply troubled. But one thing he had said stuck disagreeably in her consciousness.

"Kanji—why cannot you promise not to beat her? You would never beat a woman, not your wife, would you?" she asked softly.

He did not turn, his mouth set obstinately. "I would not wish to do so, but if she provoked me, or defied me, I might have to do so! Then she would accuse me of breaking my solemn word! You see? She would take my honor from me!"

Charita turned slightly from him, gazing also at the pool. That Kanji, her kindly, understanding brother, should say this! Was this how men felt? That they have all rights to a woman's body in bed, and could also feel free to beat her as well? She drew a shaky breath, remembering the first night Brad had held her in bed, her fear and the pain — He was usually gentle now, but sometimes she stiffened in anticipation of the pain—and he could beat her if he chose! It was a shocking thought. Her parents had never struck her even in anger, or in punishment. Always they had reasoned with her, cautioned her with gentleness.

"I do not know what to do, Charita," Kanji said. "I do not know to whom I can confide, who will advise me. I have had a frank talk with Pearl. She utterly refuses to consider marriage. She will not even be engaged to me publicly. Yet the contracts were signed!"

"What does she say of this?"

"She says that if the contracts were burned, her father would beat her mother severely, and she would be most unhappy. So my hands are tied. I can neither burn the contracts, nor force Pearl to let me announce our engagement, much less our wedding date! I am twenty-six, now, and I earn good money. Why cannot I marry and have a son? I would be so proud to be a father!"

She heard the pain in his voice and wanted to console him. Her hand half-moved toward his arm, then dropped to her lap. He wanted a son! He said nothing of loving Pearl! Was this all marriage meant to a man? And he said he would beat Pearl, should she disobey him!

Kanji finally stopped speaking, and took a deep breath. Then he said wearily, formally, "Forgive my miserable speech to you, Charita. You have problems of your own, and your husband has your loyalty. You have much trouble about his illness, and I have bothered you with my poor little problems."

She said quickly, "I am honored by your confidence, and shall not speak of it to anyone. I do not know what to advise, I am so poor in wisdom I cannot say anything. Only know that you have my best wishes for your future marriage and happiness."

Kanji stood and began to bow to her in the preliminaries of farewell. Impulsively she held out her hand to him, not touching him, but preventing him from going.

"If you will, Kanji, there is a matter of importance concerning the business and my honored husband."

Immediately Kanji was alert. He sat down again, and looked at her expectantly. "Pray tell me, you know I will listen with much attention to your words."

Charita put her hand to her face to gather her thoughts. Then she started at the beginning, the story of the two men on the same plane from Hokkaido, what they had said about the gold formula. Then she had seen them again in Hakone. Kanji listened, his face growing stern, understanding more than she said.

"They came again, and were in the garden? And

232

Livingston-san told them that only he had the formula?"

She nodded, and described the men. "And now the two men who attacked him match this description, Kanji. I think they followed him and lay in wait for him in that dark street."

She told of her suspicions, of what the Japanese policeman had reported to her of their manner of speech, their dress. "They were rough, and they did not speak in the Kyoto colloquial."

Kanji's usually calm face was expressive of his deep concern. "But this is dreadful! This cannot be tolerated. The men must be captured and arrested!"

"I think so also. But our descriptions might not be sufficient for this." Charita sighed. "It is such a relief to tell you, Kanji. Brad makes light of this, I think, for my sake, so I will not worry. Does he take enough precautions? I think the chauffeur should be with him every day. Or perhaps a bodyguard to protect him."

"Hummm. I will see what I can manage." Kanji was frowning and disturbed, obviously agitated by the danger to his employer. "He is one strong man, yes, but what is one against two or more? With your permission, I will consult a man I know on the police force, a man with much experience in these matters. Yes? Then perhaps I may with tact approach the matter with Livingston-san."

"It would be very good of you. I am most grateful." She felt relief at having confided in Kanji. He was intelligent and sensible. She stood when he did, they bowed to each other. Gently he touched her arm, then his hand fell to his side.

"Your worries are mine, dear sister," he said. "I will do whatever I can to help you."

"You are always and ever so very good to your humble and stupid sister," she said, in the conventional manner, but with deep gratitude. She saw him to the car, then went back into the house.

The maid stood waiting for her, hands folded in patient resignation, but reproach on her face. "The master-san waits you in his room, mistress-san," she said, glancing at the clock in the hallway. "It is two hours that you have been in the garden with your guest, if you forgive me."

"Two hours? Oh, my—" She went back to Brad's room, ready to give him some explanation, though she could not confide in him Kanji's trouble.

Brad was sitting at the side of the bed, the scowl on his face telling of rising temper. "Where have you been all this time? In the garden with your Kanji?" he snarled, so angrily that she was shocked.

"I did not realize it was so long. Pray forgive me," she said hurriedly. "We had much of which to speak—"

"And the time sped past! I looked out the window, and you were talking and talking! Whatever did you have to talk about? Tell me!" His voice was rising in anger. She shut the door hastily and approached the bed.

"Brad, I am very sorry to leave you so long. I cannot tell you all of which we spoke, it was in confidence—"

His face flushed with rage. "In confidence! What do you have to talk about in confidence with him? By God, Charita, you do try my patience!"

She wanted to snap that he was not overly endowed with the quality of patience, but a look at his thunderous expression quelled her flippancy.

"I do beg your pardon most earnestly," she began, her hands clutching each other. "It is most remiss of me, I should have come to make sure you were comfortable—"

Her pretty speech was interrupted as he yanked at her arm, and brought her down to sit on the bed beside him. "I don't give a damn for excuses! What were you talking about with him?"

Her blues eyes shone with reproach. "I have not seen him for several days, Brad, we had much to discuss. I wished to tell him—"

"I forbid you to confide in anybody but me!" he snarled, so hatefully that she stared at him, eyes shocked. With her mind full of Kanji's story of his refusal not to beat Pearl! And the menace to Brad of men beating him up— She could not think straight. It seemed that violence swirled about her, there was no escaping it in this ugly world. She shrank from his hard grip on her arm, and it made him more angry.

"Please—you hurt my arm," she said, as his fingers closed like steel about her wrist.

"I want to hurt you!" he flared. "My God, Charita, you infuriate me without half trying! You belong to me, do you understand that? I won't have you sitting in gardens with other men, and meeting them secretly—"

His fingers were so tight, they seemed to cut off the blood. Her arm began to tingle and then go numb. She tried to pull away, he caught her other arm and pulled her around to face him. His breath was close to her face.

"You will *not* meet Kanji anywhere, do you understand me? I don't care what you talked about, you are not to confide in him! When you have secrets to confide, tell me!"

"But Brad, please—" She tried to wrench away from him, tears of pain stung her eyes. He did not know his own strength. "You do not listen to me—" she accused, biting her lips to keep back a cry of despair.

"You don't listen to me! I have told you I will be obeyed! You are my wife—and I am not so feeble that I cannot make sure you remember that—"

With that, he flung her down on the bed beside him, and pulled at her dress. "Brad, not," she pleaded, shocked. The maid could come in anytime, though the door was closed.

He paid no attention. His face was darkened, his eyes blazed with fury and desire. He had her dress up, the undergarments yanked down, and he pressed himself to

235

her. There were no tender touches, no gentle lovemaking first, nothing but his angry, greedy possession of her. He kissed her mouth brutally to silence her when she tried to protest. He seared his mouth on hers, stifling her cries. He held her arms overhead with one strong hand as he forced himself into her body. For a long moment, painfully long, he held her to him, his other hand pulling her thighs roughly to him.

Her body twisted and writhed, involuntarily trying to escape the pain of his entry into her. She tried to pull away, but he held her tightly with his superior strength. As tears streamed down her cheeks, his touch gentled, but he did not let her go.

Wildly, he kissed her mouth, her cheeks, her throat. His body tensed, and he plunged into her violently, taking her again and again for his own relentless satisfaction.

She turned her head back and forth on the pillows. In broad daylight, he was taking her like a servant; the sunlight revealed all of her body to Brad. There was no chance for modesty and shyness, no chance to conceal herself under a sheet. Shame mingled with her pain.

His touch finally softened, but too late for her to care. He finished, and drew out, and held her close to him. "My darling," he said, but it sounded like a mockery to her. "My love, don't shut me out. I adore you, I love you."

She could not answer. Her eyes were shut tight against him, her fists clenched tightly by her stiff sides.

She was remembering what Kanji had said of Pearl. He would not give her his word that he would never beat her! Gentle Kanji! And Brad had made no such promise to Charita. Why should he? He had taken her, married her, and she was his damned possession.

Mistaking her silence for surrender, Brad was kissing her again, his arm across her body, his hand caressing her arm and waist and thigh. His kisses wandered over her throat, down over her breasts. The dress was torn off her body, and flung to the floor, her undergarments were in shreds. His fury had done that. But more—he had taken her with no more thought and care than he would have a—a prostitute, a woman of pleasure, she thought bitterly.

Yes, and he had paid for her. With the clothes he tore, with the jewels he put on her throat and about her wrists, with the house about her, with possessions that were empty to her, for they had not one-hundredth the tenderness with them that her foster parents had heaped on her for years.

Brad lay back, satisfied, falling asleep from sheer weariness. He had been violent too soon, shaking his weakened body. When she was sure he was asleep, she slid from under his loosened arm and moved to put her feet on the floor. She kept watching him, as warily as a frightened animal escaping a trap.

He did not wake. She crept away, gathering the shreds of the clothes about herself, picking up her sandals. Tears burned her eyes. She escaped to her bedroom, and locked the door. She took a long cool shower, then put on a loose robe. Her whole body was bruised, she saw the dark bruises coming out on her fair skin. Brad had done this to her, in the name of "love" and marriage.

A maid tapped on the door. "Mistress-san, your dinner, it is all ready!" she sang out.

"I wish no dinner," said Charita, and the maid finally went away.

Charita stood in the loose robe, looking out at the garden which had given her so much pleasure. She could endure no more. Her mind was so confused, she ached from head to toe. She could not go on like this. She had married him, she had been grateful to him for his care—

But he could not treat her like this! She thought of her gentle foster mother, the bright smile of welcome, the tender anxiety of her foster father. She had never known cruelty before. Death, yes, and grief. But not cruelty and pain like this.

She thought of Pearl, and sympathized with her. No, if she had it to do over, she would not marry Brad! Marriage *was* hateful!

He had shamed her, he had humiliated her. All the maids would know what he had done when they saw the shreds of her torn clothes, the state of the bed. She put her face in her hands but could not weep.

She must make up her mind, she must leave him. No woman had to suffer this. She would find some way to earn her living. Brad could have his mistresses! All he chose! And take out his anger on them! Let him pay them with jewels and bright-colored garments!

All of a sudden, in the midst of her fury, she thought of those sweet nights and happy days in Hakone. How different it had been there! How kind he had been. How he had made her feel desire and deep emotions!

But those days were gone. She could not live like this, and she would not. Charita's gentle mouth firmed with her thoughts, and her dulled blue eyes gazed out at the dusk forming in the garden in purple shadows. She had to go, that was all she could do.

16

Brad woke in the night and lay awake for a time. He missed Charita at his side and wondered if she had gone to her own bedroom. She must have, perhaps she was very weary from nursing him.

He was thirsty, and longed for hot tea and her soothing presence. He finally managed to get to the bathroom, and drank a long cool drink of water. He got back into bed, muttered at the mussed bedclothes, and stared out at the darkness until he slept again.

He woke again at dawn, and lay listening to the soft calls of the birds, rejoicing in the dew and the nectar from the flowers. It was so peaceful, so quiet here, he felt soothed.

He noted the time passing, an hour went by, and another. The maids were padding softly about the house, their feet in thick socks making little sound. He was getting hungry.

Finally Charita came in, looked at the bed to be sure he was awake. He smiled to see her lovely solemn doll-like prettiness, so charming in the dark blue kimono.

"Good morning, darling. I hope you slept well." He looked eagerly at her, patted the side of the bed. "Come and talk to me."

She did not move from the doorway, her hands were

folded in the wide sleeves. "I will see to your breakfast," she said, seriously. "What do you wish to eat?"

"Steak, potatoes," he joked.

She did not smile, she bowed her head briefly. "I will prepare eggs and bacon and rice. We do not have potatoes."

She disappeared before he could say he was teasing. He sighed impatiently. Every time he thought he was getting through to her, and they understood each other, she seemed to retreat into the foreign Oriental world he could not comprehend.

She returned presently. "The maids are preparing the breakfast. You wish to rise and wash first?"

She helped him to the bathroom, ran the tub, helped him into it with little shyness. At least they had passed that stage, he thought, wincing as the water touched his wounds and bruises. But it felt great, and he soaked in the hot tub for some fifteen minutes. He got out, with an effort, and toweled himself dry. Charita had laid out fresh pajamas. He eyed them with distaste.

"Charita, I'd like some underclothes, my gray trousers and shirt," he called from the bathroom.

He expected an argument. Instead she obediently brought the clothes to him, and disappeared again.

He felt stronger, eager to start work again. He fumed that Charita must be in one of her detached moods again. He wanted her to share his pleasure in becoming well once more. What the devil was wrong with her now?

He dressed, then went back to the bed and lay down. Charita was straightening the bedroom, drawing back the draperies to let in the late June sunlight. He saw the gardens, where she and Kanji had talked so long, and his face darkened again. She was too damn close to Kanji.

He had been suspicious of their closeness before, but had forgotten it. After all, they were not really brother and sister. But neither were he and Jacinda, and Jacinda had made advances to him, had begged him to take her. Brad's fist clenched. He had not suspected that his stepsister felt that way toward him. It must have been a temporary insanity brought on over her worries about Miles. It must have been. She could not believe that Brad would be interested in her that way. Why, he would as soon seduce a real sister!

Yet Jacinda had seemed serious. She had held his knees, begged him. She had clung to him, pressing herself against him. He felt acute embarrassment again at the memories. He must put them out of his mind, or he would find it difficult to see her again.

The maid brought his breakfast as he was thinking darkly that Kanji might feel the same about Charita, as Jacinda had seemed to feel about Brad. After all, they were not really related. Kanji was a good worker, a fine man, but he was not immune to the appeal of the senses, and Charita was a very lovely girl.

He ate slowly, silently, thinking. He knew he could get very jealous, he was a very possessive man. He didn't want Charita even to look at another man, that was impossible in his world. He must control himself, he thought. But it wouldn't hurt to keep Kanji away from her!

He finally noticed that Charita had said little that morning. The room was straightened, in neat order. She was very precise about everything, all must be in order. Even his hairbrushes stood exactly in line on the oak chest. Now she was moving to the door, her feet soundless on the thick rug.

"Charita?"

She turned, her face somber, her dark eyes not meeting his. He noted the bruised look about her eyes, as though she had not slept much.

"What is wrong, darling?" he asked anxiously.

"I must speak with you today," she said quietly, after

241

a slight hesitation, and again her small hands were hidden inside the sleeves of the kimono.

He looked her over, feeling pain at the thought of her reserve from him. They had been married almost three months, yet deep parts of her were still hidden from him. They were not as close as he had hoped they would be.

"Yes, of course." He moved abruptly on the bed, the tray slipped. Charita moved forward gracefully, rescued the empty tray, and picked it up.

"I will take this to the kitchen. Then we will talk," she said, so definitely, he was startled all over again.

"Very well. I think I'll go into the drawing room. I'm tired of this room." He tried to make her smile, she did not even seem to hear the undertone of humor. She nodded and left the room.

He managed to get to the living room, and sank down onto the couch. He stuffed a pillow behind him; he felt frail as an invalid, he thought, in irritation. He was rarely ill, and when he was laid up he felt definitely abused. He was a tough man, why couldn't he take a little beating up?

Still, he was improving. He could go back to work soon. He felt better for having dressed, it made him feel more alert. He waited impatiently for Charita to return. What the hell could be on her mind?

Charita came back into the room silently, saw where he was, and carefully took a straight-backed chair across from him where she sat with her kimono about her, her feet planted side by side in their little white socks, and her hands folded placidly in her lap.

Brad lay back, eyeing her warily. She looked cool and stubborn. "What's on your mind, darling?" he asked.

She took a deep breath, he saw the tremble of her body as she controlled herself. "I must leave you, Brad. You are almost well now, the servants will take care of you."

He shot up straight, ignoring the sudden pain in his

242

ribs. "Leave me? Hell, no," he snapped. "What the devil are you talking about?"

"Your cruelty to me," she said simply. "I cannot endure it any longer. Last night, in your anger you forced me to accept you . . . I am bruised all over—" Her head drooped in her shame, and the delicate color came to her face.

The memory of the late afternoon came back to him: her passiveness when he wanted her so badly, so desperately that he had pulled and tugged to get her closer, and yet closer.

"Oh, Charita, I may have been a bit over-eager," he admitted. "But you know what marriage is like—and you had angered me! Lingering with Kanji in the garden. I saw you talking to him. You had your hand on your heart—what did you talk about?" he added sharply.

She shook her dark head, and the pageboy softness made her look like a sad little cherub. "That does not matter now. I shall return to my parents and live there. I have decided. You may obtain the divorce."

He wanted to laugh, he wanted to snarl his fury. Instead, he lay back and contemplated her solemn face. She was serious! Divorce! He would never divorce her! He would never let her go! She was the sweetest, loveliest girl in the world, she was the only softness in his hard, tough life, and he would not release her.

"And what would you do then?" he asked.

"Work in the radio factory," she said, as though she had thought it all out.

"And marry a Japanese? You aren't Japanese, you are an American."

"I will not marry again. I will not tolerate this again." She did not raise her voice, her hands were quiet in her lap, her tone was strong.

He dropped that line of thought. "Charita, I need you,

I love you. Was I very rough last night? Then I am sorry—"

"You are always sorry when you hurt. Then you hurt again. It is the way of men," she told him, still she held that even tone.

"You sound like one of those American women's libbers," he tried to joke.

"I can now understand them," she said. "Why should they marry and endure cruelty and blows, when they can support themselves? Why be the pawn of some man, when a woman is able to live alone and do as she wishes?"

He eyed her uneasily. "Let's get down to facts," he said, practically. "You said blows and cruelty. What blows? What cruelty have I done to you?"

"No blows. But cruelty, yes. The first night, when you —you—took my body, it hurt very much."

"Darling, it usually does hurt," he said gently. "But since then—"

"Since then, it is according to your mood." Color was high in her cheeks, her blue eyes were distressed, but she persisted. "Sometimes you are kind—as in Hakone. Other times, like yesterday, it is what you will. I am bruised all over today, and my arms ache, and my—legs."

"Bruised?" he asked incredulously. "I just did—show me, Charita."

She hesitated, then slowly rolled up the sleeve on her right arm. Mutely she held it out.

"I—did that?"

Brad stared at the purple-green bruises and was sickened.

She nodded. "I tried to stop you. I told you—you hurt me. My wrist, look." She indicated where the fingerprints were clear on her wrist, in purple marks.

He swallowed. "I'm sorry, Charita. I had no idea of what I was doing. Forgive me—I'm horribly sorry."

"It is the way men are," she said, nodding wisely,

looking like some adorable doll he longed to sweep up into his arms. "You hurt, then you are sorry; but the pain lingers. No, I cannot remain. I am sorry also, Brad. I should never have married you. I was bewildered and dazed at the death of my father, or I would not have agreed to do this. I was wrong to marry you."

This was worse than he could ever have imagined. "It was not wrong, love," he tried to keep his voice even and rational. "It was the right thing to do. You needed a husband and protection, I loved you already and wanted to take care of you all my life. So we married, and we have been happy, haven't we?"

She shook her head. He felt hollow inside. She was usually so gentle and agreeable that he felt he was coming up against someone he had never known.

"No. There has been some joy but much sorrow," she said. "It was wrong to marry, knowing so little of each other. I should have returned to my foster parents and gone to work."

"In a radio factory?" he snapped. "All your talents gone to waste? And what kind of men would you have met there?"

"It would not have mattered. I shall not marry."

"You have married. You are my wife, and shall remain so!"

"No. I shall leave you today. I remained only to inform you of my intentions, so you would not worry when I departed."

"You will not leave me!" he snapped, thoroughly frightened now. "You are my wife, and you will remain."

"No. You do not respect and honor me. You do not value me. I am a new possession. You tire quickly of your possessions, I think."

"Tire of my possessions? That is idiotic, ridiculous. I have had some of my paintings and vases for a dozen years!"

He quickly changed the subject as he realized it would not do to compare Charita with a vase!

Charita's fingers circled her wrist, he knew she thought of the pain.

"Charita, love, I am truly sorry I hurt you. I don't know my own strength, and you are so soft and fragile—I am sorry. Can't you forgive me? I will try never to hurt you again."

She looked down at her feet, her face twisted in anguish, before it smoothed to control again. "I forgive you," she said, in muffled tones. "However, I cannot remain. You should marry someone—more of your own kind."

"You are my kind. You are who I wish to keep at my side all my life." He forced himself to get up off the couch, painful as his body was, and went over to her. "Charita, think carefully. We were so happy in Hakone. Could it not be that way again? I will try very hard to make you happy in that way again, and consider how to please you." He dared to put his hand on her soft thick hair, and stroke it back from her hot cheeks.

"I do not like marriage. I wish to leave you and become single again," she repeated obstinately.

He wanted to shake sense into her, but he forced himself to remain calm. This was what had terrified her before, his quick temper and unthinking force.

"Please give me time, Charita. I wish to think over what you have said. Do not leave today. Let me think about the matter, and try to consider all sides."

He was so upset he could not think clearly and he didn't want to scare her into running away. Finally, reluctantly she assented and stood up, moving away from him.

"I will remain today," she said flatly, and left the room. He went back to the couch and collapsed on it.

He felt his world had turned upside down. As though a tiger had evolved from a cuddly kitten! She was so determined and obstinate! He must think quickly and figure out what to do. He knew only that he would not let her go! He didn't want to scare her to death, or make her a prisoner in his home. What to do?

He lay and thought about it. He remembered her words, that she had little to do, that she was accustomed to working. He had let it go for the time, thinking she would take up hobbies, she could sketch, paint, work in the garden sometimes.

But that had not worked. She must have a more challenging occupation. His eyes narrowed thoughtfully. Work. Maybe that was the answer. Yet he didn't want her anywhere near the factory, going back and forth every day. It was too dangerous, with men around like those who had attacked him.

After a restless evening, and a somewhat wakeful night, Brad had evolved a plan. A particular letter Kanji had brought to him helped him make up his mind.

He dressed slowly, rather unusual for him. He was early, Charita had slept in the other room. He waited for her in the drawing room. The maid came in with his breakfast, but still Charita had not come.

"Is she awake?" he finally asked. He would have gone to find her, but feared she would take it amiss. Still—what if she had stolen away in the night?

"She wakes, I took tea to her," the maid beamed and bobbed.

"Good. Ask her to have breakfast with me here."

"Yes, master-san."

He did not mind when she bowed several times. He gave a grim smile. Maybe he was accustomed now to the over-politeness all around him. He sighed. Japan was different from America, that was sure. Yet human beings were not so different, after all. Charita had begun to resent his domination of her. Beneath the docile exterior must have

247

burned some rebellion. Well—he adored her, they would work things out. They had to.

Charita came in, wearing a pale rose kimono with a silver obi. Her hair was done in the Oriental style.

"You have slept well?" she inquired politely, sitting down opposite him.

"No, not well Charita. I was up thinking much of the night," he said bluntly.

"You should sleep! The doctor will be angry," she reproached.

At least she cared what happened to him, he thought glumly as he eyed her carefully over his coffee cup. The maid brought rice and tea, with some raw fish for Charita. He concealed his shudder over this idea of breakfast.

The maid took the trays away, and Brad sat up, putting his feet on the floor. "There are two matters I wish to discuss with you."

"Yes, sir?"

He flinched from that "sir."

"In the first place, I am most heartily sorry I have hurt you. I forget my strength. It was not my intention to harm you. Are the bruises better today?"

"They are better, I thank you." He knew he had not penetrated her defenses. The dark blue eyes looked down at the ground.

"Good. In the future, I hope you will tell me when I am too rough with you," he said gently. "I do not wish *ever* to hurt you. Sometimes my desires are too strong, and I am too quick. I hope in the future I will do much better."

Her head came up quickly. Her delicate mouth opened to speak. He went on swiftly. He did not want her to say again that she was going to leave him! His temper might turn loose!

"The second matter is this: I realize what you have said is true, that the maids are most efficient and leave you

248

little to do. However, I have too much to do. If you would aid me, it would be beneficial to us both," he concluded formally.

"How can I aid you?" Her smooth forehead crinkled in puzzlement. "You have many workers, and you have said Kanji is most helpful."

"Yes, he is." Brad sternly stifled his jealousy of Kanji. That must wait! When Charita had spoken of leaving him, she had said nothing of going to Kanji, nor did he seem to figure in her plans. Maybe the affection she held for him was only sisterly. "You see, I have entire charge of creating the designs in the factory. The orders are pouring in far too quickly for my pearly gold designs."

Her eyes were on him, her expression puzzled and wary. "I know nothing of jewelry design."

"No," he agreed calmly. "It takes time to learn this. However, I have received a commission, involving a great deal of money, which I do not have time to personally create. The same Arab oil prince who commissioned me to make jewelry for his marriage has requested something I do not have time to do. I think it is something you could design."

"I? I have never done anything like that," Charita objected spiritedly. Yet Brad noted that her blue eyes were beginning to sparkle.

He laid out the letter before him, couched in very formal English, and scanned the typed lines. "The prince wishes an elaborate Japanese screen, using my special finish. He wishes a design in the old traditional manner, yet of modern materials, something unique for his palace. As you can imagine, the palace is old and full of many valuable antiques, marble statues, oil paintings, mosaic tables. I would love to do such a screen, but I have no time."

He glanced up at her with seeming casualness. Her

eyes were blazing with excitement. Her slim hands clasped together tightly.

"You think I could create something which would please him?"

"I think so," said Brad. "You see, you are familiar with the traditional art. Yet your own designs and paintings are unique. Remember the sketch you did of Mount Fuji in the flat pattern, with the meadows and lake? I thought that might be one idea to try. You would start with a small sketch, stylized, then if it works, you would sketch it out full size on transparent papers. That could be transferred by one of our workmen to a full-size design in gold, set against a carved wood screen, perhaps of mahogany, if I can get hold of some. Just the stark gold against the mahogany."

"Oh, I do not know if I could do such a thing." But her face shone with the desire to try it, and Brad felt keen relief. "I would go to the factory with you?"

"No," he said decisively. "The factory is too noisy and full of people coming and going. The telephones ring nonstop. You would work here at home, in the workroom. I'll help you all I can, but it will be your design entirely. Think about it, imagine all kinds of designs that are typically Japanese—"

"Mount Fuji," she breathed. "A heron in the water. A torii. A pine bending to the wind. Chrysanthemums." She looked eagerly for his approval.

"Splendid! Take your time, work it out. We'll consider various designs. He wants—" Brad consulted the letter again, then handed it to her. "A six- or eight-panel screen, very splendid, about eight to ten feet tall. It is a huge project, Charita, and worth a great deal. With a commission like that successfully fulfilled, we could begin branching out into designing screens, wall paintings, porcelain flower designs."

Her face shadowed. "I do not know if I can do this —" she hesitated. "Maybe I would disappoint you."

Brad was firm and optimistic. "I am sure you can do it splendidly. I don't know anyone else who could. If you don't, I'll have to turn it down, and the Arab prince will be angry with me. They don't like to be turned down," he laughed.

She looked down at the letter, reading it soberly. He studied her round face eagerly. Would this be enough to hold her for a time, until he could convince her that he was able to treat her as she wished? It *had* to be! He would tie her to the bedpost if he had to! But he would make her stay, any way he could.

When she finally looked up and nodded reluctantly, Brad was so relieved he felt dizzy. "Yes, I will try it. I hope I will not disappoint you."

"You won't, honey. Take your time, think about it, try small sketches first. We'll go over them when you finish some." He swung his feet up, and lay back with a sigh. His head ached with the effort, his pounding blood brought on a tenseness in his shoulders.

Charita came over to him and adjusted the pillows, her face anxious and her hands gentle. "Should you not go back to bed, Brad?" she murmured.

"No, I'll get some sleep for a time. Has Kanji telephoned yet?"

"I believe not."

"When he calls, tell him to come over, and bring Pearl to take some dictation. I want the most urgent letters, tell him."

"Yes, Brad."

She padded softly away, and he closed his eyes. He gradually relaxed in the cushions, feeling how tense he had been with the effort.

Now that he had succeeded in making her stay—for a time!—he realized how terrified he had been that she

251

would walk out. He needed her, desperately. She was the one person in his life who made him feel needed and useful. How she had clung to him when her father had died, turning to him trustfully for advice.

He wanted her like that again, yet it was inevitable that Charita would mature. He didn't really want her to remain the doll-child she had been. She would always be that girl to him, but she was obviously starting to feel like a woman. Maybe that was good, he thought, his eyes closed against the bright sunlight. After all, hadn't he initiated her?

One day, she would want a child, and he wanted also to begin a family, to have a son, a daughter. The thought of Charita with a small baby in her arms brought a tender smile to his lips. She would be such a careful, loving mother.

They would have the home he had wanted without knowing he wanted it, a refuge from the tough world of business in which he had to fight to exist. A place where he could shed the hard image he maintained before the world, a place where he could lay his head down and be at peace.

Peace, calm, quiet. A trio of qualities he had always scorned. Yet, these days they looked good to him. He realized that Charita kept the house quiet and serene. Things were always in order, the maids giggled or were silent. He would hear a song in the kitchen, but no quarreling or screaming.

He felt he had changed since his marriage. He no longer wanted to pile fortune on fortune. How much did a man need?

He wanted to work, not for the money, but for the love of the designs, and to keep Charita happy with what he could give her. Yet she never asked for clothes or jewelry, and seemed overwhelmed by what he did give her.

Brad thought he was a fortunate man. He had found Charita, a loving, giving person, and he meant to keep her. She meant his life to him now, she was the love he hungered for without knowing he was hungry. He flinched again as the thought of the bruises on her soft arm returned to him. That he could have hurt her!

He must be more careful with her. She was soft of flesh, easily bruised, easily hurt, though she had concealed it from him for a time. He must be as careful of her heart as of her body. She wanted to be needed, to be useful. She would never be satisfied to be a decorative object in his drawing room, an object of passion in his bedroom.

Charita had more depth than that, and he was glad of it. They must come to more understanding. He would draw her out to tell him her thoughts, her memories of the past. He wanted to know all about her, and how she felt about everything.

They must grow closer, he resolved. His campaign of getting to know her would start at once. When he thought of how close he had come to losing her completely, he felt cold chills down his spine.

Charita padded back into the room, breaking into his reverie. "Kanji will come within the hour with Pearl and the important mail. Do you wish anything now?"

He held out his hand. "We have an hour, then, my love. Let's talk." She sat on the floor beside him, and took his hand in hers. It was a beginning, Brad felt, it was enough.

17

Brad seemed to have changed since he had been attacked. They talked more. In the evenings, Brad stayed at home, his injuries still bothered him. He would go to the factory for a couple of hours, take care of the most urgent matters, then the chauffeur and the bodyguard would drive him home again.

Charita was glad he had a bodyguard, but the presence of the silent burly Japanese man disturbed her. It meant that Brad was always in danger.

Charita had begun work on the designs for the screens in the workroom at the back of the house where the north light was good, and the windows wide and without draperies. She had made a number of random sketches. She would study them, then go over them with Brad.

They would work together sometimes in his study, he at his desk and she at the large table, and from time to time would compare sketches. He was working on a jewelry commission for an exclusive Parisian jeweler.

"This is much better than the office," he decided contentedly one morning. "I was always being interrupted at the factory. I felt I had to be on top of every problem. Now Kanji takes care of immediate problems, and saves the rough stuff for me. What a relief to be able to concentrate!"

"I am glad of that," she said shyly, smiling across at him. She bent her smooth dark head over the sketches again.

"What forms do you like best, Charita? Flowers—birds?"

She tapped the end of the drawing pencil against her lips, frowning in thought. "Flowers—yes. Roses, lotus petals. But also butterflies. The shape of seashells."

"Seashells," he repeated, staring absently at her.

"The shape of a pine in the wind. A deer with delicate horns, like at Nara. But most of all I like forms of circles, which come back to the beginning again and again, never-ending."

"Circles, shells," he muttered. She heard him still talking to himself as she bent again to her work. The scratch of his pencil was dear to her as she worked. She enjoyed being able to stimulate his mind. They did not talk much as they worked, that came later as they compared sketches. But she was always conscious of his presence near her.

As they stopped for lunch, he carried some sketches with him. At the dining table, he laid them beside her. "Look through those, darling," he said, his dark face bright with eagerness. His brown eyes shone with pleasure in creation.

She picked up the pages, caught her breath as she studied one after another. Delicately, he had sketched a seashell, evolved it into a pendant, into earrings. Circles of shells, circles of golden abstract shapes, a bracelet with a seahorse design around and around it.

She sparkled at him. "This is most beautiful! I like them all. How will you decide which to do?"

He laughed, and flung out his hands in abandon, stretching to ease the tightness of his back caused by sitting for so long. "I may use them all. I can never get enough ideas. All of these will work—in gold, I think. I have wearied of the flowers, I needed something fresh. This is it, I think. Sea creatures! Have you seen pictures of the sea anemone?"

She shook her head, and rescued the sketches hastily as the maid brought in asparagus soup for their lunch. She placed them carefully between herself and Brad. "No, I have not seen them."

Brad tasted the soup, it was hot and delicious. Charita was glad his appetite had returned. "I think I'll see if the bookstores have some good books on shells," he mused. "I could go into town this afternoon—"

"Or send Kanji or Pearl," she suggested hastily. She grew cold when she thought of the dangers he ran into when he went out of the house. Here he could be protected. Whenever he went out, she worried.

He smiled at her, understanding her intent, and touched her hand. "I'll be careful," he promised. "How did you get along this morning?"

"I have several sketches completed. We could consider them this evening. I have not had the idea for the completed design just yet, nothing seems to match for the six or eight screens."

Brad came home early that evening, with half a dozen books piled in his arms. The maid hastily took them from him and placed them reverently on a lacquer table in the living room. After dinner, he and Charita looked first at her sketches.

As he looked at them, he was the critic, not the lover. "Um. This one is too conventional," he said of a Mount Fuji sketch. "It has been done so many times, it is difficult not to make it look as it has been. Ah, I like this—" He held the sketch out at a distance, then closer to see the design.

She had sketched a mountain, any mountain, and on its crest was a single pine bent in the wind. The design was starkly simple.

"Yes, this is good. It might work for the center panel. And this—" He held it out, studied it for a time. His brown eyes shone in approval. A torii was set in the center, its ends upturned gaily. Beyond it was a curved bridge, going on into the distance. "This is typically Japanese, yet abstract at the same time. Great!"

She watched his reactions to the other designs. Often she could tell what he thought by the expression of his eyes, the length of time he took to study it. Finally he set three together.

"These three are workable," he said. "The torii and bridge, the mountain and pine, the outline of the Buddha. But how to tie them together?"

She bent over, then sat down abruptly on the floor, her face intent. She laid out the three sketches, the mountain in the center, the torii and bridge to the right, the Buddha to the left. She left spaces between.

"The Japanese like the irregular pattern of three, five, seven," she began. "Not like the American who prefers even numbers. Even guests at a dinner should be in irregular numbers. So, maybe—so—with patterns of lotus in a pond between them, or shells on a beach, or perhaps birds in the air—" She gestured to the empty spaces, her hands moving.

He looked down at the design for a long time, grappling with the problem. Then he nodded abruptly. "Yes, I think so. Let's consider five or seven panels. Work on that idea, and see what you come up with. Keep to the separate sketches, we'll tie them in later."

Brad looked very pleased and happy, and Charita felt contentment. She picked up the sketches and laid them on the table.

"Bring the book on shells, honey. Let's have a look at it."

She brought it over to the couch where he sat, and sat down beside him. They turned over the pages silently;

occasionally she would point to something, and they would study it carefully. His arm went around her shoulders. She tried not to stiffen, but she still felt constrained with him. She had not slept with him for almost a week, not since that terrible afternoon.

Sometimes she wondered if the art work was a ploy to ease her suspicions of him. She had said no more about leaving, but it was still in the back of her mind. She had always hated cruelty; the stories of beatings on the radio, or in the newspapers, or the ones of child abuse, and the ones of the torture of prisoners in Russia or Africa made her physically sick. She could scarcely endure them, and usually she read only the first paragraph and turned away.

She was aware that one needed to know of evil in the world in order to help combat it, to fight it. But she felt physically and mentally weak at the very idea of such cruelty.

Now she lived with a man who could be cruel to her! The bruises had not faded for several days, even now she still had the faint marks on her shoulders and arms, and on her legs. She dreaded sleeping with him again, though he had promised to be gentle. A man did not know how strong he was, she thought drearily.

"What are you thinking?" a voice came in her ear, quiet but imperiously demanding.

She sighed. "If one could only be a silkworm in a cocoon," she said. She thought he would not understand. His arm slid down about her waist, and he drew her against him.

"Some people find it possible to withdraw from the world," said Brad after a pause. He seemed to be considering his words very carefully. "Nuns in a convent, Buddhist priests in their temples, and so on. They seek seclusion in order to meditate and come closer to the God they worship. It is not easy. I knew a man once who tried to become a monk, but had to leave. The silence got to him, he said, he had to speak to people and relate to them, painful though it was."

She rested against him, her head down, so he could not see her face. Then he did understand somewhat, she thought.

"But you, my darling, are in this world, and so am I. We find cruelty and terror, beauty and joy, happiness and pain, all mixed up. Sometimes life seems terribly unfair. Well, nobody promised us it would be fair. It isn't."

"I know that. Only I find it difficult . . . to find where I belong." She finally admitted it aloud. "Once I thought it enough to live with my foster parents, and do as they wished for me. As long as I was obedient, and did as they wanted, I was happy and so were they. Now—I find all confusion—there is no pattern—"

She could not finish, she did not know her own mind. She had wanted to leave him, yet thinking ahead to the emptiness of her life after she left made her feel desolate. How would she feel, never again to feel his arm about her, his strength holding her, his kisses making her feel weak and strange?

"You belong with me," said Brad firmly, a little spark of anger in his tone. She stiffened, and he felt it, and calmed his voice. "You are mine, I am yours, and we are a family now. We belong together. Someday you will feel this as keenly as I do, Charita. You *must* feel it."

She could not answer him, and he bent and kissed her forehead, then tipped back her face to study her eyes. She met his gaze only for a moment, then looked away. The creases at the sides of his face deepened, he put his chin on her hair.

"Charita, honey," he said. "Don't think again of leaving me. I will not have it." His hand stroked coaxingly on her soft shoulders, down her back.

She felt suspicious of his coaxing, and his hand on her. What did he want from her? Complete obedience?

Probably! He was a man, and that was what a man wanted from a woman. No wonder Pearl, able to support herself, wanted to remain free.

Yet—yet—Charita felt secure in Brad's home, she had a place here. She was Someone, she was important to Brad, he said. Could she give up all that, to go back home and work on her own?

A telephone call came for Brad, he muttered a curse, and went out to take it. She curled up on the couch and studied the shell book and the butterfly book intently, trying to forget her problems. When he returned, they spoke of the sketches again, and his new commissions.

The next afternoon, the peace of their quiet home was abruptly shattered. Brad had gone to the factory, and Charita was about to retreat to the workroom, when a maid came to her. The maid's delicate hands fluttered in agitation.

"Mrs. Snow-san, she come to see Livingston-san, she very angry, she shouts at me!"

Jacinda had followed the girl, her high heels clicking loudly on the polished floors of the hallway. She stopped in the doorway, gazed about curiously.

"So this is what you do all day!" she snapped.

Charita rose from the chair, said with dignity, "I regret Brad is not here just now. He went to the factory."

"I was just there, he wasn't!" Jacinda's green eyes flared. "So where is he?"

Charita sighed. "You must have missed him, Mrs. Snow. He had lunch with me at one o'clock, rested for a short time, then left about two-thirty. You know, he is not yet quite recovered from the attack."

Emotion flitted briefly across the woman's face. "I know. I was worried about him. I haven't seen him, he has called me only twice. Is he really recovering?"

"Please come with me to the drawing room. I will order tea—or coffee," she added, as the woman scowled.

260

Jacinda reluctantly went with her to the drawing room. The maid bowed to them, and departed to prepare coffee.

Charita politely indicated a chair. Jacinda flung herself down, and crossed her lovely long legs. She took out her emerald green jade holder and fitted a cigarette into it with shaking hands. Her face looked weary and drawn, and whiter than Charita remembered.

Charita felt some compassion, and some anger. That she should have come chasing Brad, openly! The woman had no modesty, no sense of shame. It was an effort to be gracious to her.

"When will he come home?" Jacinda asked abruptly.

"I never know," Charita said honestly. "He comes when the work is finished, or he tires."

"About what time?" gritted Jacinda.

"Anytime from four to six, usually," Charita told her, her face polite and bland, seething inside.

"I'll wait!"

"And so will I!" came a voice from the doorway. Miles Snow, staggering and holding on to the doorframe, was standing there, his face flushed, his eyes glittering. The smell of liquor was striking in the quiet room.

Jacinda jumped up. "You followed me, damn you!" she raged.

"How else can I talk to you?" he shrugged, and stood right in her path as she tried to depart. He grabbed her arm, and his strength made her wince. Charita flinched for her, remembering the strength of Brad's grip.

The maid hovered in the doorway, in agitation, her kimono sleeves fluttering, her eyes wide.

"Another cup," said Charita, in despair. Her day was shattered. She had a horrible feeling they were going to quarrel before her, and reveal all the details of their relationship with each other—and with Brad.

"Not for me. Where's the drinks?" Miles looked

261

about, but fortunately the liquor cabinet was concealed, and Brad had locked it.

"You've had enough," said Jacinda. "And little Mrs. Brad here is busily working on her designs. We're intruding, in case you didn't know it! What are you working on, my dear?" She turned to Charita, her holder at a defiant angle.

"Merely some poor designs," said Charita, taking refuge in a Japanese style of language. "Nothing of importance."

"Brad says you're quite an artist! But of course he would be prejudiced." Her eyes were flaring with anger and jealousy. "You're just a child, you haven't had any training, have you?"

"Very little, I am sorry to say." The maid came quickly with the coffee and remained to pour for them. Charita's hands were shaking so hard she was afraid she would spill it.

"Don't take it out on her, she captured Brad, and you're furious," drawled Miles Snow, sprawled on the couch. He looked untidy, his white jacket flung open, his tie undone and his red face looked unhealthy, as though he might have a stroke.

"You have a filthy, nasty mind!" Jacinda flung at him. She drank the hot coffee in quick gulps. "You've always been jealous sick of Brad! You don't have half the guts he does, nor one-tenth the drive. You drink so you can say that's your excuse! You hide behind—"

"Please, please," said Charita, in distress. "You must not speak so to each other. Such terrible words leave marks which cannot be erased."

Miles and Jacinda stared at her, as though at some precocious child. "What the devil do you mean? I'll talk as I please!" said Jacinda furiously.

Miles absently picked up his coffee cup, drank, then made a face. "Are you sure there aren't any drinks around?" he asked plaintively. "Brad always keeps some Scotch. All right, sake?"

The maid moved at the word, Charita shook her head at her. She subsided.

"The coffee is good," said Charita quietly. "Please try the sandwiches, they will be delicious, I am sure. The cook is excellent, my husband chose him, and he was trained in a good hotel."

Miles made a face, then finally took a sandwich. Jacinda lay back in her chair, looking like an angry tigress, lacking only a swishing tail to remind Charita of a tiger she had seen in a cage. The green eyes flared with rage and suspicion.

"I suppose that's how you see keeping a man around," said Jacinda spitefully. "Keep him well fed, keep him happy in bed, and he'll stick around. Or do you keep him happy in bed? I can't imagine it! You're only a child, and he is an experienced man."

"You would know," said Miles thickly, laying down the sandwich. "Hanging around him, your tongue out. God, what a bitch! If I'd known what I know now—"

The maid was taking it all in. Charita gently dismissed her, and waited until the door closed after her.

"Now, you will gain nothing by flinging such remarks at each other," she said, in her mildest tones. "I think too much has been said. Words flung on the wind cannot be called back."

"Oh, don't start that with me!" sneered Jacinda. "We hate each other, that is the matter! I'm getting a divorce."

Miles put his hand to his face. Charita glanced away from him, biting her lips. She had been angry when he had come in, now she felt sorry for him.

"That is news to me," said Miles. "What will you claim? Infidelity of your own? You won't prove any on me! Nonsupport? I've supported you for six years in the extravagant way you love! We moved to Japan because

263

you wanted to. What grounds?" he sneered. "That you fell in love with your own brother?"

Charita hung on to her patience by sheer strength of will. They were confirming all she had feared, but it would not help for her to break down and scream also.

"Fell in love! I've always loved Brad! He was the most solid person in my life! How I could have married a weakling like you! You can't even hold your liquor! No, you have to go out drinking day and night—"

"You drove me to it! You egged me on, with your refusing me your bed! What did you want me to do, take up with Oriental women? Not on your life! Drink for me! Drown the sorrows!" He laughed hysterically at the distaste on her face.

"I don't have to listen to this. I'm going home—"

"Your home is with me! Don't tell me you like a flea-bag flat when you could be in that luxury one! You decorated it yourself—gold and silver, you said. Just like Brad's jewelry! Did you think he would see you as the prime gem of his collection? He was too smart. He got himself a wife who was innocent and pure and good— No used goods for him!" Miles was roaring with laughter, his face purple now.

"No more such talk," said Charita, raising her voice to be heard above their yelling. She was sick with their words. "Please! The fault is probably on both sides. Find fault with thyself rather than with others, it is said. Look within yourselves, to find the fault, mend it, and then you will be able to be at peace again."

"Peace, there's no peace for us." Miles stopped laughing, and stared somberly into his glass. "Only war. Huh, Jacinda? Only war. War. Fighting, yelling, bombs going off, legs and arms flying, blood spilling. War. That's all. No peace."

"War is right," said Jacinda, her mouth twisting. "It's been war from the first. Hate and war."

"No," said Miles. "You loved me at the first. You loved me. We made love night and day, wherever we were. You loved me. You said—you said I was everything to you. Family, home, love, security—what happened, then? What happened?"

The green eyes shifted, she stared unseeingly at the painting of iris behind Charita's head. Her mouth worked convulsively. She shook her head.

Loving and hating, hating and loving all at once. It was rather beyond Charita. She groped for wisdom, something to help them.

"Life is a long journey," she said gently. "The scenes change as one goes, yet the companions remain the same. Take the steps slowly and steadily, so you do not stumble. Hold up your companion, do not push him down. Life is difficult enough, our tragedies overwhelm us. There is enough trouble, without creating more."

Jacinda put her hand to her head distractedly. "Oh, don't talk, don't talk!" she cried. "It makes it worse. God, I shall go mad! What good is it? We are finished—"

"Only if you want it so," said Miles, leaning forward, his head in his hands. "It's up to you, isn't it? You walked out, you walked out before. But you always came back. You coming back now?"

"No, I am not," said Jacinda flatly. "I won't come back. I'm finished."

"So am I, then. Might as well hang myself," he said, and grinned unpleasantly. "Or is that an easy out for you?"

Charita put her hands to her ears. "That is very unlucky," she breathed. "You must not speak of death so lightly. He listens at every door!"

"How about some more coffee, honey? I'm thinking clearer than I have for a time," said Miles, and held out his cup.

Charita began to pour with unsteady hands. As the brown liquid flowed into the cup, and they were both intent on the cup and the ceremony, Jacinda dashed up and out the door, her handbag clutched in both hands. She was out before they realized it. Miles slammed down his cup and saucer, pulled himself from the couch. He was scarcely on his unsteady feet when they heard the car start. He went to the window, fumbled with the catch. It was locked, and he stared out the window as the green car raced down the graveled drive.

"She's gone," he said gloomily. "Damn it. And I don't know yet where she lives. Thought if I watched Brad's house, she would come here eventually. She did. But won't listen to me."

"Come back and drink your coffee," said Charita, feeling sympathy for his hangdog look. "And eat something more. That will help you."

"You're kind, you know it?" He came back and sank onto the couch again. He rubbed his hands over his face, the red had faded a little. She was shocked to see tears in his hazel eyes. He looked unkempt, he had cut himself when shaving, he sniffed like a child without a handkerchief.

He rubbed his hand over his nose, picked up the cup and drank heavily. He ate a sandwich.

"You know, I liked Oriental things when I saw them," he began finally. He wiped his eyes carefully with a handkerchief, stuck it away again. "I used to read Oriental poetry with Jacinda. She was different in those days, not so hard and callous. She liked it. You know, she used to call me the smartest man she knew?"

"I imagine she believed that, she seems a—a truthful woman," Charita managed to say.

He nodded. "Very—truthful. Says what she thinks, that is hard on a man. Likes to be flattered, told he is great. She stopped thinking I was great. Too many failures, too many. Can't take too many, you know it?

"I used to recite poetry to her. We sat on a beach

with our feet in the Caribbean Sea, and talked. I could recite reams of poetry then, by heart, all of it. Haiku. Well, I could make it up, right off, just like that. I wrote poems to her, she kept them. We were happy a long time, we really were."

She wondered what had happened. He rambled on, drinking coffee, eating as though starved. She had the maid bring more food, more coffee. He ambled to the bathroom, came back, and picked up the sentence just where he had left it, accurately. He had an amazing mind, she realized, as he went on and on.

He talked about Ming porcelain, told the differences between it and the other periods, went on to a story of an emperor in China and the legends of the dragon. He had a fantastic memory, once started in the tales, and could go on and on.

She glanced furtively at the clock. Four o'clock came, and four-thirty, and still Miles Snow went on, rambling, mingling stories of his life with Jacinda with fragments from his reading, his travels, history, sculpture, the Buddhist religion, theater, on and on.

She encouraged him with an occasional word. He did not seem so drunk as he had been, but he would not leave. What would Brad say when he came?

When she finally heard the car crunching on the gravel, she felt desperately relieved. Miles was sobering, Brad could handle him. Miles did not hear anything, absorbed in his own talk and an undemanding audience.

"Did you ever see a Nō play? Well, it goes on all day, and not much happens, but every movement is important, it is stylized and symbolic. You see, this actor—"

Brad entered the house, the maid was murmuring to him. Charita drew a great breath of relief, and turned with a polite smile as the door opened.

18

Brad's face was grim. The maid hovered curiously behind him. He handed her his portfolio, and she left the room, bowing low. The door closed after her.

"Well, this is a fine mess," snapped Brad. "What are you doing here? And drunk!" His tone was heavily accusing. He glanced at Charita, then back at Miles.

"He followed Mrs. Snow here to the house," said Charita, when Miles just grunted and leaned back in the big chair. "Mrs. Snow came to see you—us. Miles wished to see her and speak with her."

"Charita, you better go away and—"

"No, no, the little girl has heard it all spilled out," growled Miles, waving a big hand vaguely. "She talked sense to us. But you know us, Brad, we don't listen to sense. Never did. We know it all, the facts are all there. Facts matter, don't they? Only facts."

Brad sat down, gazing at Miles gravely. "Miles, you're letting alcohol ruin your life. What's the point of that? You had a good life with Jacinda, I thought you loved her. Now you're destroying everything."

Miles laughed abruptly, somehow a sad sound. He seemed more sober than when he had entered the house. "Do you think that is the whole problem, drinking? You're kidding. You know how Jacinda feels about you—"

Brad flushed deeply. Charita, watching, felt as though stabbed to the heart. He looked—self-conscious, embarrassed. "She had been like a sister to me," said Brad. "That is all, and you know it, Miles. She loves you. Remember when you were married, and she kept hanging on your arm? Damn it, I felt like an intruder when I came to your house after you had been married three months! You were still on an emotional honeymoon!"

He gazed anxiously at Miles. Miles, with the vacant grin on his red worn face. Miles, limply lying back in the chair, as though exhausted. Miles, looking a lot older than his years.

"Yeah," said Miles. "Yeah. The good ol' days."

"They could be the good new days," said Brad, with more patience than usual for him. "Jacinda loves you—"

"No, she hates me. Loves you."

Charita sucked in her breath in shock. Brad did not glance at her, his whole attention was on Miles. Charita folded her shaking hands together. The entire day was a nightmare!

"I represent a sort of security to Jacinda," said Brad, carefully choosing his words, it seemed to Charita. "We met at a bad time in her life. She was only sixteen, and her mother's divorce had shaken her up, shattered her world. To say nothing of the screaming and fighting that had been going on. I was enough older and on my own, that I could kid her out of the blues. We were friends. Always were, always will be."

To Charita's strained attention, he seemed to be trying to convince himself as well as Miles.

"That's your story," said Miles, gloomily. "Hate to tell you, the first to tell you, best friend and all that. Jacinda loves you, wants you. Not me, she never wanted me."

Brad stalked to the window, and back again. He had not sat down, and weary lines were engraved on his bronzed face. Charita wished he would sit, or lie down and rest. He needed rest, yet this terrible scene went on, and on.

"You're wrong about that," Brad said. "Wrong, Miles. She married you, happily. You were the smartest man she had ever met, she told me. And not just smart, you were wise. She said, *wise*, Miles. She needed that wisdom. She was a smart-aleck kid, raised wrong, never loved enough, never secure. She needed you as well as loved you. That is still true."

"It never was true," Miles told them gloomily. "Say, Brad, where's your drinks? I need a bit more Scotch. Charita only serves tea or coffee." He gave a ghastly laugh.

Brad's mouth tightened. "Drink will kill you, Miles. Your system can't take it—"

"I can take anything you can, my boy!" snapped Miles, his face flushing more deeply red. "Don't give me that stuff, I can outdrink you any day or night!"

"You're trying hard. Thing is, I'm not," said Brad. "God's name, Miles! You're killing yourself and ruining your marriage. What you have done to a promising law business is criminal! Give it up! Dry out, and start again—"

"Why?"

Miles laughed at Brad's exasperation. It was as though he enjoyed taunting him, it gave him a perverted pleasure. Charita sighed.

Brad's patience snapped. "All right, drink yourself into an early grave! Go on, and have fun! Enjoy it! But not here, don't come here again and bother my wife with your problems! If you want to drink, then drown yourself in alcohol! But don't blame me, and don't blame Jacinda. It's your own damned fault!"

"Brad!" whispered Charita, flinging out a hand to stop him. He ignored her, staring down at Miles, as though he longed to fling him from the house.

"Wore out your hospitality, did I?" drawled Miles, pulling himself slowly from the chair. "I'll be on my way. If you hear of a drowning, it'll be me!" He laughed hoarsely.

Charita caught the look in the hazel eyes, like those of a wounded dog, bewildered, lost. As Miles stumbled to the door, Charita rose hastily to follow him, and bow him out. Brad caught her arm roughly, and held her back.

"Let him go. And be damned to him! He loves to wallow in the misery he brought on himself! He's ruining himself and Jacinda, because he can't control himself!"

"Oh, Brad!" said Charita sorrowfully. She turned to Miles. "I am deeply sorry for your troubles, I am hopeful of your recovery. Please be careful now, for the sake of those who truly love you."

Miles stared down at her. "Thanks, honey. But there ain't nobody who does that," he drawled it out, in imitation of some uncouth comedian. He shrugged, and went out the door.

Charita pulled free of Brad, and followed him out. The maid stood bowing at the door. Charita called to Miles, "Be careful, Miles! Please drive yourself very carefully! And know that you are always welcome in our miserable house! Our hospitality is open to you!"

Brad would have contradicted her, his face flushing and his hand shooting out to restrain her. He stood behind her, his hands gripping her arms, as she bowed to Miles, and watched him go unsteadily to his car.

Miles got in, managed to start the car, and with a series of jerks the smart car lurched down the gravel path. Finally he was out in the road safely, and turned the corner and was out of sight. Charita, sighing, turned back into the house.

"Well! You must like him a great deal more than I had realized!" Brad shot the words at her, still holding her arms tightly.

The maid closed the door, and retreated into the depths of the house. This had been a most upsetting afternoon for her, thought Charita, gloomily. There was no hope that the incidents and harsh language would not be repeated throughout the servants' quarters for days and nights. The Americans were a constant source of interest and amazement to the polite Japanese, and all this quarreling and shouting and slamming of doors would be discussed and wondered about.

Brad drew Charita back into the drawing room, and stared down at her grimly. He repeated himself, "You must like Miles immensely!"

"Now, Brad, I am very sorry for him," she faced him bravely. "One does not desert a friend because he is sick. The personal relationship must not be broken."

"Hell! He is breaking it! Let him go down for the third time, he is doing it to himself! And he is destroying Jacinda's life."

Charita felt a deep pain in her heart. It was Jacinda; always Jacinda. She tried again, nevertheless, to reason with him. "I could not let Miles depart with curses in his ears. What if he had crashed, because of his grief and despair? How we would blame ourselves—"

"Charita, he is dragging himself down! It is his own fault!" Brad said impatiently. "I won't have him do this to Jacinda! He is ruining both of their lives!"

"It is because of his grief and—and his worries," said Charita, gazing up at him gravely. How she wished he would deny to her, and she could believe it, that Jacinda was no more than a sister to him! They were not related, nor were she and Kanji. She loved Kanji, and wished him happiness. Yet she did not wish to have an affair— She shuddered, and drew a little away from Brad. The strong musky odor of Jacinda's perfume had been on Brad's skin the night she had helped to undress him for the doctor's examination.

"Well, forget him," said Brad curtly. "I won't have him coming here and upsetting you. I'll tell the servants not to admit him again."

"Oh, Brad, please! He does me no harm. I will give him coffee, and listen to him, and ease his mind—"

"You'll have nothing to do with him!" roared Brad, and caught her shoulders. She flinched at his hard grip, and he eased it abruptly. "I'm sorry, honey, did I hurt you?"

"You are stronger than you realize," she said quietly.

"And you are so soft and sweet," he said, and bent and kissed her cheek. "Um, like a peach," he said, and nuzzled against her neck for a moment.

"Lord, I hate to think of going out tonight," Brad groaned, as he released her.

"Out?" she asked blankly.

"The dinner—at the New Miyako," he reminded her. "We'll have to leave here about six."

She glanced frantically at the gold clock on the mantel. It was five. "Oh, Brad!" she gasped. "I had forgotten it entirely!"

"That damned Miles."

"Oh, please do not curse him! It is so unlucky!" she whispered, near to tears. The thought of the huge dinner party had escaped her mind, now it returned to plague her. She had dreaded it, now she was not at all ready to brave it. The afternoon, with all its horrors—

Brad put his arm on her shoulders and steered her to the door. "Forget him—come on, honey. We'll have to change fast. What are you going to wear?"

She shook her head blankly. "I don't know—Brad— could you not go without me? It has been such an afternoon, and please—perhaps it will be all men—"

"All men? Not a chance! This is an American party," he said, and seemed angry again. "No geishas at this one!

I want you to meet my friends and business associates. Come on—let me choose your dress."

Brad drew her remorselessly with him into the hallway. He called to her personal maid, who followed them, her sandals flapping, into the bedroom. Charita would not have a chance to get out of this evening, weary and heartsick though she felt, she realized.

Brad was flipping through the dresses in the wardrobe where her evening dresses were hanging. He paused to consider a gold tissue silk, decided against it and went on to a pastel pink chiffon with bell sleeves. He finally decided against it, and drew out a cream silk gown with brocaded lotus designs.

"This is it," he said, with satisfaction. "I like the stand-up collar at your throat. When I see it on you, I'll choose your jewelry." He went off whistling to shower and change.

Charita felt a growing rebellion in her heart—Brad was choosing her clothes, her jewelry, even her thoughts! To say nothing of her friends and companions! Was this marriage—this—this slavery? Charita was silent as she bathed. She put on the white silk slip, the fragile luminous hosiery, the delicate kid sandals comprised of tiny gold straps. Brad came in as the maid was slipping the dress carefully over Charita's dark head.

Brad watched critically as the maid zipped up the back; the girl knelt to tug out the full folds of the skirt, and adjust the paneled pleats.

"Yes. You look terrific," Brad said, pleased that his wife looked so beautiful. "That style suits you. It is elegant, yet restrained, and the color becomes you. Of course, you look good in every soft color."

The pink in Charita's cheeks deepened. It embarrassed her, the way he praised her, and even more the way he gazed up and down her slim, rounded body. That possessive look, that knowing look, the way he had of making her feel he touched her all over even when he stood several feet away.

Brad studied her as the maid carefully brushed the shining hair into its pageboy style, and Charita studied her makeup and added a bit more powder to her small nose.

Then Brad went to the safe for some of the jewelry and proceeded to add to her outfit. He gave her gold earrings, a gold bracelet, heavy and engraved with a lotus design, for her right wrist. He studied the effect, then pinned on her shoulder a delicately wrought golden lotus, shining against the cream brocade. "There, that's enough," he said. "I'd like to load you down, but that delicate effect would be ruined."

She studied herself briefly in the mirror. She had another mutinous thought. Did he enjoy doing this because she would be a showcase for his jewelry? It was like being a mannequin in the store window!

She finally heard his voice insisting, "Are you pleased? Charita, do you like them?"

She managed a smile. "They are most exquisite, Brad. The ladies will enjoy seeing them, and they will envy me, I am sure."

That seemed to please him. The maid placed a stole of crocheted silk about Charita's shoulders, and they went out. Brad looked very smart in a white silk summer suit, with a black tie and black and gold studs at his wrists.

Brad was whistling tunelessly as they went out. The car followed them from the garage and down the street. Charita could see the reflection from the little mirror at Brad's side of the car. Always there were bodyguards! Their presence chilled her.

Brad would glance in the mirror from time to time, and all about him. Ordinarily she would not have noticed it, but she knew now he was not just watching for traffic.

He drove out into the traffic. Fortunately, most was

going the other way, out to the suburbs from the business district at the end of the day. The cars streamed past them as they drove into town and parked at the New Miyako Hotel. The bodyguards followed them into the hotel and into the hallway and lobby.

The hotel was beautifully lit. They stepped into the elevator, and went down to the lower floor where the dinner was to be held, a private affair. The bodyguards followed, standing at the front of the elevator, then stepping aside to let Brad and Charita past them. Their black eyes were glancing everywhere, observing everyone. They never looked at Brad or Charita, only at everyone else about them, watching for one dangerous move, one out-of-place person in the elegant surroundings.

In the far room, Brad saw his friends, and he and Charita went toward them. She felt as though she tottered in the high-heeled golden sandals, but Brad's hand was always under her arm, gripping her firmly.

He smiled in greeting as he approached his friends, and Charita stiffened her back and raised her chin. She must do him proud. She did not want him to be ashamed of her shyness and gaucheness. She was not a schoolgirl anymore, but the wife of an important businessman, a wealthy man, who wished to show the world what he could achieve.

Brad led her to the first couple, an older man and woman with white hair and formal look to their appearance. The woman was wearing a black brocade dress that rustled when she moved; her gems were diamonds, glittering in her white hair and at her throat. Her blue eyes. were frosty, like diamonds, thought Charita, and her smile was a twitch of her lips. The older man was staring at Charita, and he was smiling widely.

"So—here is the bride! My dear, we have not seen you since your wedding!" He was holding out his hand and grinning.

She touched his hand briefly. She shared the Japanese dislike of touching hands so often. She would rather have bowed, but Brad would have been furious! They were all Americans, as he had said.

She dared not wet her lips, or make some movement which indicated how shy she felt among these smart, fashionably dressed people. She managed a slight smile, and bent her head a little.

"It is good to meet you once again," she managed to say.

Brad's hand was on her elbow, moving her a little. "This is Mrs. Patterson, whom you have met," he said warningly. She smiled, murmured the appropriate words to the frosty-faced dowager.

"I'm charmed," the older woman smiled unexpectedly. "I caught only a little glimpse of you at the wedding, my dear. No wonder Brad married you! You are so lovely, so young—" the woman sounded wistful.

Brad grinned, and accepted the congratulations smoothly. He moved her on to others, Mr. and Mrs. Myers, bright and chatty and curious. They detained Charita to ask about her painting, of which they had heard. "We must see your work one day soon," Mrs. Myers requested.

Charita would have invited them over, courteously, but Brad squeezed her arm and stopped her speech. "We are planning a dinner before long, we'll arrange a little showing," he said smoothly. "Right now, Charita is working on a project for me, and her painting is not progressing! Of course, the designs are secret—"

"You sly dog," said Mr. Myers with admiration. "Caught a beautiful bride, who can work for you also!"

By the set look of Brad's jaw, and his tenseness at her side, Charita realized he did not care for that remark. She said, in her small soft voice, "I enjoy painting very much, and designing is new and most enjoyable to me. My poor work is a hobby—"

Brad cut her off. "Charita is used to the Japanese style of speech," he said quickly. "Her poor work, as she calls it, is worlds ahead of any artist I ever hired professionally. She catches on to our methods of working with amazing skill."

"You are very fortunate," said Mrs. Myers, respectfully.

Charita was wondering at Brad's words. Did he mean them? The Japanese would not praise a wife so, yet Americans were different. He was on the defensive, and she was not really sure just why. Didn't he want his wife to work?

They moved on to another couple, Mr. and Mrs. William Hartung, Brad told her. They were young and vibrant, both artists, as Brad said to Charita before them.

"Joy is an artist in pottery, and William is studying brushwork, to improve his painting in oils. I think they will show you their work one day, right?"

Brad seemed more at ease with them and Charita took this to mean he liked them very much. She paused to talk with them, and asked, "Your pottery, Mrs. Hartung, is it like the Japanese? Do you use their motifs, or create your own?"

"Theirs, at first," Joy said, eagerly. Her red hair and freckled face were not exactly beautiful, but she sparkled with life. "Now I am slowly evolving my own. I have placed some in the department stores here in Kyoto, and that is quite an honor!"

Brad introduced two other couples who had arrived, and the twelve finally sat down to dinner at a long table. Charita was glad that the Hartungs were near her, she liked Joy and felt she could talk to her. The frosty Mrs. Patterson made her feel wary, as though she were an object under a microscope.

But finally Charita was able to relax. The food was delicious and elegantly served. They began with prawn cocktails, with cocktail sauce of a delicate flavor. Then came another seafood course, a variety of raw and cooked fish with seaweed, and delicious stuffed mushrooms. Light white wines were served.

The next course, this time served with red wines, was comprised of thick steaks from Kobe, about four times as much as Charita could eat. She thought of the prices in the stores and how her parents served steak like this once a year at a fine dinner, and saved for months for that party—and she felt like shivering. With the steaks came bowls of rice. Some of the party left theirs, Joy ate all hers, with a little grin at Charita.

"I enjoy rice," she confided across the table. "I grew up in India, where my parents ran a tapestry business, in Bombay. Rice is my favorite food. When I'm ill, Bill knows all I want is rice and tea."

"I also," said Charita, answering the friendly smile. "It is soothing to the stomach, and calming to the nerves."

Mr. Myers leaned across to speak to Charita. "Mrs. Livingston—" he said, and Charita realized he spoke to her. She was still not really accustomed to her married name. "Could you tell me how you work?"

"How I work?" she asked, puzzled. "You mean—at a table or drawing board—"

Brad stopped them, with a laugh and a cutting edge of his hand, the side outward. "Oh, no, you don't, Myers! Don't say a thing, Charita, love. He's trying to find out trade secrets! We'll say nothing of work tonight, thank you!"

There was general laughter at Myers' good-natured chagrin. There were curious looks at Charita, smiles and nudges.

A woman near Charita said, "Your husband is most successful in a very competitive field, my dear! I've heard

Karl Frundsberg would give his eyeteeth to buy into Brad's firm! And he would keep Brad on as chief designer, wouldn't he, Brad?"

Brad looked inscrutable. "I have no intention of selling out," he said definitely. "You'll do me a favor in denying it most emphatically. The business is booming, no reason to sell."

The entire table of guests had quieted to hear his words. Myers leaned forward so far to listen, that the end of his tie fell into his plate. His wife frowned at him, he drew back, embarrassed.

Brad changed the subject so abruptly that the guests could not help understanding he meant no more talk about that. Charita listened in silence at the talk of foreign trade, the oil problems, the Middle East settlements, the European Common Market pricing; all flowed on about her.

These were important and successful businessmen, she realized, and some of the women were also involved. Evidently the frosty Mrs. Patterson was on the board of an oil company, her husband was someone in a television production area. All of them looked up to Brad, spoke to him with respect and even awe in their voices. They asked his opinions on all matters from business to world affairs to fashions, and listened carefully to his answers. And he was not the eldest among them, either, Charita thought with growing pride.

They respected and were in awe of success, she decided. Brad was a very successful businessman, therefore they cherished his friendship, listened to him, requested his opinions and advice. One asked, as though casually, for a meeting one day soon about adding some product to his firm. Brad nodded, told the man to phone him the next day. The man leaned back with such relief, and a wink at his wife, that Charita realized it had been most important to him.

So this was how business was done with Americans. They met in seeming friendship, to make contacts, ask for help, see men of influence. She suppressed a wriggle of impatience and boredom as the long talking went on through the meat course, into the desserts and coffee.

Charita had left most of her steak, finding it too heavy so late in the day. She thought with regret that she could not have shared the huge portion with Kanji and his father, they enjoyed it so much on the rare occasions they had it. The Kobe beef was hand-tended beef. The cows were kept in a dark barn at the back of the farmhouses. The farmer and his family shared the task of going into the barn to give the animal a quick massage. It was specially fed on hot feed.

One of the men noticed she left most of her meat. "Don't you care for steak? It's specially raised, you know!"

"It is most delicious," said Charita, carefully. "I have, however, eaten so much already—" She let the sentence trail away, with an apologetic smile.

"I hear they give the beef cows beer," said one man, and they went off on that subject, of which none knew much. Charita was silent.

That was another myth which seemed to amuse the Americans. The hot feed did not include beer, but somehow the story had started. These Americans had so many misconceptions of this adopted land of hers, she thought sadly.

Finally, as the coffee was finished, the Pattersons began to make polite sounds of leaving. Still it was another half-hour before Charita and Brad could make their farewells and also leave.

The bodyguards followed them closely. At the elevator another burly man stepped forward, and spoke quietly to Brad.

Brad listened, frowning. Charita was not close enough

to hear what they said. She did catch the words, "two men—listening—sent for me—another man upstairs—"

They departed by the elevator, only Brad, Charita and the three men on it. Brad shielded Charita with his body as the door opened. One man got out, another held the door opened, as they all cast looks about. Finally they nodded, and Brad and Charita were able to step out and go on their way through the lovely halls. People were sitting on the lounge chairs and sofas, some having drinks, chatting and laughing. Heads turned, people stared, their gazes followed Brad's tall figure and Charita's dainty loveliness as they went out, with the guards hovering about them.

"Who?" she caught the words. "Must be important. Guards? Wonder—is he a diplomat? Have I seen him on television? She's a doll, awfully young, though."

Brad paid no attention to them. He was gazing about, keenly, looking over their heads. His hand was on Charita's far arm, his arm heavily about her, sweeping her with him through the lit hallways, out into the garage. There, another guard was waiting near their car, his hand on the pistol in his holster. Brad helped Charita into the car, carefully put her skirt about her feet, then straightened to speak to the men. He was shutting the door, but she caught the words.

"Men lingering about yet? You follow them, you two. The others come with us. I want to know where—" The door slammed, she lost the rest.

She was chilled and upset when he slid into the car. He smiled down at her, and patted her knee. "I was proud of you tonight, honey. You looked gorgeous, and you behaved perfectly. You were friendly, yet cool, not giving away much. Did you like them?"

What a strange way to speak of friends! She fumbled for an answer. He did not wait to hear what she said.

"I thought you got along well with Joy Hartung.

She's a nice girl, a bit featherbrained though. Don't go out with her if she calls."

"Why—why not?" gasped Charita.

"It isn't safe," said Brad, easily. "I mean—she's liable to walk you all over Kyoto looking for pots! Put her off, if she calls. Promise me, Charita."

"I promise," said Charita, subdued. She rubbed her arms. She felt cold all over. It was a fine mess, she thought. She was told to be friendly, but not to make friends. She was instructed to behave politely, but by American standards, not Japanese. She was supposed to be careful, but Brad was the one in danger. Would there ever be a way to resolve this?

19

Brad left work early that hot July day. He was tired of designing, his brain felt numbed and weary. The heat seemed to drain him of energy. People told him that Kyoto was pleasant even in the summer, but this summer was unusually hot and the air pollution hovered over the city.

He turned in the drive, and gravel crunched under the tires. He saw Charita in the garden, and gave her a wave as he drove past.

He left the car just outside the garage for the chauffeur to put away. The bodyguards paused to make sure all was well, then their car curved and turned around, and they departed.

It was midafternoon, time for a long cool drink and some talk. They had nothing planned for tonight. He was weary of the social round. It was useful, but lately he had had less and less time alone with Charita.

He strolled into the garden to find Charita on an unpainted wooden bench near the pond. She wore a larkspur blue cotton dress, American-style, with short sleeves and open neck. She looked cool and composed as she gave him a slight smile.

"How pretty and comfortable you look," he said. A maid came out to him, he turned his briefcase and his tan summer jacket over to her. She bowed a number of times, beamed at him, showing her gold-capped teeth, and walked back into the house, her sandals slapping with every step.

Brad sank down onto the bench beside Charita and put his arm along the back of the bench. His free hand wrenched open his tie, unfastened his shirt at the neck. "Whew, was it hot in Kyoto today."

"I am sorry you were so miserable," came her soft cool voice.

He frowned. She was so distant, so polite. Was there no way to get through to her? He looked over her longingly, from the polished shining head, over her shoulders, down her slim, rounded figure, to her tanned legs and bare arched feet in small sandals. How desirable and beautiful she was; he felt passion rising in him. He looked away from her to the pool.

"Hey—we have an addition to the pool," he said, startled.

Charita smiled. "The lotus have begun to bloom. Are they not beautiful?"

"Stunning!" Several of the lotus blossoms were creamy white, one was a strange and glorious blue, another was of gold. He stared at them in fascination. Such glorious exotic blooms, lying quietly in the garden pool.

"I was sketching them," and Charita indicated the pad beside her. "They are so large, so lovely. Some time ago, a small frog jumped onto one of the pads. There—is he not sweet?"

She turned the pages of the sketch pad, and showed him. Brad grinned at the open, startled look of the little frog gazing up at him.

It gave him an idea. He took the pencil Charita had laid down, flipped over to a fresh page, and began to sketch. Charita watched curiously as his big fingers drew the frog in a pattern, wide-eyed and squat. Then he drew a stylized lotus bloom, large as a gold pin.

"And the chipmunk there," whispered Charita, fascinated as he was. She reached over as he paused, took the pencil, and deftly drew the cunning, alert face of the chipmunk. Brad laughed soundlessly. She drew a goldfish, curved and sensuous. He took the pencil as she stopped, and drew a bird that perched just over their heads.

They had no need for speech. It gave him a curious thrill to communicate without words with Charita. They were so close in their art. It was like at Hakone. She was half smiling, dreamy-eyed as she gazed up at a second bird.

She reached over as he held the pad at a fresh page, and she sketched the two birds, beaks touching. He watched her fingers flying over the page. Then finally she set the pencil down, and gave a slight sigh as she flexed her fingers.

He set the pad down and leaned with a sigh of relief against the back of the bench. He felt oddly contented all of a sudden. He had been cross, tired, hot, when he had driven through the traffic of Kyoto, smelling the polluted air, hating the crowds and blasting horns.

Now he felt as though transported to a cool paradise, of blue morning glories opened against the side of the house, just closing their vivid blue petals against the heat of the afternoon, and drooping to sleep. A few iris lingered in the garden. The tea roses shone in soft yellow, several glorious red roses bloomed, and a number of spectacular pinks.

And best of all were the exotic lotus blossoms in the pool, swaying gently when disturbed by a frog, or a golden fish bumping against their thick stems in the waters. The green pads were glossy, the petals like new silk.

Beside him, Charita sat in silence, herself like a flower, long-stemmed and fragrant and beautiful. Her slim fingers were clasped in her lap, her ankles crossed, her pose restful. Her face was closed, dreamy.

His hand slid from the back of the bench to her shoulder, and he felt her tremble with the suddenness of his touch. He caressed the shoulder gently, feeling the desire well up in him once more. How he adored her!

He turned to look down into her guarded face, into the clear blue of her eyes. He bent closer, nuzzled against her soft neck.

"Brad—not here," she said, in a smothered tone.

He put his arm about her and drew her closer. His mouth moved over her neck, pushed aside the dress, and pressed against her shoulder. Then he moved his lips up the side of her neck, feeling her shivering, and came to the lobe of her ear. He tugged at it, gently.

"Charita—my darling—"

"Please—Brad—everyone—will see us—" She was stiff in his grasp.

"Then come in the house!"

He pulled her up with him, impatient with her reserve. They had been married for months now! It was high time she got used to him and began responding!

"In the daytime?" she said, scandalized, a scarlet flush creeping into her creamy face. Her lashes drooped over the blue eyes, like the closing of the morning glory petals.

"Whenever we wish!" he teased, his passions rising rapidly. He urged her to the house, although she tried to hang back.

"Brad, I think it is not—not the thing to do—please, Brad—you shame me—everyone is looking—"

"For the love of God!" he exploded, all at once furious. "We are married, aren't we? Didn't we go through that ceremony twice, even in a Shinto temple—"

"Shinto shrine," she corrected. "Did you not—like that, Brad? Did it mean nothing to you?"

"It was a beautiful ceremony, Charita, honey," he said, gently. "I'll never forget it."

He moved her ahead of him into the house, through the hallway, to their large bedroom. Inside, he locked the door with a snap, and turned to her.

Her head was bowed, her fingers locked together before her breast. Hungrily, he drew her to him, and unlocked her fingers, and put her arms about his neck. He unfastened the dress down to below her waist and slid his hand inside the dress, to find the soft breasts, covered with the thin slip. She trembled at his gesture of stroking the breasts.

"Oh—honey—darling—" he murmured, and drew her to the bed. He took off the dress, flung the slip after it. She wore little that hot day. He picked her up in his arms, pressed his lips to her breast, ardently. His mouth moved down to her waist, to her thighs. Oh, how she made him burn!

She lay limply in his arms. Did she feel nothing? Did it take much more than his efforts to make her respond? Brad felt angry, hurt, jealous, anxious. He worshipped her, he would do anything for her. Why didn't she feel it and respond to him?

He laid her on the bed and rapidly undressed himself. Then he joined her on the sheets. He rolled over on his side and studied her, even as his hands began to go over her soft body. Her eyes were tightly shut as though she blanked him out. The afternoon sunlight streamed through the opened curtains. Her soft creamy skin seemed to glow golden, like the golden silk of the lotus petals.

He leaned over her, pressed his mouth to her shoulder, then slid his lips down to her breasts. He took a pink nipple between his teeth, and caressed it. His breath was coming faster and faster. He wasn't sure he could control himself until she was warmed and ready. But he must, he could not risk her pain.

His hands stroked over her thighs, urgently. He parted them, and slid his fingers gently to the soft lips. She shivered again and again, as he kissed and caressed her. A breeze drifted in through the opened windows, a breeze laden with the perfume of roses and other heady scents from the garden.

Her arms lay at her sides. He paused in his movements to lift her arms and put them about his body. He moved to lie over her and directed her to hold him, silently, with his movements. He felt the heat of his own body against her coolness.

He forced himself to slow down, to move with more deliberation; wild though he was for her, he knew she was not nearly ready. He kissed her, lay back to caress her with his hands and his long legs against her legs. He whispered words of love to her, against her pink-peachy cheeks, against the closed eyelids, the pink rose mouth. Finally she moved, and sighed, and her body went more softly limp against his.

Her arms closed more tightly about his neck, and drew him closer to herself. He moved on her, urgently, and began to draw them together into the final embrace. The room was silent, warm in the afternoon sunlight, with the slight breeze to cool their hot bodies.

He came to her, again, again, his body moving out of control now, plunging, aching, needing to release. Finally he could not hold it back, he finished in her, and drew out. She had not felt the aching sweetness he wanted her to feel, and it was a great disappointment to him.

He lay quietly, his arm about her, as they regained their breaths. She was shivering a little, he drew up a sheet to cover her, for her body was wet with sweat, as his was. "Darling," he murmured. "I wish you had felt it also."

"Do not trouble yourself about me," she said, in that polite little voice that made him ache to shake her.

"You are my wife, of course I am troubled about you." He forced himself to say it quietly, but a throb of anger flamed through him.

"I am realizing," she said, unexpectedly, "that I am green and stupid for you. You must be regretful sometimes that you married someone so young and foolish."

"Never!" he said, with conviction, and drew her closer to him. "Don't you realize, honey, I love you? I shall never regret marrying you, and I don't like to hear you say that. We belong together."

"But I do not please you." The shining blue-black head turned briefly from him. He put his hand on her cheek, and turned her face back to his, lying close to him on the pillow.

"Even when you do not please me, you please me," he smiled.

"That sounds like a Japanese riddle," she giggled unexpectedly, and the dimples flickered in her round cheeks.

"Then you may ponder it, oh, my little wise one, and come up with an answer one day soon." He kissed each dimple, and her little round chin, and lay back, more satisfied. As long as they could laugh together, things were not so bad. One day she would come to love him more, and not be frightened of their sexual relationship. He wanted her at ease with him.

If he had to teach her slowly, all right. He realized she was very young, and untaught, and that was really the way he wanted it. Anything she learned about marriage and sex and love, he wanted to be the only one to teach her!

Whenever Brad thought of the possibility of Charita having loved and married anyone else in the world, it made him so wildly jealous it alarmed him. He felt terribly possessive of her, he didn't want her to look at any other man. He even felt jealous of her affection for Kanji and her foster parents. He knew Charita was an innocent, yet he wondered sometimes if she had ever met and loved any other boy—or man.

He asked now, with seeming casualness, "Did you ever go out with boys in high school?"

"No, my parents would not have permitted it!"

There was something to be said for her Japanese upbringing! If she had "gone steady" with a boy, allowed him to kiss her and pet her—Brad frowned at the very idea.

"Not even to dances?"

"No, the girls went together. I usually went with my girl friend Spring Flower, who lived down the street. My parents took me, or her parents, and came for us again. We did learn to dance quite well, did we not?" There was an anxious tone to her voice.

"Beautifully, my love. I enjoy dancing with you." He moved her head over to his bare shoulder, and stroked back her hair, moving his fingers through the thick silk. "I must take you to a nice nightclub or restaurant where there is dancing. Would you like that?"

"Oh, yes! I should like that—when you have time, Brad," she hastily added. "I know you are so busy a man."

"Things should let up by late autumn, when the Christmas jewelry is completed," he said, and sighed, thinking of all the work ahead. "I thought we might go to the States for a honeymoon."

"The States!" She sounded horrified. "Not for long, though, we would not be gone long, would we?"

"As long as we wish. How about Hawaii? It is gorgeous there, with all the flowers, and the sweet-scented air."

"I should like Hawaii. But I would not want to leave Japan for very long."

She relaxed against his shoulder. He was frowning, though she could not see his face. He had often thought he would remain in Japan for a year or two, or until the business was going well. When Kanji was fully trained, he would leave the man in charge, and return to Japan only briefly, to oversee the operations. Brad had several factories in the United States to watch over, with good managers in charge. He had not gone home for a year, he must go soon. But Charita seemed to panic at the very idea. Did she realize that he meant to return home for good one day, and live there? He had thought perhaps somewhere in San Francisco, or nearby, they might build a beautiful home, near to opera, concerts, ballet, museums. She would love the museums. He must tread slowly, though, he decided. Charita had lived all her life in Japan, and it represented security to her.

One day, he vowed, he would represent security to her, and Charita would go wherever he wished.

He stroked her shoulders gently, and felt her turned and sighing, and going to sleep against him. How adorable she was, curling up like a silky kitten against him.

But the thought of his plans began to bother him.

A couple of days later, he realized he was not the only troubled person in the factory. Pearl had been sighing up a storm, and he had caught her a couple of times, with her hands quietly on the keys, staring into space. She had flushed, apologized, and worked harder than ever.

And now Kanji. Brad looked up from the orders they had been discussing, to see Kanji gazing into space. It was so unusual, that Brad stared at the younger man. His face was sad, not like the usual polite smiling mask.

Kanji started and flushed when Brad continued to stare at him. The mask slipped over his handsome features once more. "You say, honorable master, that the jewels must be shipped—"

Brad went on with the order, ignoring the honorable master title for the moment. Kanji was distressed, that was

292

evident. And several times lately, Brad had had to correct some errors in Kanji's work. Now that he thought about it, the errors had happened four times in the past three weeks, and that was unusual for Kanji. He was meticulous and very careful.

Brad felt responsible for Kanji. He had persuaded the man to come and work for him. He was not involved in the secure system of the usual labor-management arrangement in Japan. Normally, when a man obtained a job in Japan, he was there until he retired. The employer took care of him from then on, no matter how poor or how good labor conditions might become. If the times were depressed, the men were kept on, in shorter hours, or at more menial jobs, such as cleaning up the factory or the grounds. But no man was fired, no one missed his pension. He was taken care of for life.

Kanji had taken a big chance, coming to work for an American. Pearl could be expected to marry and leave, but Kanji was in a management position, expected to give his devotion and loyalty to a man of another country, not knowing if the business might fold in five or ten years, leaving him stranded.

He wanted Kanji to be happy in the work. Had something gone badly wrong, and the man was too polite to tell him? Damn the manners, thought Brad ruefully. If he had been in America, his assistant manager would probably have let him know in no uncertain terms that something had gone wrong.

Well, Brad would have to dig.

At the end of their meeting, Brad said, rather casually, "I would like to talk to you in confidence, not in the office. Where can we go to speak privately?"

Instantly, Kanji Noguchi was alert, his black eyes gleamed with bright intelligence. "Alone? Of course. Let me see. There is a tearoom in the next street. The booths are far enough apart to allow confidences. Businessmen often go there to discuss contracts."

"Good. Let's go." Brad reached for his briefcase, scooped papers into it. He got up, reached for his jacket, and put it on. To his pleased surprise, Kanji imitated his movement, snatched up his briefcase, slid into his jacket, eagerly.

Brad was tickled. Kanji learned his ways swiftly, and he was eager to please. And smart as a whip! Brad never had to tell him something twice—except about the miserable worm bit, he thought with a concealed grin.

They went out. "Pearl, I shall not be back this afternoon," said Brad easily. "Leave the letters on my desk. I want to go over them again and make sure of the details on the jewels. Any word from the Arab oil prince today?"

She smiled politely. It was an office joke, enjoyed between the three of them, that the oil prince wrote or telephoned daily to see how the work on his screens and jewels was progressing. "No word today. I will tell him that all goes well, yes?"

"Right you are." They went out. Brad was thinking with pleasure about the screen that Charita had designed. It was almost finished. The men working on the gold were in awe at Charita's finished designs. There were seven panels, the central one of an immense gold Buddha with a serene uplifting expression. On either side of him were screens of golden lotus flowers in ponds. Beyond, on the right, was the mountain with the leaning pine. On the left was the heron standing on one leg. The end panels on each side were of intricate shells and sea creatures, sea horses, squid, and delicate waves against the beach on which they lay.

Brad had discarded the torii with reluctance. It did not fit in. But Charita was evolving another one with the torii in the center, a five-paneled screen for another commission. She seemed to enjoy this work, so he let her go on with it. Inwardly he chafed a little at the idea of her working. His macho feelings, he decided, with an inward grimace at himself. He wanted to support her completely, he wanted her completely dependent on him.

They left the factory, he indicated that the guards were not to come with them. Kanji glanced back at the bodyguards.

"Is this wise, Brad?" he asked, then flushed. "Forgive me, I should not question you—"

"We haven't had any sign of men following me for more than a month," said Brad, shaking his head. "I think they were merely curious. Thank God. I don't want anything to happen to Charita. I have always told her to stay home unless she is with me."

"Charita is a good, obedient girl," said Kanji, and sighed deeply. "My little sister was raised in the old-fashioned way. That is good for a woman."

There was a faint ring of bitterness in his voice. Brad walked silently beside him as they moved past the crowds of men in the midafternoon sunshine of Kyoto.

Did Kanji regret Charita's marriage? Had he longed for Charita himself? The old jealousy was rising.

Girls passed them, some in navy blue or gray business suits, white blouses opened at the throat. Several schoolgirls in blue outfits giggled past them, giving them coy looks. An older woman, her gray hair in a knot on the back of her head, her plump body in a dark blue kimono, clattered past them in her high geta. The old and the new, thought Brad. The constant contrast of the cultures never ceased to amaze him. He would see smart shops with the latest refrigerators, washers and dryers in the windows. The next block would have men squatting on the sidewalk, cooking beef cubes and peppers over a charcoal brazier, while people stood about patiently waiting for their order to be ready.

They turned in at the tea shop. Brad looked about

curiously. The booths might have been transplanted from an American coffee shop or quick-order restaurant. But the Japanese businessmen leaned across tables to consult in low tones; a bowing girl showed them to a booth at the back of the shop. She brought their tea quickly, and a plate of cakes.

"Those are rice cakes, those are almond paste," Kanji pointed them out. He half turned, looking back toward the counter. He beckoned the waitress. "Do you have cream cakes?" he asked.

"Yes, yes, I will bring them," she beamed, and clattered away, to return with a plate heaped with cream- and chocolate-filled cakes.

Kanji looked sheepishly at Brad. "My vice," he explained whimsically.

Brad laughed. "Look out, then. More deadly than alcohol," he joked, then his face shadowed, thinking of Miles Snow.

"You are troubled about your friend, Mr. Snow?" murmured Kanji, transferring a particularly puffy concoction to his plate. "It is sad, he is a man of much chie-saikaku."

"What is that?" Brad did not recall hearing the term.

"*Chie-saikaku*—ah—that is—wisdom and ability— it is important for a merchant to have such virtues," explained Kanji. "My honorable parents say you have much of this virtue," he added with a charming blush, and bob of his dark head.

"Thank you," said Brad. "I just wish Miles had some common sense along with it!"

"Ah. One cannot have everything," and again the shadow went over Kanji's face. He drank his tea automatically, as though his mind had gone to some other matter.

Brad drank his tea in silence, wondering now how to approach the matter in a way not to offend Kanji. He ate an almond cake, found it so good he had a second. Kanji

296

was plunging into his third cream cake, eating like a hungry schoolboy. Was something really wrong?

He remembered the matters of the past weeks and strengthened his resolve. "Kanji, this matter of which I would speak is a delicate one."

"Yes, Brad? I listen carefully." Kanji set down his fourth cake regretfully, wiped his mouth, and set aside his teacup.

"Usually you are a man of cheer and optimism. Our work goes well, you have been of much help to me, so much I have been able to take more leisure to myself."

"I thank you." A little anxiety flickered over the broad face.

"However, lately—oh, hang it all," said Brad abruptly. "I can't be polite and devious and beat around it. You're upset about something, and it worries me. What the devil is wrong? Is it your parents? Are you in money troubles? Tell me, for heaven's sake!"

Kanji stared, his black eyes going round. "I—I am ashamed, that I have brought my troubles to work with me," he finally mumbled, and hung his head. "It is very wicked of me. I am covered with humiliation—"

Brad groaned, "If you say miserable worm, I'll dump this pot of tea on your head. For God's sake, Kanji, tell me what I can do to help. What is wrong with you? You are sad, and upset, and it is driving me crazy!"

Kanji bit his lips. "You are very kind, very honorable employer. My unimportant matters shall not be allowed to trouble your kind mind—"

Brad reached for the teapot threateningly. Kanji's face lightened, he managed a grin. "None of that, Kanji," said Brad. "Come on, out with it. Maybe I can't help, but my listening may help you. Is it something you can tell me, or is it too personal?"

"It is very personal, but I long to confide in someone. My parents would be very hurt, very disappointed,"

297

began Kanji, his hand on his heart earnestly. "You will not mind if I tell my miserable life to you?"

"Go ahead," said Brad. At least he had gotten through to the man.

"Many years ago," Kanji said, "my parents who had their only son wished to make contract with good, dear friends who had only daughter. This contract was made for my marriage. However, now that I am ready to consider marriage, having great position of much respect and responsibility, and flat with furniture, and even fine car, the girl says no, she does not wish to marry me."

"Then she is an idiot, and you'll be better off with someone who will appreciate you."

Kanji considered this. "No, I cannot do that," he said. "The contracts are made, and signed, many years ago."

"When you were children?" Brad was trying to understand.

"Yes, we were children. I had met Pearl just once—"

"*Pearl?*"

"Yes, it is Pearl Takahashi of whom I speak. We have been betrothed these many years." Kanji was studying Brad's face keenly now, his face sober, his black eyes dark with shadows.

"I had no idea she was engaged to you." Brad's mind was whirling. They had worked together in the office for a year, and showed no signs of affection or regard. Rather they worked together with brisk, impersonal efficiency.

"Yes, she is engaged to me. I wish to announce the marriage, and have the engagement ceremony, with a wedding date set in a year or so. Pearl says no."

"Why would she do that? Women's lib?"

Kanji nodded. "Yes, she is women's lib. It is because of her father, you see. He beats her mother much.

298

Pearl left their home and obtained a flat of her own, and refuses to go to visit them. It hurts her heart that her mother is beaten."

Brad swallowed back angry words. Kanji said it all so simply. Beaten! It was another world. Or was it? There were more and more instances of wife-beating being revealed in the States.

Kanji was going on eagerly, as though relieved to be able to spill out all his worries. "I say to Pearl, we shall just announce engagement, it will please our parents. My parents, they worry that nothing is done. They wish to plan ceremony. Her parents wish to begin preparing kimonos and obis, and wedding chests of sandalwood and bronze. Pearl says no, she will wait. She will not burn the contracts, because her father will be angry and beat her mother. She just says wait."

"Well, that isn't fair to you. You can just start courting another woman—" Brad said angrily. That Pearl! He had no idea his demure and competent secretary hid such orneriness in her neat body.

"No, I wish to marry Pearl. I—love—Pearl," confessed Kanji, his head bent. "She is most beautiful, most gracious, a lovely mind in a lovely body, you know? Only, why could she not be more like my sister, Charita!"

Brad stiffened. "How do you mean?" he asked carefully, wondering if this was the crux of the matter.

"As you know, Charita is a most fine girl, so gentle, so feminine, and old-fashioned. She obeys you, she always obeyed our parents. Never does she utter bad words. Her heart is soft and tender. But Pearl—you should not hear such language! She makes me have shame!" said Kanji indignantly.

Brad rubbed his face with his hands. "Well, this is more than a bit beyond me," he said finally. "You do want to marry Pearl, and not break the contracts?"

"I wish to marry Pearl. And my parents would be

most ashamed and shocked if the contracts were broken."

"Well—seems to me that you'll have to court Pearl. Make love to her, take her out—"

Kanji was listening to him intently. But abruptly he turned his head, and stared out into the shop behind him. The waitress was taking care of another booth, bending to listen to the order.

"More tea? We'll get some," said Brad. "Now, Kanji, about all I can suggest is that you get Pearl to change her mind by courting her, take her out to the movies and to fine restaurants, send her flowers—"

Kanji was more restless.

"What the devil is wrong?" asked Brad.

Kanji had turned rather pale. "Do not look now. But in a minute, when I have finished speaking, look toward the waitress. Then with casualness, look to the front of the shop to the central tables, at the second table. There are two men, big men, who I think followed us into the shop. When I first ordered, I noticed them. Now I see they linger, they do not order more, they look at you often."

Brad felt a chill run down his spine. Damned carelessness! Casually, he looked around the edge of the booth, as though searching for the waitress. He glanced briefly toward the central tables. The ones near them were empty. Beyond them, at the second table sat two burly Japanese men, in heavy jackets. They stared rather hard at him, then turned and spoke to each other.

They were the same men who had been on the airplane from Hokkaido. They were the men who had been at the hotel in Hakone. Damn, thought Brad.

"You see them?" murmured Kanji anxiously.

"Right. Any other way out of here?"

"I know the back way, it leads into an alley, and out into a street where taxis are to be found."

"Okay; we'll get the waitress, order more tea. I'll

leave some money on the table. While she is standing here, say nothing to me. But we'll slip out as soon as she turns her back. They will think we are staying for more tea. I'll watch their faces, and give you the signal."

It moved smoothly. The waitress smiled, brought more tea, took away the empty cups and pot. Brad watched idly, as the men settled back in their chairs and turned to speak to each other.

"Now!" he said, low. And he got out of the booth and headed for the back door.

Kanji was right behind him. The door was stuck shut. Kanji reached around Brad, gave the door a hard knock with his palm, slashing like a karate expert, and the door shot open. Both men were out the door.

"They follow," said Kanji, and grabbed a thick barrel filled with trash. Brad helped him roll it in front of the door, then they ran down the alley.

Kanji ran like a boxer, rolling and ducking; when Brad paused at the alley entrance, he pushed him, urgently, out in the street.

Taxis were there. Kanji pushed him into the seat, said something in Japanese to the driver, and the taxi shot away. Brad looked back, twisting in the seat, to see Kanji climbing into another cab. As that pulled away from the curb, the two Japanese men shot out into the alley, looking after the taxis in intense frustration.

20

Brad reached home in good time, paid the taxi driver well, and went into the house. Charita came out from the living room, smiling.

"You are home early, Brad. Oh—what is wrong?" She was scanning his face uneasily.

"A spot of trouble. Don't worry, honey. I'll have to make a couple of phone calls." He went past her with a touch to her shoulder, and back to his study.

He phoned the factory first, reported to the bodyguards. They were disturbed that he had gone out without them, and more upset that he had been followed so closely. He described the two men to them and then hung up.

He then telephoned Kanji at his flat, and was relieved to find him home.

"Were you followed, Kanji?" he asked.

"No. And you?"

"I'm not sure, a taxi was hovering behind me for quite a distance. I think we lost them in the traffic."

"You had a good driver of the taxi?" Kanji sounded very worried.

Brad grinned in spite of his tension. "A regular kamikaze of a driver! I expected to be helping drop bombs at any moment!"

Kanji did not laugh. "It was very close, Brad. You must take more care. Never again will I permit you to venture out on to the streets without your trusty body-guards. I blame myself bitterly."

"It was my own fault," said Brad. "And you did very well, Kanji. You keep very fit."

"I go often to judo and karate courses," said Kanji simply. "I must keep mind and body fit. If I can serve you, it is my pleasure."

"Thank you. You're a good man to have in my corner."

Brad hung up, thoughtfully. Judo and karate! No wonder Kanji could act so swiftly, and so powerfully. Brad remembered that hard punch at the stuck door, Kanji's swift reactions. Yes, a very good man to have on his side.

He went back to the living room. Charita was standing there, watching the door, her slim hands clasped tightly before her. He realized she was scared stiff. He went over to her, took her hands in his, bent over and kissed the tip of her nose.

"All serene, honey. Don't look so scared."

"What—happened?" she breathed, gazing straight up at him, as though to read his face.

Brad hesitated, then for her own safety he decided to tell her. Maybe it would encourage her to be careful also.

"Kanji and I went out to a tea shop to talk privately. We were followed, by the same two toughs who were on the plane from Hokkaido, and were in Hakone. You remember them?"

She had gone pale, he put his arms about her and held her to him. "Yes—I remember—well—oh, Brad!"

"Foolishly, I had not told the bodyguards where I was going. Kanji spotted the men watching us and got us out the back door. God, Kanji is some fellow!" he added, more lightly. "He tells me he is into judo and karate."

"Yes, he has gone for many years. He was of aid to you?"

"Much aid. He's a good man." Brad kissed her again, on her soft cheek. "Don't shake, that's a honey. It's all over, and I'm going to take more care from now on. I thought they had called off their dogs, but they haven't. I sure wish I knew who was giving them their orders!"

"Who could it be? Who wishes you harm?" she asked soberly.

Brad shrugged. "I could name you a dozen men offhand. Jealous of the success, and so on. But—" He stopped abruptly.

He knew of no one who wished him deadly harm, such as death. What else could anyone want?

In the States, several companies had tried to muscle in on his operations. He had shot up too far too fast to please them. They wanted to take over his companies. One man had even managed to buy some stock in his company. Brad had consulted Miles and Jacinda, and managed to freeze the man out, bought back his stock through a dummy, and kept control.

In Japan, Karl Frundsberg had been persistent about wanting to buy him out. The Pattersons had made several overtures about buying stock, helping him expand. They had been furious, in a rigid sort of way, when he turned them down flat. Yet the Pattersons and Frundsbergs both did very well in their fields, they had no need to envy him.

He thought of several other possibilities, sitting on the couch silently, with Charita in the curve of his arm. What if some Japanese company envied him, or hated him for being a foreigner in their country and making a success of his business? He knew such things happened. How would they approach him? They would try through his close associates—Kanji—or Pearl—or Jacinda and Miles. No, he would stake his life on their loyalty.

Charita finally spoke, breaking into his musings. "You have thought of someone to dread, Brad?"

"No, I can't think of anyone special, Charita," he replied. "All I know is, I want you to be as careful as I am."

"Me? But why would anyone chase me in a taxi?" she asked, in a puzzled fashion.

His hand curved about her round face, he studied the wide blue eyes. "Because you are my wife," he said bluntly. "And they might try to get at me through you. I want you to be extremely careful, Charita. I don't want to frighten you unless I have to. But you must take every care. I don't want anything to happen to you."

"Oh—Brad—could it?" She had gone pale and was trembling.

He held her close, and she rubbed her cheek against his shirt. She was such a small, sweet darling. If anything happened to her, he would be shattered, he knew it. He had never been so vulnerable in his life.

"It might. But we won't let it," he said firmly. "You will go out only with me. And we will both be guarded. Don't trust anybody—"

"But I trust Kanji—and others—my foster parents—"

"I know. And Jacinda, of course," he said.

She did not reply to that. His thoughts wandered on. Who could it be? Who would pay large sums to have him followed constantly? He thought of what Charita had overheard on the airplane from Hokkaido, and asked her to repeat it. She did, and he mulled over the words.

"It is someone after the gold formula then," he concluded reluctantly. "So it must be connected with the firm. Well, we'll have to see what their next move is. Damn, this hampers me."

"I am so sorry," murmured Charita. She drew back, and looked up at him again. Slowly her hand came up, and she stroked his cheek, timidly. "There is such weariness in your face, darling."

It was almost the first endearment she had called him. His heart leaped in pleasure. He grinned down at her, and hugged her.

"I'll get some rest, then a shower. What's for dinner?"

"I will go and see. You would like a drink?"

"Not now. We'll have some wine for dinner. If it's fish, tell them to chill some white wine. If steak, some red wine."

She nodded obediently. He went off to lie down and ponder over what had happened. He felt strangely exhausted, probably the strain and the shock of it all. After half an hour, his strength had returned, and he got up and showered, then put on a pair of gray trousers and a thin white shirt. The evenings were still quite warm.

He went out to the living room, to find Charita curled up on the couch, a sketch pad in her lap, the shell book beside her. She was wearing a simple rose cotton dress, sleeveless, open-throated, and was bare-legged with sandals. She glanced up, to study him. "You look much better, Brad."

He bent over, kissed her cheek, then picked up the pad. "I feel fine. What are you up to, honey?"

"I am fascinated by the shapes of the shells. Look at these, Brad," and she pointed to some colored illustrations on the page.

He sat down on the floor, absently, and leaned beside her thigh to look at the pictures. He could hardly concentrate, for thinking of her, how soft and fragrant she was, the rose color against her round legs. Her blue eyes sparkled with eagerness as she explained what she was doing.

The maid called them for dinner, smiling indulgently to find the big master sitting on the floor. Maybe he would learn Japanese ways soon and would sit on cushions!

They went in to dinner, to find chilled white wine at their places. The first course was of shrimp, small and pink, in a delicate soy sauce. It was followed by platters of white fish and scallops in a sauce of creamy richness. Brad ate hungrily, even the seaweed. Charita had prepared a huge green salad, she knew he liked that.

She watched him eat, with the concern of a little mother, he thought, with inward amusement. What a mother she would make! He pictured her with a small bundle in her arms, a cooing little bundle in pink or blue. He drew a deep breath. To think he had been a cynical bachelor for so long, and now he longed not only for his wife but for children as well. Just so long as they were Charita's children!

"You like this?" she beamed, as he took a second helping of the fish and scallops.

"Delicious!"

He poured out more wine for them both. He felt pleasantly flushed by the end of the meal. After the dessert of fresh strawberries piled on tiny pastry shells and covered with thick whipped cream, they returned to the living room for their coffee.

It was a quiet, peaceful evening. There were no telephone calls, no business worries. Only in the background, the shadow of the afternoon's events lingered, the memory of someone who wanted information, or worse.

Brad looked at Charita's latest sketches for the five-panel screen, approved them, and set them aside in a large folder. They discussed the next project. She would be ready before long for the more elaborate and difficult projects, those of jewelry design, he thought.

Yet—as word of the screens went out, they would probably receive more orders for them.

They went to bed early, after an hour or so of music, Chopin (her favorite) and Brahms (his choice). He went into the bedroom, to find her in bed with the light still on. Her face was a mirror of worry as he came in, she was propped against the pillows, her shoulders bare with a curve of lace framing her slim throat.

"What's on your mind, love?" he asked, as he slid out of his robe and laid it over a chair. He moved over to switch off the lights, before coming to the bed.

"The danger to you," she said simply, lying back in bed. He lay down beside her, and reached for her.

"I am sorry to worry you, but I thought you should know the danger. I'm sorry, darling."

She came willingly into his arms, and his heart gave a jump. She settled down against him, the lacy silk nightdress brushing against his bare chest.

"I wish to know all that concerns you. Yet, I am so fearful. I am a terrible coward," she murmured.

"And a miserable worm?" he laughed, teasingly.

She laughed a little, and he felt her relax. "You do not like this way of speaking. Yet I notice the Americans sometimes speak like this. They say, 'Oh, this old thing, I've worn it for ages,' when one admires a dress. Or when one compliments one on how the business goes—as one did to Mr. Patterson the other evening—I noticed that he said 'I'm afraid it will slide—it's gone up as high as I had expected and more—bound to bust!' " She imitated his booming voice and Brad burst out laughing.

"You're right! We do it also, only not the same way. I never thought of that comparison." He held her closer, hugging her as she giggled.

He brushed his lips against her cheek, then around to her mouth. Her lips trembled, then pursed against his, and she shyly answered his kiss. He forced himself to go slowly, and just held her in his arms for a time, brushing against her mouth, her cheek, her throat.

His hands began to roam over her softness, pressing against her breast gently, then around to her back, and down over her thighs. She cuddled closer to him, her body moving against his. He found it hard to contain his delight. She was responding at last! It was like it had been at Hakone.

He drew out the lovemaking, hoping against hope. He kissed and caressed her for a long time, drawing her hips against his, lying on his side casually and letting her feel him warm against her body. Her arms went spontaneously about his body, and her fingers played shyly against his spine, up and down the long back, to his shoulders, then down again. The touch tingled.

When he moved, and shifted over her, she did not cringe or stiffen tonight. She moved, naturally, under him, to accommodate his legs and torso. He supported himself on his elbows, and bent to kiss her again, her broad forehead where the dark hair fell back, down over her nose, to her lips, around to her ear and below to the sensitive places.

Her breathing was faster, her hips shifted restlessly under his. He held off carefully, only touching her gently from time to time. If he could wait long enough, tonight she might let go.

He kissed her over and over, down over her breasts and to her waist. He flung off the nightdress, and felt her heat against his. One hand slid under her back and held her closely to him. Her arms clung to his neck, she half lifted herself up, then fell back.

His other hand went under her thighs, and gently stroked over them.

"Oh—Brad—Brad—darling—" she moaned against his mouth. Her hips moved against his, she lifted herself again. She scarcely seemed to know what she did, she had never moved so sensuously with him.

He could not wait any longer. He brought them together, sliding up, and up, and she gave a great sigh, her fingers clutching his back frantically. Her head was moving back and forth on the pillow, the soft hair in his face. He buried his face in the thick silk, and pressed deeply on her. She moaned against his throat, and her body stiffened suddenly against his.

He felt her peaking, and held tight. She cried out softly against his throat, writhing and twisting in the ecstasy he brought to her. He thrust slowly, deliberately, back and forth, and she was sobbing softly, her hands slipping on his back, wet and frantic.

He found he could hold back, as she sobbed herself to quiet. He soothed her with his hands, whispering to her words of love, calming words.

"There, darling, love—it's all right—oh, darling, you're so sweet—easy, honey."

When she was quiet again, he began once more. "Ohhhh," she shuddered, as she felt the movements in her once more. He brought her quickly to another climax, she cried out wildly, her hips pressing up to him. He circled her hips, making her feel all of him, smiling into the darkness at the wildness of her responses tonight. It was worth it all, the waiting, the patience, the teaching—

She was squeezing him hard. He could not wait longer, he lay on her and let his own response come rushing into her. It brought on another pulsing reply from her, and he felt her holding him, grasping him deeply, exquisitely.

They came together, and it was wildly beautiful. His heart was beating frantically when it was over, and she lay limply in his arms, her own breathing needed gasps for air.

He lay back, rolling her over to half-lie on his hard

body. He cuddled her against his body, her legs wound with his, so he could still feel her warmth and wetness. He stroked slowly down her back and over her thighs, soothing her to rest, whispering to her.

She was limp across his body, like a piece of seaweed flung on the beach by the force of the tide. He drew the sheet over them both, it was cool in spite of the heat of the July night.

"Love," he murmured, "oh, my love, my own darling, my heart's delight—how sweet you are—how I delight in you and your loveliness—" He could not praise her enough, he adored her body and mind and heart—all of her—the silkiness of her, the sweet scent of her—

She murmured something sleepily.

"What, darling?"

"You are—so strong—so good to me—"

It wasn't what he wanted, but it would do for now. He wanted her—one day soon—to say the words, "I love you." She had never said that, he thought. But one day she would, and mean it.

She cuddled sleepily against him, and soon her even breathing told him she slept. In spite of his weariness, he lay awake for a time, smiling with pleasure at the joy they had known. Small as she was, her hips had held him so firmly, with such marvelous tightness that he felt it all through him.

It was going to work out, this marriage of opposites, he thought. She had been raised so differently from himself, they had such different ideas, but it would work out. Charita was teachable, she learned quickly, and dear heaven, how she learned! His hand went lightly over her back, her adorable back, over her hips, which had just held him.

In the future, they would grow closer. She would not be so cool, so polite and distant with him. It had to work. She belonged to him, he would never let her go.

Tonight was a good omen for that future, he decided. He could make her feel and respond sensuously to him. And they worked well together. He had been reluctant to let her work, yet she needed something to do, something to make her feel useful. Goodness knew, she was useful! He had never seen such designs as she created. She would make herself indispensable, if he didn't watch it.

Eventually, he wanted a child of her, and that would keep her plenty busy! More than one child, a son, a daughter. She would like that, he thought, and so would he. A family—he who had been without family much of his adult life. And it would be different from the earlier family he had known, bickering, quarreling, hating, screaming, fighting— No, not that, not ever again. He would not have that kind of life.

What good fortune had brought him to Japan, to find and marry Charita! If he had not gone up to Hokkaido, worried about Charita and her father, he might never have stumbled onto this good luck. The ways of life were strange—how the paths led one firmly where one had not intended to go—and the paths led to delight.

He thought of this again a couple of nights later, when he returned from work early. He had decided to have a dinner party at last, after the urgings of the Pattersons. It was the same group, plus Kanji, Pearl Takahashi, Donald Raglan, two other Japanese couples whom Charita knew and liked. Quite a crowd, but she had said eagerly that she could manage.

The house glowed with soft lights. Instead of the bright electric ones, Charita had lit lanterns all over the two formal living rooms, the hallway, the dining room, and the guest room where the ladies primped before coming out to join them. The effect was of a soft rose glow over all, and it flattered the complexions of the women.

Charita wore a long rose brocade gown, embroidered

312

in silver roses. Her slippers were silver, her jewelry amethysts set in silver. She seemed to glow herself as she greeted the guests at the door.

He was proud of her. She was poised, smiling brightly, her voice low and lovely. She remembered all the names, she directed the men to the bar to help themselves as they wished, the ladies were taken care of with whatever they wished to drink.

The dinner was well-planned also, a charming mixture of Japanese and American dishes. Shrimp, wild rice, broiled chicken, asparagus in butter sauce, green salads, wine, and for dessert an immense strawberry shortcake for each one.

Charita saw Brad smile at her, and she relaxed, there at the foot of the table. He was pleased, all was going well. She had worried secretly, but vowed she would not allow him to see her ruffled. He wanted a poised hostess, she must mature, she told herself firmly. He was an important man, she would not let him down.

Donald Raglan was a help. He was a born diplomat, or perhaps his early life had rubbed off on him. He balanced gallantry with keen interest in business, was attentive to the older women, teased the younger ones, explained Japanese customs to the Americans, and American ones to the Japanese. He spoke Japanese fluently, translated quickly for the Japanese couples, including the difficult puns, which are so hard in any language to explain.

Kanji and Pearl looked at each other and remained at opposite ends of the room. Charita felt exasperated with them both. Why didn't Kanji treat her with the charm and poise with which he treated other girls? Instead he showed himself as awkward as any schoolboy. And Pearl's nose was in the air. She looked so beautiful tonight, in her cream kimono with the pattern of pine cones on it.

Charita complimented her shyly. "It is most shibui,"

she said. "How handsome is the fabric, so elegant and restrained."

Joy Hartung caught the word, and as Pearl bowed and murmured her gratitude to Charita, Joy asked, "What is that—*shibui*? I have heard the word applied to pottery, painting—I don't understand it."

"It means—an elegant restraint—understatement—I am not sure how to say it," said Charita, frowning a little in puzzlement.

Kanji had wandered near, hovering opposite Pearl. "It means a quality of restraint which makes for an elegance of design and line. There is some color, yet not too much. There is pattern, not too much. It is an astringent taste, not too sweet. It is simple, yet not too plain, nor too gaudy. This is all I can explain."

"That is very good," applauded Joy brightly. "I like that! *Shibui*—I must remember that."

Kanji bowed to her, in response to her laughing bow. His smile was attractive, Charita noticed Pearl staring at him dubiously. Aha, thought Charita. It was good for Pearl to see how Kanji was attractive to other women. He would not wait forever for Pearl! She must be wary, or she would lose him!

Charita moved away to talk to other guests. Joy followed her, persistent as a bright butterfly in her brilliant green dress, with her flaming copper hair.

"I wish I could see some of your paintings," Joy said, at a pause in the conversation.

"There is one over there," Charita pointed out shyly. "The lotus in the pond. Brad liked it and had it framed."

"That is yours?" Joy went closer to study it in detail. "Beautiful!" They were temporarily alone in the corner of the living room. Joy lowered her tone. "Is it true about Brad's foster sister, that she has left her husband?"

Charita schooled her face to an impassive look, gazing at her painting blindly.

"I do not know all the truth of it," she hedged.

"Well," the voice lowered even more. "I just wondered, because I was going through some old neighborhood one day—someone told me that he saw the most gorgeous old pots over there—and I happened to see Brad's car. He had stopped in front of some tacky old apartments and was getting out, and she was with him—I knew her at once, that silvery bright hair, and her elegance. Well, did I stare! They went up into one of the flats. I know she wouldn't ordinarily be caught dead in that—I expect that's where she moved. They say that Miles Snow gets roaring drunk all the time and rages around trying to find out where she lives! He even called us twice from a bar!"

"I am so sorry you were disturbed," said Charita, automatically. She was flushed and distressed, yet something cold, like a knife, pierced her heart. Jacinda and Brad—going up to her apartment—

"I wouldn't have said a word," gushed Joy, "but I thought you ought to know about Miles. He is practically your brother-in-law. Well, he is raging all around, and some of the men have withdrawn their business, he can't handle it, you know—"

Donald Raglan came up, and Charita mentally blessed him. "One of yours?" he nodded to the painting. "I say, that is very good. Do you ever sell any? Mater would adore having one."

"I shall be happy to paint something for her, as a gift—" Charita managed to say the words around the pains that gripped her chilled body.

"No, no, you mustn't give things away. Sell them," urged Donald earnestly. "I'm beginning to find out at Frundsberg's how important and expensive good art really is. I always took it for granted before— Now I realize that people are willing to pay high for a good talent—"

He went chatting on, and Charita could smile and

nod, and blank out for a time what Joy Hartung had said. But later on after the guests had departed with much gushing gratitude, she lay awake in the bedroom, alone. Brad had gone to sleep in the other room, saying she must be very tired.

"And I had so hoped," Charita whispered aloud into the darkness. "I had—so hoped—"

His kisses, his gentleness, his thoughtfulness—all meant so little. He did not love her, for all his words. He probably used the words as carelessly as he had used her body at first. Now he was careful with her, because he wished the wild response that pleased him. Tears fell on her cheeks, to be wiped away impatiently with the sheet.

She had hoped for a good marriage, one man, one woman. Devotion freely returned. It was not to be. Brad was still seeing Jacinda—alone—in her apartment. And she was not returning to her husband, Miles.

In the dark hours of early morning, she felt the grip of despair tightening on her. How could she go on living like this? Up in the heights, then plunged down to the depths? How long could she endure this?

She had been starting to love him, but that must stop. She could not love where she did not trust—could she?

21

August burst in with stormy rains and cloudbursts that drenched the crowds in the streets of Kyoto and sent them scattering into the shelter of nearby stores. Bright yellow and red umbrellas bloomed on the rain-wet streets. Women clattered along the sidewalks on two-inch-high getas especially made for muddy, wet weather.

Brad felt the weather matched his mood. He could not understand Charita. One time she was so sweet and gentle and welcoming. Then for a week she would be cool and standoffish, and he could scarcely get her to respond to him. And one night after making love, he had slept, only to awake and find her quietly, desperately weeping beside him, her fingers pressed to her mouth to hold back the sounds of her sobs.

"What is it, darling, what troubles you?" he begged her over and over. She shook her head, desolately, and turned her face from him.

"I am so sorry to awaken you," was all she would say.

He damned the politeness that was like a shield between them. She would not speak to him frankly. When he stormed at her, she shrank in fear, and he had to quit that. When he begged her, she shut her mouth obstinately, and looked at him with drenched blue eyes like wet violets.

He turned to his work with relief. She had completed the designs for two screens now, and he was very pleased with the way the workmen had rendered the designs in gold. He stayed up all night then, and did the gold-plating on the silver and gold designs and was very happy with the pearly-gold results.

Now the workmen carefully fastened the golden pieces to the mahogany frame, and they shone beautifully. Brad almost hated to have the screens boxed and crated and sent off to Arabia. The workmen had been thrilled with them also, coming respectfully into the workroom where they were displayed for a few days while the mahogany frames were being completed.

The Arab prince decided not to have a shipping company handle the screens. He sent one of his innumerable cousins and a retinue of five men to Japan, to approve the screens and carry them back to Saudi Arabia with them. The cousin had wanted to meet Charita, the designer, but Brad had firmly refused. He felt he did not want those black-eyed men to stare at his lovely wife and carry back the report of how beautiful and talented she was. In fact, he thought, he would like to have her in purdah, walking about demurely in a cloak and veil! That showed how far he had sunk, he thought ruefully, with a shake of his head.

The Arab prince, the cousin, had gazed long and happily at the screens, examined them from all sides, praised them, and said, "I know my lord cousin will wish more work from your esteemed hands, Mr. Livingston. He will be most pleased with your care and the beauty of these objects."

Brad had bowed his head respectfully, and told him, "I shall be happy to hear from your esteemed lord cousin. I only hope that these screens will add to the beauty of his famous palace."

The words seemed to please the cousin. Maybe the Japanese had something there, with their careful courtesy,

Brad decided. They carried off the screens, heavily guarded, and Brad settled down to work on other commissions.

He had planned to go back to the States on business about September, but now he wrote to his factories and told them they must carry on without him for several more months. He would be lucky if he could complete the work laid out for him by Christmas. Perhaps then he and Charita could get away together to the States for a time. He wanted that badly. He felt they were drifting apart, and he didn't know why.

Brad arranged to spend as much time alone with Charita as he could. However, Jacinda had called him several times and begged him to come and see her. He had gone reluctantly, met her usually in restaurants, then taken her back to her apartment. He had tried to make her decide whether to return to the States and get a divorce from Miles, or return to Miles. But she would weep and storm and tell him he didn't understand her.

The trouble was, Brad thought, he was coming to understand Jacinda all too well, and the knowledge made him squirm. Why in the world she would mistake his brotherly concern for love and passion, he had no idea.

Another batch of jewelry was ready to be electroplated, and Brad contemplated that with a sigh. He wished he could trust someone else to do that, but he must not slip. If only he knew the gold formula, no one else could get it.

So he warned Charita he would not be home until morning, and set out that evening to work. He cleared out the factory, told the workmen not to come until noon the next day, and set to work. He had locked himself in, with only the guards prowling about. He could hear the dogs snarling, or barking, when anyone came even close to the building.

He worked through the night, electroplated the jewelry at hand with the pearly gold. Then he carefully poured out the chemicals he had used, cleaned the electrodes of all the mixtures, and set the jewelry to dry under the artificial vents. He could not use opened air vents that night, for rain was pouring down, and the vents could not be opened to the skies.

It was dawn before he finished. He was tired. He took off the white lab coat, and left it for Pearl to send to the cleaners. Then he put on his suit coat and raincoat, and departed. His head was down against the rain, and he supposed later he must have been careless. He got into the car, waved good-bye to the guard at the factory door, and started down the street. He turned the corner slowly, thinking wearily of food and bed.

He had not taken the chauffeur or bodyguard. He didn't want them waiting up all night.

Two cars were waiting beyond the corner. They blocked him off before he knew what was happening. One rushed his car, and smashed into it. Then one brawny man opened his car door and hauled him out.

They pushed him roughly into the back seat of the huge limousine behind his car. He was followed into the car by two guards. Instinctively he tried to fight them. One blow on the head with a hard stick, and Brad was out.

He came to, in a dingy gray-walled bedroom. He was laid out on a lumpy bed, hands bound before him, a bandage around his head. He felt blood trickle down his face. He blinked at the overhead light, a single dull bulb swinging from a cord in the middle of the room. A man leaned forward from the straight chair beside the bed.

"Mr. Livingston," he said distinctly. The beady black eyes stared at Brad.

It was one of the two men he had seen before on the plane and at Hakone. Brad's stomach churned. He grunted, closed his eyes as though unconscious. The man leaned forward and slapped his cheek, hard. Brad's eyes flew open again, he could not keep the hate from his look.

The Japanese face was bland and impassive. No hate was there, only the impersonal look of a man doing a job. He was big, rough-looking, and he had a heavy accent.

"What do you want?" asked Brad, in English.

The man stared at him. "You know what we want." His English was crude, his accent odd, but Brad could understand him.

"Money, I suppose," said Brad. It was too much to hope for, but they just might have kidnapped him for ransom.

Another man leaned over Brad, from the other side of the bed. He was a muscle man, too, but his eyes flashed with a keener intelligence.

"We wish the formula for the gold you make, Mr. Livingston," he said. "You will tell us now, yes?"

"Formula?" repeated Brad, blankly.

The first man struck him on the face again, with his fist. Brad's head jerked back in pain.

"You will stay here until you tell us the formula. That is what we wish," said the second man. The other man had his fist ready.

"I don't know what you're talking about," said Brad, rather hopelessly. Had his guards seen nothing? How soon would they miss him? How could anyone trace him? Not much hope—he would have to get himself out. Would an offer of money help?

He was struck again, again, on the chest, the legs. His body ached, until finally he closed his eyes and pretended to be unconscious. They muttered above him, angrily. One man brought a cup of water and threw it in his face.

Jacinda was wakened from an uneasy sleep. She didn't like her crude apartment, she missed her maids and her comforts, and good food and good whiskey. The phone ringing in her ear made her cringe, she snapped into the phone, "What is it?"

"Excuse please, Mrs. Snow. This is your man Yoshida."

Her brain snapped to attention. She sat up in her bed. "Yoshida. What has happened?"

"Excuse please, I have the sad duty of telling to you of unhappy news which is happening to your friend."

She gritted her teeth. "What—has—happened? Is it Mr. Livingston?" she said, with cold, forced patience.

"Yes, yes, Mr. Livingston-san. He get taken away in big black car."

She was all alertness, her long fingers clenched over the telephone as though she would squeeze information from it more quickly. "Where did they take him?"

"To bad district, Mrs. Snow-san. I am very sorry to tell you such unhappy news."

"Come and pick me up at once. I'll be downstairs." She slammed the telephone down and slid out of bed to grab for the first pants suit that came to hand. Her brain was working swiftly. Money. She would need a lot of money, cash.

She had been half-expecting this. She had been worried about Brad. Her men had heard rumors. She had hired several guards to shadow Brad, she thought he was not careful enough. That child he had married was taking too much of his attention. He was not his usual careful self.

She gathered up all the cash she had around, locked up her jewelry in a traveling case and put it under the bed. Then she was ready. She walked down the long flights of stairs, her mind half on Brad, half on the utter insane inconvenience of living in Japan in this horrible flat.

Yoshida and two husky friends were waiting for her in their shabby little blue car. She got in beside the driver, and they set off.

"When did they get him?" she asked, as they went.

"This morning, when he left the factory."

"No guards with him, I suppose?"

Yoshida gave a big sigh, spread out his beefy hands from the seat behind her, where he sat cramped. "No guards. Mr. Livingston-san get too careless with his safety."

"Where are they?"

"In old hotel, very bad place."

"Go in with me, all of you, and be ready for anything."

"They have four men, very bad men," said Yoshida, not complaining but telling her.

"I have much money with me. We will bargain for his life. If all goes well, you will all receive good pay, very good pay."

He beamed, showing gold-capped teeth, and spurted something in Japanese to his friends. They all beamed and looked eager. Money could buy much, she thought bitterly. Maybe a life. It had better work.

They pulled up in a poor neighborhood, beside a stinking alley. Dingy clothes hung on a line stretched from the window of one apartment building to another. Children played in the filthy piles of wood alongside the alley. They paused to stare curiously at the foreign lady in the green silk suit who stepped so fastidiously around them.

Yoshida went first, she followed, the other two hung close behind them. They went up the steps, to where a man lounged in front of a door. He stood up straight and blocked their way, his black eyes flickering with suspicion.

"I am here to see Mr. Livingston," said Jacinda distinctly. She voiced every word clearly. He glared at her.

"No here. No here."

"He is here. I will see him. Open the door!" She made her voice brusque and imperious. These people responded to authority. She nodded at the door.

323

He scowled, hesitated. Yoshida stood quietly, watching, his hands in his pockets.

"Open the door, at once!" said Jacinda, and moved forward.

He started, then slowly reached for the door knob. He opened the door, and she stepped in.

She saw Brad stretched out on the pallet-bed, his hands and feet bound. Dark bruises stood out on his face, and dried blood slashed across his forehead. She kept her nerve with an effort. His eyes blazed at her.

"What the hell are you doing here?" he snapped.

She ignored him with an effort, and turned to the toughs who had risen in fury at her entrance. They snapped at the man who had been at the door. He shrugged, looked down at the floor sullenly.

"You will release Mr. Livingston," she said, with authority.

"Why? It is nothing to you," said one of the men.

"He is my brother," she said flatly.

More mutters from the men. They stared at her with hard eyes like black marbles. Yoshida stood so close behind her, she could smell his sweaty body. But she was glad of his closeness, and the weapon in his pocket.

"Who paid you to do this?" she snapped.

No answer, only glares.

"Well, you can do nothing now, since I am here," she said. "You will release him."

"No!"

"I will pay you enough money to get you out of Kyoto, to safety. You will hide from the man who pays you. He probably pays you little enough."

The black eyes shifted, stared at one another.

Carelessly, she pulled out an envelope from her pocketbook. She let the yen notes drift to a table. Greedy eyes fastened on them. "Twenty thousand yen to let him go."

They growled at each other. She waited, strategically.

"He will not have the money with him," she said. She knew, shrewdly, that they did not anticipate money, but the gold formula. Damn, she had warned and warned Brad!

"You will leave Kyoto and hide from the anger of the man who foolishly hired you, and will leave you to the police," she said, casually.

At the word "police," they started, and glared around, belligerently.

"Yoshida, cut him loose," she said.

Yoshida started forward. One man stopped him, a hand before him, warningly.

Jacinda nodded to the pile of notes on the table. "That is half what I will give you to let him go with me."

She paused to let the words sink in.

Then she said deliberately, "I will give you that much again, when he is free and out on the street with me."

It was a gamble, but these men were for hire. They muttered, shook their heads, she waited. Then she tossed more money on the table, letting it spill there.

"Thirty thousand yen. And that again when he is free."

That did it. All that money! It was more than they saw in a year. One of the men cut Brad loose. It hurt her heart, the way Brad got up so slowly, staggering, holding carefully to the side of the bed, before letting go and standing erect. Blood ran down his sleeve. Those damned men! Cutting him like that! She wanted to rave, to rant, to curse them. But she stood rigidly, her cool brain in control.

Yoshida stood aside. Jacinda went first, then Brad staggered down the creaky stairs after her. The other men crowded after. At the foot of the stairs, she told Yoshida curtly, "Get Mr. Livingston into the car."

He nodded, took Brad gently by the arm, and helped

him into the back seat. The other men waited, rigidly, beside the car, alert black eyes on the men crowding down the stairs, eager eyes on the large handbag she carried.

She saw Brad into the car, Yoshida safely beside him. Then she reached into the purse, and took out yet another envelope. Deliberately, she spilled it, spilled the money onto the dirty sidewalk.

"The other thirty thousand yen. And I advise you to leave Kyoto!" She walked quickly on her high heels to the car. She slid inside, the driver was ready; they pulled away as the men were scrambling for the money on the sidewalk.

Her shoulders ached from tension. She turned around to look at Brad. He grinned back at her, looking boyish in spite of his weariness and pain. "Good dealing, Jacinda. How did you manage all this?"

"You've been such a careless fool, I've had you followed," she snapped, to hide her anguish at his injuries. "Now I'll get you to the hospital."

"No, not the hospital. Take me home," he said quietly.

"But you've got to have those injuries treated—"

"At home," he repeated. "I'll get a doctor in."

At the protest in her face, he smiled, leaned forward and touched her hand with his grimy, bloody hand.

"I'll get a doctor, Jacinda, don't worry. But I don't want this advertised. Your men will keep quiet?"

"Oh, yes, they know how," she said, looking significantly at Yoshida. He nodded and grinned widely. All had gone well, he still wasn't sure how!

"I don't want this all over Japan," said Brad quietly. "The fewer who know, the better. And I want the man behind the attack, not those poor fools."

"All right. Only for God's sake, take more care in the future!"

"Don't worry. I will," he said grimly. He leaned back, and shut his eyes. She gave him a last look, and turned to

326

stare forward rigidly. She was beginning to shake, now that it was over. She had taken a chance, but brazen behavior and quickness had carried it. They could have both ended up, tied and helpless, and tortured—Brad, tortured—she couldn't bear it. She nibbled at her knuckles nervously, holding back weak tears. God, how she loved him! And she had managed to save him—this time.

Brad opened his eyes, spoke wearily from the back seat. "I don't know what you paid, but I'll repay you at once. And what about your men here?"

"I promised them a lot of money."

"And I'll pay them again," he said, with a tired grin. He managed in Japanese to say to Yoshida, "I am most grateful for your skillful pursuit and aid in rescuing me. I shall never forget your most honorable actions and help."

Yoshida beamed, and bowed, his head bobbing in the small car. "It was my most humble pleasure, that my stupid self could be of assistance to most honorable Mr. Livingston-san."

"I hope I shall not need your aid again. However, it is of much comfort that men such as you are about, to help me—"

Jacinda burst out, "My God, Brad, you talk like one of them—"

"I am grateful," he said shortly.

Yoshida and his men were beaming, and chattering to each other about Brad and his ability to speak so well in Japanese. Jacinda was about to burst forth again, bitterly, in her shaking relief, that Brad was unduly flowery. But she noticed the tired frown on his face, noticed the slowness of the movement of his hand to his dirty face. How they had hurt him, shaken him. She could have killed them all! She bit her lips, and her long fingers tore at the lacy handkerchief in her lap.

"I wish I could take you to my flat," she said shakily. "You need nursing—"

"Thanks. Charita will do that. Poor kid, she will be shook up over this."

The tender note in his voice hurt her unbearably. She was biting her lips hard when they drew up in the driveway of his house. It was about nine in the morning.

The chauffeur came running, and the powerful body-guards, growling as they saw the ruffians emerging from the car. Brad stopped them with a gesture.

"They saved my life. After this, I don't move without you," he managed to say. "My fault—all my fault." He was staggering. One of his bodyguards, hesitating, finally went up to him and gave him a shoulder to lean on as he limped into the house.

Jacinda followed them slowly, churning with a mixture of feelings. She was glad she had rescued him, triumphant that it was she who had done so. She resented Charita, that the girl would have the task of caring for Brad. And she felt sick at Brad's injuries, as though the blows had fallen on her own body. And she wanted Miles' shoulder to cry on. That was the strangest of all. He would have some cynical, wry observations, and would make her laugh. Miles, oh, damn, why did he have to be a lush?

Brad said, "Wait here, men, I'll have some money for you. To express my gratitude—"

The house door opened, the houseboy stared open-mouthed at the strange procession that came toward him. Whatever had Livingston-san been up to?

22

From her workroom, Charita heard the voices raised in agitation, and came out curiously. She saw Brad staggering in the door, blood on his face, blood running down his torn coat sleeve, the guard supporting him.

"Brad!" she whispered, and put her hands to her heart. She ran forward, almost afraid to see the damage done to him.

"Don't worry, honey, it's worse than it looks. Get me to the study," he said to the guard holding him.

Jacinda was following them, looking smooth and immaculate. What was she doing here, with those tough-looking Japanese men, her green silk suit and high clicking heels an odd contrast to their rough clothes and shabby appearance? Jacinda gave Charita a long cool look.

"He was getting careless," she said, in an offhand manner. "I paid to have him followed, and this morning it was necessary. Someone kidnapped him, and was beating him up when we located him."

There was a calm pride in her voice, in the lift of her smooth blond head. Enmity in her green eyes, a glinting triumph. Charita bowed her head in silent acknowledgment of that triumph.

"You have done a most wonderful miracle," said

Charita, slowly. "I shall be forever grateful to you for your goodness and your wisdom."

Jacinda looked as though she would snap out something rude. Her red mouth thinned.

"I didn't do it for—" she was beginning, when Brad emerged from the study, staggering still, but upright. He had a fistful of yen notes in his hand.

"Jacinda, I'll pay you later, all and more that you paid out. This is for your men—" And he gave the leader, Yoshida, the money.

Yoshida bowed and thanked him profusely, and bowed himself backward hastily out of the house, before the crazy American changed his mind. The car roared off in a clatter of old parts.

"I'll call the doctor, guess that's the next move," said Brad, looking suddenly weary and haggard. His unshaven face made him look almost like the ruffians, thought Charita, tenderly. She came up close, put her hand to his face gently.

"It aches, yes?"

He pressed his hand over hers, holding it to his cheek. "It aches, hell, yes. My own damned fault. I let the guards go on home, I knew I would be late. Next time, we stick it out together. Someone is desperate for—" He stopped short, looked at Jacinda significantly.

Charita felt left out, abandoned by that look of understanding between them.

"I will telephone the doctor," she said slowly, and moved to the study to make the telephone call. She heard Jacinda speaking behind her, so cool and sure of herself.

"Do you want to press charges? I can find the men again, Brad. I think they should be arrested—"

"No, I want the man behind them. Let them go, we may find them again."

His voice was tired and stubborn.

Charita went into the study and telephoned the doctor. He promised to come at once, and she hung up. She returned to the hallway to find Brad sitting limply on a hall chair, and Jacinda touching his head, searching for the source of the fresh blood streaming down his cheek.

Charita paused. Jealousy was streaking hotly through her. She hated to see Jacinda so close to Brad, touching him intimately, her slim silk-clad body so close that Brad must be able to feel her warmth, smell the musky perfume.

Yet Jacinda had saved Brad by her cleverness and wisdom. Charita and Brad owed her much. She had rescued Brad—how? How had she known to watch over him, to set men to guard him? Why had she done it? She was a smart woman, a lawyer, very sure of herself. Yet— how had she known an attack would be made on Brad?

Charita despised herself for feeling such suspicions. Yet more than one attack had been made on Brad—and Jacinda was always about. She seemed to know his moves before Charita ever found out. How could she know so much?

Charita moved forward slowly, the outsider, instead of the wife. Jacinda was murmuring compassionately over Brad. Brad glanced beyond her, saw Charita waiting there, hands clasped.

"Is the doctor coming?" he asked sharply.

"He comes at once," said Charita formally. "Should you—retire to your bedroom?"

"Yes, I'll go there, and wash up—I feel grimy and achy. A hot bath will feel good." He got painfully to his feet.

"I wish you wouldn't move until the doctor comes. Your ribs might be broken," protested Jacinda, not moving far from him. Her hand went to his shoulder, the long fingers with the red polish on the nails went slowly over the curve of his shoulder.

"I would feel it if they were broken," said Brad shortly. "Sorry, darling, I'm tired and feeling fed up. Do

331

you mind going home with the chauffeur now? And how about going back to your own flat? I worry about you in that fleabag place."

Her face closed, her green eyes blazed. "I'll go where I please." Deliberately, she reached up, her fingers spread on each cheek. "Take care of yourself, love. I worry about you."

Jacinda was tall. In her high heels, she was almost as tall as Brad. Deliberately, she reached up, and pressed her mouth to his. The maid drew in her breath in a hiss. Charita felt a little faint. The bodyguard and chauffeur watched with interest, turning away a little in the shame of a woman kissing a man before them, yet interested.

"Darling, I hate to leave you. Let me stay and help you, I've had first aid—"

She was begging, and Charita held her breath, waiting for his answer. He put his hands on her wrists, a color had come high on his bruised cheekbones.

"You've done plenty for me today, Jacinda, I'm most grateful. I'll express it better with a few diamonds," he managed to grin. "You go off now, and get yourself safely home. I'll talk to you later."

"All right, sweetheart. I'll go." Jacinda gave Charita a little triumphant look over her shoulder. "Take care of Brad, he's very precious!" she admonished, before clicking out the long hallway to the door.

"Bath and bed for me," Brad muttered. "Charita, I could do with some food—"

She started, as one in a dream. "Oh, yes, of course. What would you wish? Tea—toast—"

"Hell, no. Bacon and eggs and coffee," he growled, and limped down the hallway toward his masculine bedroom.

Charita gave the order to the maid and followed Brad slowly to his room. He had stripped off his jacket, wincing, and now was struggling with his tie and shirt. She went to

332

him, and gently helped him remove the garments. He had trouble with his pants belt, and she unfastened that.

"Run some hot bath water, will you, honey?" he asked, with a smile as she stopped with the belt strap.

She went willingly to the bathroom, and ran his water. She wondered if he would like her to scrub his back, the way the Japanese women did for their men. But he said nothing of that as he came into the bathroom in his robe, and she departed.

He sank into the water as she was closing the door. She caught a glimpse of the bruises and welts over his lean hard body, and felt a little faint. What those men had done to him! She put her fist to her mouth, then went to set out clean pajamas, and see that his bed had fresh linen on it.

The doctor arrived before Brad's breakfast. He examined him, shook his head. "You are most lucky man," he said gravely. "A little more time, they break some bones, I think." The black hair shook on his head as he nodded briskly.

Charita was standing by with a basin of hot water, as the doctor had requested. She flinched as though in pain herself as the doctor probed. The wound on the head took most of his attention. He cleansed it with antiseptic, and took a good look at it.

"No stitches this time. You are most tough man, Mr. Livingston-san!"

Brad gave him a tired grin. "I used to be tough, I'm not so sure anymore. I'm getting tired of getting beaten up, though. Next time, I'll do the beating!"

The doctor looked serious, swabbing the blood efficiently as the wound began bleeding again. "One hopes there is no next time for you, Mr. Livingston-san," he said politely. "One hopes there is no more danger for you."

"Life itself can be dangerous," said Brad, and their eyes met in understanding.

"For some," said the doctor.

"Those are the chances of the game."

Charita wondered what they were talking about.

"You must remain quiet for several days and give your head a chance to heal," said the doctor, as he prepared to leave. "It will not hurt to rest your other injuries. You will be covered with blue and green marks for some time, but fortunately no bones are broken, no ribs are broken."

"You are most kind to come so quickly," said Brad, and bowed his head a couple of times to the doctor, as he bowed his way out of the bedroom.

Charita was a little cheered to see this. Brad seemed to do it sincerely, not mockingly, as he had done at first. The doctor was very good to leave his practice and his clinic to drop everything and come to Brad. She thought Brad did appreciate it.

Charita lingered to see if there was anything else she could do for Brad. The maid brought in a heavy tray of food, and Brad sat up to eat. But he frowned, and put his hand to his head.

"A little dizzy," he said, apologetically, and grimaced.

Quietly, Charita helped him. The maid set down the tray, and hovered to see if she could be of aid. Brad ate a little of the egg, a bite or two of bacon, drank some tea, then lay back exhausted.

"Sleep is best," murmured Charita, and motioned for the tray to be removed. She settled the pillows so Brad would be more comfortable, then moved to the windows to close the Venetian blinds.

Brad was asleep before she had turned from the windows. She contemplated him in the dimness, soberly, feeling so confused and close to tears that it scared her.

Why did he take such chances? Why was he so reckless? Dismissing the guards because he didn't want them to wait for him! If Jacinda had not come to the rescue—

And there Charita felt the more confused. She disliked and distrusted Jacinda Snow, and that long kiss on the lips she had given Brad had upset Charita. Yet she had saved Brad from a horrible fate, that torture and beating—

Brad stirred, murmured, and she stood still, waiting until he sank into a deeper sleep before leaving the room. She did not have to tell the servants to be quiet, they whispered around as though someone were very ill.

Brad slept all the day, until late in the evening. When he woke, he was groggy, his head ached like fire. For a time, he could not remember what had happened, and wondered why his whole body ached dully and stung in places.

Then he remembered, and his mouth set. He had been caught off guard. Never again, never again! He brooded about that for a time.

Charita peeped in at the door, he held out his hand to her and she entered. "Hello, darling. What time is it?"

"Almost nine o'clock. How do you feel?"

"Head aches. I'm hungry, though."

She put her cool hand on his forehead, it felt cold. "A little fever, I fear. Shall I call the doctor?"

"No, I've bothered him enough. I'd like some coffee and something light."

She nodded, and went out, softly. He managed to get to the bathroom, fought a wave of nausea, and got back into bed. One of the blows must have caught him in the stomach. Charita brought in a small tray, and plumped up pillows behind him. Her face was softly concerned, the blue eyes sad.

"I'm going to be all right, honey," he said, touching her pale cheek with his fingers, "Don't look like that."

She nodded, her head bent. He began to eat, but found the coffee about all he could manage.

"Kanji telephoned several times. I told him you still slept."

"I'll phone him tomorrow. If he phones again, just tell him to carry on, as usual. The gold-plating is done."

"Yes, he said they found the gold jewelry that was finished, and will continue the work. But he was much distressed at the events—" Her voice faltered, and she brushed her hand over her face.

"I won't be that careless again, you may be sure of that," he told her quietly. "Ask Kanji to come over tomorrow morning, about nine o'clock, on the way to the factory. We'll talk a bit."

Charita nodded. "And Mrs. Snow telephoned, and was most concerned."

"I'll talk to her tomorrow. Reassure her if she phones. Did Miles Snow call?"

Charita shook her head. Brad frowned, thoughtfully. A mad, impossible thought was taking shape in his brain, and he did not like it at all, not a bit. Could Miles have been so jealous of Brad, in his alcoholic frenzies, that he would have hired thugs to beat him up? He was one of the few who knew Brad's routine, how he worked all night on the electroplating. But Miles—a friend, a close friend, Jacinda's husband—no, he would never have done that. Or would he? Could he?

And how had Jacinda known where and how to come? Brad had accepted completely at first her story of having Brad followed. But what if she knew more about this—what if she suspected Miles—oh, damn, he didn't want to think like this!

"The egg does not please you?" came Charita's soft voice.

"It's fine, honey." He smiled, and forced himself to eat, in spite of the pains in his stomach. He wanted to recover fast. And he hated the unpleasant thoughts that plagued him. Suspecting Miles Snow! He had known him for years, he had liked the man—

Yet lately Miles had been so damned unpleasant, so

insulting. And the man had it fixed in his mind that Brad and Jacinda were carrying on an affair.

Brad would have said "ridiculous" a few weeks ago. But now, with Jacinda acting like a brat—

"Anyone else telephone?"

Charita recited, "Mr. Frundsberg telephoned to talk to you. He was most concerned when he learned you were ill." She looked guilty. "I told him you had come down with influenza," she confessed like a child.

Brad grinned. "Good girl. That's the best idea yet. Keep on with that story."

She relaxed a little. "I thought you would not wish it known about those—those horrible men."

"Right you are. Smart girl. Anyone else phone?"

"Mr. Patterson. He seemed most upset. He said he had an appointment for dinner with you, and wished to see you at the house if you could not come out. I persuaded him you were with fever. I fear I told many lies!"

"He wants to buy into my business, good investment," shrugged Brad. "It is hard to make him accept my refusal. No harm in putting him off."

"And the Arab prince telephoned, to express his pleasure at the screens. He—he remained on the telephone almost half an hour, by long distance from Saudi Arabia!" Charita looked horrified.

Brad felt irritated and angry. "He talked to *you?*" he asked sharply.

Charita nodded, her round face softly shining in the dim light of the lamp, her hands folded before her as she sat in the armchair near his bed. "Yes. He asked if I had designed the screens, and when I said yes, then he must compliment me for many minutes. It was most embarrassing."

"Damn," said Brad. Charita looked at him, blue eyes puzzled.

"You are angry?"

"Those Arab princes have too much money and too much time and too little respect for women," said Brad abruptly. "I don't want you talking to him. What else did he say?"

"A cousin of his wishes a screen, one of his wives wishes emeralds set in the pearly gold, and he wishes us to come and visit him in his palace," she recited.

Brad started to swear, then began to laugh. "Well, he can just wait! I have more than I can do, and so have you. One of these weeks we are going to take off for the States on a honeymoon, and I want the time clear for that! There is such a thing as too much success!"

Charita's transparent face was suddenly radiant. "Oh, do you believe this, Brad? My father said this at times."

He gentled, and took her slim fingers in his, smiling at her. "Yes, I believe it, now. I didn't use to. I enjoy my work and want to continue it, I get a whale of a satisfaction from it. Yet when it keeps me from spending time with you, I resent it. We'll have to strike a balance somehow."

"I should like that," she whispered, and let her fingers stay in his.

He felt contented, and calmed. They talked a bit, but when his eyelids drooped, she rose, took the tray away, and left him to sleep again.

He felt better the next day, but strangely languid, as though something inside him had sprung loose and he could not wind himself up to get going again. He didn't want to leave his comfortable bed, he enjoyed being waited on, he liked sitting with Charita and talking with her, and hearing her read to him.

And between times, he thought. He thought and brooded, and as his mind cleared from the blows on his head, he pondered the many possibilities of who was behind the attacks on him.

Patterson. Possibly. He was a cool customer and had made a heck of a lot of money, some rather shadily.

338

Miles Snow. That hurt. Brad liked the man, and used to respect him for his knowledge, the keen mind, the wisdom. And Miles had helped him immensely in the early years. Yet—Miles had burst out all that filth about Brad and Jacinda—and seemed to believe it.

Karl Frundsberg. Possible, but not probable, thought Brad. The big German had all the business he could handle, practically a corner on the German and French markets. He had made a generous offer for Brad's business, but Brad had no reason to think the man would be underhanded. He seemed bluff and hearty and good-natured, rather fatherly.

Kanji Noguchi. That had to be faced. The young man was willing to learn, eager. Yet—yet he was a tough young man, that was sure, and fond of Charita. Brad thought of the karate and the judo, and scowled. Eager to get ahead. Close to the secrets of the Livingston gold formula, yet not close enough to find out. And Livingston was a foreigner, and the Japanese were insular, tightly knit. Maybe pressure was being brought on Kanji to get that gold formula. What did Brad really know about him, except that he was smart and learned quickly, and was respectful?

Mr. and Mrs. Myers. Possibly.

Joy and William Hartung. Smart and artistic, and often broke. Quite possible, yet was it their nature to do something like this? What did one know really of others?

Slowly, over the next days, Brad went over all his acquaintances in Japan, trying to think about them from all angles, dispassionately, considering whether they would have the desire and the opportunity to do something with the gold formula. Who wanted it this badly that Brad had been followed for months?

Kanji stopped in every day. Brad found himself studying the bland handsome features of the young man, testing him casually.

Kanji passed every test. He was burningly anxious to

prove himself, he would do anything Brad requested. He was smart and practical. He brought the orders, and went over them painstakingly with Brad, making good suggestions about which man should work on which items, which orders could be put off until after Christmas, which must be done soon.

Pearl came twice and took dictation. Charita disappeared while this was going on, to Brad's irritation. She didn't have to go so far away, and sometimes he wanted to ask her a question. He finally rang violently for the maid, and asked her to get Charita.

Charita appeared, subdued in a soft violet kimono and silver obi, with silver embroidery on the violet. Pearl murmured appreciatively, "It is shibui," and Charita bowed gracefully to her.

"Charita, I want to ask you about some new designs. Don't go away, if you please!" ordered Brad irritably.

"Yes, Brad." And she seated herself at a careful distance from the bed and folded her hands in her lap.

He saw Pearl give Charita a sympathetic glance with her black eyes. Charita returned it in a shy smile, as though to say, "The man is sick; he must be humored."

It amused him a little, to think about their relationships. If Pearl married Kanji, and Kanji was foster brother to Charita—then Pearl and Brad would be sister and brother. And Jacinda—well, she and Charita and Pearl would be sort of sisters— He wondered what Jacinda would think of that!

It was intriguing. He was acquiring quite a family! And it was nicer than he had imagined it would be. At first he had resented the Noguchis and Kanji—but now— he still felt possessive about Charita, but he liked the way they had brought her up.

"Pearl, read that back," he asked. Pearl read the letter obediently. He concentrated on it, frowned. "Charita, make a note also on that. Remind me to sketch some designs for gift brooches, all in gold, one hundred alike, a second hundred in a different pattern."

Charita wrote. Pearl watched soberly, murmured to Charita, "And fifty special ones for the top workers."

"Right," said Brad.

Charita whispered, "Arigato" to Pearl, and wrote it down. They worked well together, he thought.

He felt like a pasha on his throne, pillows piled about him, a bandage like a turban about his injured head. He wanted to laugh as the two girls bent obediently over their note pads, and listened to him carefully.

"Now—the next order—one of those Arab prince jobs, Pearl. What was that letter again?"

She took it out from the pile before her and read it in her low modulated voice. Brad listened, frowning, so did Charita.

"That will mean two sets of gold screens, a pile of jewelry, and he wants some chairs set with gold. Damn. I just don't have time to design all that, and neither does Charita. I don't want her busy all the time."

"I have never done chairs, Brad," murmured Charita. "I could do more screens, however. I have more designs and sketches ready for your inspection."

"You do? Let me see them this afternoon, then. Pearl, let the letter wait. Maybe we can fill about half his order, and he'll be pacified." He rubbed his aching head absently.

A maid came in, murmured to Charita. She started up, looking surprised.

"What is it?" Brad asked sharply.

"She says that Donald Raglan has come, and wishes to see me. He is most agitated, she says. He asked how you were first, then asked for me. May I go to him?" Charita's hands, so betraying as to her emotions, were clasped before her breast.

Pearl had lifted her sleek black head alertly. The slim dark eyebrows were drawn together. Brad said, "Go and talk to him, Charita, and then bring him in to see me. We should be finished with the correspondence in about half an hour."

Her face lightened, she bowed to him twice, to his irritation. "I thank you, Brad. I shall receive him with respect in your name," she murmured, and slipped from the room.

"He is a handsome young man," said Pearl, enigmatically, looking down at her note pad.

Brad scowled. He went on dictating, with half his attention on the opened door and the hallway. He could hear a murmur of voices, Charita's and Donald Raglan's. The voice of the young man rose and fell, in some agitation; he sounded as though he paced about, for the voice came from different directions. Brad's curiosity rose.

Finally he was finished with dictation, and sent Pearl away with the letters. Promptly, Charita appeared at the door. She was flushed, her blue eyes wide.

"Oh, Brad, could you see Donald for a few moments? He is most upset. He has quit his job with Mr. Frundsberg!"

Brad stared at her. "Quit? Yes, I'll see him. Send him in, and you stay also. You—have been friends for a long time," he forced himself to say, with false cordiality.

Charita smiled radiantly at him. "I have tried to comfort him, and say he has much talent and honor. But he is most unhappy, and says that his father will send him at once to the States and make him become a diplomat, and he is not ready for such a step."

Brad nodded, not understanding at all, but very curious. Donald came in answer to her beckoning hand, and he did seem upset, his nice young face flushed, his hair mussed in a reddish tangle on his well-shaped head.

"I say, I am intruding, Mr. Livingston," said Donald, halting at the door. "You have been quite sick with the flu, I understand."

"Actually I'm recovering nicely. Come on in," said

Brad. Charita fluttered around, showed him to a chair, beaming over him as though to a favorite child, thought Brad. "What's the trouble?"

Donald clasped his hands before him, shifting on the chair. "Well, I don't know if I was fired or if I quit," he confessed, sheepishly. "We had a hot shouting session. Never knew he had such a temper! All because I saw some papers—"

"What kind of papers?" asked Brad.

"Well—I guess I shouldn't say. He was my employer. All I can say is, I don't like his business methods! A bit too shady, and I told him so. Sure, maybe most businesses are conducted like that, but I don't like it." Suddenly he looked miserable. "I guess I have too many ideals, Mr. Livingston. My father said I'll have to wake up to reality some day. But I can't believe all businesses fix their taxes, and steal correspondence, and spy on each other!" The outburst seemed to embarrass him all the more. He looked anxiously at Charita, who nodded encouragingly.

"Well, I wouldn't say they do," said Brad dryly, thinking carefully. Was this a trick? Frundsberg was capable of tricks, he knew that, but Donald seemed an honest man, certainly he was very disarming. "So you are out of a job, now?"

The handsome mouth drooped, his head nodded. "Yep. Guess I'll have to go back to the States, and start in the university again. Father wants me to study politics. Right now, I am sick of politics."

"Charita says you do designing, and like it."

His face lit up. "I'm crazy about it! But father said no artist can make a living and I'm an idiot to think so."

Brad suppressed his opinion of Donald's father. He was a starched diplomat, and made an excellent appearance for America, but Brad would never call him a wise man.

"Quite a few artists make a living at art," said Brad.

343

"And right now I'm a bit desperate for a good artist. Do you have some sketches with you?"

Donald's mouth hung open. He finally shook his head. "No—I just came to say good-bye to Charita—and to you," he said.

"Well, forget the good-byes. Go and see Kanji and have him set up an office for you. We'll see what you can produce in the way of art."

"Are you—offering me a job?" stammered Donald. "Gosh! I'd like nothing better than working for you. But I wouldn't ask—me being a friend of Charita, I thought it would look bad—I mean—"

Both Charita and Donald looked nervously at Brad. He suppressed his ever-ready jealousy, and tried to smile. "I think we can overlook any friendship, and stick to business. After all, Kanji is her foster brother, and I wouldn't know how to operate without him." He leaned back in the pillows. "In fact, you may be the answer to a problem. Charita has more than she can do in the way of our gold screens. We have a letter here—" He searched in the bedclothes, pulled it out.

Donald was sitting as though stunned, his face beginning to turn radiant. Charita was smiling, her face relaxed and glowing.

Brad read parts of the letter aloud. "You see, if you can produce some of the designs, that will save the contract and help us out immensely. Have you done any designs as large as those?"

"No, but I sure would try!" Donald said fervently. "I'm willing to try anything, Mr. Livingston!"

"Good. Charita, will you bring a couple of your sketches, ones you have made into tissue tracings, and we'll show him what we want."

Charita nodded, and slipped away, to return with the materials. They looked over them, talked about the order for the Arab prince, and Donald finally went away, stammering his gratitude. He would come to the office first thing in the morning, he didn't care about the salary, Brad Livingston was terribly generous, he didn't know how he could ever thank him enough—

Brad leaned back, very tired, when Donald had left. He shoved the letters onto the floor, and lay out, stretching cautiously to ease his body. Maybe he had done something foolish, hiring a man who had left the firm of a rival. On the other hand, he could watch Donald and see that he learned nothing vital about the gold formula. In time, he could tell if Donald was on the level, if he could be trusted.

A man had to take a chance, and Charita was happy. That was important to Brad, more important all the time, he thought ruefully. The sparkle in her eyes, the shining look of her face, that made everything worthwhile.

23

Jacinda dressed with special care that morning. She frowned at herself in the dingy mirror. She would have to pick up more of her smart clothes at the apartment today, and leave some to be washed and pressed. She hated being so cramped in this small apartment, but she would not go back to stay. She was determined on that.

Even with her firm resolve, she felt in limbo. She didn't want to return to the States, she would not go back to Miles. Brad was married and didn't seem to miss her at all.

Jacinda smiled a little, her mouth twisted into a wry grin. Had she deceived herself all this time? She was like any other weak woman, wanting a strong man to lean on. Was she kidding herself that Brad had made a foolish marriage?

Charita was really a sweet girl, she decided. Anyone who had behaved like Jacinda had deserved to be screamed at and pitched out of the house. But Charita had bowed to her husband's foster sister, and thanked her courteously for saving Brad. Jacinda *had* saved Brad, that was sure. Her man Yoshida was still on the job, impatient for more piles of yen.

Jacinda had finally gone to visit Brad, and found him still in bed. Charita had hovered over him solicitously, brought them tea and food, fluttered around Brad like a little geisha girl, thought Jacinda ironically.

But Brad seemed to thrive on that treatment. Maybe all men liked it, Jacinda said to herself, adjusting the aqua silk scarf carefully at her throat. He had caught at Charita's hand, made her sit on the bed beside him, showed off her sketches proudly, indicated a painting she had done.

"It's a wonder to me that the poor girl has time to do any work," Jacinda had said to him teasingly. "You demand all her time!"

"But I am happy to help him in any way I can," protested Charita, a pretty flushed look to her round face. Brad had grinned up at her.

"I've been a devil to you, haven't I?" he had murmured, affectionately. "It's a wonder you haven't thrown something at my head!"

Her hand had touched his head gently, over the bandage, her transparent face revealing her concern. "As though I would throw something at you!" she whispered.

Maybe Jacinda had been wrong about them. She fastened the silver buttons of the aqua and white jacket carefully, and studied her reflection dispassionately. Yes, she looked sharp and sure of herself, as always.

The marriage had looked impossible, Brad was so much older, more sophisticated, a man of the world. Charita had been a schoolgirl, naive, wide-eyed and wondering. But the girl was growing up, and Brad was softening. Jacinda had never seen him looking so relaxed and happy, as when Charita was fussing over him.

It might indeed work, but then where did that leave Jacinda?

She sighed, and snapped shut the smart white bag, and set off. Her high heels clattered on the wooden steps, down to the street. She gave a sharp look about, spotted her bodyguard sitting in a car nearby, and nodded. Then she set off in her little green car.

347

She hoped to catch Miles at home before he set out. They had much to discuss, and perhaps Miles would be sober for a change. Besides, Jacinda needed more clothes, and more money from the bank. One of these days she must come to a decision about her future.

She parked in front of the apartment building, and sighed at the smart appearance of the doorman who appeared promptly to open her car door. She murmured a greeting, and scarcely noticed the irritating bobbing of his head in respect.

She took the elevator up to the top floor, and stepped off into the golden and silver rooms she herself had decorated. She paused to straighten a picture, adjust a vase. The maid had appeared, to eye her apprehensively, giving her a wide false smile.

"Mrs. Snow-san! We miss the honorable presence of our illustrious mistress," the girl murmured. Jacinda handed over her laundry with a little scowl.

"Not so much as I miss you," she said, honestly. "Is Mr. Snow in?"

"He sits in dining room, with coffee. Is it that you will have some breakfast with honorable Mr. Snow-san?"

"Why not? Some scrambled eggs and coffee, and a couple of pieces of toast," she said, suddenly hungry.

She went back to the drawing room. Miles shot up when she came in, giving her a dazed look. He was sober, she thought, drinking coffee. His face had paled to tired lines, he was thinner, she thought.

"Hello, Miles." She seated herself in the chair opposite him at the long formal table. The newspaper was crumpled on the floor beside him.

"Jacinda. What are you doing here? Have you decided to move back?" he asked, sinking into his chair cautiously, with a sharp eye on her. Not such a bloodshot eye, she thought. Maybe her absence had made him think. Or calmed him down, she decided wryly.

"No. Just came for some fresh clothes. And a talk with you," she said. The maid brought coffee, Jacinda hesitated to say more.

"You haven't been in the office for weeks. Do you think I can keep on doing your work and mine?" he snarled.

She nodded. "If you stay sober," she snapped back. "But I didn't come to talk about that. It's another——" She stopped again as the maid came in with eggs and toast. She attacked them hungrily. She didn't eat much, she had quickly tired of the restaurant on her street.

Miles leaned back, toying with his coffee cup. She noted his thin hand, the long clever fingers, and glanced away again. How she had loved it, when he had stroked his fingers down her spine, and caressed her! It seemed a thousand years ago, yet it made her tingle to think of it.

"It's silly for you to remain away," he said, finally, gruffly. "You like your comforts. If you're going to be ornery, I'll leave. Why don't you move back in?"

"You would hate it," she said, thinking of the dingy flat. "No, it wouldn't work. And it won't be long. I'll make up my mind before long what I'm going to do."

A flicker of apprehension came into his hazel eyes. He looked at her carefully. "What—are you planning to do?"

"I haven't decided yet," she said stiffly.

"Go back to the States?" he asked.

"I don't know."

"And I don't matter?" he asked bitterly. He reached for his cigarette case and lighter and snapped it on. "I am not to be consulted? Are you planning on——" He stopped, and his sensitive mouth quivered.

Jacinda looked away, carefully. She had vowed not to be moved by his presence, by the memories that had spun between them for six years. Yet—yet— How could she help but remember? Those nights on their honeymoon

349

on a Caribbean island—purple-blue skies, prickles of stars, a slim sickle of new moon, and Miles holding her in his arms, making her feel secure and wanted and safe, as she had never been in her life before— Those warm wanton nights, laughter over nothing, talking the night through, sleeping in the hot day with only a mosquito net above the bed—

She flinched. She could not remember and remain steady in her purpose. What was her purpose? She wasn't sure herself.

She finished eating and pushed the plate away. The maid padded in, took it away, filled her coffee cup silently. How she had missed that service, the little careful touches, and even that damned bowing and smiling—

"We'll talk in the study," said Miles wearily, and stood up. She followed him, her heels clicking on the parquet floors, then deadened by the Persian rugs of his study. His study. They had His and Hers desks, they had kidded each other about that at first. In the old days.

He sat down at the desk, his long fingers played with a jade figurine, going over and over the smooth green surface. She sat down casually across from him, crossing her legs in the aqua slacks. She saw him look down slowly over her body, and knew his thoughts, as she often knew them. He wanted her.

"It's about Brad that I came," she said briskly.

He flinched visibly, and the look came in his eyes that she hated, that bitter knowing despising look.

She made herself go on. "Have you talked to him this week?"

"No," he said abruptly. "He has the flu."

"No, he doesn't," said Jacinda. "It is not supposed to be general knowledge. But he was kidnapped, and beaten up—my men were following him, and I got him away. But they managed to break open his stupid head—"

Miles was staring at her as though she had gone mad.

"Kidnapped—and beaten? When was this?" he asked sharply.

She recited all the facts, keeping herself calm, snapping out the words. "So I got him home, turned him over to his dear wife. She does seem to know what to do with him. He looked better when I went over yesterday, but he's still in bed, and the wound on his head is just healing. He was quite shaken up. He's a mass of bruises. The thing is, Miles—who would do it? Who was paying those men?"

He set down the jade figure and folded his hands slowly. His mind was going over what she had said, she knew by the absent air, the way he stared into space.

"It must be the gold formula," he said slowly. "If they didn't just send out a note for ransom—what else would they want? Yes, it must be the gold formula. Damn it, why didn't he apply for a patent?"

"He has not applied for one?" she asked, incredulously. "You were supposed to send in the application—"

He shook his head. "Brad refused to make one out. He said something crazy about keeping it in his head. Freedom of Information Act—anyone could get hold of it. You know the General Motors case recently—"

"Ah—that, but GM didn't get much satisfaction from the Japanese firm," she said absently, reaching into her handbag for her cigarettes. They both lit up and puffed away in unison, as they used to when considering a problem. Like the old days. God damn, why couldn't she forget the old days, when she and Miles had worked together so beautifully?

"It was too late. The firm was already using the information, they said it was general knowledge. And even if a fine is paid—" Miles shrugged. "It doesn't really pay for the chemical formula. I guess that was what Brad was getting at."

"He was working alone in the lab all night, electroplating the jewelry—" said Jacinda, absently, rubbing her

351

finger beside her nose. He glanced at her, smiled to see the gesture. "That was when they got him, when he was tired, coming out alone—"

"Where was the bodyguard?" he asked.

"Dismissed," she said wearily. "I bawled him out, he's too damned careless. But I think this experience will teach him. Those men are after the formula, I'll be bound. And if only Brad knows it, they'll try again, and again—"

"Yes, but who is paying those men?"

"That's the question."

They smoked in silence.

Miles finally leaned back in the swivel chair and linked his long fingers behind his head, to stare out the window. "Who are the possibilities?" he asked abruptly, in the old sure way.

"I've been thinking. Tops on my list are the Pattersons."

"Yeah. I thought so, too. Old Patterson wants into the firm badly. I'll check his finances, find out how strapped he is."

"Right," said Jacinda, relieved. "And there are several Japanese firms in competition—" She named them, he wrote them down.

"And Karl Frundsberg," she added. "You know, he's so jolly and fatherly and nice—but he has a big firm, and he had made a mint before he came here. I wonder what his background is?"

"I'll check that. I know a man in Frankfort—" Miles made another notation, then glanced at his watch. "I'll have to figure out the time to call him, always confuses me," he confessed, sheepishly.

"I'll figure that out for you, I have a pocket guide for that," she said, fighting a feeling of tenderness. He was so smart, so wise in big things, why did he have to be such a fool in little things? And wrecking himself with drink?

"Who else?" he said, absently, doodling on the pad

before him. "What about that Japanese boy working for him? Seems very smart and catches on fast. Might be the type to be in someone's pay, if he sees it will pay for him."

Jacinda had a memory for names. "Kanji Noguchi," she said, and frowned. "You know, he is the foster brother of Charita—and seems very fond of her. I wondered if he might be—well—jealous."

"Humm," Miles gave her a steady look. "I'll check him out. Anyone else?"

"Pearl Takahashi. She is a very smart girl, very smart," Jacinda said bitterly, thinking of her suspicions about Pearl and Brad. "Very beautiful, very well dressed for her probably small salary—"

"Brad pays her well, he said so. He wanted her to be free of dependence on her parents. Evidently the father is a mean one."

"Oh." Jacinda drew a deep breath. A story, or the truth? Somehow she felt it was the truth. It would be like Brad, he was terribly generous in unexpected ways.

They discussed the Myers couple, the Hartungs, several others, but they seemed remote possibilities. The main suspects, thought Jacinda, were the Japanese firms whose business was being cut into by Brad's success with the gold process.

"And they will be damned hard to research," sighed Miles. "They help each other over here. And the government often has a part financial interest in the firm, especially those exporting to the United States. I'll probably come up against blank walls. Don't expect miracles." But his face was light and eager, he was looking forward to this challenge.

"I think my man Yoshida can help," said Jacinda thoughtfully. "I wish you would talk to him, Miles. He doesn't understand much English, but I think he knows the underworld over here. He sure has the contacts. If I knew more Japanese, I could question him. But we just use the most elementary English and Japanese words."

Miles gave her a dark look. "How do I get in touch with him, may I ask?" he asked, with more than a little sarcasm. "Your man, Yoshida? Sounds like you own him."

She shrugged. "I pay him well for guarding Brad," she said frankly. "I found that Brad wasn't protecting himself, and it worried me. I thought marriage had gone to his brain. You know—Charita isn't a bad sort," she said awkwardly. "Artistic, very. Some splendid designs. I think there may even be a brain behind that pretty-pretty face."

"But you resent how Brad feels about her," said Miles.

"Well—I did," said Jacinda, not wanting to delve too much. It was too painful. "Somehow—I guess I never thought any woman was good enough for Brad. He was so—terrific—so generous, so good to lean on. And for him to marry a gauche schoolgirl—"

"She was his choice," said Miles, frowning. "You had no right to interfere—or did you think you had the right?"

She shrugged, not meeting his look. "I thought I did. But Brad set me straight about that. And their marriage seems to be working out. They have—more in common than I had thought. And you know, she does have some dress sense. She was wearing a lovely dress yesterday, blue chiffon with ruffles at the wrists, very feminine, and just the color of her eyes. If she would only wear higher heels, and put on some eye makeup—"

Miles grinned, out of the side of his mouth. "You'd like to get your hands on her, and remake her? Let her alone, she seems to suit Brad just as she is."

"I suppose so," said Jacinda, crushing out another cigarette. It had lost its taste. "Well, I guess that's all. I'm going to gather up some more clothes—"

"Why not stay here?" he asked, standing. "It's stupid to keep on with this damned fool feud—"

354

"It isn't damned fool. Damn it, I still have your marks on me," she flared, and walked out of the room, her head high.

"You're wearing your hair longer," he remarked, following her.

She shrugged. "Haven't bothered to go to the hairdresser. I've been doing my own."

"It's—more feminine. I like it—" He walked after her into the bedroom.

Her mouth compressed. She took a suitcase from the wardrobe, and reached into the closet for another pants suit. He watched in silence as she put in one, then another, then several blouses. The door was shut, the room was silent but for the swishing of the silk clothes as she folded them and set them into the case.

Abruptly he took the last blouse from her and slammed the case shut. "Damn it, listen to me! You're not walking out again! It's stupid, it's silly. I haven't been drinking much—we could work things out—"

"I'll make my own decisions!"

"Helped by Brad, no doubt!" he sneered. "Does it make you feel like his wife, to watch over him, and guard him? Did it do big things for your ego when you rescued him? I'll bet! Well, you are my wife, and your precious Brad is married to the girl he wants! Face facts!"

He grabbed her arms, and pulled her around to face him. She stared haughtily into his angered, flushed face. "Facts to you might not be the same to me! Brad happens to mean a lot to me, and if I want to have him guarded—"

He pulled her closer, and stopped her mouth with his own. She fought against him, but an insidious weakness was creeping through her limbs. Too many memories were spun between them, too many times had his hands run over her back, and too often had his palms cupped her slim boyish hips and pulled her tautly to his hard thighs.

"Miles—stop it—" she said, muffled, against his lips.

He did not bother to answer in words. His hunger had overwhelmed him. He kissed her lips as though starved for them, his mouth roamed to her taut throat, over her bared pulse— She shuddered and went limp for a moment.

His hands were moving over her urgently.

"I want you," he said, against her shoulder. "God, Jacinda, I want you—I love you—"

"I love you," she said, muffled against his throat. "I love you—and I hate you—and love you—and hate you—"

He laughed, shaken. "That's the way I feel. Oh, my darling—"

Just the sound of it went through her like a knife, that low, shaken word "darling"— So many times he had said that—and other love words, against her throat, her breasts.

His hand was unfastening the snappy jacket, feeling inside against the silken undergarments, reaching for her breasts.

"No—" she said. "No, damn it!" She wrenched herself away, breathing hard.

"Saving yourself for Brad?" he sneered, still holding her.

She struck his face, hard. She stared, aghast, at the red welt on his thin, pale face.

"I guess you are," he said, more quietly, and stepped back. "I thought you had more sense, but you don't."

She took a deep angry breath, hating herself for her own weakness. "Answer me one question, Miles," she said.

"What question?"

"Did you pay to have Brad attacked?"

He stared at her, the question slowly hitting home. "Did I—Did I—pay—my God, no! What the hell do you think I am?"

She pushed back the loosened hair, fastened her jacket again, her wary gaze still on him. Could she trust him, was it the truth? She knew then that she had come that morning just to ask that question. And she didn't know whether to believe the answer.

She didn't know. She wasn't sure if she could trust the man she had married six years ago.

"What the blazes do you think I am?" he demanded again. "Do you think I would pay to have Brad—Brad—no matter what you do! Now answer me one question!"

She backed around him, picked up the case. "What question?" she asked, keeping half her attention on him. He was teetering on his heels, the silly grin on his mouth reminding her of the times when he was drunk.

"How many times have you slept with Brad?"

She stared. Swallowed. He hadn't said "wanted to sleep with Brad—"

"None." She lifted her head and walked to the door, the case in her hand. "None, damn you!"

She walked out the door, past the curious round-eyed maid bobbing her head in the hallway. She flung open the door and went out to the elevator. Miles made no attempt to follow or stop her.

Out in the car, she was shaking. She put the case in the back, and folded her arms on the wheel. She stared ahead. She couldn't drive yet, she would crash into something.

Her confidence was shaken. Her brain was not operating as calculatedly as it usually did. If Miles had not been behind the attack, then all those names they had recited meant something. Would Miles do anything about it? Would he really investigate? Or was she really on her own in this?

And why was she shaking so? Just the touch of Miles' hands on her, and his mouth on her lips.

Why did she have to be so weak and feminine? Why hadn't she been born a man? She had started asking herself that question when she was fourteen and men had begun pawing her.

Maybe there was an answer to that one also, thought Jacinda, as she finally started the car, glanced automatically over her shoulder, swung out into the traffic. Maybe there was a reason. Maybe Miles was the reason.

But she had a lot of thinking to do before she could satisfy herself that the answer was there. She had hated men for years. Only Brad had measured up to her high standards. Only Brad—

Until Miles had come along. And how heartbreaking to find he was weak, getting drunk, hurting her. . . . Tears stung her eyes. She blinked them back with determination.

She had faulted Charita for being so young and naive. But maybe she, Jacinda, had some growing up to do. You couldn't expect people to be perfect, the way you wanted them to be. They all had weaknesses, she did too.

She had wanted Miles to be perfect, and he was not. Could she endure that? Could she love him anyway? Could she keep from loving him, now she knew he was not anywhere near perfect?

Preoccupied, she drove more slowly than usual through the traffic, her mind swinging from her personal problems to those of Brad and the gold formula.

In her legal work, Jacinda had always enjoyed a puzzle, an unexpected complication. She liked to wrestle with a difficult twist, a puzzle of personalities, a problem not easily solved. Ease bored her. She didn't care for easy cases, she rarely took them.

This would be complicated, and suddenly, in the bright August day she smiled. She tossed her lengthening blond hair in the sunlight, and waited for the impossible hoards of people crossing the street before her.

She had a challenge, and she loved a challenge. Her green eyes were bright and confident as she directed the

ittle car toward the office building, heading for her office
n the same suite as Miles' office.

Jacinda had a lot to catch up on. She had been bored
and self-absorbed for too long.

The first task was to list all the suspects and go over
he various possibilities. She hoped Miles would get right
on that also, then they could discuss it—maybe over lunch.

That might be the first step back.

24

Pearl was vastly relieved when Brad finally came back to work. It had been almost two weeks. She had seen him often, but it wasn't the same, seeing that vital, dynamic man lying propped up on pillows, getting weary after an hour of work.

They welcomed him back with flowers and much ceremony. The workmen wanted to come up and see him, and there was a little parade in and out of his office. Pearl thought he was pleased, though he grumbled to her.

"You'd think I had been gone a year!" he said.

She bowed her head. "It seemed a long time, Brad," she said softly. She deftly straightened the flower arrangement of crimson and yellow dahlias on his desk, and glanced over the tall vase on the floor that held long-stemmed chrysanthemums with huge yellow and purple heads.

"Well, let's get back to work. Is that the pile?" and he dove into the bills, orders and correspondence she had set on his desk. Another workman paused at the door, one of the venerable old men with much skill.

Brad rose from his desk, bowed twice as the old one entered.

"How excellent to have your worship return to us," murmured the man, his crinkly fine skin wrinkling as he beamed a smile, and bowed again and again over his skill-ful thin hands.

"You are most kind to welcome me. I have had good reports of your progress on the screens. My good wife sends her respects to you, and hopes her designs are the right ones for you to use with your skill."

Pearl was a little amused, but more touched that Brad spoke in Japanese, and used the flowery flattering language of these people. He had changed in these months since his marriage, she thought. He was slower, more kindly, more open to suggestions. He was not so abrupt and brusque, he listened more thoughtfully when one spoke to him, and even his speech was not so clipped as before.

The old one was pleased, his black eyes shone as he bowed again and murmured his pleasure with the designs. "It will be an honor to work on them with these poor hands," he said.

"I received telephone calls from the Arab prince. He wishes to send his commendations to my workmen for their skill and devotion in making such beautiful objects for his palace. He has ordered more work done—" And Brad sighed, unconsciously, shifting the papers. "I hope we have time to do them for the prince."

"You are most generous in your praise to this un-worthy object," said the old one, gently, and bowed him-self out, his face shining with joy at the generous praise.

Pearl thought, "Brad *has* changed. I think it is Chari-ta's doing. She has much sympathy with our ways. I like her—really. If only she is right for Brad!"

Pearl had considered her a poor thing at first, a gauche schoolgirl, awkward, shy. Now she had seen Charita, beau-tifully gowned, a gracious hostess in Brad's home, her face soft as she bent in concern over Brad, her hands gentle as she soothed him.

One could like the girl, thought Pearl. At first Pearl could not believe anyone was good enough for her marvelous boss, who had given her a wonderful job, high salary, nice flat, praise for her work. No man had ever treated her so, and—well—maybe she had been jealous. Jealous? It was nonsense, Pearl told herself severely. She was not emotionally close to Brad, he showed no signs of feeling anything for her but gratitude for good work done.

His wife was lovely, her sense of taste was shibui, her talent truly awe-inspiring. And how she had softened Brad, and given him a feel for Japanese ways and customs. It could only have been from Charita that Brad had acquired this sense of knowing when to bow to an elderly workman, when to praise in graceful words which were well-deserved. He was not nearly so curt and offhand as he had been.

Pearl moved forward as the old one left, and found the letter in the pile. "He really wants a great deal, Brad," she said frankly. "Do you want to tie up so many workmen in his projects?"

He ran his hands over his face. "How is Donald Raglan working out?"

"He has been working steadily, but I don't know about his designs," admitted Pearl. "I don't know enough about that end of the work. Kanji said he was waiting until you returned before presenting any designs to you."

"Might as well see him first, then. It will depend on how well he works. I won't have Charita slaving night and day to turn out more designs," he said, rather impatiently. "Send Donald in first, Pearl. I'll take these letters to lunch with me."

She was about to protest, but closed her mouth when she saw how drawn and thin he was. The injuries had taken more out of him than she had realized. "Yes, Brad," she said, and withdrew silently.

She sent Donald in to see him, and the young man went in apprehensively, a folder in his hands. The door was left open. Pearl found herself eavesdropping unconsciously, for she had little typing to do until Brad had caught up on his work.

"Well, Donald, how are you settling in?"

"Fine, sir. I just hope you like some of these ideas." Rustle of papers. "I—ah—was just trying out some things. Walked in the parks the other day, sketched some ideas."

"Ah yes—" Brad considered the designs.

Pearl found herself straining to hear. If Donald could do some good work, it meant much to them all. Brad had too much to do, so did Charita. They really needed another good designer.

"Ah—I like this one. Yes. Splendid. That will work out in a flat design. And this—you have a nice hand with flowers and trees. Looks Oriental, somehow. How long have you lived in Japan?"

"Eleven years now, sir."

"Make it Brad," came Brad's voice easily. "Too much ceremony around here, I can't take too much!"

Donald laughed, a rather strained sound. Pearl imagined he was very nervous. "Yes, sir—I mean, Brad."

Silence again. Kanji came in, Pearl put a finger to her lips, pointed to the open door. Kanji frowned, went to close it, she shook her head vigorously. He let it go, and came back to her. "What is it?" he whispered.

"Donald and his work," she whispered, almost soundlessly. "We hope so much—" Her bright eyes finished the sentence for her.

Kanji went to his office, to wait. She could see him going over the papers on his desk, pausing over one and then another. His dark head was bent over them. He was a conscientious worker, she thought. He seemed quieter now, more somber. They had not gone out for a long time. He asked her, she refused, and that was all.

She thought of the letter from her mother, bright, cheerful, but underneath the strain of fear. How much could she do for her? In her most recent letters, Pearl had stressed how much she enjoyed working, how she would find it difficult to adjust to marriage. "I like," she had written, "to have my little silent apartment furnished as I please. Mr. Livingston is most generous in his salary. I have several girl friends with whom I attend a movie or concert. My clothes are of the best."

She meant to lead up to it gently, that she would not marry, that she was finding a single life so satisfactory that she had no need to marry. This was a new age, she would tell them. A girl did not need to marry, she would find satisfaction in doing good work for a fine salary. She would not be promiscuous, but a good girl, of whom they could be proud, even though she did not marry and produce children. Her mouth set. They wanted grandchildren, and she was their only child. That would be a difficult hurdle.

"Pearl? Come in here, please," called Brad.

She was startled back to the present. She hurried in on her neat gray pumps, and stood demurely near the door. "Yes, Brad?"

Donald's eager young face was flushed with pleasure. Brad had laid out several of his sketches on the long worktable near his desk.

"Look at these, which ones do you like?" asked Brad.

A little wary, but flattered, Pearl advanced to the worktable, and looked at the work. She caught her breath.

One sketch was of a bold design, the head of a ruler, a haughty man with high headdress. Beside him were his shield, his sword. In the background, a fluttering fan, the indication of a lady's head.

Next was an intricate design, a mulberry tree, silkworm cocoons, the drawing of a thread into silk, and so on, showing the industry which had been a mainstay of Japanese economy for many years. It was fascinating, but Pearl thought too cluttered with detail.

Another design was of fans, many fans large and

364

small, fluttering, in many designs. The best one was of grasses, simple and feathery, with a couple of butterflies hovering on them. Other designs were of autumn flowers.

Pearl studied them carefully. She pointed out the one of grasses, "I think this is shibui," she said.

Brad nodded. "I like that, and it would work on a screen."

They studied the others critically, and finally Brad and Pearl settled on three others on which Donald could proceed with tissue sketches for screens.

"Well, that settles the Arab prince," said Brad, gathering up the sketches with the best ones on top. "Go on with these, Donald, I'll write to him and say we can produce a screen for him of your designs. Have you thought about the chairs?"

Donald looked rather dazed. "No—actually not. I thought only about doing the screens first. I was afraid— that is, I wasn't sure I could please you—I mean—I never did this before—"

"Well, after you do the tissue copies, go out to the department stores and look at chairs. And go to a few museums and see if they give you any ideas. If he wants gold-plated chairs, it should be done well," said Brad frowning. "It could get gaudy. I think perhaps sandal-wood chairs, of very simple design, then gold inlay on the back and arms would be better. What do you think, Pearl?"

"Something simple and elegant," she approved. "We do not wish a reputation for extravagant, frivolous designs."

"Right. Shibui," repeated Brad, evidently liking the sound of the word. "Take those away, Donald, and let me see the tissues in a week or so. Or, if you want, go off to the museums first."

Pearl stayed to take dictation, a long letter to the prince, then briefer letters to the other clients who waited. She gave him reports on the progress of some jewelry, one client wanted pearls reset in lighter more elegant designs than the ancestral ones.

When Pearl went out to lunch, Brad asked her to bring back a sandwich for him. She said nothing, but when she returned she brought a tea tray, with hot tea, sandwiches, and fruit. He grinned and thanked her, and went on working at his desk.

He left early, weary, and she continued with the dictation he had left. Kanji waited for her silently. Donald had gone out on winged feet to department stores and museums. His job was secure, and he was a happy boy.

Pearl said, briefly, "You do not need to wait for me, Kanji. I have my car."

"We have something to say to each other," he said, ominously, his face set, and older than she remembered. He sat quietly until she finished, then accompanied her to the sidewalk outside the office.

"I must go home now," she said flatly, turning to her car. He took her arm firmly in his, unusual for him. Usually he never touched her on the street, and rarely inside the office.

"No. We must talk. Do you wish dinner?"

Dinner would bring a waitress between them, and food to occupy their hands and gazes. Pearl nodded, "I believe I am hungry," she said brightly.

He directed her to his car, and they got in. He drove silently to a Japanese restaurant, and said nothing until they were seated and had ordered.

Pearl had been thinking, and gathering up her courage. She must make this break, and it might as well be now. If her mother was beaten for it—well, it had happened before. It made Pearl cringe to think of it, but she had begged her mother to leave her father and come to live with Pearl. Her mother had refused, horrified. It would never do. She was a traditionalist, not a modern.

The waitress set the first course before them, poured out tea, and padded silently away. Kanji spoke at once.

"Pearl, this has gone on too long. We are able to marry. I wish to marry you within six months."

She kept her eyes lowered, sipped at her tea. "Kanji, I have told you before. It is definite. I shall not marry you. I thank you for the honor," she began to say politely. He cut her off with a gesture of his strong hand.

"No politenesses between us, Pearl. I wish honesty today. The contracts are signed. Do you honor them, or are you a girl without honor?"

Shocked, she opened her eyes wide at him. His face was dark, sullen, threatening. "How can you say such a thing?" she breathed.

"I watch you with Donald Raglan. You are worried about him. You had lunch with him three days this week."

Her breath caught in her throat. "This is foolish. He is new to the work, he is anxious."

"Anxious!" he spat. Pearl stared at him in wonder. She had never seen Kanji so. He had lost his smiling charm, his boyish, disarming grin. He was dark, brooding, jealous. "Yes, he must be anxious. He comes to you and weeps on your shoulder. You realize he is American, and will not marry you?"

She drew in her breath in a hiss. She felt the blood draining from her head. She set down her fork carefully, and began to rise. His hand shot out, she felt the cruel grip of it on her arm, forcing her effortlessly back into the chair opposite him.

"You will remain here. After dinner, we shall stroll in a park—if you do not care to risk coming to my apartment." No smile, no charm. He was cold, forceful. "We shall talk, and make an end to this flightiness."

She clasped her hands in her lap. She was trembling. She had never expected force from him—even after the episode in his apartment. He seemed—hard, tough, as she

367

had never seen Kanji. She remembered his belts in karate.

"Very well. We will make an end of it," she agreed, with cool courage, in spite of her shaking hands. "I will inform my parents I am breaking the engagement. Unless you wish to do so. I realize it is not fair to you to continue the contracts. I shall not marry you."

"You do not care what happens to your mother!" It was a harsh, accusing statement.

The waitress hurried over to see if anything was wrong with the food, that they did not eat. Kanji waved her away imperiously.

"I care about my mother, yes," said Pearl, as steadily as she could. "However, if father beats her, it is her fault for remaining with him. I have begged her to leave him, I have offered her a home with me."

"You would break up the marriage of your honorable parents!" The black eyes blazed at her.

"If necessary. He must stop beating her. However—if she chooses to remain and be beaten, that is—her problem." She was biting her lips. She had never seen Kanji so, and it was upsetting her.

She thought, when Kanji would not promise to respect her and never beat her, that should have been a sign to her. He was a brute also! Probably all men were brutes!

She was better off single. At least, she knew where she was. If the nights were lonely, so be it. Better loneliness than cruelty and weeping into pillows.

He picked up his fork and began eating, mechanically, as though he did not taste. She picked at her food, and was glad when the tea was finished, the plates removed. She stood up. "I will call a taxi to return to my car," she said, coldly. To tell the truth, she was afraid of him in this mood.

"I will return you to your car," he said, and his hand closed over her upper arm, as he propelled her before him out of the restaurant. Curious glances were sent after them, though the farewell bows were as courteous as ever.

She hesitated in the car park, Kanji pushed her in the direction of the car, saw her inside, and locked her in. It might have been a protective gesture—but somehow she did not think so. Her hands clasped in her lap, over her handbag. The autumn chills were coming soon, she thought, it was almost the end of August. The night wind made her shudder.

He turned away from the city. "Kanji, my car is at the factory," she began.

"We will walk for a time in a park," he said, biting off the words.

"It is late."

"The sun has scarcely set."

What could she do? At the entrance to a park, he turned in and drove the car into a lot at the far end. Most of the automobiles had departed, it was dusk, and the sky was purple.

She did not move from the seat. "It is late, Kanji," she said, very quietly. "I do not wish to walk. Please, take me to my car."

"We will walk," he said, inflexibly, and reached into the car, gripped her arm, and drew her out to stand beside him. He locked the car with one hand, holding her firmly with the other. She glanced about to see if any help was at hand. Only the yawning gatekeeper noticed them. The park was open evenings, and he was too polite to interfere should a girl say she was unwilling to walk with her boyfriend.

"My shoes are high of heel, Kanji," she tried again. "I do not care to walk far in them over the stones."

"We will not walk far," he said, meticulously polite. But he held her arm as he drew her inside the gates of the park. They strolled slowly along the graveled paths, winding around past fragrant bushes. They came to a stone bridge, and walked up the curve to the top, where Pearl halted. She leaned on the railing, and pretended interest in the dimly seen water lilies and the sleepy white swans that paddled below them.

Silence between them. Kanji leaned beside her, between her and the gate.

The sun had set, and the dark was about them, purple blue, the dusky evening. A sleepy bird sang in a bush nearby, with piercing sweetness. A night for lovers, thought Pearl, with a pang of regret. She must harden her heart against such things. She felt the heat of Kanji's body as he stood close beside her on the curved bridge. He was gazing into the distance, beyond the small artificial lake, toward a teahouse, where the paper screens had been drawn, and laughter and music came dimly to them. The glow of fires inside from hibachi stoves, and the odor of cooking told that there was a party at the teahouse. A yellow-orange glow against the darkness of the trees.

"It grows late," said Pearl finally, when the silence began to eat at her heart. "Let me return to my car."

"Not yet," said Kanji, stirring. "I write to my parents and to yours, that the marriage is in six months. That will be February. A good month for marriage, I believe."

"No," she said.

"Not a good month?" he asked ironically. "You wish for March and cherry blossoms? It can be done."

"No, Kanji. I will not marry you."

"Yes, you will," he said. "I have waited long enough for you to mature. Marriage will mature you, and you will be happy when you have a man to master you."

His tone did not raise, he sounded faintly complacent. She moved to go past him, his hand shot out and caught at her shoulder. She stilled.

"You cannot force me into marriage," she said, bravely. "This is a modern age—I am modern—"

"I am not," he said. "I can carry you off and take you without marriage."

Fear struck deep inside her. He had said it so calmly, so coldly, so deliberately. She stared at him, unable to make out his features in the deepening dusk.

"You would so insult and deprave me?" she asked.

"If necessary. We are going to marry, make up your mind to it. I want you, you are pledged to me. I will not be shamed before my family and friends."

"That is all you care about—shame!" she flared up.

"I am a man of honor, the descendant of samurai. Yes, I care about shame. But more, you are contracted to me, and it shall be carried out. I warn you, you will not meet with Donald or any other man again. You will inform your parents obediently of our coming marriage. Otherwise—" He paused.

She turned, and this time he merely followed her out to the car. The heels of her shoes clicked, he was soundless on the gravel path. He was light on his feet, he was lean and hard, and she felt she had never known him.

In silence he drove her to the car park, and waited politely while she got into the car. He followed her a short distance, then turned off to his own apartment, and she lifted a swift hand to wipe the sweat from her temples.

Safely in her small flat, she sat down to a hot cup of tea. She was cold and shaking with fear. She had never dreamed that kind, gentle, smiling Kanji could be like this. Would he truly do what he threatened—take her without marriage, to shame her into it? Did he care so much about her? Or did he care only about his reputation? He had said not one word of love. He had said only that he wanted her.

Who would help her? Not Donald, he was too young and vulnerable. Not her parents, her mother was helpless, her father wanted the match, and despised his only child anyway.

Brad, she thought. If the worst seemed about to happen, she would appeal to him. He was kind, and tough, and he liked her. He would help her, she thought, and advise her.

Morning brought saner thoughts. She dressed carefully in a gray suit and crisp white blouse that the August heat would soon wilt, and went in to work as usual. Kanji was there before her, he lifted his head, and bowed once to her as she came in.

Donald came to talk to her gaily about what he had seen in a museum. As he was talking, Kanji came to the door, and called him.

"If you have time to talk now—" he said. "And what about lunch? There is much to discuss."

"Oh, fine, fine," said Donald, happily unaware, and went off with Kanji. Donald did not even see the cold warning Kanji gave to Pearl with his black marble-hard eyes.

Brad lingered over his desk. After Kanji and Donald had gone to lunch, Pearl went into Brad's office, and shut the door after her.

Brad looked up absently. "Yes, Pearl? What is it?"

She was wringing her fingers, her forehead was wet. "I must speak to you—forgive me—sir—it is a personal matter—but I am much troubled—"

He was on his feet in an instant, holding a chair for her. He touched her shoulder lightly, comfortingly. "What the hell has happened, Pearl? You are shaking. Is it your mother?"

She shook her head, pressed her fingers over her eyes. "It is—Kanji."

"Kanji? What is it, pressing his suit, eh?" Brad sounded amused.

"It is not—funny, Brad," she said, with dignity. "Kanji insisted on taking me to dinner last night. He said we would marry in six months, whether I wished it or not.

If I do not consent—he will—will—" Hot color came up in her cheeks.

"Will what?" asked Brad, impatiently.

"Rape me," she ended, bluntly, and hung her head in shame. "He is—different. He is cold, hard—he would hurt me—I know it— I have never seen him so icily angry."

"Kanji? I can't believe that," said Brad, staring at her. "Are you sure you understood him?"

She nodded. "He is violent inside—" she whispered. "And he has such strength—"

"Has he ever—I mean—attacked—you?" asked Brad, with clumsy delicacy.

"He has embraced me against my will," she said softly. She had never been so embarrassed and shamed. She put her hand to her face. "I do not wish to marry! Men can be beasts! And Kanji—he would beat me as my father beats my mother! I know it!"

There was silence in the office, she heard a fly buzzing around the desk. Brad cleared his throat.

"Pearl, you must not be afraid of Kanji," he said gently. "I think he loves you very much. He will be a good husband, he wishes the best for you. He would never injure you. He is not brutal."

"You do not know him," she said, disappointed. "You have not seen this side of him. Do you know of his prowess in judo and karate? He has great skill and toughness and can use it. What am I to do? Learn karate, in order to repel him?" she flared with bitterness.

Brad ruffled his thick hair in puzzlement. She stared at him with more antagonism. She might have known the men would stick together. She thought of Charita, the little she had seen of the girl, how Brad would grab her arm and pull her down on the bed to sit with him, how he ordered her about. How quiet the girl was, how obedient, even though she was an American girl.

Was Brad like that also? A man who must prove his

373

masculinity by beating up his wife? Order her about? Strike her and beat her when he chose? The new thought made her stare, silently, piercingly at him. Seeing him with new eyes, her kind boss who gave her such a good salary.

"Pearl, you are exaggerating," said Brad, with a sigh and a troubled look at her. "Kanji is the soul of decency, he has gentle, good parents. He isn't the wife-beating sort, I'd give my word on that. He would never injure you. You must not understand him—"

"It is you who do not understand," she flared. "Kanji is a Japanese man, and they must dominate women. American men, I think, are not so different. They must be tops in all—they must be the boss—" Then aghast, she put her fingers over her betraying mouth.

Brad looked grim and tired. He leaned back in his chair, and stared down at the sketch before him, one of Charita's. He touched it gently, and Pearl realized his mind was far from her.

Pearl said, more quietly, "You do not understand Kanji, I think. He is a strong, tough man, and he says he feels shamed that I will not set a wedding date. He used to say he loved me. But love—frustrated—can turn to hate. A man like Kanji can hate well, I believe. He can be violent. I know he can."

She stopped, but Brad said nothing, holding the sketch without seeing it.

He could do nothing, she thought, in despair. She was on her own. Brad and Kanji were both men, they would not interfere in each other's personal affairs. She was alone, and must fend for herself.

Pearl stood up, rather shakily, and clung to the back of the straight chair. "But I trouble you with my personal concerns," she said, with dignity. "Pray pardon me. I do not mean to do this. You must forgive my impertinence." She turned and walked out of the room.

Brad said, weakly, "Pearl—I say—" She shut the

door firmly after herself and went to get her handbag. She would go somewhere for tea, and try to pull herself together. All she could do then, was to try to avoid Kanji, avoid being with him, never be alone with him.

She could never trust him again, nor any man, she thought with bitterness and despair.

25

Donald was doing good work, Brad told Charita.

She smiled happily. "I am so pleased. He did good work in school, and his sense of design was excellent. Also, his parents are of honor and work conscientiously for America in Japan. How happy I am that he came to you."

She thought Brad was staring at her thoughtfully. They were sitting in the drawing room after dinner, she with her tea, and he with hot black coffee. He had not offered to turn on the music.

The September nights were cool. Today she had seen yellow leaves falling into the lotus pool, and the golden lotus blooms were beginning to fade and grow brown. Autumn was coming, with its red and golden touch, but brown death waited for the leaves.

"Yes, he is doing very well," Brad said, after a long pause. "And Kanji handles the office work excellently. I have been thinking—"

"Yes, Brad?" Her heart was fluttering, there was something strange in his care in speaking. What was he thinking?

"After the New Year, I think we will take a vacation in the United States. I need to visit my factories and see how they are doing."

She had thought she was braced for this idea, of the vacation in the States. However, when he actually said the words, she began to feel she was sinking into a dark well where nothing was familiar. She felt panicky. She took a sip of hot tea, another sip, thinking frantically.

Finally she said, "As you wish to visit your factories, I believe I should be in your way as you travel. Perhaps it might be well if I remain in Kyoto, or go to visit my parents while you are absent and traveling."

He frowned, and his glossy brown head was shaking from side to side before she had finished. "No, never. I shall not leave you behind me, Charita," he said decisively.

"But you have much work to do. It would distress you—"

"No," he said, more gently. "Charita, I have been thinking a great deal. You have never lived in the States. You should have that experience, otherwise you will be more Japanese as you grow older."

"That is—bad?" she whispered, her mouth trembling. She could not believe he was saying this. Did he detest the Japanese? Did he find fault with her?

"It could be," he said, cautiously. "Now, listen, honey. I'm not criticizing you. But as you get older, as we have children, I would like you to become more American. The children should grow up in America, go to school there."

"Why?" she asked, her eyes wide open.

"Why? Because—well, they will be Americans," he insisted, staring at her gravely. "They should have the advantage of an American education."

"I have been reading the American magazines," she said, setting down her delicate white porcelain teacup with an angry little bang. "And they do not think American education is so good anymore. It said one place that many Americans graduate from high school and cannot read and

377

write. Is this what you would wish for your—your children?"

A blush rose in her cheeks at the words. But she was too upset to let that stop her, the embarrassment of thinking of children they might have.

"Now, Charita! That is one isolated case, or some cases. We would make sure to send our children to a good school," he said impatiently.

"We do not even have children as yet," she defied him, surprised at herself. But it made her feel desperate to think of going to live in a strange country, away from her foster parents and her friends.

"No, but we will have one day, won't we, honey?" When he smiled at her like that, so tenderly, she wanted to melt. She looked away resolutely.

"Perhaps," she said, coldly. "However, I do not see why we must return to the States."

"I never intended to live here longer than a year or so," said Brad, shocking her. "By the New Year, it will be almost two years. I always intended to set up a factory, get it working well, then return to the States. I can return from time to time, do the electroplating or anything that needs doing, then go home again. I thought we might set up housekeeping in some city we both like—San Francisco —or perhaps Santa Fe—or somewhere in the East. Baltimore, or New York, or Boston—"

"The words are only names on a map for me," she said, her hands shaking. She clasped them tightly in her lap. "How can they be places I like? They are strange to me! Brad, tell me you do not mean this!"

He came over to sit beside her on the couch. He put his big hand over her shaking ones, holding them warmly. "Now, honey, don't get upset," he said firmly. "We have our lives before us, many years of happiness. Where we will live does not need to concern us just now. I just wanted you to know what I was thinking about."

"When you married me," she said, with precision, "you said nothing about moving to the States soon. You married me, knowing I have been brought up here, that I love my parents, that I enjoy my friends. Why do you wish me to leave them all, for a strange land, and people I've never met? Why, Brad?" Her words were from her aching heart. She searched his face anxiously.

He looked more tough, and rather exasperated. "But I am an American, Charita! And so are you, even though you never lived in the States. Your father should have taken you back to the States after your mother died——"

"Now you blame my father! My father, who lived in a world of peace and contentment here that he never found in the States!"

"I didn't mean to start an argument tonight," he said, standing up abruptly, and pacing to the window and back again. "I just wanted you to start thinking about the future, Charita! You are not your father. You will soon make friends wherever we decide to settle down. Don't let it panic you——"

"I am not panicked," she said, more quietly. "I just am thinking I do not know you very well. Never have you said that you wished to move back to the States soon. You spoke only of some vacation——"

"A honeymoon," he said, smiling again. "We never had that honeymoon, darling!"

"We went to Hakone," she said, with desolation. It seemed an eon ago.

He shrugged. "Wait until you see the Grand Canyon, and San Francisco, with its old streets— There is a fine Chinatown there, you would enjoy it."

She stared at him. Why should she enjoy a *China-town*—whatever that was—when she lived in Japan? Were all Oriental matters the same to him?

He was going on, with enthusiasm. "And we could travel to Europe, you have never gone there. I enjoy

England a great deal. There are some marvelous medieval towns, like Chester and Carlyle, with shops. And some interesting cathedrals. And France! How you would like France! The chateaus of the Loire Valley are beautiful, with their gardens and the furnishings of long ago, the tapestries with their faded colors. Yes, you might get some good ideas from the tapestries—"

He was beginning on Italy when she interrupted.

"I have an idea, Brad," she said, dangerously quiet, her blue eyes flashing.

"Yes, honey?" he asked hopefully.

"Let us move to Egypt and settle down there. It is halfway between your ideal home, the States, and Japan. We could go on vacations, you to the States and me to Japan. And surely there would be many fascinating places to visit!"

He stared at her. "That is nonsense, Egypt is hot and has very bad sanitation," he said shortly. "Whatever put Egypt into your head?"

"It is halfway between your dreams and mine," she said, rising. "I shall retire now, and let you think of Egypt!" She stalked out of the room, furiously angry, upset, near tears.

For the first time, she went to bed with her door locked against him. She was furious and weepy, and she sniffed into the pillows for a long time, tossing and turning in the bed. Brad was impossible! He had let her think they would live in Japan for many years. Now he was telling her, they would return to the States, *as he had planned long ago!*

He had deceived her. If she had ever dreamed that Brad would marry her and carry her off to America practically at once, she would have said no, very loudly and clearly. She would have returned to her foster parents, and all this grief would not have happened.

She would not have known his brutality, his forceful

lovemaking, his insistence on his own way. She would not have suffered, thinking of him with Jacinda, with Pearl, with who knew how many other women!

She tossed and turned on the warm bed, in spite of the cool September night. She rose early, to dress in a kimono, and sit at the window, and gaze out longingly at the Japanese garden, splendid with crimson salvia, and scarlet and orange gladioli, with maple leaves turning red and yellow, with trailing vines so beautiful in the sunlight.

If only she had never met Brad!

She buried her face in her slim hands. Never met him. Never known the warmth of his body in bed at night, his hands urgent on her body, his lips knowing every intimate part of her.

Never known Brad, never known his furious love-making, when his lean hard body strained to take hers. His lips on her cheeks, her mouth, her throat, her breasts. The way he taught her slowly, surely, to respond to him. The wild passion she had known in his embrace. His whispers in her ears, the words in English and Japanese, every love word for her—

Tears dripped slowly through her fingers. He had deceived her over and over. He had made Jacinda his mistress, probably, and then Pearl, probably—though Charita had begun to doubt that. Pearl was fastidious, she was cool and contained. Would she have given in to Brad, would he even have wanted to make his secretary his mistress? When Pearl had come, Charita had watched sharply for secret touches, intimate looks between them— and had found none. They were all business, though they smiled, and used each other's first names.

Jacinda was jealous of him. Perhaps she had lied when she had said that to Charita, that Pearl was Brad's mistress. Perhaps she had lied at other times. That was a new thought to Charita.

But all else was blanked out in her misery. Brad was

going to insist on taking her to the States! He had it all worked out in his mind, and that was all. Would he listen to her pleading?

She waited for him to rise, to come and bang on her door and order her to talk to him. The servants would talk, but for once Charita did not care.

She heard the sounds of the shower running, and tensed. She waited. A door banged, a drawer opened and shut. She heard the sounds of Brad getting dressed, and then his door opening.

He walked down the hall, she heard his footsteps slow and heavy. But he walked right past her door and into the other part of the house. She held her breath. His voice sounded, curtly, the maid's voice was high and shrill.

"You wish no breakfast, master-san? You go without food? Will you allow me to fix coffee quick?"

Evidently not. The front door banged, and soon she heard the car starting up on the gravel path near the garage. The car went past her window, Brad was staring straight ahead. He was driving, the chauffeur sat beside him.

He was gone for the day, without a word to her. Charita felt dazed and unreal. She was weary from lack of sleep.

She got up and went out to the dining room. She sat down, and the maid brought tea and egg, giving her a furtive quick glance before politely averting her face. All the household would know there had been a quarrel, but somehow Charita did not care today. How could he have so deceived her! Not deceived her so much, as allowed her to think she would live all her life in her beloved homeland of Japan.

She was still toying with her teacup when the maid flop-flopped into the room, her sandals louder than usual, carrying a letter on a tray.

"For mistress-san," she said politely, setting the tray down beside Charita.

Charita looked blankly at the letter. At first she had thought Brad had left a loving note for her, reassuring her. But it was not Brad's sure handwriting.

She ripped open the envelope.

Her eyes went wide as she read. It was so polite, but so urgent.

"Charita," the note read. "I beg you—come to the gardens behind the Gion restaurant where we have met before. At eleven o'clock, I beg you, not later than that. I must see you about terrible problem. Your brother, Kanji."

She started up. "What time is it?" she asked.

"It is nine o'clock, mistress-san, just after nine."

Charita flew to her room. She would meet Kanji at once, but not just to listen to his problem. She would tell him her own problem, and beg his advice.

She changed rapidly to the cherry red dress and bright red shoes. Perhaps they would help her morale. She put a compact and some money into the matching red handbag, and went to call a taxi. The maid fluttered about her, Charita waved her away.

"I go to meet my brother, Kanji Noguchi," she finally said, and went out to the waiting taxi.

In the taxi, she took out the note and studied it again. Kanji must have been in a tremendous hurry, the note was not so neat as he would have usually written, and his hand-writing looked a little unlike himself. What could be wrong? Was he having trouble about Pearl?

And why was it so urgent?

On the way, she had time to think that she had not told anyone where she was going. Also she had promised Brad she would not go out without him, except with her foster parents, or with bodyguards. But she waved the thought away impatiently. She was quite safe in a taxi, and she would meet Kanji, who was strong and brave and fine.

She arrived at the restaurant, but instead of going inside, she walked around the outside into the grounds. It was a quarter until eleven. She noticed a thick-set Japanese man behind her, going slowly in the direction of the pond, as she was doing. The garden was a favorite place of the Japanese, they liked to pose for pictures on the attractive gray stone bridge, or against the weathered natural brown teahouse on the grounds, or against the azalea bushes or the cherry trees in the spring. It was lovely today also, with the maples turning their glorious colors.

Another man was walking across the little bridge as she went toward it. It was early for luncheon; however people would be coming in another hour. It was a very popular place for older people. Young ones liked to come also, for the gardens were extensive, and the paths winding. One could go among the attractive bushes, or the maple trees, and behind the teahouse, and follow the paths along the little winding stream that wound through the grounds.

One could walk and soon be out of sight of the huge windows of the restaurant, she mused. Perhaps she had best remain close to the entrance of the grounds, so Kanji would see her.

Kanji was not around. Puzzled, she turned back toward the restaurant, and gazed toward the windows. He should be here, he was always prompt.

She sat down to wait on one of the oak benches placed near a bush, and stretched out her feet. The red pumps had two-inch heels, she regretted she had worn them. They were not as comfortable as the lower-heeled black shoes she liked. Her vanity—she should not have yielded to the wish to appear well in public. But where was Kanji?

Now she was noticing the Japanese men, coming toward her. One from the back, one from the bridge. They were short, burly, with ugly bullet heads, and hair cut short. They reminded her unpleasantly of the men on the plane and at Hakone, but of course they were not the same men.

Charita tensed as the men came close to her. It looked as though they would meet near her bench. Perhaps they knew each other. The men stared at each other, then away again, politely. The one man from the bridge passed her.

The other man came on. He came near her, then grabbed her arm, pulled her up, and clapped his other hand over her mouth. It was done so swiftly she could not draw breath to scream before his big dirty hand was over her mouth.

He hurried her toward the bushes, on the way to the bridge. She struggled, kicked out with her high heels. Her red handbag had fallen into the path. He did not attempt to scoop it up. He did not want money, evidently. He did want her!

Terror was racing through her.

She fought against his hand, tried to bite his fingers. He was too clever for that. His hand held her mouth shut.

His other arm was about her, hustling her toward the bridge. Toward the thick masses of bushes, where no one could see her, even in the bright red dress.

He pushed her into the bushes, his hand was on her throat. She saw the menace of his bright excited black eyes, his ugly broken-nosed face.

All she had remembered of what Brad said came back to her. Men after the formula. Men who would do anything. Men who had beaten up Brad!

At the office, Kanji had paused in his work to stare at a dirty white envelope which had been given to him by a messenger boy.

"Where did this come from?"

He grinned, excited, his eyes snapping. "Lady give to

me," he said, then ran away, and down the stairs again, his bare feet swift.

Kanji had gone to the door to stare after him. Donald came from his office.

"What's up, Kanji? Who was that?"

"I don't know." He gazed down at the envelope again, then ripped it open. He went over the words, then read it again.

"What is it? Pardon my curiosity, but you look—funny," said Donald awkwardly.

Kanji read aloud, "My dear brother Kanji, I beg you to come to the gardens behind the Gion restaurant where we have met before. I beg you come about eleven fifteen. I must see you about terrible problem. Your sister, Charita."

Donald was scowling. "What terrible problem could she have?" he wondered. "That doesn't sound like Charita."

Kanji thrust the page at him. "Does this look like her writing?" he asked tensely.

Donald took the page, scanned it, shook his head. "No, she writes very neatly, we used to read each other's compositions. She makes her *g*'s very rounded and—Kanji, this isn't from her!"

The men stared at each other. Kanji drew a deep breath.

"I must go—she may be in danger!"

"Where is Brad?" They swung around to see Pearl staring at them, color gone from her face. "He should know of this! Those men may have captured him again!"

"All I can do is go to the garden. Pearl, you try to get hold of Brad," snapped Kanji, with authority. "He went to see Mr. Miles Snow about some legal matters. Telephone him, send a messenger—oh, no, do not tell him where we went—it may be a trap for him—" he ended in a groan. He ran down the stairs, Donald after him, Pearl screaming after them.

"Do not go—it is danger, Kanji, I beg you—do not go!"

He did not answer, nor look back, but some exultation came in the midst of his worry. She did worry about him! Maybe that was a good sign!

Donald was right behind him when Kanji reached his car. "I'm coming with you—two is better than one in a fight!" said Donald, his friendly brown eyes blazing with excitement.

Kanji nodded, there was no time to argue. He got in, started the car. Donald was just slamming the door as the car whipped around the corner of the parking lot.

"What time is it?" said Kanji tensely. "If they wrote also to Charita—"

"Not quite eleven—five till—" said Donald, checking his watch against the clock on an office building. They said no more until they had wheeled into the restaurant grounds.

They ran around the corner of the restaurant, down into the gardens. Kanji was ahead, his brain whirling. What could it mean?

He saw the powerful Japanese man first, standing idly near a wooden bench. Beyond, something red lay on the ground.

Kanji ran down the path, toward the man. As he came, the man snapped into alertness. A warning rang in Kanji's brain. Donald was following him. Kanji did not break his stride. As he came to the man, he whipped out his arm, and knocked him down!

Then he ran on. He paused only to glance at the handbag, it looked like one he had seen Charita carry. He scanned the bushes, the bridge, the stream. In the distance —something red—Might be a bush hidden by the other bushes—or—

He ran on, Donald after him, scooping up the hand-bag. "Charita's?" gasped Donald behind him.

Kanji did not bother to answer. He was putting on speed. Through the bushes, he saw a figure struggling with another beefy man. He broke through the screen of bushes, into the open. Charita—the man's hand at her throat. She was struggling, almost down, the slim body bending like a fragile red stem—

Something blazed in Kanji, a battle fever like that of his samurai ancestors. He was at the man, his hands on the man's throat before the Japanese bully knew he was there.

Charita fell from the man's grasp, toppling to the leaf-strewn ground. Her hands went to her throat. Donald bent over her protectively, concerned.

Kanji's whole attention was on his opponent. The man had been offguard, wrestling easily with the girl. Now he had a worthy duelist. He struck out with the edge of his palm, in a karate stroke. Kanji ducked it, struck him, but hit only glancingly.

The man flung himself at Kanji's head with a flurry of arms and legs. Kanji protected himself, then turned around to parry another blow.

The man ran! He took to his heels and ran through the bushes, and across the stream, disappearing far up the other path. Kanji ran after him, then checked himself, glaring through the red haze of blood that obscured his vision. He had been ready to kill the man, the bully who had had his fingers around Charita's throat. But there was another man behind them—

He turned around reluctantly and went back to Donald, bending over the prone girl. He looked around warily for that first man. He was gone, no sign of him.

"How is she?" he snapped.

"Can't talk. She was badly choked. Poor kid," said

388

Donald, soothingly. "Don't cry, Charita. We'll get you home again. Come on, up you get."

Charita was sobbing soundlessly, tears running down her pale cheeks. Donald was holding her, his arm about her shoulders, patting her awkwardly, in brotherly fashion. "Come on, old girl, wasn't a tragedy, thank God. Come on, let's get you home to Brad. Whatever did you come for?"

Kanji stopped scanning the bushes, and looked at her, his mouth tight. "Did you get a letter also?" he asked.

She nodded, unable to speak for now. She touched the handbag Donald had slung carelessly on his arm.

"Let's get her to the car. I don't like this place," Donald complained. "What happened to the other creep?"

Kanji went ahead of them, watching out for him. The other man had smartly disappeared. But someone else might be about— He had a distinctly uneasy feeling that someone watched from somewhere, perhaps from the wide restaurant windows.

They avoided the restaurant again, climbing the path that led past the stream and waterfall, up toward the parking lot. Charita was crying quietly, and Donald was soothing her, with boyish gentleness. Kanji kept his whole attention on the cars near them, any men who might come near, his black eyes alert, his body tensed for attack. But no one came near them, though several parties going into the restaurant stared with polite curiosity at the little group heading for the car.

Charita sat between the two men in the car. Donald was still soothing her quietly, skillfully, as though he had practice at this, thought Kanji, curiously. Kanji kept watching the road as he drove, worrying that they might be cut off by two or more cars. Those men kept attacking and attacking. Brad must be more careful—

At the house, Brad was not there. Kanji hesitated,

then said, "We must wait for him here. I will call Pearl and see if she has reached him."

The maid was clucking over Charita, the state of her clothes, muddy and leaf-strewn, and her pale face and tears. When she saw the red finger-marked throat, she gave a shocked exclamation, and said they must get the doctor.

Charita sank onto a sofa in the living room. One shoe fell from her foot, she made no attempt to put it on. Kanji went to the telephone and called the office.

"Pearl, we have Charita here, she was attacked," he said, as soon as she answered. "Where is Brad?"

"He was at Mr. Snow's office. I will call him—he was calling the police—where are you now?" she asked, in a very agitated way.

"We are at his home. Please ask him to come."

"Is she—is Mrs. Livingston—all right?"

"She was hurt, but yes, she is all right." Kanji wanted to say more, but finally hung up. Pearl must call Brad.

Brad arrived within half an hour, the doctor had already come. He was pale with shock. Kanji was pleased to see that he had his chauffeur drive him, and the bodyguard was in the back seat. He strode in, looking about.

"Where is Charita?" he demanded at once.

"In the bedroom. The doctor and maid attend her. Please, when you have seen her, we must speak to you," said Kanji, forcefully.

He had obtained the letter from Charita, and he had his own to show Brad also. He paced the room slowly as he waited. Donald watched him gravely, longing to ask all sorts of questions, but too trained in the diplomatic to ask.

Brad returned shortly. "She has been hurt—her poor throat—why did she go to the gardens?" he asked, puzzled.

Kanji picked up the letters from the table. "This is the letter she received, saying it was from me. This is the letter which was sent to me. Donald agreed with me that it was not Charita's writing."

Brad picked up the letters, read them, paling even more. "Good God, so now they are after her!" he groaned, and put one hand to his head. "The men—what did they look like?"

Kanji described them, but it meant little to Brad. Two Japanese toughs, looking much like other toughs of the Kyoto underworld, probably paid to do a job.

"But why go after Charita?" asked Brad again and again, pacing the floor, watching for the doctor, ruffling up his hair in agitation. "Why? She does not know the gold formula."

"Perhaps they hoped to hold her for ransom, the formula," suggested Donald, the most contained of the three men. "That has been done before. They know you would do anything to get her released."

"But they were choking her—the man was holding her in a merciless grip," said Kanji, feeling the hot anger rising in him again. His hands clenched. "I wish I had him in my hold! He would know how I felt! The old days were best. A man could go out and find and kill his enemy!"

Donald and Brad stared at him. "Hey, calm down, Kanji," said Donald, getting up to stand near him compassionately. "You're a civilized being, you know. We'll get the police on it."

"They can do nothing," said Kanji, shortly. "A man must protect his family, or he is a poor thing! Charita is my sister. How dared they drag her into the bushes and treat her like—" He stopped, biting his lips. He shook his head. "Very well, we report it to police. But I will speak to my contacts in the underworld, and see if I can learn anything. They shall not go unpunished!"

Brad had picked up the letter to Charita, and scanned it. "You are sure this is not your writing?" he asked Kanji.

Kanji whirled on him. "My writing! How dare you

say this to me! I would not take her into danger! No, it is not my writing!" he repeated hotly.

"Hey, now, cool down, both of you," said Donald, worriedly. "Of course, Kanji did not write that. Brad, you must think of the danger to Charita. Is there anywhere you can send her until this cools down?"

"She shall not go away from me!" said Brad, and stormed away to the bedroom to see to his wife.

Kanji shrugged his hard shoulders, and went out to the car. Donald followed him, watching him but saying little as they went back to the office. Kanji was hot with fury again, this time against Brad, and there was hurt in his anger. How could Brad think this of him, how could he even entertain such a thought? It showed how little Brad really trusted him!

And poor little Charita, with her throat so red and raw, and her blue eyes brimming with tears—and that slim body so close to death. Someone would pay for this! A life for a life, thought Kanji, grimly. The insult to his family would be wiped out only in blood.

Donald said, still scanning the letters, "You know, I think I have it figured out, why you got a letter also." He pointed to a line in one, then in the other. "Looks like Charita was to come at eleven o'clock. You were told to come at eleven-fifteen. An odd time, isn't it?"

Kanji came out of his absorption, to stare at the letters. "Identical instructions, except for the time," he agreed slowly. "But—why?"

"They acted fast," said the younger man. He tapped the letters, his face as shrewd as that of his father working out a diplomatic problem. "They meant to strangle Charita, perhaps leave her body in the bushes. You would come—presumably alone—and find her body. What would the police think?"

Kanji stared at Donald, his fingers gripped the pages. "That—I had killed her—Charita?" he whispered.

Donald nodded. "Thank God I came with you. And we were in time," he said simply. "Someone's careful plotting went screwy. Kanji—someone is after Brad, and Charita, *and you*," he added with emphasis.

"But who would believe I would harm Charita—" Kanji began. Then he thought of Brad's fury. "Ahhhh—to make trouble between us—and Brad? As well as harm us both by murdering Charita—his wife and my sister!"

"I'm afraid so," murmured Donald, with regret.

"They will pay," said Kanji violently. "They—will—pay! The insult to my family—the harm to Charita—and the deeper harm meant—" He flexed his fingers.

"Leave it to the police," Donald advised, but without much conviction.

Kanji stared ahead, through the mist of blood-red anger that filmed his eyes. No, not the police. He—Kanji—would make them pay—in blood.

26

Charita felt very terrified and crushed. Her throat hurt for days, she did not even try to speak the first couple of days. Brad hovered over her, but that irritated her, for he kept asking questions.

For some reason, Brad seemed to think that the letter might have come from Kanji.

"But that is not his writing," whispered Charita painfully.

"Then why did you think it was?" he asked.

"I thought . . . I was tired . . . and weary . . . all I thought was to meet him—" She was near to tears, but he was relentless in his questioning.

Charita asked a question in her turn. "Why did they —those men—try to—kill me? Why, Brad?"

"I don't know, but I'll find out," he said grimly, his mouth white-lined in anger. "You don't know the formula, and I thought that was what they were after. If they are going to go after you and other persons—just at random —my God, I don't know—" He shook his head, lapsed into silence and thought.

Charita had nightmares of a man trying to strangle her and racing after her through dark woods. She would awaken, wet with sweat, and trembling with fear, to reach out for Brad in the darkness.

He woke one night as she touched him. "What is it, darling?"

"I was afraid—I dreamed—" She crept into his welcoming arms, and put her face against his hard throat. She felt his hands soothing her into sleep again. He said gentle nice things, then.

"Poor love, my poor darling, it's all right, you are all right now, I won't let anyone come near you —"

But in the daylight, she was alone. He went off to work, and warned her not to stir out without him. It was lonely, just staying at home, and being afraid even to go out into the garden.

Brad had hired more guards, and one roamed the grounds at night with a huge fierce guard dog. Charita was as afraid of the fierce guard and his dog as of the men who had attacked her. Who knew what men would do? They were all bullies and had strange ideas.

In her fear, she could not confide even in Kanji. He came over one day to talk to her, to get more of a description of the men. She told him what she remembered, he wrote it all down carefully. He looked cold and strange to her, not like her smiling elder brother.

"Do—do you think you might be able to find the men—" she asked timidly.

"I might," he said shortly. "Now, do you remember any marks on their faces? Any scars or birthmarks?"

She shook her head. Her mind was a blur of fear and frenzy. The minutes in the garden had hazed in her mind.

In her fear, she turned back to the safety of her childhood. How little she had known of danger then! Her parents had kept her safe and secure. The thought of their little home in the village, its brown warm walls, the sliding paper doors in the summertime opened to the wind and the scents of the garden—all seemed like a dream to which she would like to return.

If only she could go back, to the days and years

before her father had died, before she had married Brad, before she had known danger and the fear of a violent death!

Finally one day she called her parents. It took a time for the long-distance call to go through. But her mother answered at last.

"Mother! It is Charita!" cried Charita, as though her raised voice would reach farther. "How are you?"

"My dear little Charita! How goes everything with you?"

"Not well, Mama! Oh, Mama-san, such a terrible thing has happened!" and tears filled Charita's throat, still sore from the attack.

"Terrible! What is it? What has happened to my baby?" her foster mother cried dramatically.

Charita was about to burst out with the whole story. Then she hesitated. It was a long story, and it involved Brad and his secret gold formula. She could not tell all about that.

"Charita? My pet? What is it? Your father has just come in for luncheon. Tell him all about it!" her mother commanded.

Charita heard the voices in the background, thin and reedy by distance. Then her foster father spoke. "Charita, my dear. What troubles you?"

"Oh, it is a long story, Papa-san," she said. "I regret troubling you. Many things have happened. I was—was attacked in a garden, and a man tried to choke me to death. But Kanji and Donald Raglan came to my rescue, and I wish I could see you!" The words poured out.

"Tried to choke you! A thief? A man who attacked you—what were you doing in the garden?" Her father sounded upset and incredulous. She heard her mother chattering to him in fear.

"It upset me," said Charita. "I had to call you—and

talk to you. I wish I could see you! I do not feel secure—it is not like the old days—"

"I do not understand this at all," said Mr. Noguchi firmly. He understood the things that one could feel and touch, and he understood much about reverence to one's ancestors and the gods. But this babbling of a woman disturbed him. "Where is your honorable husband? I would speak with him."

"He is at work, he is all right," said Charita hurriedly. "I just—I just called—to talk to you—to know that you—love me—" And she started to cry.

That upset Mr. Noguchi, and he had his wife get on the phone to soothe Charita with loving words. There was a hitch in the conversation when the operator broke in. Then she apologized, and let them go on.

But Charita realized she was upsetting her parents without getting the reassurance she needed. She wanted to sit between them on a sofa, and have them hold her hands, and say gentle words. She wanted to go back to her childhood—but there was no going back. She was a married woman.

"I wish I could see you," she blurted out. "If only I might see you and talk with you."

"You must come and visit with us," said Mrs. Noguchi, tenderly. "Ask the permission from your honorable husband, and come for a good visit. It will be our joy to receive you."

"I would like to come, Mama-san." Charita wiped her face, her handkerchief was soaked. She smiled into the telephone. "It is good to talk with you, Mama-san. You have been well?"

"Yes, we are as always," was the serene reply. "Your father is quite well, though he works too hard for our miserable lives. You will speak to your good husband, and ask his permission to come to see us?

Perhaps he will come also, we would welcome him in our poor home."

"I will ask him," but Charita thought he would not go. Work was so important to him, he was busy all the time.

She sent her love, lingered a little, then hung up. She felt homesick now, after hearing their loving, anxious voices. She huddled on the sofa, and could not force herself to go to the workroom and invent designs.

Brad found her like this when he came home after five. "Charita, what is it? You are so pale and white?" He came over to kiss her tenderly.

She stared at him resentfully. It was all his fault, that he had married her, and taken her away from the comfort of her home. "I am all right," she said. "I would speak with you this evening, however."

He gave her a dark look, nodded curtly. "I'll go get a shower and change," and went off.

He came back in about half an hour, headed for the ice bucket and whiskey. He drained half a glass, and came to sit with her. He studied her curled-up figure, in the blue and silver kimono, and sighed.

"All right, what is it?" he asked.

She studied the ends of her sleeves. "Have you had a good day?" she evaded.

"Reasonable. No, damn it, it was bad. I caught Kanji going through my papers."

She sat up straight, her wide blue eyes aghast. "You—what?" she cried.

"You heard me. I would have trusted him with my life. But there he was, going through the papers of some tests I made on my new gold process," he said curtly, and drained the glass.

Charita continued to stare at him. "You do not mean—you cannot mean—you must trust Kanji! He is a man of much honor!"

"All I know is some damned peculiar things are going on, and he seems to be in the center of them!" said Brad bitterly. "I was training him to be a manager of the whole works, and then I find him at my desk, going over papers!"

"What did he say—what was his reason?" asked Charita anxiously. "Surely he had a reason for what he did?"

"He said the Arab prince had telephoned about another order, and he could find no record of it— But those papers had nothing to do with orders." Brad got up and went to pour another drink.

"But surely he could not know that," said Charita, gently. "He must have been looking for the order—"

"Oh, you would defend him if you found him sneaking into the factory at three in the morning!" Brad burst out angrily. He turned from the liquor cabinet and faced her, his eyes darker than usual from anger. "Kanji can do no wrong. You love him, he is your big brother! Even when he wrote you a letter, asking you to meet him in a garden—you forgot all precautions, you never told me—"

"He did not write the letter!" she burst out, appalled. "I told you—it was not his writing!"

"You thought it was, you went right off to meet him—carelessly, without consulting me—"

Her mouth tightened. She said, with an effort, "You said, it was a new gold formula. Do you not mean, the pearly gold one?"

"No," he said shortly, taking a drink. "I have another formula about worked out, of a reddish gold, quite different. I have been experimenting with various combinations, and the papers with the tests and their results were on my desk. Pearl had called me to ask about something, I went out for a couple of minutes, then down to the worktables to talk to one of the men. When I returned, Kanji was going through that desk, and looking at the papers."

Charita put her hand to her face. It was a continuing nightmare that would never end. Worse and worse—

"Kanji would do nothing without honor," she repeated wearily. "He is a man of honor—he would not do this, Brad, please believe me. I have known him all my days—"

Brad turned away abruptly, and went to stare out into the dusk of the garden. "I'm thinking of closing up my operations here, and going back to the States," he said.

"Oh—no—no!" she gasped.

"Yes. Too many things have happened. My life in danger, and yours. I think that time on the runway—you remember?—when you were pushed down and almost run over by a baggage truck—that was no accident. Only my closest friends knew of our arrival. Kanji—Pearl—Jacinda and Miles. Only them. Yet the attempts on your life, and on mine, began at once."

She sat still, in horror, staring at his back. "And you—think—Kanji—"

"What else can I think? And damn it, I don't know the Japanese." His tone was even, quiet, more terrifying for that. "They have closed faces, they smile and don't mean it. They cover hate with courtesy, they bow and smile, and could knife you in the back."

"Brad!" He was talking about her people, the people with whom she had grown up! She could not believe it.

He drained the glass, set it down wearily. He turned back to sit down in a big chair, and stretch out his long legs.

"Forget it for now, Charita. I'm tired. I'll have to wait until I'm calm, and come to some decision. But by God, we're going back to the States, where I can understand businessmen, and know what is going on!"

"And in the States, everyone is honorable, and means

exactly what he says?" she flashed bitterly. She had been reading the American magazines he brought to her. "And the government is always honorable and just—no matter how many bribes are given and taken under the table? And there is no cutting of throats? Brad, I am not a young idiot. In every country, there are dishonest men, and methods. I am growing up, no matter what you think of me! And I know Kanji Noguchi, and I know he is as honorable and fine as any man in the States! You wrong him, and I am—am disappointed in you!"

"I am disappointed in him," said Brad, ironically. "Don't try to understand business, Charita."

She drew herself up. "I am a woman, so I am not supposed to think!" she flared. "Well, I do think, and I know who I trust, and I know what business methods I prefer! Go back to the States, but you will go alone!"

He gazed at her, and never had she seen him so impersonal, so deadly cold to her. "Don't challenge me, Charita," he said, softly. "It won't work."

She put her hand to her face. She felt dizzy and sick with her emotions.

"I wish I could go home," she whispered.

"Your home is with me, wherever I am!"

"I telephoned my parents today. I told them—I said I was anxious and terrified— They asked me to come and remain with them for a time."

His jaw tightened. "You are going nowhere," he said, definitely. "Especially not to your foster parents! Don't think about it, Charita. I will not permit it!"

The maid came in, smiling to show her gold-capped teeth. "The dinner is ready for master-san and mistress-san," she chanted.

Brad got up, and went over to Charita. He helped her up, and it must have looked like courteous behavior. Only she could feel the iron of his arm, the grip of his fingers.

"I am quite ready for dinner," he said.

During dinner, he made polite talk. He asked about her designs. When she said she had done no work, he smiled, and said, "You must get more rest. You have worked hard." But his eyes were cold and angry.

She did not know what she ate, she pushed the dishes from her after a few bites. Brad ate stolidly through one course after another, but he was angry, she thought.

After dinner, they sat in the drawing room. He played records to cover their silence. She finally got up to go to bed, sick of the pretense.

He looked up. "I'll come in presently," he said coolly.

She wondered what he would do if she locked the door. Break it down, probably.

She went to bed, and lay waiting for him, angry, helpless, wishing she had never married him. A woman was a poor thing, she thought, her fists clenched on the thin blanket. She could not fight the man who most oppressed her! Her husband. She was supposed to do exactly what he wished, and refrain from doing what he did not wish.

Brad came in presently, in his pajamas and robe. He took off the robe, and set it on a chair, and slid into bed with her.

"You would be sorry if we went to America," said Charita, continuing her thoughts.

"Sorry?" He sounded surprised, she could not see his face in the darkness. "Why should I be?"

"The women in America do not always obey their husbands! They learn to be—independent—and think for themselves! And they—they walk out—if they wish—" Her voice faltered into silence.

"And do you think you would learn to be independent?" He sounded amused, rather than angry. "Do you

402

think you would learn to walk out on me? Forget it—we are married for life!"

She did not answer. He put his arm under her, and drew her over to him. Her body was stiff and unresponsive. When he put one hand to her throat, and caressed it, she shivered, remembering the hard, cruel fingers of the man who had tried to choke her to death.

"Does your throat still hurt, darling?" asked Brad anxiously. As though they had not quarreled! As though all were smooth between them!

"Sometimes," she said briefly.

He leaned over her, and kissed her throat, a little butterfly kiss. "Poor throat," he whispered. "My poor little hurt darling."

He sounded as though he meant it. Yet he was so cruel he did not want her to go to visit her parents! He made slanderous remarks about Kanji! She tried to whip up her anger against him, but he was caressing her with his lips and hands, and her weak, treacherous body was giving in.

He could be so sweet and loving when he wanted his way! His hands could be so gentle, smoothing over her silky flesh and touching her skillfully to rouse her passions.

She tried to remain passive when he kissed her mouth, slid his lips over to her ear, and nibbled teasingly at it. But the lips were doing their work, and the warm hands, and the hard body pressing against her soft one. She wanted to fight him, to show she was cold to him, but she could not do it.

Suddenly, she wanted him also. She wanted him close and tight and hard against her, needing her, collapsing against her, suddenly helpless and weak in his masculine need. She put her hands on his back, and he came over to lie on her.

Their bodies were moving smoothly together, as

they did more often now. Her fingers pressed urgently on his spine, and slid up to his neck, curling in his thick hair. She thought, "What if I should have a baby of this? What would I do then? Would I go where he wished, weakly, because he was my husband and the father of my child?"

Yet—yet she did not want to leave Japan, and the security of her family ties, the friends she had made. How could Brad want to take her away? She knew he was jealous and possessive, that he resented her love for others. He wanted all her love for himself—

Her love— The thought struck her suddenly. She loved him! She could not help herself, she had never thought about it much. But she loved him, even when he hurt her, or angered her, or bossed her about, or was jealous and peevish with her. She loved him, and she wanted his arms about her, and his smile to shine upon her, and his caresses to heat her—

Brad was whispering to her, "Oh, my darling, my love. Oh, you are so sweet and adorable. Come closer to me, move your hands on me—oh—like that—like that—oh, love—God, I love you—"

He was moving more frantically on her ready body. She received him, and they seemed to move like one creature on the wide bed, hands slipping and lips urgent, limbs striving to come closer yet—

She felt it come. She felt the rush of passion, the mindless need in her, that wanted him closer and tighter and harder in her. She felt herself crumpling up, crying out, clutching at him, in the infinite need of a woman for the one man she loved—and they came close, and completed, and it was beautiful for them both, in the final moments. Soaring, infinitely alive, pulsating, touching the heavens, before releasing, and gliding slowly, slowly, down to the earth once more.

He sighed deeply, and moved off her. "You are

more marvelous all the time, my love," he said, and put his arms about her, to hold her close. His body was wet and warm and shaking, she cuddled close to him, and put her head on his chest. She could hear the heavy pounding of his heart, the way the beat finally slowed down to normal.

He slept, but she lay awake for a time. How bitter it was, they matched so well physically now. But mentally and spiritually they were far apart.

Why could he not understand her? Was she so different from American girls he had known? Did he resent so much that she had been brought up in Japan? Why did he want to take her away from her family and friends and make her live in a strange land?

He did not care that much about his homes there. He had been indifferent about them, he had said how many times they had moved. A different school every year for ten years, he had said. No one town was home to him. Why then did he want to "go home" to America?

He was jealous and possessive. Maybe he did not want her to have anyone else in the world to depend on. Maybe that was it. He had refused definitely to let her go to visit her foster parents. Nor would he go to the States without her.

And his suspicions of Kanji! Her anger rose hotly, for all her weariness. To suspect Kanji of deceit and fraud and cheating and stealing! How could Brad! Kanji was the soul of honor! And Kanji had served Brad devotedly.

Charita sighed lightly, careful not to wake the husband sleeping now against her. Her hand automatically brushed back his hair from his forehead, how soft and silky was the hair. She loved him—yet—how could she live like this? How puzzling was life. There were no simple answers.

She searched in her mind for some fine piece of

Oriental philosophy to help her in this time. Was there no wisdom that could guide her?

She thought and thought, lying awake with the intriguing idea of finding some bit of sane advice from the masters.

But all she could come up with was the Book of Ruth from the Old Testament. How Ruth had gone with the only close family she had, the mother-in-law, Naomi, to a strange land, where they had to endure hardships. And there she found her lasting happiness and a new fine husband to give her sons. "Whither thou goest I I will go, thy people shall be my people—"

Charita grimaced. She did not want that advice! She liked the people and family that she had.

27

Jacinda Snow was in her office going over a contract between a Japanese firm and an American one, studying the intricate details of it, when her Japanese secretary came in.

She bowed low.

"Yes?" snapped Jacinda. She had asked not to be disturbed. She looked up with a frown.

"I beg your pardon, Mrs. Snow-san," murmured the discreet girl. "Mr. Karl Frundsberg is on the telephone, and begs most urgently to speak with you."

"Oh—yes. He called yesterday when I was out," murmured Jacinda.

"Yes, Mrs. Snow-san."

"All right. Put him on." Jacinda was curious. What did the big smiling German want with her? He had his own firm of lawyers from Germany, most efficient and expert, specialists in international dealings.

Mr. Frundsberg was on the line when she picked up the telephone. "Good morning, Mrs. Snow. Pardon me for disturbing you! I need to talk with you most urgently," said the smooth accented voice.

"Well, I'm quite busy today—" she began.

"Could you meet me for dinner this evening, cocktails and then dinner?" he asked. "The business is pressing. I hope to interest you in taking on this matter."

Her curiosity won. That, and the fact that she was weary of dining alone, and then going home to a horribly depressing flat. Soon, she must make up her mind what to do about Miles, and that decision she was evading.

"Very well—" They named a time and place, and he thanked her effusively before hanging up.

She was dressed today in a smart navy suit with green blouse and earrings. It was sufficiently elegant to do, so she forgot about the dinner until evening. She drove her little green car straight to the restaurant, and parked.

Jacinda went inside, alone, her head up, watching for Mr. Frundsberg. He came up behind her from the bar.

"There you are, I hope you did not have to rush, Mrs. Snow." He was smiling, affable.

"No, everything worked out fine, thank you." She eyed him warily as he seated her in the bar, at a small table far from the busy bartenders. "Gin and tonic, thank you."

He ordered for her, and again for himself. The waiter set their drinks before them and hurried back to his customers. It was an American-style bar, and they were accustomed to making American-type drinks. Jacinda tasted hers with appreciation.

"All right?" Frundsberg smiled.

"It's good, thanks. You can't get good gin everywhere."

Under her long lashes, she appraised the man. He seemed bigger than usual, close up, sitting across the small table from her. She was a tall woman, but he was much taller, and his hands were lean-fingered, strong. There was pure muscle in that large body, the wide shoulders. He was about forty-five, husky, well-kept. She had never heard about any wife or mistress, but in

Japan people were more discreet than in New York or San Francisco.

"I will apologize briefly for being so persistent," he smiled. "You are a businesswoman. You understand how some matters can come up so suddenly that they must be dealt with at once."

"Yes, of course."

He moved his glass on the small table, took a peanut and ate it, as though not realizing what he did. "My firm is dealing with a touchy situation. There is an American firm based in Houston, Texas, which is interested in handling our jewelry. My lawyers are most efficient, I am not disputing that. However, one man has managed to antagonize one of the Houston people—you know how that can happen."

"Yes, I understand." She did not understand at all. Surely with his many contacts, he could get another German firm for this deal.

He proceeded rather cautiously. "I know that you and Mr. Snow have much business, more than you can handle. Yet, I would make it well worth your while, to handle this matter for me. It means a quarter of a million dollars worth of jewelry. And we are interested in expanding into the field in America."

Jacinda hesitated. "I am not sure you should continue, Mr. Frundsberg. You know, it could mean a conflict of interests. I handle the contracts of my foster brother, Mr. Bradford Livingston, and his jewelry firm."

"Yes, and he is also interested in the Houston firm," smiled Mr. Frundsberg. "However, I understand that you and Mr. Snow have separate concerns. You—ah—are living apart. May I inquire tactfully, if you mean to separate your business? That is, are you going to take over all the business of Mr. Livingston, or is Mr. Snow?"

Jacinda was shocked and startled, but her poker

face stood her in good stead. She gazed down at her glass thoughtfully. She and Miles had flung many things at each other, even that. Miles continued to handle the Livingston matters, and Jacinda was involved in some of the contracts. How did Frundsberg know they were considering severing the partnership and dividing the contracts?

"Our personal affairs are as yet unresolved," she said, with reserve. "Yet I think no matter what happens, I shall continue to handle the work of my foster brother."

"Forgive me if I seem to meddle in what is not my concern," he said smoothly, a glitter in his piercing blue eyes. "If you do—ah—separate from Mr. Snow and divide the business, must I then go to Mr. Snow to handle the Houston matter? And how soon will you know?"

Her mouth compressed. He was watching her keenly, she did not want to show her anger at him.

"I really could not say, Mr. Frundsberg," she said frigidly.

"But it is urgent for me. I beg you—let me have some hint—"

"We may not separate," she blurted out.

"Ahhh." He leaned back, his eyes half-shut. She could not tell if he was disappointed or merely thoughtful. "Your husband is a brilliant man, Mrs. Snow," he said respectfully. "I understand he specialized in Oriental studies, even while he was obtaining his law degree. You are—ah—not so interested in them, I believe?"

Now, how did he know that? Jacinda's keen mind began to click. How did Frundsberg know so much about her personal affairs? And their backgrounds? Unless he had been doing some investigating? And why had he ordered an investigation? Was it routine? Or far beyond that?

She began to remember. Brad had notified her to

meet him at the airport with Miles and Pearl. Frundsberg had been there—to go to Tokyo. Had he taken that plane? It seemed to her that he had not, yet it all was a blur in her mind. Charita's injuries, her anger that Brad was considering marrying such a schoolgirl—

Frundsberg was going on, leaning sympathetically toward her. "I understand Mr. Snow has had a problem with alcohol for many years, that you have left him before, Mrs. Snow. I am so sorry about this. If you will forgive an older man his presumption, may I say—he will probably never give up his habits. Men do not often change their colors, you know. Of the two of you, it has struck me that you are much the stronger personality. You have wisdom, courage, toughness, much needed in your profession."

She did not jump with joy. She wondered why he was flattering her. Even if he thought so, it was not exactly tactful of him to say so.

She emptied her glass, he lifted his hand to the waiter. "No more," she said brightly. "I am starved! I wonder if we could go in to dinner, if you don't mind?" She half got up. He had to rise also, and a flicker of annoyance crossed his bland features.

But he had to go along with it. He shook his head at the waiter, and escorted Jacinda in to the large dining room. She pretended great interest in the menu, chatting over the dishes, discussing what to order. But that did not take long, and after the waiter had left them, Frundsberg started in again.

"It has struck me from the first that you are the strong one in the marriage and in the partnership," he said, not seeming to realize he was being too personal and offensive.

"Oh, Miles is a very intelligent man," said Jacinda, concealing her fury behind a bright smile. "That was what attracted me to him. We have our differences, who

411

doesn't? But we always come back together again. We probably shall again."

He frowned, as though that did not please him. "Again? Surely it is more wise to break off completely a relationship that distresses you both?"

"We are much involved in our law firm," she smiled again. "As you may know, the firm of Snow and Snow is becoming widely respected in Japan. More offers are coming to us. In fact, we are so busy, we will probably not be able to take on anything more, Mr. Frundsberg. I would advise you to look for another firm. Perhaps another German one."

That did not please him at all. He nibbled at his salad, she ate more heartily, pleased at this clash of wits. She wondered what he was after. This was the biggest puzzle she had had for a time, and it pleased her to try to work it out.

"I understood you and your—ah—foster brother, Mr. Livingston, were very close to each other," said Mr. Frundsberg. "And his marriage did not please you. Is that about to break up?"

Jacinda pretended great interest in her steak. "Break up? I should say not," she said briskly. "I never saw two people so crazy about each other."

"Ahhh," said Mr. Frundsberg. "So—he is most fond of her? She seems so young, even juvenile, if you don't mind that I say it. You are—forgive me—more of his mental equal."

"Oh, Charita is quite bright," said Jacinda. "Very pretty, also. Not mature yet, but she is young. She learns quickly."

"And he confides in her much," said Frundsberg.

Jacinda thought of the gold formula, and said quickly, "About social matters, not business, I should say." And she added, "About some matters, Brad is very close-

412

mouthed. He believes the fewer who know about a matter, the less possibility of it being revealed."

"And *you* are one of the closest to him," smiled Frundsberg.

She shrugged. "As his sister—"

"Foster sister. In fact, no relation at all," said the man. "I believe your father was briefly married to his mother."

She was startled again. Few people knew that exact relationship. How did this man know about it, unless he had had his investigators probe closely. And that was all years ago.

"As you say," she said. "However, Brad and I have always been close, fond of each other. Like a real brother and sister. However, there are some things he does not confide in me," she added, deliberately.

Frundsberg ate his steak and rice in silence, bent over his plate. She found she did not like him very much at all. He did not look fatherly and benign today, for some reason. She looked secretly at the little golden watch that Brad had given her. How soon could she leave?

She wanted to talk to Miles. Urgently, she wanted to confide in Miles and hear what he thought of this.

"You were not living with your husband," said Frundsberg abruptly, "at the time of the two attacks on Mr. Livingston? I wondered—has your husband ever shown much jealousy of this—close relationship—that you have with Mr. Livingston?"

Something clicked again in Jacinda's mind. It was important, what he had said. She wanted to examine it. She poked again at her steak, and laid down her fork.

"I think we have talked enough of personal matters," she said quietly. "My opinion is that our firm is too busy to take on your business. I strongly advise you to look elsewhere."

She rose to her feet, picked up her handbag. He was on his feet, all apologies.

"I have offended you! Forgive me, Mrs. Snow! Please sit down again—you have not finished your dinner." He reached for her arm, she evaded him deftly, smiling brightly. The Japanese had something with their big smiles, it concealed much, thought Jacinda.

"I have thought of an appointment I must keep, forgive me for leaving you. Please continue your dinner, I must go," and she scooted out so fast she left him holding his big dinner napkin and looking furious.

Her heels click-clicked on the parquet floors. She bowed low to the manager of the restaurant who hastened to hold open the door for her, looking worriedly back to Mr. Frundsberg. She went out, got into her little car, and was off. She had a funny, giddy feeling that she had escaped.

The car seemed to turn by itself up to the section of the city of her smart apartment. She had parked, and gone up in the elevator, before she realized what she was doing. She must talk to Miles! If only he was home—

She unlocked the door, the maid came scurrying, her face amazed to see Mrs. Snow-san.

"Is Mr. Snow in?"

"Yes, Mrs. Snow-san, he just come in, he is in drawing room." The maid bowed again, and again, in her smart crimson kimono. How nice she was, thought Jacinda, never a word nor a snide look when Jacinda chose to descend upon them.

Jacinda walked into the drawing room. Miles was sitting in a big chair, his face buried in the evening paper. A glass was set at his hand, but it was more than half full.

He lowered the paper, to stare, then cast the paper to the floor. He got up, paused. "Well—Jacinda."

"I have to talk to you, Miles!"

"Well, I'm here," he said, simply. He was gazing over her, his hazel eyes clear, unclouded with drink. His face was not as puffy as before. "I like your hair—that way," he said, rather shyly.

She touched the longer strands self-consciously. "Do you? I thought I'd let it grow longer for a while."

She sat down in her pretty silver and gold drawing room, with an unconscious sigh of satisfaction. This was her setting, not that dingy flat where she existed at nights.

The maid padded in, and bowed. "Mrs. Snow-san wishes a drink? Will she wish a dinner?"

Jacinda grinned a little to herself at the thought of the excellent steak she had deserted along with her dinner companion. "Yes, I'll stay for dinner, thank you. No drink." She waited until the maid had bowed herself out, and shut the door.

"What's wrong Jacinda?" Miles looked faintly worried. "You look flushed. Nobody been chasing you, has there?"

"Chasing me?"

"I guess I was thinking about poor Charita," he said. "Brad is considering returning to the States, he is so upset. Attacking that poor child!"

"Yes—I know. She was terribly shaken," said Jacinda. "No wonder. It must have been horrible for her. Miles—I had dinner with Mr. Frundsberg tonight."

They both had quick impatient minds that leaped from subject to subject. Miles showed no surprise at her swift change.

"What did he want?"

"It's what he didn't want that worries me. Miles, he knows too much."

"Oh—how so?"

She described briefly their conversation. "Do you re-

415

member—in the airport when we went to meet Brad and Charita coming back from Hokkaido—did Frundsberg take that plane to Tokyo?"

"No," said Miles.

She stared at him. He elaborated.

"You remember I went back for Brad's luggage? Well, I met Frundsberg coming out of the airport. He was with a burly Japanese man, they were talking, Frundsberg was giving him a bawling out. They were talking low, in Japanese, I couldn't get it all. He said something about the man bungling it. I didn't think more—Jacinda. That attack on Charita—" Miles was staring at her, in growing excitement.

She nodded. "I was thinking the same thing." She ruffled her hair absently. "Let's go back over the whole story. Miles, Frundsberg knew about both attacks on Brad. Who else would have known but us, and Charita, and the police, and—"

"Let's start at the beginning." Miles went over to the desk, searched out pen and paper, and sat down. "Okay. First, we hear from Brad that he is returning to Kyoto with his fiancee—"

"Earlier," said Jacinda, in mounting alarm. "First, when Brad decided to go to Hokkaido to see the professor and Charita. Who else knew about that? He told us in confidence."

"But Frundsberg was around," said Miles, nibbling at the pen. "I remember—we took him to the airport, remember? And you were saying it was not Brad's concern, why did he bother about the girl and her father. Frundsberg was meeting a plane, he said. He came over to speak, then left."

They stared at each other, Jacinda's eyes were sparkling with the glee of a small child on a treasure hunt.

"All right, write that down. Then next—the return. Who could have known?"

"Pearl—Kanji—you and I—and I had to put off a dinner with the Pattersons—Frundsberg was invited that evening also—he could have heard about it—"

"And he was at the airport. And Charita was knocked down, and the baggage truck was backing up when Brad stopped it."

They carefully went over every detail with the thoroughness of two lawyers who had worked together for years. By the time Miles had three pages filled with his small, careful handwriting, they were building up a damning case against Frundsberg. He had been around at major events. He knew about two attacks against Brad, even though few people knew about the second attack.

"And Charita told people he had the flu," said Miles. "So if Frundsberg knew it was an attack—"

"Then there is a good chance," concluded Jacinda, "that he was behind the attacks, that he had reports from his men!"

"It is possible," said Miles. "Very—possible. But what is possible is not enough to go to court."

"The hell with going to court," Jacinda was beginning, when the maid called them to dinner.

They had to be cautious of their conversation during dinner. But afterward they retired again to the drawing room to continue. "Miles, we have to talk to Brad, to warn him," Jacinda urged.

He glanced at the clock. "After nine. We'll tell him first thing in the morning. Frundsberg can't do anything tonight. Let's go over this all again. We want to be pretty damned sure, as sure as we can be, when we talk to Brad. Knowing him, he'll take after Frundsberg with both fists!"

"We can't have that," said Jacinda, frowning. "Brad is strong, but I'll bet Frundsberg has half the underground working for him. Think of all those men involved in the attacks—"

"Stay here tonight," urged Miles awkwardly. "I

won't—I mean—you're safe here. I hate to think of you going to that awful neighborhood."

"How do you know where I live?" she snapped.

"I followed you twice," he said simply.

She was angry, then she laughed. "At least, you didn't hire a tough to follow me!" she teased him.

He looked relieved. "Jacinda—you will think about staying here again, won't you? If you won't sleep with me—I guess I can bear it. But I hate to think I have driven you out to that sleazy place. Do stay."

"All right." It pleased her oddly to give in to him. "I don't want to go there anyway. I think I'll close up the place and move back tomorrow. I miss—" She was going to be cynical and say she missed her comforts. At his look—"I miss you," she concluded simply. "It's deadly dull without you, Miles."

He was flushed, his hand moved toward hers, then dropped. "I have missed you like hell," he said. "You make me angry, but I'd rather be unhappy with you, than happy with anybody else."

"That's the way I feel."

She got up and went to sit on the arm of his chair. His arm slipped awkwardly about her waist. She leaned over and pressed a kiss on his brown lanky hair, the lean jaw. "I guess I must love you," admitted Jacinda in a low voice, as though afraid of being overheard in her confession. "I can't get along without you. I think of crazy, funny things to say, but you aren't there, and nobody else would understand them. I worry about things, and I can't talk them over with you."

"I feel the same way. Half alive. Miserable. Jacinda —don't be angry—but you don't love Brad—that way, do you?" He looked at her cautiously, as though afraid she would blow up.

She shook her head. "No. Never, Miles," she said, sure of herself at last. "I love you—like a husband, a lover, a companion, a friend. Brad is like a brother, a lean-on-him brother. I like to think he's around. But you know —I think Charita is a good match for him. She's rather a nice girl."

He leaned his head against her breast, and she put her hand on his head and pressed it closer. She didn't feel cold and sarcastic tonight, but all warm and melting. Maybe she had been alone too long, but somehow she meant all these things she was saying, and it was a relief to say them.

"We'll talk to Brad tomorrow morning," said Miles, more sure, his voice muffled against her breast. "We have to get this all straightened out."

"Tomorrow," agreed Jacinda.

"I've quit the heavy drinking," he went on. "I couldn't blot out any damned thing. Jacinda—if you come back to me—"

"I'm back," she said, and smoothed her hand gently over the back of his neck.

"And you don't—love Brad?" he asked bluntly.

She grimaced, unseen. "He has always represented strength to me, love I could lean on. The brother I never had. Yes, I love him, but not *that* way, Miles. You are the man for me, the only one who stirs me, the only one I can talk to and say anything—we match each other, Miles. We fit—like—"

"Two halves of a whole?" he suggested, holding her more tightly. "I drank—to forget the half of me that was cut off—I couldn't stand the pain."

"You won't have to again, my love," said Jacinda, uncaring that she sounded sloppy and sentimental. Damn it, she could be romantic if she wanted to! "You are a part of me. I can't leave without hurting—"

"If only we had said this before," he groaned.

She looked into his hazel eyes, cupped his flushed

419

face with her long clever fingers. "Didn't you tell me once, a story about going through fire—to purify love?"

"I would go through hell—"

"We did, darling. And now we are out the other side. Right?"

He kissed her fiercely in answer.

28

Charita had been feeling more and more upset and panicky. She felt stifled with Brad, he was so dominating. He wanted to boss her all the time.

She had to stay indoors now, he said, until "the matters were all cleared up." When that would be, he did not know.

She felt rebellious and tearful. She snapped at him, and he was angry with her. "I know what is best for you, Charita!" he kept saying. "You must be safe!"

Well, she did not feel safe. She wanted to go home to her parents and return to the serenity and calm security of their household. The peace of their tiny garden and pond. The comfort of their love and gentleness.

One afternoon, she telephoned the railroad and asked about train schedules. She asked about the times of the bullet train to Okayama, and the regular train on to Hiroshima. The maid peered in the door of the study several times, Charita frowned at her severely, and she padded away again.

She wanted to go home. She wanted very badly to go home. She had been thinking of the time she and her parents had visited the shrine at Miyajima, the beautiful red torii in the sea, and the marvelous large theater for the Nō plays.

The more Charita thought about it, the more she

wanted to go home to her parents. That afternoon, she searched out a map and studied it. She could go by bullet train to Okayama, then take the local train to Hiroshima. From there, she could take the ferry to the island out in the Inland Sea. There she would wander about for a little time.

When she had regained some peace and serenity, she would return to the mainland, telephone her parents, and they would come and pick her up. They would go home to their little village on the Inland Sea, and she would be safe. What would happen later, she refused to consider.

Maybe she would leave Brad forever. She wanted to think carefully about that. She loved Brad, but she wasn't sure she liked marriage very much. She loved him, but he stifled her. And she didn't care about wealth and social position, and being a hostess—

Though it had been rather fun to entertain his friends, to plan the meals and flowers— She put that thought away.

She wanted to go home! She was afraid. She had never felt such fear in her life as when that man had tried to strangle her. Before Brad had come into her life, she had not known fears like that, dangers like that.

She blamed Brad for that. She refused to think how he had come to her and her father on Hokkaido, had taken care of matters with his big comfortable hands and calm manner, how capably he had managed everything for her. She refused to think how good he had been to her, how he had married her instead of sending her to her relatives in the States.

Charita thought only, panicking, of the terror that had come into her life. He had brought it. Brad and his jewelry, and his millions of dollars, and his gold formulas. She wanted no part of wealth, it brought sorrow and danger and great trouble.

She would go home and think about it. Maybe she would leave him forever, and he could play around with other women—

She packed a small case and hid it under the bed. That evening the maid kept staring at her worriedly, but Charita frowned at her, and shook her head.

The next morning Brad fiddled around, looking for his briefcase, pausing to talk about a dinner they would give the following week. She thought she would scream before he finally left the house. He sat in the back of the car, and waved and grinned at her as the chauffeur drove him out.

She waved back, feeling like a deceitful hussy. Then she dashed back into the house and telephoned for a taxi. The taxi arrived, and she was ready, in her neat blue schoolgirl uniform and cap.

The maid clattered after her, as Charita went to the door, carrying her handbag and small case.

"Mrs. Livingston-san, where you go? Do you have permission of honored husband? What shall I tell to him when he demands where you are?"

"I am going home to my parents," said Charita firmly, and walked out to the taxi. The maid wailed after her.

"What I tell honorable husband?"

She did not answer. The taxi driver looked curiously at the schoolgirl getting into his cab, looked more closely at her. Not a Japanese girl as he had thought at first, but an American, with her creamy complexion and blue eyes.

She spoke to him in good Japanese and directed him to the train station. They drove rapidly, he knew the hours of the train. He let her out at the wide-pillared entrance, opposite the New Miyako Hotel, and she looked briefly at that hotel. Her wedding had taken place there. She swallowed, and went into the train station.

She pushed her way politely into the crowd waiting to board the bullet train. She knew that many of those on the platform waited to see relatives and business associates leaving, and to bow to them respectfully as they left, no matter how short the trip. She got on board as soon as the train stopped at its little marking, and found her reserved seat. She sank down, thankfully, and wiped her forehead with her handkerchief.

She had a moment of panic when a man came into the compartment as the train began to pull out of the station. He was tall, brown-haired—was it Brad? Oh, no, he could not have followed her. The man turned, grinned at one of his companions. He was a tall man, Australian, she learned later from his accent as he and his friends called back and forth across the train aisle to each other.

They seemed so friendly, so loud and amiable and so very big! She had never seen such huge men, with such brownish red faces, so robust and weatherbeaten. One man must be over seven feet tall, she thought, as he stood to let a plump Japanese woman past him in the aisle. The woman looked like a cuddly doll next to the huge man.

Charita finally relaxed in the seat, watching nervously for the station where she would get off. The announcements came clearly in Japanese and English at each station, and well before each station. She was able to follow them easily, she was relieved to find.

A girl came through with coffee; she did not want any. Nor was she hungry. She felt a little sick at her stomach from nerves. When she got home, Mama-san would feed her rice and tea, that was all she wanted. Tears came to her eyes, at the thought of the comfort and calm concern they would show to her, her Mama-san and Papa-san.

She glanced at the beautiful gold watch that Brad had given her. It was so neat, so lovely, so accurate. Did

Brad know she had left yet? She had wondered if the maid would telephone him and tell him she had left.

But he had not come, he had not stopped her. She was safe.

Idly she noted that there were two husky Japanese men in the seat behind her. She had seen them when she had turned to the girl to refuse coffee.

Brawny, with those ugly short haircuts. She frowned. Whenever she saw men like that, she would think of those two men who had attacked her. And the men on the plane, and the ones at Hakone.

She shivered. She would forget all that. Leaving Brad would solve that.

Did Brad know she had left? Would he miss her terribly?

The lines on his face this morning. He wasn't sleeping well. Sometimes she could soothe away those lines and make him smile. She would put her hands on his cheeks, and kiss away the lines, and he would relax in her arms in bed.

She frowned away the thought. Her parents would be so happy to see her—

The next station came, the train pulled in neatly to the right place marked on the platform. How accurate they were, always pulling up just to the right place, so people would stand at the right place, and get into the right car and get to their seats.

Her thoughts made the time fly. Finally the station of Okayama was announced, and she got ready to get off. She must leave the train and get the next regular train to Hiroshima. It would be a worry, she had rarely traveled alone. Always her parents were with her, and sometimes Kanji, and lately Brad. Brad always took charge of matters, she never had to consider where she was going and how to get there—

She might miss that, she admitted. She thought of

that terrible time she had gone up to Hokkaido alone, to reach her father. It had been a nightmare—clutching her case and her tickets, asking again and again where she must go.

Coming back had been so easy, with Brad in charge.

Brad. He did look tired and weary. He did not sleep enough. He worried so much about the business and about her. Would he worry when he found she had departed? She knew he would. She bit her lip, then gathered up her case and her tickets and handbag, and prepared to leave the train. They had gone along the Inland Sea, and her seat had been on that side of the train, though she had scarcely noticed the beautiful scenery. On the next train she must look well at the scenes that unrolled before her and enjoy them. It was one of the reasons she had come this way.

She hopped neatly off the train, and started along the platform. Someone brushed against her, muttered, frowning, as he strode along past her. She turned, to see where he was going.

And behind her were the same two chunky Japanese men, their ugly hairdos like wire brushes on their heads.

One man was looking right at her, she met his gaze, and panic went through her.

She turned around, swallowed, and went down the stairs, holding her case carefully. Deliberately she went slowly, and allowed others to stream past her. But these two men stayed right behind her. Whenever she casually half turned, she saw them just behind her on the stairs.

She had half an hour to get her next train. She went to the magazine counter and looked through magazines. They went also, saying nothing, but purchasing nothing. She left abruptly, and went to the train platform for the regular, slower train to Hiroshima.

Then she began to feel choked up and panicky. The

men were right behind her, and had purchased tickets for the train. They followed her into the same car.

Maybe it was coincidence. Charita tried to convince herself that it was. They were going the same way. It was the best way to go to Hiroshima. But, they carried no luggage, she noted.

Maybe they were going to Hiroshima on business for the day. Men did that.

She sat quietly in her seat, the men two rows behind her. She tried to concentrate on the beautiful blue Inland Sea as she caught glimpses of it from the train. She noted the rice fields, the fish ponds where fish were raised. She looked at the trees, changing to their lovely autumn colors. Maples turning to red and gold. Picturesque pine trees, some over hundreds of years old, bent by the winds off the sea into odd shapes and designs. Fields of chrysanthemums of brilliant yellows and lilacs and purples.

She tried to think about colors and shapes. There, that scene was beautiful, that little house in natural wood, with a wooden torii leading to their private shrine. How lovely, like a design. She drew out a sketch pad from her handbag and sketched it. Brad would like that, she thought.

Brad. She put the pad away, feeling a little lost. If she did not return to him, what would he do?

He did need her—a little. She did some designs for him, and he had been pleased, and praised her. But of course, he had Donald Raglan now, who would do designs—

Yet Brad had seemed to want Charita to continue them.

And who would see to it that Brad got enough rest? People were always telephoning him or calling at his office, and asking him to do things for them. He drove himself so hard.

For the first time since her panicky flight from the

house in Kyoto, Charita allowed herself to think of it from Brad's point of view. He would be badly upset. He protected her—too much, she thought. But he thought of her good. He worried about her.

What would he do? Oh, dear, thought Charita. He would probably leave his work and come charging after her! She must telephone him from her parents' house, and tell him she was fine, that she was visiting them for a while—

She bit her lips to keep back tears. She wanted to feel secure again. She wanted to feel placid and calm. She would tell that to Brad—but it would hurt him.

He thought she felt secure with him. It would make him feel very bad that she did not feel secure in his protection.

And he would be angry, and hurt, and maybe he would not sleep well. He would be cross and tired, with no one to soothe him. Even Jacinda and Pearl did not understand when he was like this. They were afraid of him, and shrank from him when he yelled. Charita knew that at those times he needed to be comforted, and soothed, and told to get some sleep. Music helped him, and she would turn on the record player and put on some Brahms and some Beethoven. . . .

But who would do that for Brad?

She was so preoccupied with her thoughts that when Hiroshima was announced, she jumped in her place. She gathered up her case and handbag, and plumped her hat on her short black hair. She prepared to get off.

The Japanese men followed her. But she had convinced herself that they had business in Hiroshima: They were not following her, she was being foolish.

She took a taxi to the ferry, and bought a ticket. It was while she was standing in line, waiting for the ferry to unload its passengers and let the next ones get on, that she saw the men. She had turned to smile after a little boy chasing his ball, and she saw the same two men standing in line about four people behind her.

She swallowed. One man met her gaze, with a bold, curious look. The other looked away, in the distance, toward the boat.

Charita felt her heart sinking, her palms were clammy with cold fear. Surely they were not following her, surely it was coincidence, strange, but it could happen.

They were let on to the boat. She found a seat near the front, and watched as the boat was loaded. Finally they set out, and she glanced about to find the men in seats near hers. They were bulky, husky, standing out in that crowd of holiday-makers and reverent old people going to the shrine at Miyajima on the Inland Sea. She hoped against hope that the men would not get off when she did.

The wind that September day blew cold across the sea. Charita shivered in her thin blue coat. She clasped her cold hands together, and scarcely saw the blue beauty of the water, the scarlet and gold of the maples on the island as they approached the shrine.

The vermillion torii was an awe-inspiring sight, now they could see it from the boat. People crowded on deck, leaning over the rails to murmur and speak of it reverently. Charita was so nervous and overwrought that she could not join them.

Somewhere in the back of the boat she caught a glimpse of a large man, who looked a little like Karl Frundsberg. He had graying blond hair, he was tall as Frundsberg. Probably not him, thought Charita, numbly, thinking of how she had thought she had seen Brad on the train.

If only someone friendly were in sight! She had never felt so alone, so cold and afraid. She did not know what to do. Perhaps it would be better to remain on the ferry and return to the mainland. Yet—yet she had determined to go to the shrine—and people would think it odd if she stayed on the boat and did not get off, as others did.

The boat landed. People streamed off, and so did Charita, joining the queue as they left. She clutched her case, which had seemed light at first, and now seemed to weigh a ton. She left the boat and went into the boat dock, and out the other side, heading determinedly toward the shrine. She had a vague but fanatical notion that the gods of the shrine would protect her.

The crowd streamed out and scattered. Some went to get food, some tourists stopped at the shops for postcards and curios. As the crowds thinned, Charita glanced back over her blue-clad shoulder.

The two hulking Japanese men were just behind her. Their dark, expressionless eyes watched her every move.

If only she had not left Brad!

The thought jumped into her mind and would not be dismissed. She had brought trouble on herself, with her obstinacy, and with her desire for the old security, which was gone forever. Charita trudged on, her steps heavier and heavier and slower and slower. If only she could go back, and start this day again—and do it differently—

She had been childish and unwise to leave Brad. She was immature, she thought forlornly. Thinking to run home to the security of her parents' home. There was no going back. One could not turn back the clock.

She was a married woman. Brad was right when he said she was very young. She had been foolish. She had put herself into more danger, and Brad would be terribly upset. She did not know what to do. Should she turn back?

The men were just behind her. She went on, toward the shrine, noting the vermillion torii shining in the late afternoon sunshine.

The day had gone by, and it was very late. She could never get to the mainland, call her parents and have them pick her up—all before dusk. And who knew what would happen in the dark streets of a strange town?

She paused to gaze at the torii, admired its proud position in the blue waters of the sheltered lagoon. She sat down on one of the benches and pretended interest in the Nō play going on, the slow, dignified movements of the chief actors, the singsong tones as they spoke the lines, the music of the backgrounds.

Another time she would have been fascinated. Now she stared blankly, thinking frantically how to get out of this situation.

A few Japanese people were there, and more tourists. She wondered if she could appeal to them. But just as she had settled on a kindly looking older man and his wife, they moved on with a laugh. "I can't understand a thing," she was complaining. "What in the world are they doing? All these foreign ways—"

He smiled indulgently, and they moved on. Charita remained in her seat, her case at her feet.

Then in the distance she saw the graying blond head of the big man again. He had half turned toward her. It *was* Karl Frundsberg! She stared at him, he did not seem to see her. She jumped up. She would appeal to him, he would take care of her.

He was leaving the theater as she went after him. She hurried but could not catch up with him. The two Japanese men were following her, at a close thirty feet behind.

Frundsberg left the crowds behind him and in great strides was climbing a steep cliff behind the theater. He had almost disappeared into the bushes and trees. Charita called after him in dismay.

"Mr. Frundsberg—Mr. Frundsberg! Wait for me—"

He did not see her. He did not turn. Charita began to run. The men behind her did not run, but their walking pace increased. Her heart was pounding, her breath caught in her throat, her mouth was open and parched. She realized she had not eaten since breakfast, and she was thirsty and hot and scared.

She ran up the cliff path, turned the corner, and was out of the sight of the tourists below. They were milling about, looking at the shrine, examining the booths of goods and booklets and postcards.

Mr. Frundsberg must be this way, there was no turnoff—

She went around another curve, and almost bumped into the big German.

"Oh, Mr. Frundsberg, there you are!"

"Well, Mrs. Livingston," he said, smiling. He did not seem surprised. His piercing blue eyes glittered at her in the orange of the setting sun.

"I'm in such trouble! There are two men following me," she cried out, coming up to him.

"Where is your husband?"

"He doesn't know I have come. I am on my way to my parents, they live about thirty miles from here," she confided. She set down the case with a sigh. The men seemed to have stopped somewhere, they had not come around the curve. She glanced back nervously.

"That was foolish of you, Mrs. Livingston," he said, his voice quiet and deep.

"Yes, it was. I'd like to go back to Kyoto," she said, fervently. "These men—they followed me on the bullet train and then to Hiroshima—"

She paused. He had come up to her. The men behind her came around the curve.

"I have her," said Frundsberg, and put his hand over her mouth. He grabbed her arm and whipped her off the path. "Were you followed?" he asked the men.

Charita squirmed and struggled against his arm. He seemed made of steel. Panicky, she realized— He was talking quietly and confidently to the two men—his men!

Her wide eyes glared accusingly at him. He smiled down at her, almost caressingly.

"You walked right into my hands, you know—Mrs. Livingston!" he said, and laughed softly.

She bit at his hand, and his fingers closed cruelly tight on her chin so she could not open her mouth.

"None of that," he snapped. "I don't care if I push you off this cliff or not! Hold still!"

His tone had changed. It was hard and cruel and callous. She tried to struggle against him, but all she could do was kick out futilely with her soft shoes. He did not even seem to feel her kick his shins. His mouth was hard as he barked orders at his men.

"Watch the path. I thought I saw Livingston down below. Keep him away from here until I get the girl away."

Brad? Brad might be near, near enough to help! Charita almost stopped breathing with relief. Then fear stirred again.

Three men against one! She had led him into a trap! If Brad was indeed near, and following her, Charita might have led him right into the danger he had sought to avoid for them both.

All her fault, she told herself, still struggling valiantly, though his arm was steel-tough about her. All her fault! Her childishness and impulsiveness had brought Brad into more danger.

Oh, Brad, I am sorry, she said to herself. I am so— sorry! I didn't mean to hurt you, I didn't mean it! I am young and stupid—

Why did Brad love her? She was a child, a fool. She thought of his injuries, the bruised body she had nursed, his bleeding head—and could have wept. What could she do to prevent it from happening again? Nothing. They had her powerless.

29

When Brad reached the office, Pearl was standing near the door of his office looking concerned. Kanji and Donald were nearby, watching the door as he came in.

"What's the trouble?" he asked.

"It's your maid, Susuki," said Pearl. "She says that Charita has left home—she is on the line—"

Brad stared at Pearl, he felt the blood leaving his head, making him dizzy. "What are you saying?" he asked sharply. "She just waved me off, she was at home—"

"Please—talk to the maid—she is most urgent—" Pearl grabbed the telephone and handed it to Brad.

"Yes?" snapped Brad into the telephone. "This is Livingston."

The maid sounded tearful and agitated. "Oh, please, Mr. Livingston-san, I try to make her stay! Mrs. Livingston, she walks out with suitcase and gets into taxi. She says she is going to honorable parents! You know about this?"

Brad wet his lips, they were suddenly dry with fear. "No, but I'm going after her! She doesn't realize—" He was about to slam down the phone when the maid's high-pitched voice came again.

In her agitation, Susuki's English flew out the window. "I get pardon, Mr. Livingston-san, to make trouble and delay honorable self. I must tell you—Mrs. Livingston-san, she telephone to railroad yesterday. She say, how to get to bullet train, to Hiroshima. Then she not go right to parents. She go to shrine at Miyajima!"

"Brad, I'll go after her," said Kanji urgently, stepping forward. "If she has gone to my parents—"

Brad waved him silent. "To Miyajima!" he said sharply to the maid. "Tell me carefully—what did she plan to do?"

"Oh, Mr. Livingston-san, it is this way. She get bullet train to Hiroshima, then—no, no, excuse please! First she get bullet train to Okayama. Then regular train to Hiroshima. Then ferry boat to island which is Miyajima. Then to see shrine where is the glorious torii and place where Nō plays are given." The maid was very agitated, but managed to be precise, and Brad silently blessed her. "After that, she return to mainland, and go to honorable parents, when she will call them by telephone to come and pick her up."

"Good girl," said Brad. "I'll follow your directions—only I'll go by car. There is a direct highway, and I can't expect to get those trains—"

"Please to bring her back safely," said Susuki, calming a little. "Very nice mistress-san."

"Thank you, Susuki, I'll bring her back," promised Brad, grimly. And he added to himself, "And give her a good shaking, for scaring me to death!"

He hung up, glanced about. Donald and Kanji were silent, troubled. Pearl was wringing her hands.

"The trouble that she makes," wailed Pearl. "She is a child—forgive me, but she does not think of others!"

Brad patted Pearl's shoulder, glanced at his watch. "Put off my appointments, that's a good girl. I'll go right off in the car. She will probably be all right, but she could get mixed up. She isn't used to traveling alone."

Kanji wanted to go along, Brad shook his head, and was running down the stairs.

Donald peered from the window, watching the street. "No, he's alone, didn't take his chauffeur or bodyguard," he reported gloomily.

"There's Mr. Snow—and Mrs. Snow, driving up," Kanji, reported, joining him in the window. "Wonder if they will see him—no—he's around the corner—"

In a couple of minutes, the high heels of Jacinda Snow sounded in the corridor. She and Miles came in together, looking taut and excited, Kanji thought.

Pearl bowed politely to them. "I regret Mr. Livingston-san is not here, he has just left," she was saying.

"But he has to be here!" cried Jacinda. "We have something terribly important to say to him—where did he go?"

"After my foolish sister, Charita," said Kanji grimly. "She has gone by herself to the Inland Sea, and then to my parents, without asking permission from Brad. She is very—"

"Gone!" whispered Jacinda. "But Mr. Frundsberg has left Kyoto also—on the bullet train—my man just reported—"

"Frundsberg!" said Kanji. "What has that to do with—do you mean to tell us—"

Jacinda nodded, Miles was nodding also. "We've been fitting it all together. Frundsberg knows too much. He knew about both attacks on Brad, and only a few knew about that. I figure he was behind the attacks, he and his men. He has tried to buy Brad's firm—to get the gold formula—"

"And Brad has gone after Charita!" Kanji looked at Donald, both nodded at once. "And alone! By the gods, he will be in deep trouble—even with a weapon—"

"We must go after him!" Donald was picking up his

jacket, slipping into it. "Come on, Kanji. He can't be too far ahead of us—"

"I'll come also," said Miles sharply, so surely that both men stared at him. "Frundsberg is a cunning rascal —Brad doesn't know what he has been up against—"

"Kanji—do not go! There is much danger—" Pearl grabbed at his arm as he started for the door. Tears shone in her dark eyes. "Send the bodyguards—you could be hurt—"

"It would matter to you?" he asked softly. He touched her cheek briefly, then shook his head. "I must go, and quickly. Wait for our calls. If we do not return by dusk, go to the house of my sister and wait there."

She nodded, dumbly. He looked at her, long, then turned away abruptly. Talking about this must wait, but his heart was beginning to sing with lightness and hope.

"We go now, in my car. It goes fast," he said curtly.

"I'll come also," Jacinda said, picking up her handbag. "I can help—"

"No," said Miles, definitely. "You wait at the house, take any calls that might come. Pearl, you do the same here. We'll need people here for any contacts— Come on, Kanji!"

The three men ran down the steps, Miles in the lead. Kanji, wondering, followed Miles, amazed at the change in the man. And Jacinda had meekly stayed up there, on his orders! Maybe things had turned for the better. Now Jacinda came down the stairs, and waved at them as they drove off. She got into her little green car; Miles peered over his shoulder at her.

"She should be all right," he muttered. "Her man is following right behind. She's a smart woman, you know?" He sounded proud and loving. "Has a half a dozen characters working for her, and keeps them all in line!"

Kanji politely kept his thoughts to himself. A woman keeping tough men in line! It revolted him! Still, Mrs. Snow had managed to figure out the man behind Brad's troubles. Then he gave his thought to keeping the car on the right highways, and what shortcuts he could take to get to the Inland Sea.

It was a trip of several hours. They spoke little. They were concentrating on catching up with Brad, who was probably driving like a maniac, despite the speed laws.

Brad was driving as fast as he could, but the highway was crowded. And he could not drive as fast as the bullet train went, which was more than one hundred miles per hour. Still—he could make time on the next stretch, he figured, and the regular train was slower. And Charita would have to wait for the ferry—

Fear and anxiety drove him on. Why had Charita left him so suddenly, without one word to him? If the maid had not telephoned him, he would not have known of her departure until he got home tonight! She had said not a word—she had just stood and clasped her hands tightly together, and gazed at him with dark blue violet eyes.

Come to think of it, she had said little this past week. She had done little work, but he had thought she was resting. He had hated it, that she had been attacked, and the sight of her bruised throat had made him want to hurt someone badly.

But Charita—to leave him! And he had wanted her safe and secure at home.

"Was that it," he muttered to himself. "To be confined at home all the time? She loved to get out. I should have taken her out more. Damn it—if she had only said something! I spend too much thought on work, and not enough on her. No wonder she was upset—she must think I'm some sort of monster, neglecting her— I wanted to get done, so we could get away together, be alone—"

The attacks on her. His mouth tightened, and his foot went down harder on the pedal. He wanted to get her home safely once more. He resented it that she turned to

438

her parents. She had asked to visit them—he had refused. That should have been enough.

Yet she loved them, adored them, felt safe with them. He sighed deeply. He should have talked to her reasonably, told her he didn't want her to go anywhere without him. Instead, he had issued an order, and she had resented it.

But to leave him like this—without a word—

Would she have left the traditional letter?

Surely she planned to return! Another fear struck him. Charita did not mean to leave him finally, did she? She just wanted a visit to her parents—didn't she? She was not thinking of leaving Brad for all time?

Surely not. She would not—she loved him— At least, he thought she had come to love him some. She was childish, immature, yet sometimes in her response to him he had sensed something deeper, more lasting. A growth, a gentleness that was womanly, a sensitivity to him, a concern over him—

He sighed, wiped his forehead of sweat. Finally he had come to the ferry, and thank God, one was in. He took his ticket, and drove on board, and waited. He got out of the car restlessly, and struck up a conversation with an elderly Japanese man who paced the deck with his placid gray-gowned plump wife at his side.

"You know where this leads?" asked Brad, in his slow precise Japanese. He waved to the island before him.

"To the shrine," said the man, showing a little puzzlement.

"It goes to the shrine of the great torii?" asked Brad.

"Yes, you can see it now. See how it shines red in the blue waters." The man waved his thin, tapering hand. The Japanese people seemed all to have such artistic hands, thought Brad—except their toughs. "You go to see our shrine?" he asked politely.

"I am following—my wife," said Brad, with difficulty. "She came to see the shrine, and I wished to see it too. So I decided to come also."

"It is there," said the man, clearly not understanding why they had not come together, as he and his wife had come. "We come each year, to pay our respects." He beamed at Brad.

Brad bowed two and three times, and thanked him. The afternoon shadows were growing longer, as the ferry made its slow, dignified progress through the blue waters, toward the torii gateway. Cameras were snapping as the tourists admired aloud the beauty of the gate in the water, the vermillion colors stronger in the orange lights of the sun.

Which way to go? He turned to his acquaintances. "Which way does one go to visit the shrine? Where are the best sights to see? I am not familiar with this honorable place."

"Ah," the man sucked in his breath in pleasure at the idea of directing a foreigner to see the fine sights. "One goes to the right, after the dock, that way. One follows the path along the sea, then to the large theater where the Nō plays are given. From there, one can see the magnificence of the torii in the waters. I believe your honorable wife will be there, witnessing the Nō plays." He smiled widely.

"I thank you very much for your good advice."

"One cannot drive the car very far," added the man. "You may be wise to park it soon after driving off the ferry. If you forgive my presumption," and he bowed again.

"You are most kind and thoughtful."

Brad thought afterward that he had not stopped often to speak to a Japanese in this manner. He leaned on the railing with the elderly couple and talked to them as the boat pulled in. The man then advised him, in a fatherly manner, to get into his car and be ready to drive off. "For the ferry empties and then fills with much rapidity," he said.

Brad took his advice, with bowing and gratitude, and got into the car. Charita was right, these people were very kind and thoughtful.

He was just wondering if he should invite the little couple to join him in the car and get off that way, when he saw them enter a snazzy little Datsun ahead of him, and prepare to drive off. He waved when they waved, the little lady gave him a crinkled smile from her parchment-lined face.

He felt warmer and not so bewildered and lost when he drove off the boat. He would probably find Charita here, and when he did, soon, he hoped, he would have a good talk with her. If she wanted to proceed to visit her parents, he would take her, and stay overnight with them. Maybe that would soothe Charita, and calm her down. He could not imagine her taking off like this, it just wasn't like her. She had never really defied him and gone off on a trip without permission.

He could not imagine what had gotten into her, unless she was more terrified than he had thought. He remembered the sadness in her eyes, how she had sat in silence for some recent evenings. He should have drawn her out, talked to her, reassured her.

He parked his car next to that of the little couple, and soon left them behind, with his giant strides eating up the path toward the shrine. It was quite pretty, he thought, but he was anxious to find Charita. He soon came to the place where the Nō plays were given. He was surprised at the size of the place. Silence reigned, broken only by the tinkling of music from the side of the stage.

He stood at the side, in the back of the theater, and looked around. There were quite a few Americans and other foreigners there, he examined the parties carefully. Charita might have found some new friends; she was a sweet girl, and very open and friendly in her shy manner. Too trusting, but she made friends readily.

She was not there. He walked around to the other side, and looked some more. He had not dreamed so many people would be around.

He should have asked the maid what Charita was wearing. If she had worn her bright red dress, he would see her readily. But no bright red dress did he see, except some kimonos. That was another thought. What if she were wearing a kimono? At a distance, she would look Japanese.

He went again over the crowd. Then he saw a movement at the back, on the other side, where he had first stood. A girl in a navy blue schoolgirl uniform with a blue hat on her dark head was running.

He started toward her. She was following a big gray-blond man—a very big man—looked like Frundsberg.

He passed the small Japanese couple, they nodded and beamed. He bowed to them, then went on to the back. He didn't want to yell, the reverence of the people listening to the lines of the play was overpowering.

Charita was climbing a cliff at the back of the theater complex. She turned a curve and was lost to his sight. Damn. But Frundsberg would help her, if he was the man—

Then Brad noticed the two brawny Japanese men following Charita, moving rapidly as she put on speed. They were almost running now up the steep path, two thugs with ill-fitting jackets, and short ugly brush haircuts—

Like those other men! Toughs, bullies—

Brad found himself panting for breath. The exertion, and more, the anxiety, were getting to him. He ran up the hill, following the two men. He turned the corner—

Charita was there, yanked off the path, in Frundsberg's grip. Her blue hat had been knocked off, and her blue-black hair shone in the setting sun. And her blue eyes—staring at him terrified over the big hand clamped on her mouth and jaw—

The two Japanese men attacked. Brad went on guard. He had his elbows out automatically—his fist chopped at one jaw. The man staggered, fell back. The other man slashed in a karate chop. Brad ducked, and plunged his fist into the iron-hard stomach. The man grunted and grabbed at him. Brad stepped back, dancing lightly on his feet, his senses alert.

So this was it—Frundsberg behind the attacks— Brad had no time to think. Both Japanese men were after him. He drew back his arm, seemed to turn, then when one man came at him, Brad let him have it on the jaw. The man went down hard on his back.

He turned to meet the attack of the second man. The man was much shorter than Brad, but heavier and more cautious. Brad measured him, they circled each other warily. He saw from the corner of his eye that Charita was kicking out wildly at Frundsberg, making choking sounds in her throat, fighting him— Bless her brave little reckless soul!

He put everything into the karate chop, and just grazed the man's cheek. The man ducked back, weaved warily in front of Brad—

"Livingston!" It was Frundsberg's heavy voice. "One more move, and I'll shoot your wife!"

Brad backed away, dared a glance in her direction. It was true. Frundsberg held a short revolver at Charita's head.

"You wouldn't—" Brad said slowly. "You fight dirty—but murder—"

"Too much at stake," said Frundsberg, his mouth curling. "You should have sold me the gold formula when I offered you a million. Too late now. I'll take it anyway!"

"Let's talk about it," said Brad slowly. "Call off your

bullies, Frundsberg. I don't want to have to knock them out." He talked more confidently than he felt. But playing for time—maybe someone would come up here. Frundsberg would hardly dare shoot them in front of a wide-eyed Japanese crowd.

There was a gleam in Frundsberg's eyes, a maniacal gleam. It died slowly, and he gradually released his grip on Charita's jaw.

As soon as she was free to speak, Charita said, "I'm sorry, Brad. I was foolish and stupid—to come here—"

"Shut up," said Frundsberg, harshly. He still held her by the neck, his gun at her forehead. "I'll do the talking. Livingston, you sign a paper here and now—and give me that formula. I know it's in your head."

"We'll talk about it," said Brad firmly, his wary eye on the two Japanese bullies. The man on the ground was sitting up, fingering his jaw, eyeing Brad darkly. The other man seemed uncertain.

Brad sat down on a rock, said, "I'm reaching for a cigarette," and slowly put his hand in his pocket. Frundsberg was alert, then gradually relaxed as Brad got out cigarettes and lighter. He lit a cigarette. Brad felt burning mad at Charita's still being held in the man's grip, but he had to endure it. He must talk sense into the man. Frundsberg could not kill—unless he was insanely angry, too angry to think of the consequences.

"Let my wife go," said Brad quietly. "She can come and sit beside me."

"She stays here," said Frundsberg. "I want that formula. Tell me, or better yet, write it down."

Brad pretended to think it over. Damn it, why didn't some people come up here on the cliff? Then he realized why, the sun was setting, sending purple shadows across the cliffs and orange flames across the Inland Sea. The vermillion torii glowed beautifully in the light. Brad could just see it from his rocky perch. He gazed at it thoughtfully, it had stood there for many years, probably, and people had come to look at it, and revere it and gaze at it—like that nice older couple.

Charita's hands were clasped tightly together. She looked at him, hopefully, not moving from where Frundsberg held her. In her gaze was hope—wonder—was it adoration? He must not think about that. He must think how to rescue them.

"I could write it down," said Brad slowly. "But how would you know the proportions were right?" He was considering. "You might be unsure of them—I might not give you the right amounts. Or you might think I was not telling you the truth—"

"You'll write another paper," said Frundsberg, biting off the words. His German accent was stronger this evening, as though he were reverting to another, less suave, civilized self. "You'll give me control of your company— better yet, you'll turn it over to me."

"I would—for my wife," said Brad, quietly. "But people would wonder, wouldn't they? They would wonder why a successful business was suddenly *given* away to a stranger."

"You and your young wife are weary of Japan," said Frundsberg. His eyes sparkled. "You are tired of the alien life here, dealing with the slow, stupid Japanese workmen. You have decided to sell out, and return to the States—where you belong!"

"Um, that might work," Brad pretended to think about that. Charita's eyes implored him silently. She was not risking another word, standing patiently in the grip of the big man. "Hum—yes, it might. I'll reach into my pocket for a pad of paper and a pen—" He slowly reached into the jacket. He longed to get out his revolver from the holster, but the German gun was pointed unwaveringly at Charita's head.

He began to write on the pad. The three men watched

445

him cautiously. Would no one ever come up that path? Surely the guards would come to make sure all had left the park before they closed it for the night.

He wrote slowly, scratched it out, frowned, then wrote again.

"What are you writing?" asked Frundsberg impatiently.

"Hmm—the contract—for a sale—it has to sound right—"

"I want the gold formula!" snapped Frundsberg. "Write that out first."

Brad pretended to be bewildered. "I thought you wanted the contract for the sale of the company—" He frowned at Frundsberg. "Which do you want first?"

"The gold formula," groaned Frundsberg. "Do you have to be so stupid? I want the formula! Write it down, and in exact amounts! I will know if it is right. I know the work you have been doing, I have bought some jewelry and analyzed it in my laboratory, I have a general idea of what you are doing—"

Brad scribbled at the paper, paused to ask questions, in a labored way. (Would the guards never come? Would someone come up the path? Any distraction. He had lit another cigarette—it was burning between his fingers—)

When the three men burst around the curve and came upon them, Brad leaped up. He did not even see at first that it was Miles Snow, Kanji and Donald. He saw people coming, and it was his chance. He jammed the cigarette in Frundsberg's face. The man cried out, put his hand to his face, and Brad flung Charita away from him. She sprawled on the ground, and Brad went after Frundsberg savagely.

Kanji and Donald and Miles went after the two Japanese thugs. Miles had one of them quickly, he was attacking with his fists, the way he had in boxing class. He had one on the ground, and was pounding away at him, as Kanji slashed away at the other man. Donald was dancing around them both, crying, "Let me have him, Kanji! Let me have him!"

Kanji grunted angrily, and his hard palm slashed at the man. The blow connected, the man went down like a fallen ox.

Brad was circling Frundsberg, jabbing in punches savagely whenever he could. The man faced the setting sun, Brad went after him, closing in with quick punches which kept him bewildered. The man was older, but fit. Brad had the advantage of his fury and a wild desire to hurt. The way the man had held Charita—what he had had his bullies do to her—those attacks—

Frundsberg made a last effort. He struck out with hand and foot at Brad. Brad evaded, and closed in with a lightning blow at the chest. He had noted that Frundsberg kept protecting his chest. The man grunted, and bent over in agony. Brad knocked the side of his palm against the back of the man's neck, and he went sprawling over the rocky ground.

Brad watched to make sure he did not get up. Then he looked around, and did a doubletake. "Miles! Kanji—and Donald!" he said, surprised. "What in hell are you doing here—"

"Jacinda," said Miles, ruefully. "She put it all together. She had just figured it out that Frundsberg was probably behind the attacks. We came to see you this morning—" He ended in a shrug, a little spoiled by the dazed movements of the man he was pinning to the ground.

Donald went over to help Charita from the ground. Tears were running in dusty rivulets down her cheeks. Brad went over and took her in his arms, and held her close.

"Oh—Brad—I am so sorry—I caused such trouble," she wept into his jacket. "And you were—in such—danger—"

He held her tightly against him, voiceless with relief. She had been in danger, not him. When he thought of that gun at her head, he went cold.

Miles stirred the body of the big German, waited until the man sat up. "What shall we do with him?" he asked, in a detached way. "Shoot him? Send him over the cliff?"

Kanji gave him an odd look. "Sounds good. But the police might ask many questions," he said dryly.

Donald intervened. "I think Mr. Frundsberg should leave the country," he said, sounding amazingly like his father. "I believe when he thinks about it, he will sell his business here, and return home to Germany. It will be— very unpleasant—for him—with everyone knowing how he tried to kill Charita and Brad."

"Hum," Brad looked down at Frundsberg, now sitting up sullenly, wiping his dusty face. Brad kept his arms closely around Charita. "I'd like to put him in prison, let him sweat out a long trial."

"What evidence is there?" asked Miles, ever the lawyer, examining his bruised knuckles thoughtfully. "I think Donald is right. You want to leave the country, don't you, Frundsberg?"

The big German glared.

"Brad?" whispered Charita, clinging to his jacket with both fists. "I want—to go home—please?"

"Home—to your parents?" he hesitated, holding her. "If you really want—"

"No—home—to our house, please? I want to go home—to our house—" She was crying quietly into his shirt, and he curled his arms more closely, protectively, about her, his heart leaping for joy.

"Then we'll go home, honey. We have a lot to talk about, but we'll work it all out, my darling, I promise you."

448

She nodded, her mussed hair rubbing against his shoulder.

Miles and Donald and Kanji were holding a little conversation.

They finally turned to Brad. "I think we best let these creeps go," said Miles. "I'll start action to have Frundsberg deported. Our evidence will make that certain—"

"I'll go," said Frundsberg hastily. "You don't have to smear my name!" He tried to sound haughty, but it came out in a whine.

Brad just wanted to get Charita home. And he had a hunch that now they knew Frundsberg was behind the attacks, the attacks would stop. "Let him go," he said wearily. "I want to get Charita home. We'll talk to the police tomorrow."

"One moment!" Kanji's voice was hard and cold. He had a knife in his right hand.

As the others stared, Kanji caught Frundsberg's head in his other strong hand. Quite deliberately, he slashed at each cheek. Blood ran down the blocky face. Donald gasped in shock.

"Kanji—my God!"

"Paid—in blood," said Kanji. He released the man, stood back, and wiped his knife clean on the German's neat suit. Frundsberg was groaning, his hands unbelieving on his face. He fumbled for a handkerchief, put it to his face, as the blood spurted. The scars would be deep, thought Brad, in primitive satisfaction.

"What—" said Donald. He eyed Kanji nervously. "What the devil—"

"For what he ordered done to Charita. I vowed to wipe out the deed in blood. It is done," said the Japanese man quietly, and his knife glittered in the dying orange flare of the sun. Brad shook his head in bewilderment, and belatedly protected Charita from looking at the

449

man. Frundsberg was wiping and wiping at the blood, growling at the pain.

Kanji was studying the two Japanese men. "I will know you again," he said coldly. "I know your faces. You will leave Kyoto territory and never return. Or it will be the worse for you!"

They ran down the path, glad to be away. Frundsberg followed them sullenly, ignoring the small party that followed him. Miles went ahead, Brad and Charita behind him, then Donald and finally Kanji, watching alertly that no one tried anything.

They got on the ferry. Charita huddled in Brad's car. Kanji said he would drive them home. Miles and Donald could drive his own car. He thought Brad had had enough driving and anxiety for the day.

So they went back to Kyoto. On the ferry, they saw the little elderly Japanese couple. Brad smiled and waved at them, and the man came over to him.

"You have found your wife? That is good. Keep her close, and next time you come, perhaps you visit the shrine together, eh?" the old man said, tactfully ignoring the tears on Charita's face, and the way she clung to Brad. They leaned on the rail and watched the awesome torii growing dim in the distance. Dusk hung over the blue waters of the Inland Sea.

"Yes, next time we come, we will come together. The place—is a blessed one, is it not?" said Brad slowly.

The crinkled face drew up into a smile of pleasure. "Yes, it is a blessed place, it is full of good spirits," said the old man. "So it is with the beautiful places of the earth. The happy gods live there, and grant us many blessings when we come to bow before them."

Charita managed to say, "You are right, venerable one. The place had blessings for us, and good spirits. We are—most glad—that we came."

Brad drew her close in his arm, and hugged her, as

the old man went back to his plump wife, and together they watched the island disappearing in the dusk. Charita put her head on Brad's shoulder.

"I prayed for some good to come, I did not dare expect that you would come, Brad," she said, in a low voice. "When you came, I knew my prayers were answered."

He pressed his cheek on her hair. "I think I have never been so frightened in my life," he said simply.

30

Charita slept in Brad's arms in the back seat of the car most of the way home. She awakened with a start as Kanji halted the car in the driveway of their house. It was past midnight, the neighborhood was very quiet.

It looked like every light was on in the house. The butler flung open the door, peering out anxiously as Kanji led the small procession inside. Brad and Charita followed, and Donald and Miles were pulling up in Kanji's car. Jacinda's car was parked on the street, and behind it was Pearl's car.

Charita shrank from seeing them all. She was so tired, so shaken. But one must be polite—

Brad kept his arm about her, that helped. She walked into the brightly lit hallway, and the first person she saw was her foster mother.

"Oh—Mama-san!" cried Charita, and flung herself into her mother's warm plump arms.

They closed about her, as gently and sweetly as they had when she had come, a terrified three-year-old child, to their home. "Now, Charita, you are home. You have been naughty," scolded the sweet voice. "How afraid we were for you!"

"We have been most worried," said Mr. Noguchi's precise calm voice behind them. He patted Charita's shoulder gently. "All this is much trouble. We came to see what was wrong with our girl-child."

"Oh, Papa-san, you are too good to this unworthy child," whispered Charita, grasping his hand gratefully.

"Looks like we have a big audience," said Brad, happily. He grinned at them all, his tired face smoothing out. "Come on in, and hear the story, all of you! I'm starved. How about some hot tea and cold drinks!"

Susuki was hovering, an anxious eye on her mistress-san, obviously wondering about her reception. Brad gave her a wink, Charita wondered what that was all about. The servants scurried about, procuring sandwiches, some hot rice, tea, ice, bottles of whiskey and sake. They brought in trays, and everyone helped himself.

Brad seemed too tired to talk. "Well, let me say what I know," said Jacinda imperiously, her face radiant and relieved. "Then you can go on."

She told them about Frundsberg, and his part as she had worked it out. Then Miles took up the story, how they had followed Brad, what the outcome had been. The Noguchi family listened wide-eyed, and so did the servants, hovering about. What a story! How much gossip would be in the neighborhood in the morning! They did not mind staying up for this excitement!

"So it *was* Frundsberg behind the attacks on Charita, and on you, Brad," Kanji summed it up thoughtfully. He looked older tonight, more mature, the smile quite gone. "Well, the police must be informed. I will go to the station tomorrow—"

"I'll go with you," said Miles, quietly. "As Brad's lawyer, I can give them the legal angle on all this. Formal deportation orders should be made out, and charges made. If he doesn't leave the country—"

"I think he will leave, but yes, the police should be informed." Brad ran his hand over his forehead. Timidly, Charita sat down beside him, and put her hand on his hand. He smiled down at her, and put his arm about her.

"All this trouble, my poor darling," he said. "No wonder you wanted to run away from all this."

His eyes begged for reassurance. She smiled up at him, and put a secret pressure on his fingers. "I was most foolish to run away. One does not solve problems by running from them. I was so terrified—I had nightmares—all I thought of was going to the security of my parents' home."

"It caused much trouble," said her foster father ponderously. "However, all seems to have ended in joy. We are most happy for you. Forgive us for coming. Mr. Livingston-san. We worry about our cherished though foolish daughter."

"It was immensely good of you to come. You must stay for as long as you can spare from your work," urged Brad. "Charita has missed you, and your wisdom might have helped solve this puzzle sooner."

Mr. Noguchi looked gratified, though he tried to hide it. "No, no, I am not a solver of puzzles. I am a poor ignorant man—"

"Who has fathered a most intelligent and discerning son," said Brad quickly. "I cannot believe all this smartness of Kanji comes from his mother, good though her mind is." He grinned at them both.

Mrs. Noguchi tittered at the compliments, politely hiding her laughter and pleasure behind her hand. But her bright eyes and the fond look at Kanji gave her away.

Then Charita noted something odd. Odd to her anyway. Jacinda and Miles were sitting beside each other on the other couch, and his hand was over hers, very subtly, hidden by her skirt. And Jacinda sparkled as Charita had never seen her before.

"Well—this is a long night," said Miles lazily. "I think you will pardon us for taking off. It's past two in the morning. Come along, Jacinda." And he drew her up with him.

Were they back together again? Charita held her breath, fearing an explosion from Jacinda. Instead the woman smiled down at Charita and Brad.

"I was going through many problems also," she said, and Charita stared up at her. "Brad—Charita—I think my problems are working out well. I always felt that—" She swallowed, and her lovely throat swelled convulsively. "That Brad was a very—dear—helpful—*brother* to me. I am—most grateful—for his advice."

"You worked it out, Jacinda," said Brad, a little awkwardly. Charita felt his arm about her tighten a bit.

"With a little help from Miles," said Jacinda with a smile. "Well—what excitement! Brad—we'll be in touch tomorrow on the legal problems. Charita—my dear —I think you are just right for Brad. Take care of that tough guy! May you both be—very happy!"

"Thank you, Jacinda," said Charita, in grave wonder. The woman *had* changed. Her gaze was soft green on her husband. Charita moved to get up, as they started for the door.

"Don't get up. We'll find our way out. And Charita —my dear—I shall advise you about clothes! I want you to throw away that schoolgirl uniform, it is dreadful for you! You are a married woman, you know."

"Jacinda!" warned Miles. Jacinda tossed her long blond hair and laughed.

Charita stood up as Brad did. "I am most grateful for your advice, which I believe is good," said Charita, and dared to smile at Jacinda. She was amazed to receive an answering smile, and a careless little pat of her cheek, condescending, but friendly.

"We'll have a nice shopping trip," said Jacinda. "Call you soon, darling. Brad, sweet, get some sleep! You look a sight."

"We are most grateful to you for all your compliments," said Brad, dryly, and bowed to her. The Noguchis looked on, wide-eyed and puzzled. Donald laughed, and got up also.

"Brother Brad, we'll see you tomorrow about the legal matters," said Jacinda. "I'm ready to drop, Miles!"

"Then I'll get you home. Donald, how about a ride? You live out our way, and you don't have your car with you—" Miles nodded at him in a friendly manner.

"Oh, thanks, fine. I'll come right along—" Donald turned to Charita, took both her hands in his. "Charita, I'm so glad—you're all right. Couldn't be happier."

"Thank you—for all your help," whispered Charita, her mouth trembling.

Brad shook his hand firmly. "And our thanks to you—for help in the rescue. I never was so glad to see anyone arrive than the Marines charging up the hill."

"It was great fun—when it was over," said Donald ruefully. "Only Miles and Kanji did all the rough stuff. They didn't leave anything for me. Oh—Miles—Mr. Snow, are your ribs all right? That was quite a punch—"

Jacinda turned quite white, and put her hand gently on Miles' arm. "Your ribs—oh, Miles! What did you do?"

"Knocked out a very tough guy," said Brad. "Take him home, and make sure he sees a doctor tomorrow if he has any pain."

"I'll do that. Come along, Miles—I'll drive," said Jacinda, and drew him out with her.

Pearl had been sitting quietly near the door. Brad gave her a thoughtful look as she got up. She was trembling.

Instead of speaking to her, Brad turned to Kanji. "You also, Kanji, you had better see a doctor. He didn't get a knife in your shoulder, did he?" He spoke so Kanji's parents could not hear, but Pearl could. Her beautiful eyes went huge and disbelieving.

"You—were injured?" she breathed. "You—were hurt?"

"No, not really. Nothing much," said Kanji brusquely. "I will take you home, it is too late for you to drive alone."

She looked at him, he stood hard and aloof, a samurai, thought Charita with immense pride.

Pearl wet her lips, her gaze could not seem to leave Kanji's. "I—would like that—if you—please?"

Kanji gave a little jerk, as though shocked. Then he bowed deeply to his parents, murmured farewells. He opened the door for Pearl and followed her out. Charita could not help it. She ran to the door, held it open, peered out hopefully. Brad was just behind her.

In the moonlight, they saw Kanji's big hand catch at Pearl's, hers moved to his. Hands clasped, they walked to his car. He set her inside, tenderly. He gave them a brief salute, then got in the driver's seat, and the car zoomed away.

"Oh, Brad, do you think—" Charita breathed hopefully.

"I think he is very much a man, and Pearl may begin to appreciate him," said Brad gruffly.

"I was *glad* when he hit Mr. Frundsberg with his knife!" said Charita. "The way that man tried to hurt you, and all of us!"

"He will carry the scars forever," Brad told her, and grinned down, a little shakily. He closed the door thoughtfully. "Kanji is a great guy, one of the best—to have on my side! A man of his word. You know, it is nice to have a brother like that."

"He is a fine man," agreed Charita quietly.

"Your parents must be weary. Chasing over here because we had a little spot of trouble. They are good souls."

"They have ever been good and considerate of me."

Brad put his arm about her shoulder and guided her gently back into the drawing room. "I know you folks are tired," he said slowly, so they would understand. He knew how he was when he was weary, he could scarcely make his way in a foreign language. He spoke very slowly in English. "Before you retire to your rooms, I would like to drink a toast with you."

"A toast?" questioned Mr. Noguchi, politely. "To your safe return? I will drink it gladly."

The butler, though weary, brought more glasses of sake, in the tiny glasses made for the drink. He handed round the glasses, all took one, and waited for the toast.

Brad looked at the liquid as though finding inspiration in it. "To the fine sister who brought me to Japan, my sister, Jacinda," he began, and Charita felt a little pang of jealousy, which she tried to stifle.

"To the fine people of Japan who made me welcome," and he paused again, and turned to Charita.

"And to the beautiful wife who will keep me here because it is her home, and she loves it, and has caused me to love Japan also," and he grinned down at her teasingly.

"Oh—Brad—do you mean it?" she asked softly.

The Noguchis were lifting their glasses soberly as he whispered, "Yes, I'll tell you all later."

They drank. Mr. Noguchi was inclined to make a speech, but his wife nudged him, and he made it short. "To our fine son and daughter, Brad and Charita, and may they live long and happily in this beautiful land they have made their own. Long life, success, happiness, many sons," he said solemnly.

They all drank to that. Then finally the elder couple tottered off to bed, in their comfortable Japanese-style room which Susuki had made ready for them. Before they slept, they agreed that Charita had a fine man, who understood her, and they might now be easy about her future.

In the master bedroom, Charita was almost too tired to undress. She stripped off the blue-uniform dress, and looked at it with distaste. "Jacinda is right, I am a woman now, and must dress like a woman."

Brad was grinning. "I could have told you that, honey."

She wrinkled her nose at him engagingly, and he had to stop and kiss her nose and then her soft pink lips.

"Tomorrow I will tell you—if you wish to hear—why I foolishly ran away today," said Charita with a sigh, as she reached for her white eyelet nightdress with the blue ribbons strung through the bodice.

"Tomorrow we will have some talking to do," agreed Brad, soberly, as he stripped off his clothes, and stretched, before donning pajamas. "You never quite realized why I wanted to protect you, Charita. I'll explain all that. It is rather dangerous to have wealth."

"I know it now," she said, with a nod, slipping into bed, and lying back. "Brad—did you mean it—about staying in Japan?" Her blue eyes were eager, for all her weariness.

"Yes, honey." He flicked off the lights, and moved into bed beside her. "I began to realize fully today, how Japan has wound itself around my heart, as well as you, my little wife! You know, it's great. Having parents like the Noguchis, who care what happens to us. And a brother like Kanji—"

"And a sister like Jacinda," said Charita bravely. "She is very clever and smart, and she is—kind."

He put his arm over her, and felt her curling up against him. "I wouldn't call Jacinda kind," he said dryly. "I could spank her sometimes. But she is coming round. And she and Miles are back together. He is right for her."

"Umm. You see— Brad—about my leaving— I cannot continue as we have been. I need the warmth and support of my family and friends," she said earnestly. "I know from what Donald has said that in America it is not

459

always this way. The boys and the girls also are brought up to manage for themselves. They are encouraged to be —to be independent. I was brought up to depend on my parents and my brother and friends. In trouble, we turn to each other."

"I see. Yes—I am beginning to realize that. A difference in training from babyhood," he said, holding her closer. "Well, you know, Charita, I rather like it. I've been an independent cuss. But today—when Miles and Donald and Kanji came chasing after us— And we found your parents and Pearl and Jacinda waiting for us—and Susuki was almost crying when you left—it all began to come together."

"How is that?" she asked, holding her breath in eager anticipation.

"I like it," he said, in a sort of satisfied way. "I like it—that your parents were so worried and came after you, dropping everything. And Jacinda was figuring everything out. And Pearl was shaking—did you notice? She was so concerned."

"I think she was concerned that Kanji might be hurt," said Charita thoughtfully. "I think she loves him without knowing she loves."

"My idea also. And he is crazy about her. Well, they will work things out," said Brad, thinking with a grin of how Kanji went after something. Quite a guy.

"He is a fine brother," murmured Charita, rubbing her face against his chest like a warm kitten.

"And Donald is a fine friend."

"And my parents are good and kind."

"We are very fortunate," said Brad. He smiled as he felt her cuddling against him and going off to sleep. They would talk tomorrow—and the next weeks—he would get away with her on a honeymoon again! But somehow he thought the worst kinks had been ironed out.

He was finding a curious delight in having Kanji

s a brother, a dependable man, a hard fighter, a nice uy. And Donald was unexpectedly reliable and a good rtist. Pearl—why she would be his sister-in-law! And acinda and Miles back together again.

He had been alone for a long time, a loner, auto-natically suspicious of others. The shared danger had rought them all close together, and never again would e feel alone in the world. And if Charita felt this need o have others about, he would share in that, and his wn life would be wider and richer for it.

People needed each other, he thought. Not just usband and wife, but the wider family, the circle of riends. He was ashamed that he had been suspicious of le Pattersons, Mr. and Mrs. Myers, the Hartungs. He vould make it up to them, for his silent withdrawal from lem. They would have parties, picnics, beach expedi-ons. Going out to those shrines, that would be great, rith Mr. Noguchi to explain things, and the "good spirits" rotecting them.

He thought of his new gold formula, for the red-old. There would be more expansion in the works, maybe e would bring in the Hartungs if they were interested. .nd Kanji might have someone dependable to recom-lend to help manage the work force.

He would take Charita to the States on business ips, he did not want to be parted from her for weeks at time, and he had to go back to visit his factories. But ley would make them fun visits, not all work. They ould stop off in Hawaii on the way over and back, and wim and play on the beaches. More fun and relaxation his life and hers, more—more togetherness.

Charita stirred and sighed in his arms. "Brad, are ou asleep?"

"No, honey, not yet."

"I was thinking. I was very wicked to make so luch trouble. After this, I will remain at home and wait for you, like a good wife, and not be sullen and disagreeable. It is—it is bad for me to wish to get out more."

He smiled in the darkness and kissed her nose. "Too bad, honey. I've just been planning ways for us to get away. Take you to the States on business with me. Holidays in Hawaii. And there are so many places in Japan we want to see. Perhaps your father could take more time off from work, with the permission of his boss—know the man, we might arrange it. He and your mother could show us beautiful places—like that shrine today. Go to Kabuki plays, and see temples—I'd like that, wouldn't you?"

She seemed to be holding her breath. "Oh—Brad—do you mean this? It would be such heaven, like reaching paradise on this earth!"

"I can't think of anything I'd like more—to have paradise on earth—with you, my darling." His deep voice was moving.

She stroked her hand lovingly over his shoulder and arm. "You are very good to me. I—I love—you—so much."

"And I love you, my love, more than anyone in the world. Believe me?"

"Yes," she whispered, and their lips met in perfect harmony and happiness.

They had come a long way, through two cultures, to reach each other. But they had made the most difficult part of the journey, and the rest would be easier, and their lives richer for the troubles. Each had so much to give to the other, thought Brad. A good life, a beautiful life, with surprises and beauties at each turn of the pathway.

And the best would be his own Golden Lotus, slowly unfolding her petals to show him her heart.